Scarlett Bailey has loved w
Before writing her debut novel, *The Night Before Christmas*, she worked as a waitress, cinema usherette and bookseller.

Passionate about old movies, Scarlett loves nothing more than spending a wet Sunday afternoon watching her favourite films back-to-back with large quantities of chocolate. Currently she lives in Hertfordshire with her dog and very large collection of beautiful shoes.

Also by Scarlett Bailey:

The Night Before Christmas

Married by Christmas

Scarlett Bailey

EBURY
PRESS

3 5 7 9 10 8 6 4 2

First published in 2012 by Ebury Press, an imprint of Ebury Publishing
A Random House Group Company

The Random House Group Limited Reg. No. 954009

Addresses for companies within the Random House Group can be found at
www.randomhouse.co.uk

A CIP catalogue record for this book is available from the British Library

The Random House Group Limited supports The Forest Stewardship Council
(FSC®), the leading international forest certification organisation. Our books
carrying the FSC label are printed on FSC® certified paper. FSC is the only forest
certification scheme supported by the leading environmental organisations,
including Greenpeace. Our paper procurement policy can be found at
www.randomhouse.co.uk/environment

Printed and bound by CPI Group (UK) Ltd, Croydon, CR0 4YY

ISBN 9780091946968

To buy books by your favourite authors and register for offers visit:
www.randomhouse.co.uk

For Adam, with much love from me.

Acknowledgments

Thank you so much to Gillian Green, Hannah Robinson, Emily Yau and all the team at Ebury who make it such a pleasure to work with them. Thanks also to my lovely agent and dear friend, Lizzy Kremer, and to my family and friends who do not mind me talking Christmas to them three hundred and sixty-five days a year.

The Proposal

The sun was just about setting as Anna Carter and her boyfriend Tom Collins finally reached the summit of Ivanhoe Beacon, the tallest point of the Chilterns. Tom's parents' overly enthusiastic Labradors charged around their legs in a series of haphazard circles before Napoleon caught the scent of a rabbit, and Nelson chased after him, both of them barking so loudly that any chance of actually catching one was obliterated by the din.

'I'm worried about that jumper I got your gran, now,' Anna said, her breath misting in the cold air, as she looked out over the stunning view of the Buckinghamshire valley, bathed in coppery gold, which stretched out below them. It was a perfect Christmas scene – snow globe worthy – of the village, gilt-edged with snow, the spire of the tiny jewel of a church sparkling in the crook of the hill. 'I mean yes, pastel pink is a good colour for a lady of a certain age, and it will go so nicely with her hair and her eyes, but what if she thinks I'm being patronising, what if she thinks that *I* think that all old ladies wear pink, and that I don't see her as person, just as a walking – tastefully dressed for her age – corpse?'

'A what?' Tom exclaimed, laughing, as he rubbed his frozen hands together, then checking his pockets once again, probably for his gloves, Anna assumed, although he still neglected to put them on. 'Granny may be eighty-nine, but the very last thing she is is a walking corpse! She was challenging Dad to a drinking game when we left to walk the dogs. She will certainly outlive us all, and she *loves* pink. You worry too much, Anna. She will adore your gift, just as much as she adores you. And if she doesn't she will say she does and exchange it in the New Year like most sensible people do. Everything will be fine.'

'But it won't be fine, will it?' Anna protested, looking at Tom, who in the dying golden light, his reddish hair shining and his cheeks ruddy from the cold, looked like a particularly handsome fallen angel, a person who was born to be good, but couldn't quite help getting into the occasional spot of trouble. 'This is our first Christmas together, my first Christmas getting to know your family. I want them to like me, and to know how much thought I've put into their gifts and that I've got it exactly right, so that they . . . you know, like me and don't secretly discuss why on earth *you* are going out with *me* whenever I'm not in the room. It's Christmas, it's *got* to be perfect.'

'Why do people put so much pressure on themselves at this time of year?' Tom asked her, shaking his head, genuinely bewildered by all the fuss. 'It's just another day, another big dinner and a load of money down the drain. Really, it's no big deal.' His grin faded as he watched Anna's face fall. 'What? What have I said? I was trying to make you feel better!'

'It's just . . .' Anna hesitated, as she struggled to find the right words. 'Look, I know it's silly, and frivolous, but to me . . . when I was a little kid, Christmas was the one time of year when everything seemed shiny and . . . exciting and magical and just for those one or two days everything was fine. And I suppose I'll always feel that way. This is my favourite time of year and I don't want that to change because I've killed your family with salmonella or offended your granny with the wrong jumper. This is the time of year when good things are meant to happen.'

'It is?' Tom put his arms around Anna and pulled her into a slightly awkward hug. Given that she was wearing his mother's ski jacket, which was made for someone a good deal taller and rounder than she was, at that moment, she most precisely resembled a duvet. 'Because as far as I'm concerned the good thing has happened already when I met you. And besides, my family already love you. How could they not? You arrived laden down with colour co-ordinated gifts, each wrapped in a different paper for every guest, you've volunteered to cook Christmas lunch for fourteen, a job my mother hates, as it very much interferes with her sherry drinking, *and* you've made my mother's only son a very happy and altogether much more organised man, who no longer forgets everyone's birthday, not even the dogs'.'

Anna looked up into his eyes apologetically. 'I know I'm a nightmare. I'm controlling and overanxious and constantly organising everything that moves. I'm sorry.'

'You're not a nightmare.' Tom grinned fondly at her, touching her rose-frosted cheek with the back of his frozen hand. 'You're extremely high maintenance, but you are not a nightmare.'

'It's just . . . it's just . . .' Anna gazed out across the valley, the twinkle of faraway headlights dipping and disappearing between hedgerows, as the whole world went home to be with loved ones on Christmas Eve.

'It's just, you're the sort of girl who likes things the way you like them,' Tom spoke for her. 'And I sort of like that about you, even though you do colour co-ordinate my pants.'

'I just think you know where you are with colour co-ordination. Particularly when it comes to scheduling when to do laundry, you get to cerise and you know it's time to put a wash on . . .' Anna began, before she broke into a chuckle. 'Sorry again.'

'You are *my* perfect girl, Anna, any time of the year,' Tom told her fondly, with more than a touch of pride. 'Even your imperfections are perfect.'

'Thank you.' Anna leaned her cheek into his hand. 'It

is so nice that you get me . . . What imperfections?'

Tom laughed, tossing his head back so that the very last remnants of the sun bathed his face in amber light.

'Oh you know: the endless list making, the constant diary co-ordination, the way you break into my phone and put reminders in my planner for me . . .'

'I don't break into your phone! You don't have a password on your phone. I keep telling you to get one. I even made a list of difficult-to-hack passwords and set a reminder for you to look at it on your . . . phone.'

The two burst into laughter. Anna playfully pushed Tom away and found herself backing into one of the dogs, who for some reason had made it his business to be tangled up in every available pair of legs he came across; Tom's grandmother said she was convinced he was dead set on getting her a hip replacement,

'Dog!' Anna yelled, giggling. 'Don't stand about, run!'

Tom grinned as Anna took off through the snow, Nelson barking and leaping excitedly at her heels, eventually bringing her to the ground in a good-natured tackle, which quickly became rather amorous on the part of the dog.

'Tom!' Anna shrieked and giggled at once as, pinioned to the ground, she suffered Nelson's enthusiastic attempts at a French kiss. 'Come here and defend my honour!'

Tom hauled the sizeable animal off Anna and threw an imaginary stick for him to chase – a ruse Nelson almost always fell for, even though he was now almost five. Tom knelt down in the snow next to Anna, who looked happier and more relaxed than he'd ever seen her, with her blonde hair fanned out around her, her eyes sparkling with mirth.

'I love you, Anna,' he said, rather more seriously than he had ever said it before, which was a total of thirty-nine times since the first time six months ago, Anna happened to know. (And had made a note in her diary in case she should ever forget.)

'What's wrong?' she asked, suddenly anxious as he helped pull her up out of the snow and on to her feet, just in time before Nelson got back from his ill-fated mission. The dog fixed his eyes on Tom, his tail wagging crazily until he threw another stick.

'Nothing,' Tom said. 'It's just, just then I realised that it's really true. I really do love you.' He smiled happily, but Anna frowned.

'So before then, before that moment all the other thir– times that you said you loved me you weren't really sure?'

'Yes. No. Oh God, Anna!' Tom rolled his eyes. 'Stop analysing everything I say, I'm trying to be romantic here!'

'Sorry.' Anna was contrite. 'Proceed.'

Tom took a breath. 'Well, I can't just be romantic on command, that's not something you set a reminder for in my diary, is it?'

Shaking her head, Anna made a mental note to delete the reminder she'd set for 13 February at the first available opportunity.

'I love you too,' she said, testing the words on her tongue. Tom was the very first man she had ever said them to, and they still felt unfamiliar and a little alien, like they weren't words that were ever meant for her.

'Do you?' Tom asked her, taking her hands in his and looking into her eyes. Anna was surprised to see her confident self-assured boyfriend looking suddenly nervous and uncertain.

'Of course I do,' Anna said gently, smiling at him. 'How could I not? Have you met you?'

'You're not that forthcoming with the romance yourself, you know,' Tom said. 'Most girls I've known have been so needy and "I love you, do you love me", but not you.'

'Really?' Anna was genuinely surprised, but then again she supposed she hadn't needed to make a list for how many times she said the three little words in question. 'Well, I do. I do love you Tom. It's just that I've never had anybody to say it to before, so I suppose I'm not familiar with the etiquette.'

'That's so you.' Tom smiled. '"Not familiar with the etiquette".'

'Oh, sorry again—'

Tom stopped Anna before she could say more. 'Stop

saying sorry for the things I love about you, otherwise I might have to change my mind.'

'Your mind about what?' Anna asked him, intrigued and then alarmed.

'I've been trying to tell you something since we got up here,' Tom said, pleased that he finally had Anna's full attention.

'Why?' she asked him anxiously. 'Because all I'm saying is if you were planning to dump me you should have done it before I arrived at your parents' house for Christmas. I bought a goose, Tom, a goose. There is a dead goose the size of a whale in the chest freezer in your garage. It would be exceptionally rude of you to dump a girl who's preparing to feed your family for the next month—'

'Were you there when I was talking about how much I love you?' Tom interrupted her. 'You know, about five seconds ago. Stop it, Anna! I'm not dumping you!'

'What then?' Anna asked him. 'Have you got a sexually transmitted disease?'

'What!' Tom shook his head in despair. 'You know what, I'm just going to do this.'

Anna stood watching as Tom fumbled in his pockets again, this time producing a small box, which he opened to reveal a respectably sized diamond ring, of at least a carat, glowing faintly in the dying winter sunlight.

'Oh!' Anna said, clasping her hands over her mouth.

'Good.' Tom nodded at her self-imposed gag. 'Now

keep your hands there until I've finished.'

Wide-eyed, Anna nodded as Tom dropped to his knees.

'Anna Carter, the moment I saw you when you opened the door at our friend Liv's birthday party eight months ago, the moment I set eyes on you, I knew you were the one for me. You are the funniest, kindest, most beautiful, sweetest, most compulsively obsessive and overanxious person I know. And, as previously mentioned, I love you. And even though I am certain that Anna Carter organising a wedding is going to be one of the single most terrifying things I have ever witnessed – or experienced – and may in fact bring about the end of the world as we know it, I am prepared to risk it. Which is why I want to ask you, will you marry me?'

Anna stared at him, her hands still clamped over her mouth.

'Now is the time when you say something,' Tom prompted her, 'especially as I've got a horrible feeling I've knelt in sheep's poo.'

'A full year before my deadline too,' Anna said, happily releasing her hands and gasping in a breath of icy air.

'Pardon?' Tom asked her.

'My life plan,' Anna explained, referring to the wine-red ring-bound notebook of mostly lists that she kept constantly at her side. She wrote in it every night, ticking off the things she had done, adding the things she needed to do. It included at its very back her life plan. Tom was familiar with it; he was one of the few people she had ever felt brave enough to show it to, a couple of months into their relationship when he still thought her controlling and obsessive traits were kooky and cute. And although it had made him scratch his head and look confused, he had not run, half naked, out of the door when he'd read her plan for a fairy-tale Christmas wedding, complete with an illustration of the dress, which she'd done aged nine. The plan was simple: married by age thirty-one, two children by thirty-five and a million-pound house in Chiswick to go with them. Which had been reason enough for Anna to decide to be in love with him then and there.

'Oh yes,' Tom said, clearly a little disappointed, if not surprised by her reaction. 'So that's a good thing, right?'

'Totally brilliant,' Anna said, looking at the ring some more, not quite able to bring herself to touch it. 'Completely wonderful in every way, Tom.'

'So you are going to say yes?' Tom asked. 'And I am going to be able to get up out of the sheep's poo, before the dogs come back and Nelson tries to have sex with me?'

'Oh yes!' Anna laughed, her eyes glittering with tears of joy. 'Yes, I say yes. Yes, Tom Collins, I will marry you.'

'Thank God for that,' Tom said, clambering to his feet, just as the Labradors skidded cheerfully to a halt at his heels. He added proudly, 'Try it on, I stole one of your dress rings when you were in the bath and traced round it.'

Anna slipped the ring on, where it sat, perfectly at home. Perhaps it was a fraction too big, but it was a neat square-cut diamond, in a simple platinum setting – exactly her taste.

'What are you thinking?' Tom asked, slipping an arm around her thickly padded waist and kissing her on the ear.

'I'm thinking there's an awful lot I've got to do if we're going to be married by next Christmas,' Anna said.

Almost One Year Later

Chapter One

Something was not quite right, Liv thought, as she watched Tom squirming in his pale gold upholstered Queen Anne chair while Anna fretted. Anna was dressed as immaculately as ever, her blonde hair tied in a chignon at the nape of her neck, her taupe patent leather heels exactly the same shade as her skirt suit. Liv thought – as she often did – that Anna looked like a cross between Grace Kelly and Marilyn Monroe, though she had been as careful as ever to attempt to hide her bombshell curves behind sophisticated clothes. Anna always worried that people would think she was nothing more than a dumb blonde, but it was a foolish person indeed that made the assumption.

Liv glanced down at her own pair of grubby Converse and wondered, not for the first time in her life, how it was Anna always managed to look like a princess in waiting, no matter what the occasion, while Liv always looked – as her mother had persisted in telling her fondly, since she was about five years old – like she had been dragged through a hedge backwards. Really it should have been the other way around. Anna was the one who had turned up at school halfway through the autumn term, aged nine, having been taken into care and placed in a local kids' home. While Liv's family was like one out of a storybook: her parents owned a large detached house with a big garden, were kind and loving and would do anything for her. Liv had grown up with the sure and certain knowledge that she would almost always get whatever she asked Santa for (except for the pet python – she never did get that).

Liv still remembered vividly the day that Anna had arrived. Before the new girl had been brought into the class, their teacher had given them a long speech about sparrows. It had been something to do with a flock of brown sparrows, who one day were joined by a single white sparrow, who, because it was a bit different and not brown, they eventually pecked to death, for reasons that were decidedly unclear. Neither Liv nor any of her other classmates could work out what this possibly had to do with them, until eventually their weary and sparrow-pecked teacher came straight out with the news that Anna was living in a children's home. Thirty nine-year-olds had all but rubbed their hands together with glee as they anticipated the arrival of their new disenfranchised victim, who was bound to be a target for torment if ever there was one. But when Anna arrived she hadn't been anything like what they were expecting, even then, fresh from all she had been through.

Yes, her uniform was worn out and second-hand, and her shoes had clearly been bought from a supermarket, but with her long golden hair rippling down her back, Anna had stood tall and proud before them, as Miss Healy introduced her, radiating a mixture of sadness and dignity that had made all the boys fall in love with her at once and all the girls want to be her best friend. Why Anna had picked Liv for the latter position, Liv still didn't know. Liv had never looked like a storybook princess. At age nine, her thick, unruly dark-brown hair had been cut short and spiky like a boy's by her own stubby nail-bitten hands, after deciding she longer wished to brush her hair. Her school uniform was always awry and her expensive shoes always scuffed two minutes out of the box. Yet she would be eternally glad that Anna had chosen her to be her friend. That morning at break the two of them had formed an instant and indestructible bond, which had lasted their whole lives since, eventually resulting in them becoming more like sisters. Chalk and cheese they might be, but Liv knew Anna would do anything for her, and she would do the same for her friend, no matter what it cost her. Which was why Tom's strange and distinctly un-Tom like behaviour today worried her deeply. The wedding was imminent. If anything were to go wrong now, well, Liv was sure that Anna would never recover.

As Anna waited, tapping one perfectly manicured forefinger on the arm of her chair, for the venue's flower arranger to present her with her vision for the table arrangements, Liv knew that Tom's discomfort wouldn't have escaped her notice. And that as they sat here, in the very room where in a little over a week's time they would all be toasting Anna and Tom's union, she was more than aware that Tom looked restless, anxious, like he had somewhere much more important to be. Which didn't make sense, Liv thought, uneasily. Tom adored Anna. He had done since the moment he'd set eyes on her, around eighteen months ago when Liv had invited her new friend from her kick-boxing class to her birthday party. And it was hardly surprising – most men, when first confronted with Anna's mass of thick golden hair, her curvy figure and long legs, were usually blown away. Then when they got to know her they'd find she had intellect and humour in equal abundance. But then soon after that, that she was obsessively organ- ised and a little bit controlling. Actually extremely controlling. Not that it was Anna's fault really. It was her way of adjusting to the chaos of her childhood, Liv understood that, but until Tom there had never been a man in Anna's life who got it.

Tom though had stuck around, and the more he had gotten to know Anna, the more he liked her. Anna's lists, her plans, her constant striving for perfection and her need to control almost everything around her, frightened most men off within weeks, despite how beautiful she was. And if she'd been asked to put money on it, Liv would have thought that sporty, but super easy-going and relaxed Tom would have been running a mile from her obsessive compulsive friend within weeks. Instead, he'd seemed intrigued by her, in turn fascinated and amused. Gradually, Liv had watched her new friend fall in love with her oldest and best friend. Aware that their lives were about to change for ever, Liv had done her best to conceal her mixed emotions as Anna and Tom grew ever closer, knowing that if anyone deserved a man like Tom, it was Anna. They were so good together, everybody thought so. So why did Tom now seem so distracted so near the wedding?

'So,' Jean the florist was telling Anna, as she opened a rather dog-eared and aged-looking photo album. 'For a Christmas wedding, my brides usually love this combination of holly, ivy and mistletoe displayed in this fishbowl vase. It looks very very festive and yet modern and chic.'

It was Liv's turn to squirm as she watched Anna stare blankly at a photograph of someone else's wedding.

'I don't think,' Anna said very slowly and sweetly, 'that flowers in fishbowls are *quite* for me, not that they are not lovely for some people. It's just that if you remember my email, sent to you on the eighteenth of November at fifteen forty-eight, you'll recall that I asked for roses? Big fat red roses?' Anna unleashed her best smile, reserved for the people that were testing her compulsive need to have everything exactly the way she wanted it the very most. 'Here, let me give you a copy, because sometimes those pesky little emails just wander off and go missing, don't they?' Anna produced her wedding folder, an orange highlighter pen from her special highlighter-pen pocket in her bag, and retrieved a copy of said email from the dated files marked 'Correspondence (Venue)' which she passed to Jean. 'So let's just go through this, shall we? As you can see, it's composed in easy-to-read bullet points . . .'

Jean blinked at Anna, and closed her photo album with a distinct slap, clearly offended that her trademark 'festive plants in fishbowls' weren't considered to be up to standard. This was her fault, Liv thought, momentarily distracted from Tom's odd behaviour by Anna's anxiety. Not that Anna's face wasn't a picture of serenity. But Liv knew the signs and knew the murderous thoughts that were almost certainly running through Anna's head. She should have made her delegate more.

'You can't try and do everything,' Liv had told her the day Anna had broken the news of the wedding. It was last New Year's Eve. Liv had got back to the flat first, glad to have escaped her lovely, but energy-zapping family, and to finally be back home with a precious week off work to do nothing but watch bad TV and eat the poor quality junk food that she would never in a million years dream of admitting she loved. She'd just put the kettle on, and lined up a family-sized bag of Wotsits, when Anna let herself in the door. For once she had been without Tom.

'Happy New Year!' Anna had said, bounding into the kitchen. 'How's the family, did they miss me? I missed them. Tom's family is lovely, but it's an awful chore having to be on my best behaviour for all those days and not reorganise the kitchen or colour code their airing cupboard.' Liv had been about to respond when Anna had hugged her literally off her feet and spun her round. 'Why am I wittering on, Liv . . . this is going to be the best year ever because . . . Oh Liv! I'm getting married! To Tom! He asked me to marry him and it wasn't a joke or anything, he meant it and everything and I said yes!'

'Wow!' Liv had said, her eyes widening as the news slowly sunk in and she got a breath back. 'Wow, Anna. Wow.'

'Are you pleased?' Anna had asked her, not able to fail to notice the distinct lack of enthusiasm in her 'wows.'

'I am, of course I am,' Liv said, willing herself to catch up with the news. 'It's just . . . Oh that's amazing news. I'm so happy for you. You're going to be married! To Tom!'

The two women had hugged again, and the second time Liv put on a much better show of being pleased, because this was Anna, and she wanted to be pleased for Anna.

'I know,' Anna had said, skipping a tiny bit. 'And there is so much to do! Think of the lists! And the pie charts, and I'm certainly going to need a spreadsheet and maybe a PowerPoint presentation!' She rubbed her hands together in glee. 'I'm going to need millions of Post-it notes, all the colours!'

Immediately, Anna set about making lists, sitting on the living-room floor of the flat they shared, with a newly bought bound notebook and a set of coloured biros, which she must have picked up on the way home for just this purpose.

'We're supposed to be going out, remember? Dancing? Bringing in the New Year? Not making lists that can easily wait until tomorrow,' Liv had said, a touch petulantly. 'Especially as this will be our last *ever* single girl New Year, Anna.'

'I know, and we will, I promise. But just let me make a pre-list. A list of lists, please, Liv. You know how excited I get by a new notebook.'

Sighing, Liv had sat down on the floor next to her friend, crossing her legs, noticing a hole in the seam on the inside thigh of her leggings, and tugging at it to make it a bit bigger.

'I'm really pleased for you and everything,' she'd said, despite the heavy weight that was descending steadily downwards in her chest.

'But?' Anna looked up at her, her pen hovering mid-air.

'But what?' Liv asked.

'That sentence was definitely going to end in a "but",'

Anna said. "'I'm really pleased for you and everything but . . .'" But what? Please, please, don't say you're not happy for me and you don't love Tom, because if you don't approve you realise I can't marry him, don't you? Your disapproval could seriously ruin my life, here.'

Liv had sighed, picking up the blue biro and slotting the lid of the green one onto it, just because she knew it would drive Anna mad.

Honestly, she couldn't quite make sense of her own feelings at that moment, and although Anna was quite right, there was a 'but', a massive huge 'but', it wasn't exactly one that she could communicate then, or indeed ever now that Anna and Tom were forever. Because you didn't do that, you didn't tell your best friend moments after they told you they were getting married that you were really pleased for them and everything BUT you'd been secretly in love with their fiancé since the first moment you'd set eyes on him, weeks before he'd even met Anna. Or that you'd only invited him to your birthday party, and made a fool of yourself by wearing an actual dress, because you'd rather hoped that it would be you he'd be kissing passionately on the sofa at ten to two the next morning, and not your flatmate and best friend. (And the person who had always best fitted the description of soulmate.) No, you definitely did not add that particular 'but' to the end of that particular sentence in response to that particular announcement. Not unless you were OK for life as you knew it to end for ever and ever less than sixty seconds later.

Liv really had done her best to get rid of her feelings for Tom as he became more and more of an integral part of Anna's life, really she had. She had told herself it was just another silly futile crush in a long line of silly futile crushes, exactly like the time she'd decided she was in love with Marcus upstairs, even though Marcus upstairs was living very happily and very monogamously with his life partner, Brian. But the truth was the more Liv got to know Tom, the deeper and more hopeless her affections became.

And now it felt like she was losing both the people she most cared about in the world for ever and there was nothing for it but to keep her chin up, have a stiff upper lip, be the kind of best friend that Anna always was to her and continue to let Tom treat her like one of the blokes down the pub, even ever so occasionally giving her short dark hair an affectionate ruffle, like she was his kid brother. There really was nothing else for it but to ride it out until the ache in her heart finally faded, only it was now almost a year on and Liv still felt exactly the same.

'But . . .' Liv had said heavily last New Year's Eve. 'If you take on organising every aspect of your own wedding with the same crazy controlling freakery you do everything else, you *will* literally explode. Take it as read that I'll help you. You just need to concentrate on the things that really matter. Like getting drunk with your oldest friend in about an hour's time?'

'It *all* matters!' Anna had said, distracted. 'Right, blue for the dress, green for the venue, red for flowers, black for catering, or do you think pink for the dress?'

'Er, we are caterers,' Liv reminded her. 'I'll cater your wedding. I might even give you a discount.'

'But you are the chief bridesmaid!' Anna had exclaimed. 'You can't be cooking in puffed sleeves and an Empire line dress!'

'Firstly,' Liv had said, 'thank you for asking me, I'm honoured, and, secondly, over my dead body will there be puffed sleeves and, thirdly, I will plan your menus, I will pay for it, I will prep it and then we can let our loyal staff cook it for you, and come to the evening do. It can be the Simple Pleasures wedding gift to you, after all, without all your hard work I'd still be doing Sunday roasts in a pub.'

'Nonsense,' Anna said. 'You are a cooking genius. It's only a matter of time before the world truly recognises your talent.'

'Which is why you'd be a fool not to let me at least take catering off your hands. Who else in the world knows you like I do?'

Anna had crawled across the floor and hugged her. 'Thank you. I'm so happy,' she'd said, beaming. 'I'm not used to being this happy. Normally when I'm happy something always goes wrong. Sometimes I think it's better not to be happy, and then you are never disappointed. Oh God, what if everything goes wrong?'

'Anna! Nothing will go wrong,' Liv had reassured her. 'Tom is one of the good guys. And he really loves you, anyone can see that. Now please put away your pens and your lists and let's go out and have some fun! For one thing I've only got twelve months to find a date to your wedding.'

'OK,' Anna had relented. 'But re the catering, could you do me a menu by the end of the week, and can we have monthly updates to check on progress?'

'Anna, it's not even January . . .' Liv began, knowing it was pointless to argue.

'I know, but can we?' Anna asked her.

'Yes, we can. And for God's sakes, get a florist to do your flowers. What the hell do you know about flower arranging?'

Famous for being one of the few people in the world that Anna listened to, Liv had made her concede control of the reception flowers to the venue florist, saying she might as well make full use of the services she was paying for. And so this moment of supreme awkwardness was in fact all Liv's fault.

'So as you can see,' Anna said, ever so politely, biting her lip, 'I want roses, deep, dark red roses, fat ones, old-fashioned fat roses, with dark green glossy leaves, a hand-tied natural-looking bunch of those every three seating places and, in between, petals scattered across the table, and candles, exactly the same colour red, alternating with the flowers. So that's not a problem, is it? To have it like that, *exactly* like that?'

'Give the woman a break,' Tom said, shaking his head, getting up suddenly and pacing to the full-length window, where he looked out across the grounds. Liv winced as Anna's head snapped round to watch him, her blue eyes full of concern. That's what all this nonsense to do with the flowers was about. She was trying to get Tom interested, to get him to take part. But for the last week or so he'd been anything but, all his apparent joy in his forthcoming nuptials seemingly seeping away. And Anna being Anna didn't know how to ask him what was wrong, so instead she went into crazy Anna overdrive.

'Look,' Liv said, leaning forwards and smiling pleasantly at Jean, 'you can get the fat roses, can't you? In that shade of red, and the candles, can't you? That's easy these days, right?'

'Yes, I can. I was just offering an alternative,' Jean said, clearly still a little wounded. 'That's what I'm here for, to offer ideas . . .'

'I know.' Liv smiled warmly. She leaned forwards and added with a conspiratorial air, 'And your alternatives *are* lovely, just not what Anna has in mind. Anna has had her table arrangements in mind since nineteen ninety-one. And you, of all people, know what brides are like, right? Mental.'

Jean said nothing, but her expression indicated that she'd seen more than one Bridezilla in her time.

'Also about the specific type of ribbo—' Anna began to interrupt, but Liv held her hand up to stop her, the only person in the entire world who could get away with doing that.

'The thing that is so brilliant about you Jean, is that you do know more about this than anyone, so who better for Anna to trust her table-setting dreams to than you?' Jean thought for a moment, and seemed unable to come up with any names. 'So, we know we can leave you to do everything as per the email, down to the last letter, and everything will be just fine. It will be more than fine, it will be a dream come true. A dream that *you* made come true.' Jean nodded and smiled, her hurt feelings instantly healed by a little of Liv's diplomacy. 'Great, now I need to have a look at your kitchens, and have a chat to your chef about your equipment, see if there's anything I need to bring with us for the day. OK?'

'Perfectly fine,' Jean said pleasantly, smiling at Anna, whose eyes were fixed on the back of Tom's shoulders. 'I must warn you that Chef is not thrilled at being ousted from his own kitchen for the wedding.'

'Well,' Liv said as she got up, touching Anna briefly on the arm. 'Chef can comfort himself with the knowledge that not catering this particular wedding will almost certainly extend his life by at least ten years.'

Liv paused, leaning close to her friend.

'Anna,' she said, 'just try to relax, darling. If you don't, all these months and years of planning will have been for nothing. It will all go by in a flash and you won't have noticed any of it, not even the reindeer-pulled sleigh that's taking you to the church, which you somehow managed to get Whipsnade Zoo to lend you for the morning.'

'It wasn't that hard. They don't open on Christmas Eve, I gave a considerable amount of money to the Save the Tiger fund and I'm paying the reindeer keeper an extra bonus. Everyone is happy, even the reindeer, who get more of their favourite feed. And I know, that's what everyone says, about it all flying past, but it won't for me. I've made a list of times when I have to pause and take stock: just before the ceremony, during the vows, speeches, photos, first dance etc. I'll be making mental memories!'

'Are there any other kind?' Liv asked her fondly.

Anna smiled at Jean. 'Thank you. I don't mean to be so demanding. It's the nerves, you know. And I always expect the worst, it's a bad habit of mine.' Anna glanced anxiously at Tom.

'Hey, Tom!' Liv succeeded in getting him to turn back from the window. 'Restrain your bride while I go and check out the kitchen, OK?' she said. She met and held his gaze for several seconds, attempting to psych–ically add the message *And at least look like you're having a good time* to the end of it, but Tom only stared at her blankly. It was clear that his mind had been elsewhere, somewhere very different from talking about wedding flowers. But where, or with whom and why?

That was the question that worried Liv.

Later that evening, after a long bath, and a large glass of red, Anna looked at Tom as he lay on his bed staring at the spot on the wall just above the TV. He'd said he had to go back to his place tonight, he had a big meeting in the morning, and Anna had accompanied him, unthinking. But now she was getting the distinct impression that he hadn't really wanted her to come.

'Hello,' she said pleasantly as she buttoned up her cream linen pyjamas and got into bed. 'Hello there? Anyone in?'

Tom smiled, albeit half-heartedly, and held out his right arm to her, which Anna gratefully scrambled into, resting her head against his chest and listening to the steady beat of his heart under his white T-shirt for a few moments.

For a while they had always gone to bed naked, or started out with clothes on, which during the course of their progress to bed would be discarded across the flat. Later, when Tom had drifted off, Anna would get up, pick up the clothes, hang, fold and pop them in the laundry as required, seeing it as a triumph of nature over nurture that she was able to be spontaneous even to that extent. But recently – was it recently? – a few months ago perhaps, they had started going to bed in nightclothes. And one night they had gone to bed without even kissing each other goodnight. Anna, who, before Tom, had limited experience of relationships that lasted longer than the seven days it normally took her to do some poor man's head in, wasn't sure if this was a normal thing, this cooling-off period, this calming down of passion. She would have asked Liv, but Liv had made her swear, soon after she started seeing Tom, not to tell her about anything she and Tom got up to in the bedroom.

'Why not?' Anna asked her, bemused. 'Finally, I have something to tell you and you don't want to hear it, why?'

'Because . . .' Liv had squirmed, looking like a restless little girl. 'Because it's been two years since I've had a proper boyfriend and, happy as I am for you, one of the main reasons I like you is because you always had a worse sex life than me. Now you have somehow lucked into a really great one, I don't need to further heighten my personal inadequacies by hearing about it!'

'That's not the main reason you like me!' Anna protested. 'We met when we were nine! The main reason you like me is because I do all your laundry and pair your socks. Oh please, Liv. Who am I going to ask about sex if not you?'

'Um.' Liv bit her lip, her dark eyes narrowing. 'You could try Mum? Call her. She's constantly trying to talk to *me* about sex. "How much sex have you had, Olivia?" "Are you having any sex, Olivia?" "Are you sure you aren't gay, Olivia? You know we wouldn't mind at all. Ask your brother, he's completely gay and Daddy and I love him just as much, Olivia!" You know, all the things that mums are not supposed to ask their daughters unless they want to mentally damage them for life. Give Mum a call, she adores *you. You* are her favourite.'

'I think I know why you haven't had a boyfriend for two years,' Anna had said, gently. 'Not because you aren't beautiful. With those massive brown eyes, and incredible skin and that kick-boxing-toned body of yours, you are stunning. And not because you seem to insist on wearing boys' clothes, and no make-up and having a hairstyle that looks rather like you accidentally wandered into a lawnmower. It's because you behave like every man you meet is your mate, the bloke you want to go for a pint with. You need some mystery, some allure, some waxing, some eyeliner and some . . .'

'Deep seated psychological flaws?' Liv countered with a smile. 'It does seem to have worked for you. Being mental.'

'I'm just saying, you don't realise how gorgeous you are,' Anna said.

'Thank you.' Liv had hugged her. 'But you still can't talk to me about you sex life. And that's final.'

And so Anna had gone on a journey of discovery with Tom without the aid of her best friend's opinion, on which she usually relied on so heavily, even secretly making a list of sex things that she liked, and sex things that she thought Tom might like and doing her best to check them off every time they made love. Had the honeymoon period been too short, had Tom lost interest in her already? Had she lost interest in him? After all, if it wasn't for his strangeness recently she would have been perfectly happy to curl up with her head on his chest and drift off to sleep and not mind at all that they hadn't done anything on either of her lists in more than two weeks. Perhaps, Anna found herself wondering ever so quietly, almost in secret from herself, marrying a man with whom the fires of passion had already died out could be considered, in some quarters, a mistake, but she quickly hushed that particular thought and filed it away mentally in her secret but overstuffed drawer labelled 'Now You Are Just Being Insane'.

Things that had been going so well, and so right, couldn't just suddenly go so wrong. Could they?

'What's up Tom?' Anna asked him quietly, after several seconds of silence during which they both pretended to watch TV.

'Up?' Tom asked vaguely.

'Today at the Manor, you seemed really uncomfortable. Have you got cold feet? If you tell me now that you've got cold feet, then perhaps I will need only ten years of therapy, prescription drugs and alcohol abuse to recover.'

'Me?' Tom hugged her a little closer. 'Why would I have got cold feet? I'm marrying you, the singularly most perfect woman I have ever encountered in my life. The only woman in the world who irons her PJs before getting into bed and, most importantly of all, the woman that I love.' He kissed the top of her head reassuringly, but Anna noticed the forefinger of his left hand tapping insistently under the covers.

'Look,' she said, sitting up away from him and pushing her mass of hair off her face. 'If you've changed your mind about marrying me, I completely understand. I am a terrible pain the arse. I know that. And you, you are a catch, Tom. Six foot two, with that body and those arms, and that chest . . . You've got a good job, you're kind and funny. You could marry any girl you wanted. So if you've changed your mind about me, even though it will kill me, and I will never recover and will live the rest of my life utterly heartbroken parading around in my spectacularly expensive wedding dress, which by the way cannot be returned as it's already had one set of alterations, like some modern day Miss Havisham until I eventually wither away and die, I *will* understand.'

Finally, Tom looked at her and the expression that Anna saw there didn't do anything to reassure her. It was one of uncertainty and something else, something she couldn't quite pin down. 'I still want to marry you, Anna, nothing's changed, I *promise* you.' He clicked off the TV, leaving the room in soothing darkness. 'Now come on, come here and give me a cuddle. I've got a six a.m. start in the morning and I need to get some sleep.'

But something had changed, Anna thought anxiously, as she lay awake staring into the dark, as Tom's breathing eventually relaxed and evened out. Tom had changed and for the life of her Anna couldn't work out why.

Chapter Two

'Which is why we need to follow him,' Anna told Liv the next morning, with some urgency.

'I beg your pardon?' Liv stared wide-eyed at her best friend. She was holding a colander rather defensively, Anna noticed, as if she might feel the need to whack her near-hysterical friend over the head with it. 'Anna, what on earth are you talking about?'

They were standing in the exquisitely appointed basement kitchen of an oligarch-owned Kensington mansion, where Liv was in the early stages of preparing a very seasonal dinner party for their clients in the last job that they had to do before closing up shop to make final preparations for the wedding. Anna didn't often come on site: usually she'd be in the office, keeping on top of the finance and administration side of their partnership, as well as the marketing and PR. While Anna could cook – and cook well – her natural domain was the office, while Liv only really felt at home in the kitchen. Normally, she would arrive first to get a feel for the kitchen and then their small but loyal team of sous chefs would arrive some time later, a well-oiled Liv-trained machine of military precision, which had so far pleased all of their clients without fail, bearing in mind they had yet to cater Anna's wedding. So Liv had been surprised to see her when Anna turned up barely an hour before preparations were due to begin in earnest, ranting on about following her boyfriend.

'Aren't you listening?' Anna persisted. 'Tom, he's changed. He's not happy-go-lucky, "sure, whatever you say" Tom any more. There's something really, really wrong, Liv. And I know you've noticed it too. I saw the way you were looking at him at the venue yesterday. It was like everything was perfect, everything was going to plan, right on schedule and then the one thing I didn't think about, the one thing I didn't make a contingency plan for has happened! Liv, I think he's gone off me. I think he's met someone else.' Tears sprang into Anna's eyes as she voiced her darkest fear. 'Someone normal.'

'No!' Liv protested automatically. 'No, not Tom. He just wouldn't. He'd do a lot of very stupid things, but he wouldn't ask you to marry him unless he really wanted to marry you, he wouldn't. I know him too, remember, he's besotted with you.'

'You see, I knew it,' Anna said, not really listening to Liv's attempts at reassurance, she was so caught up in her anxiety. 'I knew that it wouldn't last, that it would all go wrong. I tried really, really hard to think of everything that might go wrong, but I never thought of this, Liv. I *really* thought he liked me, I let myself believe it. But what was I thinking? Why would Tom want *me*? I'm weird, and constantly anxious. I write lists *about lists*, I never let my hair down and just enjoy life . . . and I can't dance.' Anna looked miserably at her neat little feet, which were shod in expensive-looking brown suede boots. It was true. Although with her body Anna looked like she should have the lithe grace of a ballerina, combined with the heated rhythm of a South American salsa dancer, whenever she attempted to take to the floor it was like watching a car crash in slow motion. Even people who didn't know her covered their eyes and looked away. And Anna had been pretty sure that at their last wedding dance tutorial, Ivan the Argentinian tango expert had been very, very drunk. 'Liv, do you think he's calling off the wedding because I am so terrible at dancing? I mean I made the teacher actually cry at our last lesson. He actually cried, Liv. In *despair*.'

'OK,' Liv said, putting down the colander and gripping Anna firmly by the shoulders. 'First of all, Tom has not called off the wedding. All he's done is be a bit moody.'

'You see!' Anna said, pointing at Liv accusingly. 'See, you *have* noticed it too. And the thing is there is so much to do if I'm cancelling the wedding. I mean we need to stop that food order, before it's too late, and, well, we can kiss goodbye to the deposit on the venue, and the dress, Liv – what am I going to do with the dress? It's a *Christmas* wedding dress . . . Have you got a pen, I need to make a list.'

'Shush!' Liv said, putting her arms around Anna and doing her best to physically calm her. 'Anna, come on, get a grip. This is me you are talking to, me. Your voice of sanity, remember? If I thought that something was really wrong, I'd tell you, wouldn't I?' Mutely, Anna nodded into her shoulder. 'Look, I'm sure you are wrong about this. I'm sure you are,' Liv said with a conviction that Anna could not know came just as much from her refusal to believe that Tom could do such a thing to Anna, or to her in a weird kind of way, because, well, she could stand him being in love with her best friend, but anyone else? Liv wasn't at all sure she could stand that.

'But he is being moody,' Anna said, pulling back to look Liv in the eye. 'And for Tom that's massive, isn't it? He never worries about things. For him to be moody, then something has to be really wrong.'

'Look . . . I . . . He . . . The thing is . . .' Liv tried, starting several reassuring sentences, but the truth of the matter was she agreed with Anna. Tom hadn't been able to look Anna in the eye for days, which could be put down to pre-wedding jitters, but, more than that, he hadn't been able to make eye contact with Liv either, not even one of his usual fond 'what is she like?' rolling glances that he occasionally sent Liv's way when Anna wasn't looking.

'You think it too, don't you?' Anna said, always able to read Liv like she was an open book, with one marked exception.

'No,' Liv said firmly, tightening her grip and looking Anna in the eye. 'No, I don't. I think that whatever it is, it won't be another woman. That's just not Tom.'

'But look at this!' Anna dipped into her bag and showed Liv Tom's archaic and battered Filofax, which he kept on because he was forever losing his phone in the back of taxis, and on the tube, and also because Anna enjoyed buying him pre-organised inserts for it, detailing things like family birthdays, holiday dates and most recently the times and places he had to be for the wedding.

'You stole his diary?' Liv gasped, her expression a mix of impressed and horrified. 'You, Anna Carter – who never ever does anything wrong – stole your boyfriend's diary!'

'I didn't steal it,' Anna said, thumbing to today's page. 'He left it lying around, in his bag, which was under the stairs . . . behind his mountain bike. Anyway, look!'

Liv took the bag, and read the entry that Anna was pointing to.

'Martha, 2 p.m. PE KHS'.

'Right,' Liv said slowly. 'So? It'll be a meeting, something to do with work.'

'So? What do you mean "so"? Who is Martha?' Anna

asked her. 'Never in the whole time that we have been together has he ever mentioned a Martha, not once. And now suddenly he's having a meeting with Martha. How many people called Martha work in football journalism? I'll tell you how many, none. I know. I Googled it. Martha,' she spat. 'It's a typical slut name, if ever I heard one.'

Liv paused for a moment, taking a breath, resisting, only just, the impulse to slap the hysteria out of her friend. This was typical Anna, it always had been ever since Liv had first gotten to know her at school. Anna was like a swan: on the surface she appeared beautifully serene, calm and in control, but just underneath everything was working frantically away, trying to keep her life from clattering over a waterfall. Both the truth, and the tragedy, was that Anna did not need to be so afraid. Even when she and Liv had first met, and Anna was sharing a room at the children's home with a girl who bullied and stole from her, the worst of her life was behind her, because what could be worse than being abandoned by your mother when you were a little girl? And since then she'd worked so hard, done so much to drag herself away from that precarious existence, excelling at school, and at university, at the expense of making a wide circle of friends, of meeting men, or being much like any other twenty-something, until she had a home, a business, a rock-solid best friend and fiancé all before thirty, and all bang on or ahead of schedule for her life list. And yet whatever Anna did to secure herself a future, it was never enough. It would never be enough to make her feel safe, and Liv was the only person in the world who really understood that.

'Anna!' Liv demanded her friend's attention. 'Remember the Regina Clarkson incident?'

Anna nodded, chewing anxiously at her peach-coloured lips. 'Right, well, if you were wrong about Regina Clarkson, then you can be wrong about Tom too. And besides, Google isn't God you know, it doesn't know everything. And seriously, I am fairly sure that in the history of the universe there has *never* been a slutty Martha.'

'Well, there is now,' Anna said, calming down a little. Although the Regina Clarkson incident had surely been one of the lowest points of her life, it was proof that she was sometimes spectacularly wrong about everything. 'Look, I know I'm not famous for being intuitive, but I just know it in my heart that something is terribly wrong with Tom. And I don't know why I'm surprised. I've always known that I could never be this lucky. And now I've got to prove it, otherwise I will literally explode. I've got to know, Liv. You know I can't stand not knowing what is going to happen.'

'I know, I know,' Liv said, making Anna look her in the eye, 'but Tom isn't your mum. He's an amazing guy,

I know he is. And whatever is going on, it won't be the end of you and him. I know it won't be.'

'But I don't,' Anna said quietly. 'And I need to. So will you come with me, to spy on him? Like any best friend of a woman who wants a relationship based on trust with her future husband would do. Please?'

Liv sighed heavily. 'Right, well, even if this Martha is his secret girlfriend, which she isn't, how on earth do we find out what PE KHS means?'

'Pizza Express near Kensington High Street,' Anna told her quickly, reacting to Liv's expression of surprise at her rapid decoding skills. 'What? I made a list of all the possible and most likely combinations it could be in order and then made a few calls. Pizza Express was third on my list. I called to confirm the booking, and his name was right there.'

'You are wasted in catering,' Liv said. 'When all this is over you need to start up another business as a private detective. Or a spy. MI5 would kill for you.'

'The point is,' Anna said, 'I know where we have to follow him to because he's taking his tart for a cheap lunch before shagging her in some motel room. Oh!' Anna gasped, her imagination running away with her. 'What if she's a prostitute! What if Tom's got a secret hooker habit? Or what if Martha is code name for Martin. What if he's secretly gay! Oh my God, we haven't sex in weeks; I think he's secretly gay!'

'Regina Clarkson!' Liv shouted what had become

their 'safety phrase' in her best psycho-chef voice. 'Tom hasn't got a secret hooker habit, gay or otherwise. This is Tom we're talking about. He doesn't have to pay for sex! He can have any girl he wants . . . not that he wants any girl but you, and even if girls constantly do throw themselves at him, he wouldn't even look at one. I mean he told me, a couple of days ago in the pub, that night you stayed in to do the accounts, that even when they had all those glamour models at the foot-baller's book launch, practically getting their chests out for him, he didn't even . . .' Liv took one look at the expression of horror on Anna's face. 'OK, fine then. Let's go and spy on him.'

'I'm pretty sure that's not entirely necessary,' Liv said, folding her arms as Anna flattened herself against the wall outside Pizza Express, the collar of her raincoat turned up and her shades on, despite the distinctly overcast December day, which had an air of gloom that couldn't even be lifted by the strings of brightly coloured lights that criss-crossed the busy street, packed with last-minute Christmas shoppers.

'Get here!' Anna mouthed at her, gesturing at her watch, as Liv reluctantly joined her at her side, her hands in her pockets. 'It's five to two, they'll be arriving at any moment. If we stand behind this column, we can get a good look at them, before they see us.'

Obediently, Liv stood behind Anna as she peered

out behind the column, scanning the mass of faces that crammed the street for the one face that belonged to her, or that at least she had thought belonged to her. Racked with an increasingly familiar anguish, she waited for that glimpse of Tom's reddish-blond hair that always rose above a crowd like a beacon, that particular gait he had, one of total self-ease, the confident roll of the shoulders that had always made Anna feel so reassured. That she, Anna Carter, could be loved by someone so normal, so established and at ease in the world, made her feel much better about herself, and gave her hope that after ten or twenty years of marriage a little of Tom's normal would rub off on her.

'Maybe we should just go,' Liv said, her chin resting on Anna's shoulder, as the pair watched the thickening mass of people. 'Maybe Tom's changed his plans, his mind even, and anyway I'm pretty sue that you and me hiding round the corner in wait to catch him up isn't going to help matters when . . .'

'When what?' Tom said, appearing behind them. Ever so slowly Anna and Liv turned around to meet his gaze. It had never occurred to either of them that he might approach from the other direction.

'Tom!' Anna said, whipping off her glasses. 'What a lovely surprise! What you doing here?'

'I think you mean what are *you* doing here?' Tom said, frowning uncertainly. 'What are you two doing lurking behind pillars outside the place where I am meeting . . .' Tom trailed off as if he'd only just remembered that he was the one with the secret.

'We're checking up on you,' Anna said unhappily, because there didn't seem to be any point in lying any more. 'We here to find out what you are up to, Tom, because we both know it's something, something big, that's giving you second thoughts about going through with the wedding.' When Tom tried to speak Anna held up her gloved hand. 'No, don't deny it. I've tried asking you what's wrong, but you won't tell me. So I had no other choice but to try and find out myself.'

'Wait a minute.' Tom ran his fingers through his hair as he tried to take in what was going on. 'How did you find out about this? Did you steal my diary? Anna, have you been spying on me?'

'You left it lying around,' Anna said, defensively. 'I was updating your wedding section when I came across this meeting.'

'I left it "lying around" in my backpack, behind my bike under the stairs!' Tom exclaimed, but perhaps not as crossly as a man who had nothing to hide might have.

'What choice do I have when you refuse to talk to me?' Anna asked him. 'Answer me that!'

'To trust me?' Tom exclaimed, looking hurt, and putting both Anna and Liv to shame in one easy move. 'You are about to marry me, Anna, and yet you don't trust me?'

'It's not that I don't trust you,' Anna said, unhappily. 'It's just that something's different, you are different and I need to know what's happened, because . . . I still don't quite believe that someone like you could really, really want someone like me. There, I've said it, and now you've made me sound all needy and insecure.'

Before Tom could reply a tall bright-red-headed woman, about Anna's age, dressed in a full-length faux-fur leopard-print coat, appeared out of the grey crowd of shoppers, glowing like a beacon in the dull city afternoon, and flung her arm around Tom's neck, kissing him firmly on the cheek and leaving an orange outline of her full lips, utterly unaware that at that moment the strange women watching her were thinking exactly the same two things at exactly the same time: *yes*, you can get a slutty Martha after all, and *yes*, it would be possible to turn that coat and its contents into roadkill with one judiciously applied shove under that oncoming bus.

'So sorry I'm late, darling,' Slutty Martha gushed, pulling a face, oblivious to her audience. 'You know what it's like getting a cab at this time of year and, darling, I *couldn't* do the tube, not even for you.'

'Martha,' Tom said awkwardly. 'Um, this is my friend Liv, and this is Anna . . . my fiancée.' The redhead's plucked brows soared into her hairline at the news, but nevertheless she smiled as pleasantly as someone who's face had clearly been paralysed with Botox was able to, and held out a hand to Anna to shake, which Anna eyed as if she were considering biting it off.

'Anna, this is Martha Tyburn,' Tom said, his cheeks blazing with colour. 'We were at uni together.'

'Anna,' Martha said, finally grabbing Anna's hand from where it languished at her side, and shaking it hard. 'I had no idea you knew! Well, I must say you are being awfully calm about it. Well done you, if it was me I'd have him strung up by the testicles by now.'

'Know what?' Anna said, snatching her hand away and thrusting it deep in her pocket, exchanging a wary glance with Liv.

'She doesn't know,' Tom mumbled, looking in the opposite direction, as if he were contemplating his chances of making a run for it. 'I haven't told her yet.'

'Know what?' Anna all but shouted, causing one or two of the passing shoppers to glance her way. 'What don't I know, Tom? Please tell me, because I can't take it any more!'

'Oh dear,' Martha said, with obvious relish. 'I'm afraid our darling Tom here has gotten himself into rather a pickle.'

'What the hell have you done, Tom?' Liv asked him, with more than a little menace in her tone.

'I got married!' Tom blurted out, almost shouted in the street, as the Christmas lights twinkled above their heads and the Salvation Army band started playing 'Rudolph the Red-nosed Reindeer'. And yet all of that noise and bustle receded in an instant and all Anna could hear were those three little words hanging in the air.

'No,' she said, so quietly it was scarcely more than a whisper. 'No, you mean you are *getting* married. To me. In a week's time.'

'Anna.' Tom said her name softly, taking her arm and leading her away from Martha and Liv, into the relative privacy of a shop door.

'I mean I got married almost eight years ago now.' Seeing the expression of shock that was spreading over Anna's face, Tom could only keep talking. 'In America, in Vegas actually. It was in a lap-dancing club. I never ever thought it was actually legal; it was more just a joke than anything. But there it was nagging away in the back of my mind, so a couple of weeks ago I thought I'd get Martha to check it out for me – she's a solicitor, does family law. I brought her the scrappy old bit of paper I signed afterwards to take a look at. It's difficult to read because I knocked a pina colada all over it, but anyway Martha took one look at it and, well, it was bad news. She told me it was legally binding, even if it was officiated by the club's barman. As far as the law is concerned I am still married.'

Anna stared blindly at Tom as he took her face between his freezing hands and delivered the final blow.

'Anna, I'm so sorry but I already have a wife. She was a showgirl.'

'But her name wasn't Lola,' Martha added helpfully.
'No, Mrs Tom Collins is one Charisma Jones.'

'Dough balls?' the waiter asked. Anna looked at him
blankly, her mind still reeling from the news that it
simply could not compute. Ever since she was a little
girl, Anna had always prepared herself for the worst.
She had always lain awake every night, making list
after list of every conceivable thing she could imagine
that could go wrong, believing that if she thought of
it first, somehow she would stop it happening. There
had been only two things in Anna's life that she had
failed to see coming. Her mother disappearing and her
fiancé already being married to a Vegas showgirl.

This was her fault, she told herself, she didn't have
a good enough imagination.

'No, no thank you,' Anna said blankly, looking at an
equally shocked Liv, who was mutely holding her hand,
her jaw set tight in an expression of repressed anger,
seething to be free, most likely in the form of a swift
steel-toe-capped-boot kick to Tom's more vulnerable
parts. Tom sat across from them both, on the opposite
side of the table, his palms facing down as he studied
the surface intently, struggling to know where to begin,
while Martha sat back in her chair, sucking on the end
of a biro, like Mae West brandishing one of those old-
fashioned long cigarette holders.

'I was twenty-two when it happened,' Tom began

eventually, feeling obliged to fill the leaden silence. 'Just graduated from uni, full of all these big ideas of how I was going to change to world with my novel. Win the Booker, the Pulitzer, the Nobel.' He attempted to meet Anna's eye line and failed, as she continued to examine the tiniest details of the paper napkin that she was folding and refolding with her free hand. 'You know, Anna. I've told you how I wanted to be a novelist, that I never really meant to get into journalism at all, it just sort of happened. Well, back then I was full of it, full of myself and my incredible talent and I knew that I was going to be the next big thing in the literary world, I knew it. Trouble was I didn't really have much to write about, what with my growing up a vicar's son in rural Buckinghamshire. The most exciting thing that had ever happened to me was getting so drunk one Saturday night that I fell off a windmill and broke two ribs.' The briefest hint of a smile crossed Tom's face before he remembered the exact level of the trouble he was in and continued his story. 'So, anyway, I decided to have an adventure, strike out on my own, go and search out life and make it happen. I wanted to be crazy, and wild, like all the best writers. I wanted to be Ernest Hemingway, Jack Kerouac, Brett Easton Ellis, you know. In my head I wasn't a nice, middle-class Home Counties English boy, I was American and edgy. And so I saved up for a summer, worked in a pub, took out my savings and caught a plane to LA. My plan was to travel across America, take in the sights and sounds, live a little bit dangerously, become a man, I suppose.' Tom sucked in his bottom lip. 'To be honest I was a bit of a pretentious dickhead.'

'He so was,' Martha interjected, cheerfully, pointing her pen at Anna. 'We went out together for a bit. It was like dating Kafka. All style over substance, darling.'

Anna opened her mouth and then closed it again. Nothing he was saying made any sense. It was as if she were listening to a completely different person talking from the one that she thought she knew. Tom had never even mentioned his trip to America, let alone his marriage, his showgirl bride. He had never said *anything* about it at all. There hadn't been one single clue that could have flagged up the possibility that this might have happened. Not even when Anna had told him she was adding Barry Manilow's 'Copacabana' to the DJ's playlist. How was it possible that her laid-back, easy-going, happy-go-lucky boyfriend, who loved footy and kick-boxing, and Sunday afternoons in the pub, and very occasionally a spot of hang-gliding off the Chilterns, could have neglected to mention a wife. Until now? A mere week before their wedding.

Wedding, Anna thought to herself, gripping Liv's hand even harder. There would be no wedding now. How could there be?

'Anyway.' Tom paused, steeling himself for the next part of the story. 'I met up with some other travellers in LA and they were heading to Vegas, so I thought, well, I thought, why not? Vegas, prime Hunter S. Thompson territory, it's a town made for me. I don't know if you've ever been to Las Vegas, but it is the world's single most odd place. There's a soundtrack playing all the time, wherever you go, music blasting out from everywhere, free drinks available in the casinos twenty-four hours a day, and if you can afford it anything, and I mean *anything*, you can think of that you might want is there for you to buy.'

'So you bought a wife?' Anna spoke for the first time, her voice sounding tight and strained, feeling very much like she was caught in some surreal delusion.

'No, no.' Tom shook his head firmly. 'No, I did get a job though, as a barman in a cabaret bar, off the main strip. I'd never been anywhere like Vegas before in my life, it was like . . . Charlie wandering into the Chocolate Factory. Like you know, all you've ever had is Mars bars and then suddenly there's this world of exotic tastes, and you want to try them all.'

'Are you calling me a Mars bar?' Martha asked, amused, earning herself a steely warning stare from Liv, who seemed keen to hit someone and wasn't all that fussy who. That seemed to put Martha in her place for the time being at least.

'So you worked in a strip club?' Anna asked him, wrinkling up her nose in distaste. The very idea that women were willing to take their clothes off for men

they didn't know to ogle at horrified her, and the idea
that Tom liked that kind of thing was even worse. Not
her Tom. Not her wholesome boy-next-door Tom, who
wore jogging bottoms to bed and hadn't even tried to
look at her naked in weeks, Anna thought, her mind
reeling, thoughts pinging crazily round her head like
the bells on a slot machine. No wonder Tom didn't
want to marry her. Whenever they made love, even at
the beginning, the lights were always out.

'No, it wasn't a strip club,' Tom reassured her. 'It was
a cabaret bar. Where the tourists with slightly less
money would come for dinner and a show. There were
regular artists, singers, magicians and a troupe of
dancers, male and female. Dancers not strippers.'

'Dancers that kept their clothes on?' Anna asked
him, insistently.

Tom sighed, heavily. 'Topless showgirls in Vegas are
as common as . . . a roulette wheel. After a while you
stop even noticing they've got their . . . breasts on show.'

Anna's eyes filled with silent tears, and she discovered
she couldn't look at Tom any more. It wasn't the fact
that he'd ever looked at other women, or even been to
bed with them, that hurt. She'd known when she'd met
Tom that there was no way she could be the first
woman in his life. It was just discovering where she
was on the scale of glamour and excitement that Tom
had been used to. Between scantily clad dancers and
Martha in her fur coat and quite possibly no knickers,

Anna was fairly certain she came far down on the list in terms of allure and excitement. Anna had many virtues – lovely skin, great hair, what she had been reliably informed by impartial sources was an impressive body, and her personal hygiene standards were exceptional. But even so, she wasn't the kind of girl who set pulses racing, she didn't have . . . *sex appeal*.

'So this . . . dancer, this woman that you . . . married. It was just a drunken one-night stand then? A stupid bender that ended in "I do"?' Anna asked him, uncertain of which answer would be worse.

'No,' Tom said heavily. 'It wasn't a one-night stand, she was my girlfriend. I thought I loved her.' He paused, reaching across the table to touch Anna, who in turn backed further into her chair, withdrawing both her hands and folding them in her lap. 'Like Martha said, her name was Charisma, Charisma Jones. But the Real McCoy was her nickname because she didn't need implants . . . Anyway, she was a solo dancer in the troupe, and you've got to understand, even if I thought I was Johnny Depp, I was still just this kid from Buckinghamshire. I'd never seen anything like her, tall and tanned, with this long black hair and an amazing body that . . .' Tom stopped himself just in time. 'I thought she was stunning, like the sort of girl you only see in magazines. And she thought I was this funny English kid with a cute accent. I made her laugh. It's not like we dived into bed together the second we set eyes on each other. I was working there for weeks, before . . . well, before anything happened. And when it did . . . I'm sorry, Anna, I know this is going to hurt you, but I fell for her. Or at least I thought I had. I had never, ever felt that way about a girl before. She consumed me.'

Anna closed her eyes, as she thought about the way Tom was with her. So sweet, so attentive, so gentle, so kind and understanding, but she was almost one hundred per cent certain that she had never 'consumed him' in the way this mysterious figure from his past had. Anna had never had that kind of power, that raw magnetism. 'After a couple of weeks, I moved into her condo and, well, I forgot about everything else – my book, my career, my family, my friends, all my dreams and ambitions. My whole life became about working in the bar, watching Charisma dance, knowing that at the end of the day she would be taking *me* home.'

Anna turned her face away from him so she didn't have to see the faint smile of the memory in his eyes as he thought about this 'Charisma' person.

'Tom,' Liv said, her expression tightly shut off, in her bid to protect her friend without betraying her own feelings. 'I really think Anna could do with less of the details.'

'I'm sorry. I'm just trying to explain how I got caught up in this fantasy. It wasn't real, it was never going to last, I know that now,' Tom said, attempting and failing to get Anna to look at him. 'I was just a kid back then. I had no idea what life and love was really about. What Charisma and I had, well, I thought it was love. But it had a lot more to do with passion and lust.'

'The things that *we* don't have?' Anna asked tightly, prompting Martha to snort coffee through her nose and almost choke to death.

'We have both those things,' Tom said. 'In buckets, and more important things besides, like friendship and trust and . . . things in common.'

'Trust? Oh yes, that's right, I'm supposed to trust you. Silly, insecure, needy me following you around when you have nothing to hide but a . . . what was it? Oh yes, a *wife*,' Anna said, forcing herself to look at him, to look at the person that up until this morning she had believed she knew inside out. 'So was it a romantic proposal? I suppose it had to be more glamorous than kneeling in sheep poo on the top of a hill in the freezing cold. I suppose that was magical and fantastical too.'

'There was no proposal, not really,' Tom said, uncomfortably, clearly dreading completing his story. 'We were out, on yet another crazy big night out. I hadn't even wanted to go. I was exhausted, I wanted to sleep, but Charisma always went to town when she had a night off from dancing, dragging me up and down the Strip. I don't know how we ended up in the lap-dancing club.

I don't remember much of it except that we were talking to the barman, Charisma seemed to know him somehow, and then suddenly she's telling me how he used to be an Elvis impersonator. How he's still licensed to perform marriages and that we should get married, right there and then. None of it was real, it was like a joke, a dream, if anything. Suddenly Charisma has some flowers from off the bar in her hand and the barman gave us a pull from a can for the ring. We were stood on tables, and everyone was cheering and laughing and we were *married*. It didn't seem real. I never really thought it *was* real. I swear to you, Anna. I thought it was just a joke.'

'Not even when you signed the certificate?' Liv asked him.

Tom shrugged. 'I don't even remember signing it. I think the only reason I took it when I left was as a souvenir, a memory of that time of my life. I almost wish I hadn't. I almost wish I'd just left it at her place, and then none of this would have happened. I'd have forgotten all about it and you'd have . . .'

'Ended up married to a bigamist,' Anna said, bitterly. 'What could be more perfect?'

'Anna, look. Martha's going to help me sort it, it will be fine.'

'And then what?' Anna asked him sharply. 'What happened next in your first marriage?'

'And then . . . and then we woke up the next day

and went to work. I don't think we even talked about it. I think less than two weeks went by before we got bored. She got bored of me, and I got bored of waking up every day with a hangover. When I finally phoned home, and heard how worried and upset my mum was, well, that was the first time the real world crashed in and I realised that I'd been stuck in a fantasy, where nothing was real.'

'Except for Charisma's tits, by all accounts,' Martha joked crassly.

'Martha, you're supposed to be helping me,' Tom said, angry.

'Sorry, darling,' Martha said, pinching her lips together like a naughty schoolgirl attempting to stifle a giggle.

'So.' Anna paused for a long moment, not at all sure that she wanted to know any more. 'How did it end?'

'It went downhill from the wedding, actually. We continued living together, going to work for a couple of weeks because, well, because I think we were both a bit embarrassed that the magic had worn off quite so quickly, it was like we couldn't look at each other even. It was almost like someone had told a terrible joke and we were the punchline. And then one Sunday morning I woke up and she'd left a note stuck in the mirror frame. It said she was off to New York to try and make a go of it as a proper actress. She'd always wanted to be on stage, before the money in Vegas sidetracked her. She said that she was glad that she'd met me because I'd reminded her what was really important in life.' Tom smiled vaguely. 'I remember not being exactly sure how to take that, after all did she mean being married to me reminded her to go and have a proper career? Anyway, there was no forwarding address, no number, no nothing. At the end she'd written "Goodbye and good luck, Tom, be happy." And kissed it, so that she left an imprint of her lipstick on it – Firecracker Red, that's what she always wore.' Tom adjusted his expression of fond remembrance, perhaps just a little too late, as he became aware of Anna's expression. 'She was gone for good and, to be honest, I was relieved. She'd done what I had been unsure how to and ended it. I never thought about the marriage, the certificate. I never thought it could possibly be real in the real world, in the UK. No one is more surprised than me to find out that it is.'

Anna nodded, tapping her teaspoon against the tabletop three times as she absorbed the story of her fiancé's first marriage. Taking a deep breath and straightening her shoulders, she looked at Martha.

'What next then, an annulment? It will all be done before the twenty-fourth though, won't it? It will be easy won't it? A formality. A technicality. A signature and a stamp and it's done, right?'

Liv sat up in her chair, surprised by Anna's response.

'You mean you want to go ahead with the wedding, after finding this out now, Anna? Don't you need at least a little time . . .'

'No,' Anna said, quite calmly, her face set like marble. 'I mean, yes, yes, I want to go ahead with the wedding, and no, I don't need time. This happened eight years ago. It's not like Tom's cheated on me, or gone behind my back. Yes, it would have been nice if Tom had thought to mention it to me before now, but it doesn't change him, or me, or us. Or the fact that we plan to get married. All the arrangements are in place. We just need to iron out this one little glitch and then we can get back on track and put it all behind us.'

'I agree, and that's why I'm meeting Martha here today,' Tom said, with some relief, finally able to take Anna's limp hand in his, oblivious to the turmoil raging under the surface of her bone-china complexion. 'To find this out. To sort it out, so that you and I can get married, just like we planned. Just like I want to.'

'I'm afraid it's not going to be quite that easy, darling,' Martha said, wincing with more relish than regret.

'What do you mean?' Tom asked her. 'You said you'd sort it.'

'I know, and I will.' Martha smiled. 'But it's going to take a lot longer than a week to get you out of this mess, sweetie. Look, I'm sorry, guys, I really am, but you have to face up to the facts. Your fairy-tale Christmas wedding? It's off.'

Chapter Three

Liv peered through the inch-wide gap in the door for about the tenth time in fifteen minutes. Anna was still sitting on the edge of her bed, her palms flat on the immaculately made bed, staring at the wall, which was where she had been since they'd gotten in through the door an hour ago. Anxiously, Liv paced up and down the hall, uncertain of what to do next. What were the usual steps when one's best friend found out that her fiancé (who one was secretly in love with) was still married to a long lost Vegas showgirl? There wasn't exactly anyone that Liv could ask, and she didn't think NHS Direct would have much to offer. Reluctantly, she took her phone out of her bag and called the only person in the world that she could think of, and who was very much a last resort. Liv called her mother.

'Goodness,' was the first thing Angela Walker had to say, when, sitting on the bottom of the stairs just outside the flat's front door, Liv relayed the whole sorry sordid tale to her. 'That *is* a pickle, isn't it?'

'Yes, Mum,' Liv said, admiring her mother's unerring talent for understatement. Like when her elder brother Simon had declared at the age of fourteen that he was gay, and Liv's mum had looked him in the eye and said, 'Well, you're going to need new shoes, for starters.' 'It is a *bit* of a pickle.'

'Poor Anna,' Angela said, thoughtfully. 'That Tom seems so nice too, exactly the sort of young man *you* need in your life – have you had any, by the way? Young men? Anything at all on the horizon, any interest, slightest sniff, passing glance?'

'Yes, Mum.' Liv sighed heavily. 'Yes, because what I really need in my life right now is a man who is secretly married to a stripper.'

'I think it might be your hair, you know,' Angela went on regardless. 'I think if you grew your hair just a little bit you'd look so much more womanly, unless of course you don't want to look womanly, and that's fine too. No need to hide in the closet with me and your father, darling. We are excellent parents to gays, just ask Simon and Greg – Greg thinks of me as his second mother you know. Ooh, you should ask Greg about your hair, he said light gold highlights for me and it's taken years off—'

'Mum,' Liv interrupted her firmly. 'Please can we just stick to Anna. She's completely distraught, like I've never seen before, not even when we were kids and everything that happened with her mum was still new. It's like she's catatonic, sitting there staring at the wall. You know how important her plan is to her, how she goes haywire if things go off schedule. And this is her wedding, her Christmas wedding. She's been planning it since we were ten, before probably. I think she's completely lost it and I don't know what to do with her. Slap her? Pour cold water over her, maybe?'

'I could be wrong,' Angela said, slowly, 'but I *think* that's what they prescribe for mating dogs that can't be parted. That or a sharp stick up the bum. Now, let me get this straight, the wedding isn't completely off, it's just postponed while Tom gets someone to track this stripper down?'

'Yes, well try to at least,' Liv said, trying to remember exactly what Martha had told them earlier that afternoon, clearly relishing every terrible moment. 'According to that dreadful Martha woman, UK law states that because Tom hasn't seen or heard from her for more than five years he can divorce her without her consent, but he has to show a judge that he's *tried* to find her and with a reasonable amount of effort and time, which isn't looking her up on Facebook or Twitter, which she isn't on, anyway, not under her last known name, Tom says. Even under Nevada law, where he could get the marriage annulled without her signature, the law *still* requires him to do a due diligence search for her, which takes at least six weeks. And the wedding is only a week away. The only way he could get everything sorted in time would be to take the papers to her and get her to sign them in person, which he can't do because . . .'

'He doesn't know where the slapper is,' Angela

finished for her, adding sadly, '*What* a pickle. Poor Anna, I bet she's in a state. She hasn't called me.'

'I'm so worried about her, Mum,' Liv said. 'You remember, when she first came to stay with us, that first Christmas? When she was still so quiet from living in the care home, still missing her mum, even after what she did to her. Remember, how she sat there with that little pinched white face, while we all pulled crackers around her and showered her with presents she didn't want, because all she wanted was her mum? Remember how I begged you to take her in for the holidays because she was just so . . . broken? And what started out as a two-week stay ended up as for good, you and Dad jumping through hoops to be approved as foster carers, everything we went through to see her finally rebuild herself, fragment by fragment?'

'I do remember,' Angela said fondly. 'And I've never been more proud of you, putting a girl you barely knew before yourself at Christmas time and taking her in so willingly as your sister. And I've never regretted it for a moment. Anna is as dear to me as you and Simon, if only she felt like she was part of our family, as if she could lean on me and your father. All these years and she still says "thank you for having me" after she's been for a visit, like she's just a guest and not our daughter.'

It was true, although Liv, Simon and her parents had taken Anna into their hearts, it was always Anna who remained slightly apart from her foster family, even to this day, as if she expected them to reject her at any moment if she put a foot wrong.

'The thing is,' Liv said.'The thing is, that little pale girl at the Christmas table, that's what she looks like now, Mum, only worse. Back then I could always make her laugh. Now she looks like the world's crumbled away from beneath her feet. And it has in a way; all Anna has ever had is her life plan. And suddenly that's all gone wrong. I don't know what to do, Mum. It's even worse than the Regina Clarkson incident.'

'Right, I'm coming down,' Angela said.

'No, no, don't come. There's nothing you can do, I just . . . I don't know what to say to her.'

There was a long silence on the other end of the phone while Angela thought.

'The thing is, this is Anna. I've looked after her since she was nine years old and I know that no matter how much you want to make things right for her she won't let you. Her independence has been her survival tool, it's what's kept her together. We need to let her do what she has to do and be there for her when she needs us. I know it's hard for you to stand by . . . My little Olivia, always wanting to fix things, always bringing in strays and wounded animals, taking care of everyone but herself . . . and her womanly needs. But Anna is a grown woman, in a very grown-up relationship, and this really, as dreadful as it is, is between her and Tom. This is, after all, their life we are talking about, not yours.'

Liv said nothing for a moment, surprised that her mother was not only making sense, but actually being perceptive. Of course this wasn't up to her; of course she wasn't going to be able to fix it – the real question was why she thought she could? She'd been so wrapped up in Anna and Tom for the last year, so involved in their romance that perhaps she'd started to feel a little bit like it was hers, wished it was even. But it wasn't, far from it. Tom wasn't hers, and never would be, and, at the end of the day when all was said and done, neither was Anna.

'Christ, I seriously need to get a life,' Liv said, with mild horror.

'I have been saying that for a while, darling, and also laid. I can't help thinking you'd have a much more laid-back personality if you had more sex,' Angela reminded her gently. 'Now, Mrs Henderson who runs our Rock Choir, she's got ever such a lovely son, he's got a bit of a wonky eye, but if you squint he looks just like Hugh Grant . . .'

'Bye, Mum,' Liv said hastily before Angela resumed her normal service of unremitting psychological torture reserved only for her natural-born daughter. 'Thanks, and love you!'

Liv started as she hung up and found Anna in the doorway, staring at her like an apparition, her complexion matching her trademark pale clothes, the stark hall lighting casting strange shadows on her face.

'I know what I'm going to do,' Anna said perfectly calmly. 'It's fine. It's simple really. I'll go to America, find Charisma and get her to sign the papers, and then the marriage can be dissolved and I can still get married on Christmas Eve.'

Liv opened her mouth, and then closed it again, for the first time in her life truly speechless.

'It's simple,' Anna continued, her colour gradually returning with her strength of purpose. 'I've had a look, I can get on the ten o'clock out of Heathrow, but I'll have to leave soon. Will you come with me in the cab, I'll pay, I just don't want to go on my own.'

'Um, but, the thing is . . . what about Tom? Have you talked to Tom?' Liv asked her. 'Told him what you are doing? Surely this is something you need to discuss with him? Shouldn't he be sorting out his own mess?'

Right on cue the doorbell went, and Anna and Liv stared at each other. They didn't even have to look at the figure that loomed behind the stained glass window to know that it was Tom.

'I'm not talking to him,' Anna said, holding the palm of her hand up against the door, as if she could keep it closed with sheer force of will. 'He's not coming in!'

'Anna, you have to talk to him!' Liv was confused and exasperated. 'You're planning to fly halfway round the world because you want to marry him, why on earth wouldn't you talk to him?'

'Because . . . even though I still love him, if I look

at his stupid stripper-marrying face right now I might kill him, and then I'll go to prison and the dress will definitely go to waste, and the reindeer keeper won't get his Christmas bonus and he's using it to buy his son a PlayStation, that's why. I'm thinking of the reindeer keeper's son.'

'You *have* to talk to him before you go through with this hare-brained plan of yours, you have to,' Liv exclaimed. 'At least give *him* a chance to fix things and take control.'

Anna chewed hard on her lip, as the debate between logic and irrational reactions raged in her head.

'But what if I do accidentally kill him?' she mumbled eventually, glaring at the door.

'I'll help you dissolve his body in the bath in acid. We'll find any old person to marry you, you'll get the dress, the reindeer, the kid will get his games console, you'll have the party followed by a quickie divorce.'

'A quickie divorce – they got married in Vegas, home of the quickie divorce and yet, they are *still* married. A week before my wedding they are *still* married.' Anna seemed to consider Liv's offer of accessory to murder quite seriously, shrugged and went to the front door, pausing before she opened it to ask, 'Where do you buy that much acid anyway and what about the enamel on the bath?'

'We'll cross that bridge when we come to it. For now, try talking to him. I'll leave you to it,' she added, hurriedly, keen not to get caught in the middle of this particular moment. She let herself into the flat and then hovered behind the front door, standing on tiptoe so she could spy through the peephole, straining to hear.

'I'm not talking to you, remember?' Anna said, tightly, forcing herself not to look at Tom, because he looked sad and apologetic and like he needed a hug, just like his dog Napoleon did when he'd been caught out chewing his way through an antique chair leg. 'I thought you might have gathered that from the way I tipped that cup of coffee on your head, slapped you hard around the face and walked out.'

'I *did* get that,' Tom said. 'I'm just not sure exactly why.'

'Er . . . already married to a stripper when you are about to marry me?' Anna said, blocking his attempt to make it over the threshold and into the building by moving first to her right and then left. It was already dark outside, and it had begun to rain quite heavily, adding to Tom's look of bedraggled remorse. Screwing her mouth into a tight knot, Anna resisted the urge to ask him in and make him a hot chocolate, and then curl up in bed and fall asleep on his chest, which right at that moment was what she wanted to do most in the world.

'*You* said that it wasn't as if I cheated on you,' Tom reminded her, hesitantly. 'You said it all happened eight years ago and that it doesn't change anything now, and that you still love me and we can still get married.' Smiling at her, he took her gently by the shoulders and manoeuvred them both inside, finally getting out of the rain. 'When did that very sane and reasonable attitude to my very stupid and ridiculous mistake go out the window?'

Anna finally looked into his eyes – the rain had plastered his hair to head, and was running in rivulets down his cheeks. Without thinking, she pulled the sleeve of her sweater over her hand and wiped his face dry.

'We are getting married in a week,' Anna told him. 'For the last year – for at least the last twenty-odd years – I've thought and dreamed and planned every last detail of getting married, and it's going to happen in a week. And even if I can take discovering the fact that you've been married before to the wife that time forgot, I can't take finding out that your amnesia about past spouses is going to trash every single one of those hopes and plans and dreams. And I'm not prepared to accept that it's happened, not yet.'

'But . . . Oh God, Anna, I know I've ruined everything. And I'm sorry, so sorry,' Tom said. 'But what else can I do? Surely you must see I've done everything I can think of? And in a few weeks it will all be sorted and we can get married right away – in the New Year – I promise you.'

Anna took a deep breath. 'I've planned a Christmas wedding Tom, a *Christmas* wedding. My dream Christmas wedding, exactly like the one I first talked about the very last night that I spent with my mother when I was nine years old. You know, don't you, how much this means to me, that I didn't just pick this date out of thin air? You do get that, don't you? I've booked reindeers, Tom! Reindeers!'

'Anna,' Tom said her name softly, pulling her into his chest in an embrace., her hot cheeks crushed against the wet of his jacket. He held her tightly against him until a little of the tension eased from her stiff, unyielding frame. 'I do get it and you don't need to tell me I've fucked up, I know I've fucked up. I know I probably don't deserve you after this, but listen, when you think about it, you'll see that I'm right. It's not *when* we get married that matters, it's that we get married at some point. OK, so we can't get married in a week, but all we have to do is postpone for a bit, we'll hire a detective to look for Charisma so we can prove we tried and then, well, how about a Valentine's wedding, we could probably get everything sorted by then.'

'I don't think you usually have a reindeer-pulled sleigh at a Valentine's wedding,' Anna said into his chest, willing him to say something that would make the knot of uncertainty and anxiety in her chest melt away and for all the things that mattered to her so very much not to matter any more, because that would be the easy option, the approach that any sensible, pragmatic person would take. Much easier than trying to explain to Tom why cancelling their wedding now would break her heart. 'Listen, when I was a kid and everything was going to crap all around me, and I was stuck in the home, where the other girls beat me up and made my life a misery, I made myself this silly little girl's promise about a fairy-tale Christmas wedding, a silly dream that I promised myself would one day come true. And I know it's stupid, and frivolous, and shouldn't really matter now. I know that. But even though I know I'm no longer that little girl, in my head, she is still there, staying awake all night in the home because she's terrified about what might happen if she closes her eyes . . . I just . . . I don't want to let her down, Tom. She got let down a lot.' Anna hesitated before confessing her other worry to Tom. 'And I don't know, I get the feeling that if we don't get married this Christmas it just won't happen at all.'

Tom cupped her face in his cold hands, kissing the tip of her nose, and Anna melted into him, feeling a wave of relief that he understood.

'Now you are just being silly,' he said and Anna froze.

'Silly?' she asked.

'Yes!' Tom chuckled again. 'Why wouldn't we get married? We're not cancelling the wedding, we're just postponing it. Of course we'll get married one day.'

'One day?' Anna looked crestfallen. 'So that's it,

you've given up. It's over, it's postponed and we'll get married "one day"?'

'I just don't see what else I can do,' Tom said, uncomfortably.

Anna sighed, wondering why the plan that she had pretty much already implemented hadn't occurred to him.

'Martha said you need Charisma's signature to annul the marriage in time. So it's obvious! Fly to New York to find Charisma and get her signature so the wedding can go ahead!'

Tom sighed, which wasn't exactly the romantic, 'do or die, never give up, anything for you' response that Anna was hoping for.

'Well . . . I mean look, let's be realistic. Even if I did do that, the chances of me finding her are virtually nil. She left Vegas for New York eight years ago, she could be anywhere in the world now. And if I go off on some crazy wild goose chase all that would mean is that we'd be apart at the very time we need to be together, and if I didn't find her, which I won't, you'd be even more disappointed and there'd be even less time to cancel stuff and get back the deposits. And I know it's a pain, but I promise you, *promise* you, that I'll get all of the deposits refunded, rebook everything exactly as you want it and we'll get married *next* Christmas, how about that? Just think, a whole extra year to make me do wedding-organising stuff!'

Tom's smile faded in direct proportion to how quickly the expression of acute disappointment and hurt spread across Anna's face.

'If you won't do it, I will,' she said, turning on her heel and going back into the flat, unwittingly almost flattening Liv behind the front door, which rebounded off her nose.

'What?' Tom followed. 'What do you mean, Anna?'

'I mean, the flight's booked, the visa's sorted, I'm about to pack my bag. I'm going to New York to try and sort this mess out and make sure we get married by Christmas, because I'm not ready to let this go, Tom. I can't stop trying until I know there is no hope left. I just can't. I'm not that sort of person. Now, Liv's coming with me to the airport, so you'd better go. I'll let you know when I have any news.'

'Wait,' Tom said, struggling to keep up with the rapid turn of events. 'You've booked a flight, already?'

'I want to marry you, Tom,' Anna said. 'I want to marry you this Christmas. And I haven't given up hope yet.'

'Then, right, well, book me a flight too, we'll go together,' Tom said, realising far too late that he had done and said much, much less than Anna had expected from him.

'The flight's full now, it's too late,' Anna said. 'Look, go home. Stick to your schedule for the wedding, help

Liv with the final details. Let me at least try and get this sorted out.'

'But, Anna,' Tom said, 'it should be me doing this.'

'I know,' Anna said sadly. 'It should be. But it isn't, is it?'

'Do you think you're doing the right thing?' Liv said, watching Anna make her final arrangements. Tom had only been there for a total of ten minutes but somehow it felt like everything had changed, and if it felt like that for her what must Anna be feeling like?

'Of course I am,' Anna said. 'If I don't do this, if I don't at least try and sort it all . . . I'm not the sort of person to give up because something is a bit difficult, am I? If I were then I would never have made it this far.'

'I know, but the way he looked when he left. Like . . .' Liv tried to put into words the look on Tom's face, but she couldn't find the right ones and she couldn't help worrying that in her determination to fix things, no matter what, Anna had inadvertently broken what she and Tom had. Perhaps she had gone too far this time, even for Tom? But still, he hadn't tried to stop her, he hadn't said, 'If you do this it's over between us.' He'd just . . . looked bewildered.

'You really need to talk to him some more.'

'I know and I will,' Anna said. 'But for now a few hours apart, some time to get our heads straight, is just what we need. I mean we haven't even talked about why he never mentioned being married.'

'Exactly!' Liv paused for a second while she examined her motivations for what she was about to say, and decided that she was saying it to be a good friend. 'Don't you think you should be talking about whether or not you should be getting married instead of rushing across the Atlantic to try and make it happen? A lot has happened and only a short time before the wedding. Don't you think you need to talk about why you are finding out about this now, instead . . . Well, I don't really know how to describe what you are doing any other way than madness.'

'That's one opinion,' Anna said, hurriedly rolling her underwear into neat little saugages which lined up in her case, and then swiftly reorganised them into similar coloured groups, without even giving it any conscious thought. 'But on the other hand, nothing has happened at all. Nothing that a signature can't undo straight away.'

'I just wonder if you need to try more to communicate what you really feel,' Liv tried again, her mother's advice about leaving Anna and Tom to it ringing reproachfully in her ears.

'I do need to communicate with him, and I will,' Anna said. 'Which is where you come in, because while I'm not here you have to be me. Once I know where I'm staying, I'm going to need that awful Martha woman to FedEx me the papers, and you are going to have to make sure the wedding stays on track. It's lucky really that we are mostly the same size, because there's a final dress fitting that I'll need you to go to, and you'll have to take over all the last-minute arrangements for me. Of course I'm a bit taller and bigger in the bust than you, but I've thought of that – all you need to do is stand on a book, wear my bra and stuff it with socks, that should work.'

'Anna . . .' Liv was seriously considering deadlocking the front door and throwing away the key. 'I wouldn't be your friend if I didn't ask you one last time. Are you sure that you are really prepared to go to the United States of America, population three hundred million and counting, to try and find a needle in a haystack, in order to still marry Tom in a week's time?' 'I know how much this means to you, but you've got to look at the big picture here. You've got to look at this incident in the context of your entire life. If you still love Tom, and you still want to marry him, he will still be here in a month or two or three. The world won't stop turning if you don't marry him on Christmas Eve!'

Anna stared blankly at Liv, as if she'd just spoken to her in Swahili.

'You were on the other side of the front door when I was talking to Tom, you know why it matters to me, you know that without having to eavesdrop, you know better than anyone. You are the last person I should be justifying this to.'

'I know, I know, but I just want to protect you from making a mistake. What I'm trying to say is, are you sure you are being rational?'

'No,' Anna said, turning on her heel and going back into her bedroom. Liv watched as Anna took her suitcase down from the top of the wardrobe and laid it open on the bed, then opened a drawer and transferred a selection of already neatly folded clothes, which Liv knew would be a pre-prepared capsule wardrobe, perfect for impromptu trips to the US of A. 'No, I'm not being rational, or logical. I'm doing what my heart is telling me to do. And like I said to Tom, where would I be today,' Anna continued, 'if I'd just given up trying when things got a bit tricky?'

Liv shrugged. That was a hard motivation to fault even if in her heart she knew that this time Anna was going too far.

'Look –' Anna paused for a moment, holding a bouquet of freshly ironed socks labelled Monday to Sunday, retrieved from the drawer in date order '– I've given a year and a half of my life to Tom so far, and most of it has been really great. It's been the nearest I've had to normality since you and your family took me in and I know how lucky I am that he wants to marry me, even though I am not some Amazonian sex worker who enjoys gluing tassels to her bits and bobs and sliding up and down a pole. Tom still wants to marry me, and I want to marry him, so why not do everything I can to make it happen the way that I want it? To marry him on Christmas Eve, exactly as planned, not in six months' time, or however long it takes for him to get his effing act together.' Anna paused again, re-collecting her composure, which just for a moment had shown signs of cracking.

'I'm getting married by Christmas, Liv, if it kills me. I am not going to let this one thing that I have always wanted, all of my life, be swept aside by some . . . some big-titted tart!' Anna lifted her chin in a moment of defiance, before Liv saw that familiar uncertainty in her eyes again.

'Look after him while I'm away, won't you?' Anna asked her. 'Maybe pop round on the way back from the airport and see how he's doing. Help him understand why I'm doing this, because I know he doesn't.'

'Shouldn't you be the one to do that?' Liv suggested.

'I'm going,' Anna said, glancing at her watch. 'I've got to now.'

'Anna,' Liv tried once again, 'this is madness. Where are you even going to start?'

'New York of course,' Anna said, rolling her eyes. 'Where else?'

Chapter Four

Anna supposed she was lucky to get the very last seat on the flight, which had been almost fully booked when she'd begun the reservation process, although she was slightly put out that she was sandwiched between a charming if slightly more robustly built than was comfortable lady on her left, sporting an 'I Heart London' T-shirt, and whoever it was who'd managed to reserve the last aisle seat on her right, in the seconds that it took for the website to process her payment. As Anna smiled at the lady, who was already tucking into a packet of crisps, cheerfully brushing crumbs off her ample bosom, she wondered if perhaps she should have gone mad and shelled out the several thousand pounds for first class after all. She had thought of it as she'd sat there, at the kitchen table, toying with her never previously used emergency credit card (because, after all, if ever there was an emergency this was it), while she was doing her best to process everything that had just happened, bypassing the nervous breakdown stage. Why shouldn't she wallow in the disintegration of her life whilst lying on a flat bed and being brought endless amounts of gin? Anna asked herself. But the same

Anna who'd often gone without meals and knew how to make five pounds last all week would not allow such wilful frivolity, not even under these exceptional circumstances. After all she still didn't have a room booked in New York. It would be the early hours of the morning by the time she arrived, nearer to three or four by the time she'd gotten through customs and found a cab – who knew how much she might have to spend to secure a room in a decent hotel, or what it might cost to start to look for Charisma, or even how long it might take for her to admit that she was engaged in a wild goose chase of epic proportions, accept defeat and go home. So, as much as it pained her, Anna had made the sensible choice, the Anna choice, to wallow in her misery in economy class, even if it did mean silently resenting the person who'd nabbed the very last aisle seat seconds before she could for the entire seven-hour flight.

Boarding was almost complete and Anna was starting to feel optimistic about getting her aisle seat after all when she heard a male voice approaching, and knew, just knew, that he was coming her way, intent on sitting next to her and irritating her for the next seven hours and fifteen minutes.

"Scuse, 'scuse me, love, yep, yep, if I could just squeeze past here ... thanks, thanks, oops sorry! Cheers, brilliant, thanks!' The next thing Anna knew, a large and weighty rucksack had been deposited unceremoniously on her lap, while the owner of a pair of jeans whose button flies were rather disconcertingly at her eye level, spoke to her as he stowed something away in the compartment above their seats. 'Don't mind if I just . . . just while I? Thanks, love. Brilliant.'

Unimpressed by being referred to as 'love', Anna hefted the rucksack, which she was sure wasn't official hand-luggage size, onto its owner's empty seat, hurriedly rooting around for the headphones that she was now certain she would need to block out her less than appealing travel companions.

'Oh thanks.' An arm, with a tattoo of a dragon winding its way around his forearm, reached down and grabbed the bag. It was followed by a torso in a red and white checked shirt and then a curtain of long straight dark hair, belonging to a man who Anna quickly realised, with swiftly multiplying horror, she knew, and what's more, desperately wished with all her heart that she would never meet again.

Wondering if would be possible to avoid detection, and the inevitable ensuing humiliation that was bound to follow for the full seven hours of the flight, Anna grabbed the in-flight magazine, opening it at eye level, so that it covered the entire right side of her face, hopeful that her unexpected travelling companion wouldn't notice that she appeared to read only with her right eye.

'Managed to get my ukulele on,' Miles Harker, owner

of the jeans and tattoo, and the unwitting co-defendant of the single worst date Anna had ever been on, said, as he unzipped his bag and threw a battered-looking old-school iPod onto the seat. 'But they made me put my guitar in with the luggage. I said to them, if you hurt my baby, man, you've not only ripped out my heart, but you've basically fucked my life. Didn't seem that bothered.'

Anna sat stock still, staring at the back of the seat in front of her, trying to come up with a plan, any plan to avoid detection. Perhaps if she managed to somehow slip on the eye mask one-handed, whilst still keeping the magazine in situ, and then maybe she could drape that crappy blanket thing they gave you over her face, he'd never know who he was sitting next to. Bitterly, Anna wondered why, out of all the people in the world, it was Miles Harker who'd bagged the last but one seat on the midnight flight out of Heathrow, next to her. Of all the seats, of all the flights, of all the terrible times to bump into Miles Harker, the universe had decided to put him here, now. Perhaps he wouldn't notice or remember her, Anna thought, wildly hopeful. After all, though he'd had a starring role in it, it hadn't really seemed to bother Miles that together they had experienced the worst blind date in the history of bad blind dates. It was a faint hope though. Of course Miles would recognise her, not because she was especially beautiful, but because the last time he had seen her she most certainly hadn't been. In fact, if anything she had mostly closely resembled a living Picasso, her features swollen and misshapen and relocating themselves to quite the wrong position on her face.

Anna winced as she felt Miles's weight ease into the seat next to hers and jammed her legs into 'I Heart London's in a bid to ensure they didn't brush against Miles's, for fear that he might somehow recognise her knees from the power of touch alone.

'The Big Apple, huh?' Miles said amiably, clearly yet to notice that he was being most decidedly blanked. 'So good they named it twice, and all that. I've been before of course, but not like this. *This* trip might be the most important thing I've ever done, and if it's not, well it's a hell of a city to drown your sorrows in, right?'

Anna wavered, torn between her innate inability to be rude, even to men who had previously almost caused her sudden and untimely death, and her desire to be anywhere else on the planet right now.

'Hello?' Miles persisted cheerfully, resolutely failing to take offence. 'Anyone in?'

Anna sighed and reluctantly, lowered the magazine.

'Hello,' she said heavily, unable to bring herself to look him in the eye.

'Shit, it's you!' Miles exclaimed, apparently happy to see her, pushing his dark hair off his face and grinning. 'Angie, right? No . . . Alice . . . no . . . something prim and a bit Julie Andrews . . . Oh that's right, *Annie*! It's

Annie! Bloody hell, what are the odds? Hi, Annie, how are you, over the rash thing now? Shit, I'm really glad you're not dead, that would have been a bummer. Like, imagine the karma, dude!'

Anna rubbed her hand across her forehead, acutely aware of the sudden interest all the other passengers in their immediate vicinity were showing them.

'Oh, it wasn't that kind of rash!' Miles said, catching the eye of a woman across the aisle who was staring at them with naked curiosity, perhaps imagining that they couldn't see her ogling them at less than three feet away. 'Not a sex rash, it was an allergy rash, actually more of an allergy swelling. Like, you know, anaphylactic shit, wasn't it, Annie? I bought her a cocktail, without knowing she was allergic to kiwis, her lips blew up like a pair of massive fish lips, then her head ballooned. It was totally gross. There was a rash all down her neck, and she almost stopped breathing. I had to take her to A&E. Spent all night there while they gave her a shitload of drugs. We couldn't even talk because, well, Annie sounded a bit like the Elephant Man; she looked a bit like him too, bless her, once the hives came up, size of golf balls. I mean normally, yeah, I do spend the night on a first date, but not normally with one of us on life support.'

Miles grinned as he turned back to Anna, his stubble darkening in the creases of his smile, his blue eyes twinkling.

'Anna,' she said, miserably. 'My name is Anna. Not Annie.'

'Wow,' Miles said, as if he'd only just really looked at her, turning his back on the woman across the aisle to study her determinedly stand-offish profile. 'You look a lot better without your head swollen to four times its natural size. I've got to be honest, I wasn't surprised when you didn't call me. I mean apart from me nearly killing you with exotic fruit extracts, it hadn't exactly been the world's hottest date, anyway, had it? I think that's why I bought you the cocktail; I thought it might cheer you up a bit. Shame neither of us knew you were allergic to kiwi. How someone gets to the age of thirty without ever having encountered kiwi, I'll never know.'

'I was twenty-eight,' Anna retorted. 'And I never liked the look of kiwi – it's furry on the outside and green on the inside, that's just not natural. And anyway, I was completely cheerful on that date, as cheerful as any person could hope to be whilst having their eardrums violated in the kind of dive that Dettol was invented for.'

As the plane began to taxi towards the runway, Anna remembered all too well how uncomfortable she'd felt sitting, in her white linen dress and neat heeled pumps, in a bar in the West End, which was situated in some basement of a pub that felt, for polite middle-of-the road pop fan, Anna, a little bit like being trapped in the noisy part of hell. Simon, who was just as much of a brother to her as Liv was a sister, had sworn blind when he'd set her up with the singer from the band that he was planning to employ at his wedding that Miles Harker was her perfect man.

'I'm telling you, darling, this man is exactly what you need,' he'd said over a Sunday lunch at Angela's house. 'He's like your very own human antidote, and he's extremely good-looking too and quite well built. The arms, oh the arms in a cut-off shirt are to die for darling. If I wasn't an almost married man . . .'

'Then why don't you set him up with Liv?' Anna had asked Simon. Angela nodded enthusiastically in agreement at her suggestion. 'Liv's single, and she's much nicer than me. People like her.'

'Liv,' Simon said, winking at his sister. 'Already has her eye on someone she's just met at the gym.'

'Oh really?' Angela said. 'What's her name?'

'And think of the sex,' Simon said, neatly deflecting Angela's attention away from her poor daughter. 'I can see you two together. Him rugged and rough-hewn, you angelic and prim. Him passionate and base, you uptight and sort of frigid. I bet you'd have really great sex. Besides, apart from Liv, you are the last single straight woman in the whole of London.'

Anna was not remotely persuaded by the promise of great sex, sex was something she'd had limited experience of and what's more, what little she had encountered was decidedly underwhelming. What had finally clinched the deal was Simon's description of her as the last single woman in London. What if Liv did hook up with her mystery man, what would her life be like then, not to mention her plan, which at the time had only allowed her a scant three years to find a man, fall in love, go out with him, swap keys, move in, wait to be proposed to, have a decent engagement, get married at Christmas (as per childhood dream) and allow a year of togetherness, before having the first of two children. No, it hadn't been the promise of hot sex that had finally persuaded Anna to go on a date with Miles, it had been cold hard fear.

All Anna had known about Miles, as she'd hurried through Leicester Square one summer's evening to meet him, was that he was a musician, a singer/songwriter to be precise, played in various bands and did quite a lot of high-profile session work to support himself financially, as he worked on breaking his own career with the sort of single-minded determination that Anna admired, even though she thought it was the law that once you were over the age of twenty-five you could never be a pop star.

First impressions were pleasing, Anna had noted, when she stopped just across the street from where Miles was waiting for her, bang on time, leaning up against a wall, his hands tucked in his pockets, one biker-booted foot resting against the wall, the other tapping away to some tune that only he could hear. He was tall, the very same muscular arms that Simon had waxed lyrical about were on display, encased along with the rest of his very promising-looking torso in a plain black V-neck T-shirt. He was very far from her usual type, which Anna had to admit was a nebulous concept, and one she hadn't entirely nailed down herself, what with his tattoos and his longish straight dark hair, which on that evening had been tied back into a pony-tail, showing off a small silver hoop through one ear. He was undeniably handsome though, with a strong profile, a good Roman nose, a defined jaw. And as Anna waited to cross, she couldn't help but notice that the girls that walked past him on that summer's evening almost all gave him a second glance, and some gave him two or three. One had even walked a few steps past him, paused and then turned on her heel to walk back in the other direction, hopefully tossing her long hair over her shoulder on the return trip in a bold, if failed, bid to get his attention. Miles had not noticed the girl, remaining deep in thought about something, or possibly, now that Anna knew him a little better, napping, as she was fairly sure he never thought very deeply about anything very much.

Still her hopes, while they had not been sky high, had not been at rock bottom either, as she crossed the road to meet him, wondering what this man in his torn jeans and biker boots would make of her, with her golden hair neatly coiled in a bun at her neck, sporting a pristine white linen pencil dress and a pair of matching heeled peep-toed pumps.

As it had turned out though, Anna would never know what Miles thought of her, because they'd spent the first hour of their date unable to hear each other over the dreadful noise, and the next eight hours in Accident and Emergency while a team of doctors tried their level best to stop her from suffocating on her own tongue.

Still, at least Miles had stayed with her for most of the night, until the dawn broke over the city, and the steroids and antihistamines kicked in sufficiently for the hospital to finally let her go home, armed with an epi-pen just in case she ever encountered a kiwi again. And he had insisted on escorting her in the cab until it reached her address, even making it wait while he walked her to her doorstep, where they had stood awkwardly for a moment or two, Anna's lips still too misshapen and swollen for her to be able to say anything coherent, even if she had wanted to.

'So I suppose a goodnight kiss is out of the question?' Miles had joked rather sweetly, Anna had thought, given that she looked like some fish-cum-hippopotamus nuclear fusion experiment that had gone awry. 'I'm really sorry Anna, I didn't know . . .'

'It's fine,' Anna had said. 'How could you, when I didn't? Just bad luck that's all.'

Or that least that's what she'd said in her head. In reality it came out in a series of grunts and wheezes that Miles seemed to get the basic gist of as he smiled, and kissed her on her bumpy, red and swollen cheek.

'Call me, yeah?' That was the last thing he'd said to her as he'd gotten back into the car, and as Anna had pressed a packet of frozen peas to her lips and sat down in front of the telly, relishing being able to breathe again, she fully expected, hoped even, never to see or hear from him again.

But of course, yes, *of course*, after having discovered that Tom was still married to a showgirl he barely even knew, and deciding to fly to New York to try and do her best to salvage the situation, *of course*, fate had decided to sit her next to Miles Harker of the Kiwi Cocktail Near Death Date Debacle affair for seven hours. *Of course* it had. And now, like so much else in her life, Anna realised there was nothing else she could do but grin and bear it.

She tensed, bracing herself back in her seat, as the plane, now at the head of the runway, gathered speed, its engines roaring as they finally lifted into the air. Anna didn't mind flying, but the taking off and landing parts she wasn't so sure about.

'So,' Miles said, leaning dangerously close to her as Anna waited for the plane to stop climbing and banking and level out. 'You look great, by the way. Really, really

. . . smart. And your normal-sized lips really suit you, if you don't mind me saying.'

'Thank you.' Anna breathed a sigh of relief as the plane settled into its journey. She tucked the magazine back in its pouch and decided that enduring twenty minutes of small talk now might mean she'd get the rest of the time to sleep or watch a film before escaping Miles, hopefully this time for ever.

'And?' she said, with her best effort at a smile. 'Why are you going to New York? Business or pleasure?'

'Destiny,' Miles said, his eyes sparkling. 'You know I write songs, right? Simon would have told you when he made you go out with me. Well, I write stuff, record it, and sometimes I stick it on YouTube – I've been doing it for donkeys – and then a few months back I wrote this song, "Fire Girl", stuck it up there, thought no more about it, turns out it's had like three hundred thousand hits or something. You might have seen it?'

'No,' Anna said, apologetically. 'I don't really know what YouTube is for, but then again if it was up to me I'd still use a pen to write a letter and then post it via pigeon, so . . .'

'Fair enough,' Miles said. 'Anyway, there's this New York band, not famous, not yet, but with a reputation, you know, a following. Their lead singer jacked it all in a few weeks back, apparently found God and decided to become a monk or something, and they need a new frontman. This morning in my inbox was a message from their drummer, asking *me* if I wanted to go and audition for them. And now I'm on a plane. To meet my destiny. Or crushing, expensive disappointment and bankruptcy, one or the other.' Miles's eyes, which Anna noticed were such a vivid blue they were almost violet, shone with a small boy's excitement, crinkling pleasantly as he relished the prospect of what could be his big break. Anna wondered vaguely if he was still single, thinking to herself that if he was, she should introduce him to Liv. Liv would like him. In fact why had Simon never thought of setting him up with Liv in the first place? Oh that's right, there had been the mysterious new man at the gym that Liv had been holding a candle for, whatever happened to him? After that one occasion Liv never mentioned him again, and if he'd been important Liv certainly would have told Anna about him.

'Bankruptcy?' Anna asked.

'Well, maybe not quite that dramatic, but I had to sell some amps and pedals to get together the money to come, and I bought the ticket a few hours ago. I've got literally no idea where I'm going to crash when I get there, or what I'm going to do between now and the audition, but you've got to grab opportunities when they come, haven't you? Roll with the punches, go with the flow, all that sort of stuff.' Miles dropped his gaze for a moment to his hands, twisting a silver ring around and around the thumb on his right hand. 'Of course, if I don't get it, I'll be stuffed. I've sold most of my gigging equipment and I can't afford to replace it without work, which I won't get if I haven't got it. But well, I had to take this chance, didn't I?'

'Honestly, no,' Anna pointed out, perhaps a little bluntly.

'What do you mean?' Miles asked her, baffled. 'What do you mean I didn't have to?'

'Well, I mean that you didn't have to gamble your equipment and your livelihood and come to New York at the last minute for something that most likely won't work out,' Anna said. 'You could have said no, you could have kept your gear, and known that you'd at least be able to take the next gig that was offered to you, and keep on paying your bills.'

Miles stared at her. 'But this is the New York Rock Department – the NYRDs – this is like the next big thing. This could be it, this could be my big break. What I've been working towards all my life. I'd be crazy not to go! You must see that?'

'*Could* be,' Anna said. 'That's the key word there. *Could* be your big break. I mean, no offence, but you're thirty, and I think, from what I can remember, that Simon said that you have a pretty great career for a musician: regular session work, gigging, playing for all sorts of bands, travelling all over the world. That's kind of amazing and in your business that *is* success. Think of the number of guitarists who don't make any money at all, who work in Pizza Hut and dream about having the life you do.'

Miles shook his head. 'No, no, no, Annie. You've got that all wrong. The reason I've made a career out of music is because I've never stopped following my dream, my ambition, never ever not for one second. And in the process, I've built up a career. I've never, ever got anywhere by taking the sensible option.' He smiled at her, light dancing in those azure eyes. 'And I'm sure as hell not going to stop taking chances now, not ever. That's not what life is about at all. It's about grabbing the moment, experiencing every single second to the maximum, without worrying about what comes next. Look at us!'

'Us?' Anna quizzed him. 'There is no us, and it's Anna, by the way. I have mentioned it before. Once or twice.'

'Yes there is an us, Annie,' Miles said, ignoring her. 'There is an "us" right now on this plane, you and me, together. Both of us setting out on an adventure. Until this plane lands we are in it together, and who would ever have predicted that when I blew up your head to the size of a watermelon and almost killed you? That's what I love about life, the unpredictable, the unforeseen. That's what makes it so interesting. So, yes, if I get an incredible chance out of the blue, it's yes. I'll risk everything to take it.'

Anna thought about what he said, shaking her head with regret.

'I hate the unpredictable,' she said with a small smile, reaching up to undo her hair, which felt uncomfortable and tight. She shook it out over her shoulders, running her fingers through its golden waves, and added, 'I hate being taken by surprise, not knowing what's coming next. I hate curve balls and bends in the road. I like to know exactly how everything is going to be, always.'

'Really?' Miles said, turning away from her as she loosened her hair, as if somehow he was witnessing something he shouldn't see. 'I mean, really? Why is that though?'

'There are a lot of reasons,' Anna said wearily, faintly surprised to find how easy Miles was to talk to when he wasn't forcing her to listen to heavy rock or poisoning her. 'My mum, or sudden lack of her, the whole Regina Clarkson incident, but probably most recently the news that the man I am supposed to be marrying in my dream picture-book, Christmas fairy-tale wedding in two weeks' time is already married to a stripper.'

In an instant the woman across the aisle was enthralled once again, and I Heart London closed the book she'd been pretending to read with an eager snap, resting it in her lap.

'You're engaged, and about to be married?' Miles asked her, more surprised by that news than he was of Tom's unexpected ex. 'Blimey, your life really *has* moved on since I saw you. I mean of course it has. It's just . . . married? That's . . . really serious.'

'Not quite married,' Anna reminded him. 'Actually, right now, very, very far from being married. And I don't blame you for being surprised. I never thought anyone would want to marry me either. I mean I look OK, I scrub up quite nicely, but as soon as you get to know me you realise I am a nightmare. I don't mean to be. I try pretty hard to be all the things that people like – funny, spontaneous, relaxed, easy-going, popular. But I'm just not that person. I'm controlling, obsessive, compulsive and I can't dance . . . I overcommit far too early.' Anna shook her head miserably, finding that now she'd started pouring her heart out to Miles, it was hard to stop, despite the many pricked-up ears all around them, whose owners had stopped watching the in-flight movies in order to listen to them. 'You know what, I did think that our date was the worst date I've ever been on, but actually the fact that you tried to kill me with a kiwi is probably the only reason you are willing to talk to me now, because when you've got a tongue the size of a salami it's hard to annoy a person. Any other man I've dated in the past who discovered me unexpectedly sitting next to him on a long-haul flight would either have paid to upgrade to first class or got off the plane before they locked the doors. See? Listen to me? I'm annoying.'

'No you're not,' Miles said, looking a little baffled by Anna's sudden gush of words. 'Shaken up, and a bit insecure maybe. Verging on needy. But who wouldn't be in your shoes. The dude asked you to marry him and didn't mention a wife, man, that's just bad manners.'

'Exactly!' Anna said, wagging a finger at him, enthusiastically. 'Exactly, that's what he is, he's really, *really* rude. And it's not like I chased him, he chased me. He turned up at Liv's party, kept looking at me, made conversation with me, even though I mainly talked about food hygiene standards, kissed me on the stairs outside the flat, in this really unexpected way, because one minute I was asking him what he thought about organic versus free range and the next he had me pinned against a wall. And then *he* was the one who kept on going out with me, again and again, until I started to think of him as my boyfriend, and *he* was the one who asked me to marry him. The one who got a ring, and let me book the church, which to be honest we were always going to get because his dad is the vicar, and he's supposed to be marrying us, but still it's the principle, and the venue, and the dress and everything else I've been doing for more or less a whole year. And then, *then* he waits until now to remember to tell me he'd already got married before by accident.' She found herself twisting in her seat, leaning forwards to look Miles in the eye. 'You're a man, what does that mean, do you think?'

Miles backed away from her a little, obviously rather taken aback by Anna's sudden intensity.

'I don't think it means he doesn't love you, if that

helps,' he said, squirming a little under Anna's intense gaze. 'I think he'd probably forgotten about it, or told himself it didn't matter, or hoped it would work itself out somehow without him having to say anything.' This didn't seem to placate Anna, whose otherwise creamy complexion was now sporting two bright red spots of colour burning furiously on either cheek, and whose eyes narrowed dangerously.

'And,' Miles added hurriedly, 'when you think about it, the very fact that he has told you now, that says a lot.'

'Yes, it says that he's a—' Anna's fuming was swiftly interrupted.

'In love with you enough to face up to your very considerable wrath even though he must have known that it could cost him your relationship,' Miles finished for her. 'That although he realises what a massive fuck-up he is, he cares enough to tell you the truth eventually, to face you down and do the right thing. Perhaps you are looking at this all wrong. After all, how easy would it have been for him not to tell you about the stripper at all, to just do nothing and let the wedding go ahead. I think the fact that he's told you now shows that he truly loves you.'

Anna blinked at Miles, sucking on her bottom lip as she tried to take in what he was saying. 'You're one of those, aren't you? One of those types. Liv is one too. Optimistic, romantic, idealistic. It's because nothing really bad has ever happened to you so you don't know . . .'

'Know what?' Miles asked her.

'That you have to keep looking, waiting all the time for the next bad thing,' Anna said. 'It's your only chance of stopping it from happening. Except that I didn't see this coming.'

'Maybe you need to start looking out for all the good things,' Miles said, spreading his fingers as if he were casting a spell to illustrate his point. 'Like the fact that the man is trying his best to do the right thing now, he hasn't lied or run away, he's just made a mistake.'

'I suppose he *was* seeing a solicitor about it when I tailed him to Pizza Express,' Anna said thoughtfully, causing the 'I Heart London' lady's eyebrows to soar skywards. 'I suppose he was *trying* to sort it out, in his own cack-handed, shambolic way. It was much too late and with frankly the sluttiest solicitor that I have ever seen, but still he *was* trying . . .'

'There you go then.' Miles smiled. 'And did he get it sorted? An annulment or whatnot? Is this last-minute trip an all-expenses paid apology to help you calm down before the big day?'

'No,' Anna said, sitting back in her seat and looking around, as if she'd just woken from a dream or a trance, and was realising exactly where she was and what she was doing for the very first time. 'No, he didn't, he couldn't. It would have meant postponing the wedding which is why . . . Well, to cut a long story short, I booked a last-minute ticket to New York to see if I could find his wife and get her to sign the papers in person.'

'Sweet Jesus,' I Heart London muttered audibly.

'I thought you said you weren't spontaneous,' Miles said. 'That's radical! That's the most spontaneous thing I have ever heard! You go, girl.'

'No, Miles, no.' Anna shook her head. 'It's not spontaneous. It's desperate, and controlling and crazy and really it should be Tom that is sitting on this plane, doing this. I pretty much asked him to try and he pretty much said don't be so ridiculous, and yet I am still here sitting on this plane being ridiculous because I just can't let it go. And the truth is I don't know if I will have a wedding when I get back because probably around about now –' she checked her watch '– Tom will have realised exactly how mental I am and he'll be running a mile.'

'No, he won't,' Miles said, unexpectedly taking her hand. 'He'll think how lucky he is to have such an amazingly romantic, spontaneous, optimistic, brave and incredible woman, who still wants to marry him, despite the high levels of fuckwittery that he has recently displayed. If he loves you that is what he will think.'

'Do you really think so?' Anna asked. 'Only no one's ever called me amazingly romantic or spontaneous before, in fact I'm fairly sure that I am the opposite of all of those things.'

'How can you be, if you got a plane at moment's notice to try and save your wedding?' Miles asked and, when she thought about it, Anna supposed that he did rather have a point, which somehow frightened her more than reassured her. She'd spent the majority of her life working hard at containing all the thoughts and feelings that she was afraid might give her away; the idea that she had somehow unwittingly let all those defences disappear without a second thought for the consequences alarmed her. Except . . . except if Miles was right, if that was the way Tom saw her, saw her trip, then perhaps, just perhaps, that might be a good thing?

'You must love him very much,' Miles said. 'Your Tom. You must love him a great deal to go through all of this for him.'

Anna sat back in her chair, leaning her head against the rest.

'Yes,' she said. 'I do. I do love him. He's the first man who's ever made me feel . . . safe and normal.'

'So,' Miles said, looking at his watch, as Anna realised they had barely been in the air for half an hour and she'd already poured her heart out to a man she barely knew. 'I think I'll check out a movie or three.'

'Me too,' Anna said, relieved that the conversation was over by mutual consent. She noticed, as she plugged in her headphones, Miles giving her a fleeting sideways look, before he settled down to watch some slasher horror, which he probably thought would be a good deal less terrifying than listening to her rant on.

Anna sighed heavily, debated over a romantic comedy featuring Anne Hathaway and then opted for the horror film too. After all, right now a good deal of screaming and anguish, and foolish decisions to go down into the cellar armed only with a torch, seemed like a much more accurate reflection of her love life than Anne Hathaway kissing boys in Central Park. There really was only one thing for it, Anna decided darkly. The only thing she could do as soon as she got to New York was to turn around and go home again and face up to the fact that Slutty Martha had been right, there was no way she would be married by Christmas.

Chapter Five

'Hello, Tom. Yes, I know what time it is, and the thing is, you see, is that, um, well . . . Now that Anna's gone to New York and left me in charge of the wedding, the last thing she told me to do was to check on you and make sure you were OK.' Liv rehearsed under her breath as she waited for the lift that would take her to Tom's riverside apartment. Funny, she thought to herself as she watched the LED numbers count down to the dawning of the impossibly awkward situation she had found herself in, when she'd first visited Tom's flat, almost two years ago now, she'd never imagined that one day she'd be turning up at just after midnight, under this set of circumstances. Nope, of all the things she had imagined, which had been legion, and mainly involved her and Tom engaging in naked kissing, never, ever had she imagined this scenario. Maybe Anna was right, maybe the only way to get through life was to try and think of every single worst case scenario before fate could get to it.

Liv remembered the first time she'd set eyes on Tom. She'd just laid out her instructor with a particularly powerful roundhouse kick to his solar plexus, screeching like a banshee as she landed on the crash mat, to find this tall, gingery-blondish, strong-looking man grinning at her with naked admiration, which wasn't something that Liv was all that used to. When it came to attracting men, Liv realised at some point around the age of seventeen, she and Anna were as bad as each other, although in completely different ways. For although boys, and then men, were usually initially attracted to Anna, with her legs and breasts and hair, quite soon her particular little tics and foibles, fierce intellect and anxieties would mostly scare them away, and those that had stuck around for longer were invariably the sort of lowlife who liked going out with beautiful but insecure women principally to do their heads in. Liv's problem on the other hand was quite different. A little shorter than Anna, with dark olive skin that she'd inherited from her Italian grandmother, her curves were more subtle, her soft brown eyes, fringed with black lashes, less instantly arresting, and her short spiky black hair, which she liked because it was easy to look after and suited her delicate heart-shaped face, was less obviously sexy than Anna's Rapunzel locks. Also Liv wasn't the sort of girl who knew how to be girly, which despite her problems, Anna instinctively was. If Liv met a man that she liked, she'd either talk to him like he was her new best mate, or not talk to him at all. And, as in Tom's case, if she managed to develop a rapport with him at all, she'd live in the vain and foolish hope that one day he'd suddenly see her in a new light and wonder to himself why on earth he hadn't fallen for this dark, exotic and rare beauty before, sweep her up into his arms, crush her to his chest and then make mad passionate love to her forever more. Well, for at least an hour or two anyway. The trouble was this particular scenario had never quite panned out for Liv. She'd had a couple of proper boyfriends – one had been at school, and the other had been a few years ago, a guy she'd met at five-a-side, a sweet enough man. They'd got on pretty well, and Liv had been really rather fond of him, even if he was two inches shorter than her five foot two and his pet name for her was 'mate'. Then one morning he'd sat up in bed and announced that he'd come to a point in his life when he felt that it was time for him to really move on with his life, to commit to a relationship, to get married and have children. And that, he told Liv, holding her hand and looking into her eyes, was why he thought it was time they broke up. She was, he told her, a great girl, a brilliant laugh, a total mate, but she just wasn't the sort of girl he imagined himself marrying. Since then Liv had come to accept that she was the kind of girl who on the inside was a hopeless romantic, but who on the outside tended to be the girl that men bought pints for and then turned to for advice about other 'proper' girls.

Her hopes had been high when she'd met Tom

though, about six weeks before his first fateful encounter with Anna, because she could have sworn that the first time he'd seen her that afternoon, screaming like a fishwife, there had been a twinkle of attraction in his eyes as he'd looked her up and down in her sports bra and Lycra shorts. A little overwhelmed by his charming grin, which made sweetly asymmetrical dimples either side of his mouth, and his sheer physical presence, Liv had done two things. Firstly, she developed an instant crush on him and, secondly, she decided to go for her policy of never speaking to him at all, mainly on the grounds that she was fairly sure he was far too handsome to talk to using actual words.

Tom on the other hand had had other ideas. He sought Liv out for sparring, complimenting her on her sharp right hooks and precise uppercuts, and showed her some of his own techniques, which frankly weren't quite as good as Liv's, but she'd pretended to be impressed by his prowess. After about three weeks of friendly hellos, and mostly kick-boxing-related chats, Liv had come out of the women's changing room one evening, her hair still damp from the shower, to find Tom waiting for what turned out to be her.

'Fancy a drink?' he'd asked her as if it was the most natural thing in the world for a man like him to ask a girl like her for a drink. Most likely he wanted to ask her advice on girls, Liv had told herself as she had mutely nodded her acceptance, or perhaps he thought, she actually was just a very short, slightly bosomy boy.

'You're good,' Tom had told her in the pub, handing her the gin and tonic she'd asked for as they took a seat. 'Better than you let on, most of the time. Have you ever thought about competition?'

'Why?' Liv had asked him warily. Was that why he'd asked her for a drink? Did he want to manage her or something? Or bet against her in some elaborate gambling scam?

'No reason,' Tom chuckled. 'I just wondered. A girl as good as you, you could win stuff, I think.'

'Oh, I don't know,' Liv said. 'It's just a good way of letting off steam. My job's quite . . . high pressured. This helps me relax.'

'Not the typical sort of hobby for a girl to pick,' Tom had said.

'Well, I'm not a typical sort of girl,' Liv had said before she had time to think of how that sounded, but Tom didn't seem at all thrown by her retort.

'I can see that.' He'd smiled at her, and Liv had been almost one hundred per cent sure it had been a flirting sort of smile. A few weeks had gone by with Tom and Liv becoming friends, stopping for a drink after sparring once or twice a week, sharing jokes, talking about their jobs, their families and friends, with one notable exception – Liv had not mentioned Anna, her foster sister, best friend and flatmate. For reasons that she didn't care to dwell on, Liv decided not to tell Tom anything about Anna or Anna anything about Tom, not even to mention that she slightly liked him as a person, let alone had a dangerously deep crush on the man, because Anna would instantly want to know everything about Tom and then before Liv knew it she'd be making a list to check compatibility and weigh up pros and cons, and within an hour Liv would have a statistical probability of how successful a relationship with Tom was likely to be in real terms. And that was one thing Liv didn't want to know, she didn't want to lose that sense of hope and expectation just yet.

She did mention him to Simon, one weekend when the three of them had been home visiting Mum. Simon had been trying, with his usual dogged determination, to set her up with some long-haired musician type, apparently convinced they'd be perfect for each other, and the only way Liv had been able to make him stop was to mention Tom. But even then she refused to divulge details. She didn't want to jinx it. The way Tom looked at her, the way he smiled at her, the way he brushed against her when they were putting on coats or picking up bags, Liv was sure that the first-kiss moment could only be days away. All she needed was the right ambience, the right setting and an excuse to wear that tight little red dress her mother said made her look like a girl for a change, and a pair of heels. Which was why she hit upon the idea of throwing herself a birthday party, to make an occasion of the date she usually tried her best to forget as an excuse to invite Tom home without looking like she was asking him out.

Anna had taken some persuading, and some reassuring over red wine and white sofa clashes, cheesy footballs in the deep pile scenarios, and people going around the house and touching stuff. But as soon as Liv had given her the green light to make lists, she was on board. Tom was invited and available to attend and everything, everything was in place for that first kiss to take place, and for Liv's secret romantic dreams to come true for once in her life.

The night of the party came and the scene was set. Liv looked fairly good in her red dress, the subtle curves of her cleavage swelling over the scoop neckline. She sported just a little mascara and eyeliner to bring out her eyes, and a dusting of glitter on her dusky skin. Negotiating even two or three steps in her high heels was more of a challenge, but Liv told herself she only needed to keep them on for that first-impression moment with Tom, the moment when he realised that he loved and wanted her, and then after that she could kick them off and go about in her flip-flops.

For most of the evening, Liv hovered by the front door, opening it every time the bell rang, hoping to find Tom there, speechless as he took in her ensemble and realised that she didn't scrub up too badly as it turned out. But as hour after hour dragged by, with the party in full swing in the other room, the several glasses of wine Liv had partaken of to bolster her courage began to take their toll, and after three hours of constant door management, she had finally had to take a break to go to the loo. She'd just been wiping away her excess eyeliner with a piece of tissue paper when she heard the bell go again. More than a little tipsy, it had taken her several seconds to guide her feet into her shoes, several more to remember which way the lock on the bathroom door turned to open, and crucially several more than that to make a dignified and almost sexy progress up the hallway in four inches of stiletto to open the door.

Crucially for her future prospect of happiness, Liv was too late, and by the time she made it, the door was already open. She felt herself deflate against the wall as Anna opened the door and Tom set eyes on her for the first time, her golden hair rippling down her back, her figure-hugging if demure cotton dress, her slim, golden brown calves. And in that one instant Liv could see that Tom was smitten. And even if, like most of Anna's encounters, it only lasted until Tom realised that she wasn't being ironic, she really was that insane, then it would still be too late for Liv. If Anna was the sort of girl who made his jaw drop, then all her silly romantic fantasies and dreams that he'd been interested in her had been just that. And any hope that Liv had fostered in her heart that the only reason Tom hadn't actually asked her out on a date yet was because he was a slow burner had been crushed when, half a bottle of hastily consumed cava later, she discovered Tom and Anna engaged in a considerable amount of kissing in the hallway, scarcely forty minutes after they had first set eyes on each other. Then there had been the discovery that Tom was still there the next morning, making Anna breakfast in bed in his boxers, grinning and winking at Liv as she bumped into him in the kitchen as if they were just good friends, which they clearly were, followed by the slow months of denial leading up to last Christmas Eve and the inevitable proposal. Liv had had almost a year and a half to get her head round the fact that her latest crush was not into her, and it was time to move on, again. But still that dogged little splinter of affection that had worked its way into her heart the very first time she set eyes on Tom persisted in festering away, and so far she had completely and utterly failed to not be in love with him

Which was why it made all this drama over the Vegas Showgirl Secret Wife so hard not to take personally, and why Liv would rather be anywhere else in the world than travelling up the eighteen floors to Tom's flat to carry out Anna's request to make sure that everything was OK, whatever that meant at this point in their lives, and take care of Tom. But there it was, she and Anna had always been there for each other, always done what the other one asked. And poor, unhappy, confused Anna could not know that she was forcing Liv to take care of a man who she wanted to kiss and slap in equal measure.

It took several long pushes on the buzzer for Tom to finally come to the door and, when he did, he looked terrible. His eyes were bleary and bloodshot, his hair was tousled, and flat on one side, as if he'd been lying on the carpet despairing, which he probably had, judging by his crumpled shirt. He really was upset about everything that had happened, and Anna was not here.

'She went to New York,' Tom told Liv miserably, holding out his mobile phone as if it was somehow proof. 'She just flew off on the spur of the moment to save our wedding. It should have been me, Liv, but I . . . I let her go. And now she's on a plane somewhere out there and I can't talk to her. I can't explain to her that I didn't mean to let her down and if she'd given me just one second to get my head round the idea of course I'd have gone to New York on a wild goose chase if it made her feel better. I've let her down, haven't I?'

Taking a deep breath, Liv followed Tom into his flat, into the large modern kitchen-cum-living space that opened out onto a steel and glass balcony with views across the Thames. It really was a beautiful flat to be depressed in.

'I can't believe this is happening,' Tom told her,

shaking his head miserably. 'I can't believe that one silly mistake, made years ago, is going to ruin everything now! It's not fair. I mean, I got married in a bar, for crying out loud! Not a chapel, not even a chapel with some bloke dressed as Elvis doing the vicar shit. I got married in a lap-dancing bar, with six topless brides-maids, while out of my mind on tequila. How can that be legal? And now I'm going to lose her. My stupid, stupid mistake has messed up the one thing she's always wanted, the one thing I so wanted to give her and I'll lose her.'

Liv waited for a moment or two, just to make sure that Tom didn't have anything else to say. But all he did was stand there on his real oak floor in his bare feet, looking forlorn, making it hard for Liv not to hug him, which she knew she could have done quite legitimately, because they were officially friends, but which she refrained from because of the also wanting to throw him over the balcony thing. I mean a Vegas showgirl in a lap-dancing club? If she'd known about that from the off, she'd have realised straight away that Tom was never going to fall in love with her and months and months of secret misery and heartache could have been averted. But what really made Liv have to stifle murderous thoughts towards Tom was the realisation that despite everything her heart rate still trebled whenever she looked at him, which was probably a good enough reason not to hug him in itself.

'To be honest, Tom, you could have maybe mentioned it a *little* bit sooner,' Liv said, holding her thumb and finger up to illustrate her point. 'I mean, you know Anna, you get her. You know that she was always going to have a meltdown about this. If you'd told her say, when you first got together, or engaged, or even six months ago, then she could have limited her insecurities to the fact that you still have an incredibly glamorous wife, and probably got most of them out of the way by the time the annulment came through *in time for the wedding*. It's the leaving it to the very last moment part that's sent her fruit loops. You know she can't cope with the unexpected, you know she does literally everything in her power to make sure that never happens.' Liv paused, looking at Tom, his head hanging, his shoulders slumped, his arms limp at his side as he realised that he did know all of that, and he probably knew exactly what Liv was going to say next. 'You let her down, Tom.'

'I know,' Tom said. 'I know I did. I just ... I honestly had forgotten about Charisma completely, you know. It was a joke almost, a crazy thing I did when I was young. I really, really didn't think it was real. Which I know makes me an idiot, but it's true. Has she called? Has she sent you round here to dump me?'

Liv shook her head, went to the sofa and sat down. Outside London unfurled along the riverbank, glittering merrily, a city in preparation for Christmas, bristling with lights, like one huge Christmas tree. Funny how it did that, London, made itself look so beautiful, when scratch even a little beneath the surface and you would find darkness and loneliness and chaos. But it was always the surface that counted in this town. If everything looked right, then it was.

'Anna still wants to marry you,' Liv said, forcing herself to look at Tom, who was now seated opposite her, hanging his head. He looked up. 'She wouldn't be on this escapade if she didn't.'

'Really? Are you sure? When she realises that she's never going to find Charisma and she comes back, do you think she'll forgive me and marry me? In the spring maybe? Or the summer?'

'I think she will, honestly. It's just . . . you know Christmas and the whole thing with her mum. It has this massive significance for her, because of what happened. I think she sees it as a sort of talisman, Christmas. It's been her worst and happiest time, and I think this wedding was meant to . . . bring a chapter of her life to a close, so she can start a new one with you. That's why she doesn't want to delay it, or have it at another time of year. Anyway, ' Liv said slowly. 'She's still pretty determined to marry you on Christmas Eve and until she says otherwise I think we have to assume that it will happen. She's left me in charge of everything. I even have to go to her dress fitting in a couple of days, which, by the way, you'll have to drive me to. It's in bloody Surrey for some reason and you know how I feel about driving.'

Tom stared at Liv for a long moment, the synchronised lights of his black and silver Christmas tree changing mechanically on his face.

'Why didn't she tell me about this whole new chapter thing? Why didn't she say that when we talked earlier?' he asked her, repeating the words out loud as if he had to hear them to believe them.

'Because I'm not really sure that she gets its herself, probably,' Liv said. 'You must understand how she feels though? Because if you don't, you don't get Anna. Don't forget, this is Anna who when she was nine years old her mum popped out to the shops on Boxing Day and never came back. Her mum, Tom. She may have been a terrible person, a drunk and a drug addict, but she was still Anna's mum. The one person in the entire world who was meant to make her feel safe. Ever since Anna's been doing everything she can to stop feeling like that again. She'd never leave anything up to someone else unless . . .' Liv had been about to say 'she completely trusts them', but thought better of it as the implications weren't great. And besides, the look on Tom's face wasn't exactly the one of concerned sympathy she'd been expecting. He looked completely stunned.

'Anna told you she was brought up in care, didn't she?' Liv asked. 'I've heard her talk about it to you, and about when she came to live with us. Hundreds of times.'

'Yes,' Tom said, rubbing his hands over his face. 'Except she told me her mum died of cancer, her dad wasn't on the scene, so she got taken into care and then you guys fostered her. That's what she told me, *that* was bad enough.'

Liv was silent, uncertain of what to say. She was familiar with Anna's pat story, the one that explained away a good deal of her unusual life without having to dwell on the seedier aspects, like the fact that neither she nor her mother knew who her father was, or that her mother had done some pretty unsavoury things to pay for her addictions. But never once had she supposed that Anna would keep the truth from the man she was going to marry, the man she was trusting with her heart for the rest of her life.

'Oh,' Liv said. 'Well, I mean it is pretty shocking. And she's done so well to put it behind her, and to move on and become the person she is. That's probably why she didn't tell you, because, you know, she wants you to know the person she is now, despite all of that. I mean, she told you about Regina Clarkson, right?'

Tom stared at her blankly. 'About what?'

'More of a who . . . not important, anyway,' Liv said, anxiously remembering how, one dark night when they were about fifteen, she and Anna had agreed they would only ever tell the men who were the loves of their lives about the Regina Clarkson incident, as a true test of their love and loyalty. 'Well, so. There. You see, that's why she went. That's why she didn't talk to you. Basically, she's frightened to death of losing you.'

'Me or her perfect wedding, with the roses and the reindeer and the dress,' Tom said heavily, knocked sideways by Liv's unwitting revelation.

'You, you moron,' Liv said, getting up and crossing over to where Tom was sitting, his head in his hands. She knelt in front of him and lifted his chin so he was looking into her eyes. 'Tom, you clicked with Anna the second you saw her. I know – I was there. And it was the same with her. The two of you, you are a perfect match. OK, so you've both neglected to mention some fairly relevant information from your pasts, but perhaps that's a good thing. Perhaps that means that now you are both starting on a clean page, on equal terms. Don't be angry at her for going, for taking charge, because she is doing her best not to be angry at you for forgetting about your stripper wife.'

'Dancer,' Tom muttered. 'She was an exotic dancer.'

Suddenly acutely conscious that she was touching Tom's face, her lips only a few inches from his, Liv dropped her hands and sat back on her heels.

'Dancer, whatever,' she said. 'Besides, you're right. There is no way she will find Charisma in that great big city, even if she still lives there, even if she still uses the same name. I mean this is Anna we're talking about, not Columbo. In a few days she'll be home again. And then you two can talk things through and reschedule the wedding. In the meantime, let's just do what she wants and wait for her to come to the same conclusion on her own. And I bet you, that as soon as she lands, she'll be desperate to speak to you. OK?'

Tom nodded, and then quite unexpectedly gathered Liv into his arms and held her in a tight embrace. 'You know what, Liv,' he said into her hair, 'I should have fallen in love with you instead of Anna. It would have been so much less complicated.'

'As if I'd ever think that way about you,' Liv scoffed with bravado, whilst on the inside she ever so quietly shrivelled up and died.

Chapter Six

It hit Anna, just as they were driving down to Manhattan, across the Brooklyn Bridge, exactly where they were. There it was, New York, laid out before them, bristling with countless buildings festooned with lights, a glamorous siren, bedecked and bejewelled, arms outstretched ready for seduction. How different it felt from London, Anna realised as their cab driver sped them through the night, with varying degrees of sensible driving, ranging from dangerous to suicidal. She couldn't quite put her finger on what the difference was, except that perhaps London was so old, so layered with history and dirt and life upon life, that her beauty was altogether more matronly than this ultimate showgirl of a city. In London, the city felt aloof, apart from its inhabitants, a grand old dame who tolerated the mass of life that crawled all over it. But when she looked at Manhattan, sparkling and sexy, it was if this city was setting out to entice her from the very start, and for Anna it was perhaps her first experience of love at first sight.

For several surreal moments, Anna felt like she was driving in a big yellow taxi straight into the movie of her own life; she could almost hear the soundtrack playing in the background, and the gravelly tones of the movie voiceover man.

'She came to Manhattan to search for the impossible, never realising what she would discover here would change her life for ever . . .'

'So where are we going?' Miles asked Anna, pulling her abruptly out of her reverie. It wasn't that she had intended to still be with him after they'd cleared customs, it was more that they'd gotten off the plane at the same time, their luggage arrived on the carousel at the same time, they'd stood in the queue for passport control, one behind the other, Miles taking her bag while she slipped off her coat to go through the X-ray, and when eventually they had emerged into the arrivals lounge at JFK at almost three in the morning, it occurred to Anna that this was one of those times that it was better to be with the devil you knew, even if the last time you'd seen him he'd accidentally poisoned you, than the devil who might mug you at gunpoint in some dark alley somewhere. That was if New York had any dark alleys. From what Anna could see of it, it positively bristled with lights, a veritable jewel, glowing with life, pulsating against the night sky, looking like the world's most glamorous Christmas bauble, which should be placed atop some cosmic Christmas tree.

'Um, to a hotel?' Anna said, realising that her habitual forward planning had somehow abandoned her the moment she'd gotten in the cab.

'Which hotel though?' Miles asked her. 'The driver needs to know apparently.'

'And you say you don't know where you are staying?' Anna asked him, tearing her eyes away from the view to turn to him.

'Not sure,' Miles admitted with a shrug. 'I hadn't completely gotten to that stage yet, of knowing where I was staying. I was thinking of finding a twenty-four-hour diner and staying up all night drinking coffee and writing a song, and maybe getting somewhere to crash tomorrow. That was sort of mainly my plan. But then again, I don't know where there is a twenty-four-hour diner, so it wasn't exactly set in stone.'

'Excuse me.' Anna leaned forwards in seat so that she could talk to the driver. 'We need a good, safe hotel in the middle of Manhattan, where would you recommend?'

The driver said nothing, keeping his eyes on the road as he undertook a truck, narrowly avoiding death by central reservation.

'OK . . .' Anna shrugged, uneasily. This was exactly the sort of uncertainty in life that she didn't enjoy: the idea that she had no idea where she was going to rest her particularly tired and confused head for what little was left of the night gave her no sense of anticipation or adventure, just one of uncertainty and dread. 'Well, the Hilton? There's bound to be one of those, or maybe . . . an Intercontinental?'

'Try that,' Miles said. 'I'll come with you, help you check in. Make sure you've got a room, before we say goodbye.'

'Really?' Anna smiled at him. 'That's actually really nice of you.'

'Ah it's just me stocking up on karma really,' Miles said, brushing her words away. 'I mean I've almost killed you once already – if I heard on the news you'd been murdered on arrival I'm pretty sure there's no way I'd do well at the audition. Besides it'll give me time to keep an eye out for that twenty-four-hour diner . . .'

The Intercontinental, which towered above them in a seemingly endless succession of floors, turned out to be fully booked, even though it looked like it should be able to accommodate an entire universe under its roof.

'It's the time of year,' the charming, but tired-looking night concierge, Horatio explained sympathetically to Anna who, desperate for a bed, looked stricken by the news. 'The whole world comes shopping in New York for the holidays. Really, to get a decent room in Manhattan at this time of year you need to book months in advance.'

'But I didn't know I was coming until today,' Anna told him unhappily. 'Or yesterday, I'm not really sure what day it is any more. All I know is that when I got up this morning I had a life plan, and now I have no idea what's going to happen next . . . and . . . and . . .

all I want is a shower and . . . and . . . a bed.' Heavy crystalline tears filled her eyes, one rolling heavily down her cheek as she turned away from Horatio and struggled to gain her composure. 'I'm sorry. I know the last thing you need at this time of the night is a British woman having a nervous breakdown in reception.'

'It's no problem,' Horatio told her, kindly. 'Look, let me ring around a few places for you. I know everyone there is to know in the hotel business in this town; if I can't find you a room then no one can.'

'Really?' Anna asked him, her lashes webbed with tears as she dabbed her nose delicately with a tissue. 'Would you do that for me? That is so kind.'

'Sure thing,' Horatio told her, a little bashfully. 'Can't have you crying on your first visit to this great city of mine, can I? Take a seat in the lobby, I'll get some coffee brought to you while I check out what the deal is. And what about this –' Horatio looked Miles up and down with a good deal less empathy '– gentleman. Will he be needing a room too?'

'No,' Anna said at once. 'He wants a diner to sit in.'

'No,' Miles said, almost at the same time. 'I'm just making sure that the lady is safe and secure before we part ways.'

'Well, then,' Horatio said, 'coffee for two then.'

'Clever,' Miles said, as Anna sank gratefully onto a corporate-looking sofa, long, cubist and red, letting her body sink into its limited softness, her head lolling awkwardly on the too low back. It had been surprisingly tiring, not sleeping on an aeroplane for seven and some-thing hours, draining all of the energy out of her, so that really all she could do was wonder what she was doing sitting in a hotel lobby on the other side of the world based on an impulse that was even more unlikely and stupid and foolish than the idiot who married a showgirl whilst out of his mind on tequila.

And even though she and Miles had done nothing more than exchange a few civil words for the rest of the flight, in between watching endless films and eating food in trays that would certainly give them indigestion, Anna had found it a strain sitting next to him never-theless, wondering if she should be thinking of things to say to him that would prove she wasn't insane, or perhaps, given that she'd somehow poured her whole heart out to him before the plane had barely even taken off, things to not say. Then again Liv always told her she seemed much more normal when she wasn't talking. Pondering which things she should or should not do had kept her on edge for the entire flight and unable to drift off to sleep for any significant period of time. Except, that was, when she woke, after who knew how long, with a sudden start, to find that her head had been resting on Miles's shoulder. Roused by the sound of her own snores, Anna had been horrified to see that she had left a small patch of dribble darkening his shirt. Fortunately, despite her high-decibel rattling,

Miles had remained fast asleep, arranged far too prettily for a boy, his head lolling slightly to the left, his rather attractive mouth remaining firmly closed and dribble free. He hadn't seemed to notice her incursion on his shoulder, her damp patch of drool, but the fear that it might happen again, and this time she wouldn't be so lucky, was enough to stop Anna from daring to attempt sleep again for the rest of the journey. And now she couldn't find a bed to lie on and Miles was accusing her of being clever of all things.

'What's clever?' Anna asked him, blowing a puff of hair out of her face and watching it descend into her eyes again, before repeating the procedure.

'Hey, listen.' Miles spread his hands as he sat in a decidedly square armchair opposite her, stretching his long legs out in front of him. 'I'm not criticising you, if I had your guns I'd do it too.'

'My guns?' Anna said, uncertainly, sitting up a little and twisting her long hair into a rope, which she tied in a loose knot at the base of her neck. 'What are you talking about, Miles. I don't have guns!'

'Babe, you are armed and dangerous!' Miles told her, chuckling.

Anna blinked at him. 'Do you have to call me "babe", because, you know, I'm not your babe. Or anyone's babe, really. And also, what are you talking about?'

'The hot chick ammo?' Miles said, genuinely stunned that Anna didn't know what he was talking about.

'Come on, don't pretend you don't know that about yourself?' Anna shook her head. 'Annie, you're beautiful, blonde, built.' Miles verged on illustrating his last point with an ill-advised gesture involving cupping both his hands in front of his chest, but managed to pull out of it at the last moment, when he saw the look on Anna's face. They both knew what he had been thinking though and Anna crossed her arms protectively over her front, pressing her lips into a thin line of disapproval.

'*And,*' Miles soldiered on, despite the certainty that he was about to get shot down in flames, 'you're, you know, lost in New York, in the middle of the night. All I'm saying is yeah, sure, why not rock out a heat-seeking flirt missile, and get some poor unsuspecting dude to sort things for you?'

Anna shook her head, rolling her eyes at the ceiling and sighing.

'You know your trouble, Miles,' she told him. 'You're a dinosaur. You're such an unreconstructed rock star in your own little head. You think women are objects, without any brains or purpose beyond trying to trick men into doing things for them by flashing their cleavage! My God, I run my own business, I own my own flat, I have done since I was twenty-three – I don't need a man to do anything for me, but if I am lucky enough to come across a gentleman who is willing to help me out, out of the goodness of his heart, then I thank my lucky stars. The world is not full of leather-trousered, eyeliner-wearing sexist pigs, you know. Some people, even a few men, are actually simply decent.'

Baffled, Miles looked like he was thinking about arguing with her and then thought better of it. 'All I'm saying is that *I* would, if *I* could, but it doesn't work the same way for men. I mean, I can talk a girl into a lot of things but probably not into, say, doing my laundry or filing my tax return. And that is the main difference between the sexes.'

'Oh my God, you are such an arsehole!' Anna exclaimed, almost laughing she was so horrified. 'Thank God for the anaphylactic shock that saved me from your nineteen-seventies mindset clutches. And just so we're clear on this, I wasn't flirting, or playing damsel in distress or anything else. I was thanking a very nice person for doing something very nice that he didn't have to do.'

Miles bristled at the insult. 'Yeah, and if you didn't look the way you do, toss you hair over your shoulder, do that cute little pouty thing and have those big blue teary eyes, then he probably wouldn't be doing it now. Do you think he'd be sending you coffee and ringing round hotels if you were say twenty stone and eighty-five?'

'Yes!' Anna exclaimed. 'Yes, I *do* think that, because he's a nice person, who cares about other people. Which, until about three minutes ago, I thought about you. I thought that offering to stay with me until my room was booked was an act of chivalry. Oh my God, are you trying to tell me this is your way of trying to get me into bed?'

'No!' Miles protested, a little too loudly in the quiet lobby. 'No, I gave up getting involved with crazy chicks after the last one I dated broke into my flat with a knife, and anyway I don't fancy you. I mean you look good, yes. But being near you is like being in the same room as one of those spiders that bites your head off after they've had sex with you.'

'Even your insults are about sex!' Anna was exasperated. 'Look, if in your little delusional head you think I've been flirting with you, then you are very, very much mistaken, which makes you the crazy one. I don't flirt, I'm famous for not flirting, I have literally no idea how to talk to men in a sexual way, which is why when one of them asked me to marry him, I had to make sure he wasn't saying it for a bet. And yes, even if he is still married to a stripper, I am still with him and I would never, ever, *ever* cheat on him. So just get that thought out of your head right now. There is no sex for you here, mister.'

Miles and Anna stared at each other, a gradual sense of the surreal quality of their early-hours argument dawning on each of them at precisely the same rate of insidious horror.

'Are we drunk?' Miles asked her quietly. 'How and

when did this all start, again? Because I don't remember getting drunk.'

A tray of coffee was deposited at their table by a miserable-looking young woman, who scowled at them as she dumped a pot of sugar sachets as a resentful afterthought.

'Look, I can't remember how we started arguing, and for the record I am not trying to hit on you, Anna, or anything of the sort. You've got your man, and you've travelled across the Atlantic to try and keep him. I see that as proof positive that you are off limits. I just wanted to look out for you in the big city, you seemed so upset on the plane, and I thought for Simon's sake, someone should keep an eye on you. He's a mate, and you're as good as his little sis, right?' Anna nodded, rather ashamed that that far more noble motivation hadn't occurred to her. 'I'm sorry, I didn't mean to offend you. I'm just . . . a bloke.'

'That's true,' Anna said. She took her coffee and drank it too quickly so that it burned the inside of her mouth. Her expression softened as she realised that she was actually glad not to be alone for her first hours in New York City. 'I am glad that you are here,' she added eventually. 'Thank you.'

'Anna, we tried dating and it ended in a near-death experience, so shall we just say, here and now, that we are friends and that's it?' Miles said.

'Miss?' Horatio appeared at her side before Anna

could answer Miles. He hunkered down so that they were at eye level and rested his chin on the arm of the sofa like an adoring puppy dog. 'I made a few calls, there isn't much going, but I can secure you a suite at the Algonquin. It's only five minutes from here and – don't tell anyone I told you this – it's much nicer than this dump.'

'A suite?' Anna said uncertainly, thinking of exactly how much heat her emergency credit card could take.

'It's all they've got,' Horatio said apologetically. 'And that's only because some celebrity cancelled at the last minute. But I know the concierge there, so I managed to get you a reduced rate of eight hundred and forty-nine a night. The room's free all weekend, and into next week, so if you want you could book it out, which might be advisable, depending on how long you're planning to stay. In the meantime, I've got friends keeping an eye out for anything cheaper that might come up, so we can always move you, if you know . . . you leave me your cell . . .'

'Eight hundred and something dollars? A night?' Anna said uncertainly. It seemed like a lot. Anna liked the finer things in life – she liked her nice clothes, and her shoes, and her hair products and a decent bottle of wine, and she liked that the ring on her finger said she was marrying a man who didn't mind spending a healthy amount on a diamond. But everything she had she worked for, barely ever using credit, and the little girl who'd had nothing as a child still found it almost impossible to spend so much money on what was, after all, a bedroom. 'And that's the only room in the whole of New York?' she asked Horatio.

'Apart from my room,' Horatio said, smiling shyly at her. 'It's the only room in Central Manhattan that I'd be comfortable with a pretty lady like you staying in. Alone.'

Horatio glanced at Miles, who instantly bristled with that kind of male competitiveness that emerges from nowhere, whether or not there is actually anything to be competitive over.

'Listen,' he said. 'Take it, between the two of us, the cost won't be so bad.'

'Between the . . . I'm not sharing with *you*,' Anna said horrified, to Horatio's obvious satisfaction.

'No, you don't have to, it's a suite. That means there'll be a bedroom *and* a sofa, at least. I need a place to stay, to practise before my audition, and you need a base while you're searching for the sex worker married to your fiancé, so . . .' Horatio raised a brow and Anna tried her level best to physically kill Miles with a look, bitterly disappointed that her telekinetic powers weren't quite up to scratch. 'So, it makes perfect sense for us to share, right?'

'But you don't have any money,' Anna reminded him.

'I've got money,' Miles said, indignant. 'Some. And

when I've been signed by this band, I'll have a lot more. The NYRDs make good money.'

'Oh, the NYRDs, they're cool man,' Horatio said. 'You up to replace Jake Evans? The one that found God and became a monk?'

'Yeah,' Miles said as the balance of rapport changed entirely and now, all of a sudden, the men were best buddies. 'If they're looking for a lead singer who definitely won't take a vow of celibacy, then they've come to the right place, know what I'm saying?'

Horatio guffawed, slapping Miles on the shoulder.

'That is sick, man, those guys are going places.' He grinned. 'They were on *Letterman* a little while back.'

'Yeah, I know,' Miles said, his easy self-confidence flickering for just a second, as Anna caught a glimpse of exactly how much this chance meant to him. 'Obviously, it might not pan out, but you've got to hope for the best, right?'

'Sure.' Horatio nodded enthusiastically. 'You'll smash it, you'll see.' He glanced at Anna as if he'd just remembered she was there. 'So you two want this room or not?'

'Yes please, I suppose,' Anna said reluctantly, looking at Miles. 'Although you'll stay on the sofa, you'll keep your pants on and you do not interfere with what I'm doing in any way, shape or form. Agreed?'

Miles held his hands up. 'Agreed! I've already told you you're completely safe from me, Anna,' he assured her.

'I'll tell them you're coming over,' Horatio said. 'Ask for Sebastian, tell him I sent you. So the guy you're going to marry is already married to a hooker?'

'Erotic dancer, actually,' Anna said. 'Charisma Jones, have you heard of her?'

Horatio shook his head. 'Nope, but I knock off at five if, you know, you want to hook up for breakfast?'

By the time Anna and Miles finally made it into their suite, which was styled in what Anna could imagine was classic modern New York chic – modern clean lines, muted colours accented with orange, everything square and positioned at neat right angles – completely at odds with the grand old glamour gilt, marble and crystal of the lobby, Anna was so exhausted, so confused by life in general, that she didn't even have the energy to cry. Which, considering she had somehow found herself in a luxurious hotel suite in the most exciting city on earth with a man she barely knew, and not her already married husband-to-be, was exactly what she wanted to do.

After trudging into the bedroom, dragging her suitcase behind her, Anna sat heavily on the edge of the bed and switched on her phone, which after a moment or two locating a network finally buzzed into life, imperiously declaring seven missed calls from Tom. It would be just be about 9 a.m. there now, Anna thought, checking her watch, which was still stuck on London time, somewhere in the uncertain future. Tom would have certainly discussed things with Liv, and by now he'd probably have had a chance to think about what she was doing. The question was, how did he now feel about it and her? Would he be thanking his lucky stars that he'd had a fortunate escape from a such a textbook psycho, or would he be bowled over by the romance of her grand gesture, as Miles had suggested? It came as something of a surprise to her that she really couldn't tell how Tom was going to react once the dust had settled, she couldn't even imagine it. Funny how they'd gotten to this point in their relationship, literally inches away from the altar and there was so much they didn't know about each other. And not just the stupid ludicrous things like pre-existing wives and reckless mothers, but the other stuff too. They'd spent almost every day together for the last year and a half, and yet Anna could not imagine what was going through Tom's mind now, and she was certain that he couldn't even begin to guess what she was feeling, because her chest was racked with such a jumble of emotions that she didn't even know herself. For a second Anna thought about calling him, but only for a second, because as exhausted and befuddled as she was, she knew that at that precise moment in time she had absolutely nothing to say to him.

Anna kicked off her shoes and lay down on the bed, her head fizzing with exhaustion.

'You going to sleep?' Miles asked her, pausing in the doorway.

'If I can,' Anna said, the sudden sadness in her voice weighing down her words.

'Look, get some shut-eye,' Miles said gently. 'Things will seem better when you've had some sleep, they always do.'

'I'll try,' Anna said, turning her face from him.

'And then when you're refreshed you can start looking for this Charisma woman,' Miles said. 'Where are you going to start looking for her anyhow?'

Anna closed her eyes and discovered a symphony of bright lights dancing behind her lids, as she heard the bedroom door gently closing.

'Honestly, I haven't got the foggiest,' she said.

Chapter Seven

Anna's watch told her that it was almost midday back at home when she finally opened her eyes again to find a thin watery light seeping in through the thick curtains. The seemingly endless night in which she had arrived in New York was finally over, and a new day was dawning, which was hard not to feel optimistic about. Getting up, she went to the window to find several well-proportioned flakes of snow wafting downwards towards the street and that the building across the road was swathed in fairy lights which still twinkled in the grey of the early morning. There was something more, also. Something that Anna could detect even from her lofty suite, high above the city with the sidewalk well out of view.

There was an atmosphere here that she had never felt anywhere else before, like a low-level electrical buzz that charged the air with an extra fizz. Even pressing one palm and her nose against the window, Anna struggled to make out the street below, but suddenly, inexplicably, she felt excited. Here she was in perhaps the greatest city on earth at the best time of year, Christmas time, her time. The only time when Anna could look back at her childhood, and know that once, a long time ago, she had truly been loved by her mother, that one Christmas she remembered when everything had been perfect.

The alarm on her phone had sounded, alerting her to the fact that her final dress fitting was about to commence, which meant that by now Liv should have arrived at the home of her dress designer, Dana Dabrowski, and would even now be slipping out of whatever maddeningly boyish outfit she insisted on wearing, and into Anna's beautiful dress.

Anna sighed wistfully, sinking down onto the bed. She had mixed feelings about letting someone else put her dream dress on, but there you were, needs must. And at least it was Liv who was to be her surrogate. In all of the world Anna didn't think there was another person who she would have allowed within six feet of the dress. The two of them were so close that really it was the next best thing to putting it on herself.

Bracing herself, Anna pushed her tangled hair out of her face, getting her bearings as she looked around the room, remembering that she didn't have the suite to herself, and somewhere out there, there was a man she barely knew, lurking about and quite possibly naked. Still in her crumpled and travel-stained outfit that she'd arrived in, Anna smoothed down her skirt, tucked her shirt back in and went to look for Miles. He wasn't hard to find, as his largely nude form was the first thing Anna saw when she opened the bedroom door. He'd crashed out on the sofa, without bothering to convert it into a bed first. She could see, however, that he had removed his shirt and jeans, and quite possibly his underwear, although Anna was grateful for the fact that she couldn't tell that conclusively, as a sheet – that he must have found in a cupboard somewhere – was just about covering his modesty. He lay on his stomach, his face buried in the sofa cushions, one arm trailing loosely on the floor, like a little boy who'd fallen asleep mid-play. Frankly, Anna could have done without being confronted by his naked torso and bare legs at that time of the morning, or any time of day for that matter, considering her position. After all, how quickly would she lose the moral high ground with Tom if he knew that she was sharing her hotel room with a virtually naked man? It would make his past-wife misdemeanour seem positively tame by comparison. Not that Miles wasn't nice to look at. The contours of his arms, as distastefully tattooed as they were, and the muscles in his back were pleasant to observe in an objective sort of way, if one didn't mind objectifying half-naked men whilst they were unconscious, which Anna found with some small surprise, that she didn't.

Realising perhaps a *little* late that she was dwelling rather inappropriately, she half-closed her eyes, as if that made her looking less real, and squinted her way back to the bedroom, firmly shutting the door behind her.

She would have locked it too, but there didn't seem to be a key. Well, she thought to herself, at least Miles looked out for the count, so she'd be safe for a little while. Anna took her iPad out of her bag and booted it up then used Facetime to call Liv, having, just prior to boarding the plane, emailed her wedding dress designer to make sure that Liv would be online when Anna arrived in New York. Despite her emotional and physical exhaustion, the last thing Anna had done before she had allowed herself a few hours of sleep was to secure access to the hotel's Wi-Fi connection, in preparation for this morning's video fitting. Was it a good thing, Anna had wondered to herself, before she finally drifted off into exhausted oblivion, that somehow she always, without fail, managed to be quite so prepared, no matter what the circumstances? She told herself the same thing she always did when she became a bit worried that she was bordering on becoming pathologically organised, that it was just her. She did whatever it took to avoid surprises, and just look what kinds of stuff hit the fan when she didn't know what was coming. Secret ex-wives, that was what. There were only two long rings before Liv answered, peering out of the screen, as if she were looking down a rabbit hole. 'There you bloody are!' she whispered, her mouth lagging a little behind the words that came out of the phone.

'Why are you whispering?' Anna asked her in a whisper.

'Because I'm standing in Madam Dabrowski's bathroom in my pants,' Liv hissed. 'Whispering seems somehow appropriate. Why are *you* whispering?'

'Because I don't want to wake . . . anyone,' Anna said, deciding at the last moment not to mention anything about nearly naked Miles languishing on the sofa. Liv was one of those people who was compulsively honest, a trait that Anna both loved and admired in her, but it was imperative that Tom did not find out about her New York lodger. As tempting as it was to make him jealous by flashing around her very own personal rock god, Anna didn't want to risk either Tom being so cross with her that he called off the wedding entirely. Or even worse, not being jealous at all.

'Where are you staying?' Liv asked her, confused. 'In a dorm?'

'No, in a suite in the Algonquin, it was all they had left,' Anna explained. 'But the walls are surprisingly thin.'

Liv looked sceptical, but, as ever, took Anna at her word, falling back on the unwritten and unspoken law that they never, not ever, told each other a lie.

'Well, anyway, as I'm standing in my pants here, can we just cut to the chase? I tell you what, top of my list of "Things I Thought I'd Never Do" is me, stuffing your bra with tissues, lots and lots of tissues, in order to try on your wedding dress. Nope, never saw that coming.' Liv held the camera away from her at chest height so that Anna could see the full extent of her humiliation. 'I think this might be the single lowest point of my life. Well, apart from that time I thought Danny Evers had left a Valentine's card in my locker and it turned out it was meant for you.'

'Leeev!' Dana Dabrowski's voice came from the other side of the door. 'You come out now, we put on dress, yes? I have next client in thirty minute. She not like Anna, she a real fat beeeetch.'

'OK, I'm coming, I'm coming!'

Anna found herself staring at Dana's bathroom ceiling for a few seconds, and wondered vaguely if she was reposing on the toilet lid, before Liv propped her up somewhere, perhaps on the sink, and slipped on a red silk dressing gown that Dana kept hung up behind her bathroom door. She crammed her feet into Anna's simple white satin wedding shoes and tottered uneasily across the bathroom tiles with Anna back in her arms.

'There you are!' Dana said, as if she had just laid eyes on Liv for the first time, hugging her to her ample bosom, which Anna found herself getting an alarming close-up of.

'Hello, Dana!' she called out a little loudly, thinking she might need the extra volume to make herself heard over Dana's considerable cleavage. 'I'm here.'

'Anna!' Dana released Liv and her heavily made-up eyes, complete with false lashes, peered out at Anna from the tablet. 'The things they can do these days with the technology,' she said wresting the device from Liv's hand. 'Well, come then, come, my Anna. Come with Dana and I put you on the mantle, yes? And you see how beautiful your dress is. Your friend Leeev, she a little short, and a little flat around the chest, but she give you the idea and you know you can trust me to have all the measurements just right for you, yes?'

'YES, I KNOW I CAN TRUST YOU,' Anna said, speaking extra loudly, and slowly, forgetting that Dana was Polish and not deaf, and in fact had a better grasp of English than many English people did, a secret that Anna knew because she'd heard Dana on the phone to someone, speaking without a trace of an accent, unless you count upper-middle-class Surrey. All the eccentric broken English was an act for her clients, it seemed, and as a person who spent almost a lifetime composing a persona that she thought people would find most easily acceptable, Anna didn't mind Dana's act in the least, in fact she positively loved her for it. It was a little bit like meeting another member of a secret club. Many people, Liv and Angela in particular, had been surprised when Anna had tracked down the obscure dressmaker in the deepest darkest corner of Surrey instead of going classic Vera Wang or Sarah Burton at Alexander McQueen. But Anna had been adamant, knowing exactly what her vision for her dress was, and knowing she would only really achieve it if she found a dressmaker who could interpret it for her.

A client had told her about Dana, showing her her own wedding photos featuring her in a 1950s-inspired bright red dress. It was a miracle, the client had told Anna. Somehow this crazy little Polish woman had seen into her head and made her vision a reality. After that, there was no way Anna wanted anyone else to recreate her dream for her.

It had been a *bit* tricky, getting to Surrey once a month, but it had been worth it and Anna couldn't wait to see the final finishing touches that Dana had put to her dress. This, perhaps even more than the wedding day itself, was the moment that she had been waiting for. This was the moment that the drawing she had done of her wedding day when she was nine years old became reality.

'You step in, yes?' Dana told Liv. 'You need to take a big step, yes? Like a spaceman on moon. No stepping on the fabric, you step on the fabric, you die. Yes?' Dana delivered the death threat with a smile and a merry twinkle in her eyes, but Liv was totally sure that she meant every word. Conscious of her best friend peering at her expectantly from the mantelpiece, she gripped Dana's hand and took a huge and ungainly step over the yards and yards of material, that at the moment looked like nothing more than an ungainly mass of white froth on the floor and wobbled uncertainly into the small circular void that was waiting in the centre of the whirlpool of duchess satin and velvet.

'Good, now, are you steady?' Liv nodded and Dana let go of her hand, then bent down, her cheek perilously close to Liv's bottom, as she fussed around at her feet, gently pulling the dress up over her hips and waist, and finally her enhanced bosom. 'Breathe in!' Dana commanded and, as she obeyed, Liv felt all the air, and life, being compressed out of her as Dana laced her into the dress with brutal efficiency. This was one way to die, Liv thought, as she was certain she felt her ribs cracking under the strain of the boning of the corset, but perhaps it was the best way to go, smothered to death in her best friend's wedding dress. At least she'd be a very thin – very pretty – corpse.

'There.' Dana took a step back, clasping her hands together. 'You pleased, Anna, yes? You in love with your Christmas princess dress?'

Pursing her lips, Liv glanced in the mirror, preparing to be horrified by what would surely be the awful juxtaposition of seeing herself – eternal awkward tomboy – crowbarred into a world of hyper girliness. For a second or two she wondered who the beautiful woman was staring back at her. She looked straight out of a fairy tale. And then Liv gasped as she realised it was her own reflection, her jaw dropping as she saw herself as never before. If there had been a man present, by all the laws of the universe and romantic comedy, he would have instantly fallen in love with her, having suddenly been made aware of what a great person she was inside, particularly now she had a cleavage.

'Oh my God,' Liv whispered, looking down at the dress, and then back up at her reflection. 'I look . . . *beautiful*.'

'Oh it's perfect!' Anna called out from the mantel-piece. 'Dana, you've done it, you've made my dream dress! It's so exactly what I wanted, I'm going to cry. I am crying, these are tears. Liv don't you cry, not unless you've got waterproof mascara on. What am I talking about, you never wear mascara. Blub all you like. But not on the dress, salt stains.' Liv smiled to herself. The last thing she felt like doing was crying. She felt like laughing out loud, and she would have, except that she was certain Anna and Dana would take it the wrong way.

'Take me closer,' Anna commanded from the mantel-piece, her hands clasped together under her chin. 'I want to see all the exquisite details!'

Liv stood perfectly still, watching herself in the mirror, as Dana picked up the iPad and began to pan it around her.

Anna really had imagined something magical and even Liv, whose idea of dressing up, excepting her ill-fated attempt to get Tom's attention, was wearing a sparkly top with jeans, couldn't help but be enchanted by the garment. It really was the perfect dress for a Christmas Eve wedding, the *only* dress for that one particular day of the year in fact, and now that Liv had seen it, she couldn't imagine that any other dress – or any other day – would do. The white velvet bodice, which had been shaped to fit Anna's ample curves exactly, was covered in fine silver embroidered snow-flakes, hundreds and hundreds of them, each one a little different from the last and each with a tiny crystal at every point, which sparkled and shimmered under the lights. By rights it should have looked ridiculous – like some mad gypsy bride meets meringue confec-tion – but the snowflake theme was so elegantly created it was breathtaking. It flowed its way down to where the full duchess satin skirt began, the opulent material gleaming faintly beneath the final layer of chiffon that Dana had floated expertly over the top, and which was hand-embroidered and beaded with the same incredibly delicate gossamer design right down the hem. There Dana had let the chiffon fall a little longer than the underskirt, and then had meticulously cut around every single snowflake, with delicate precision, creating a beautifully ragged hemline that melted into a short train. It was the kind of dress that Liv would never have been able to imagine herself, but now she had seen it, could never imagine anything more beautiful or perfect.

Liv lifted her head above Dana's bustling, barely conscious of Anna's exclamations of delight and satis-faction as Dana proudly showed her what seemed like every individual stitch, and noticed how her tawny skin contrasted with the pristine white of the gown, how the bodice cinched and accentuated the curve of her waist and hips, and how, with her cheeks a little flushed, her dark eyes sparkling, her nude lips parted as she gazed at herself, it turned out that actually, she was quite gorgeous. Shame really that a girl couldn't get away with wearing a kick-ass wedding dress to work, or the supermarket, or kick-boxing, if a kick-ass wedding dress was what it took to make her look like a girl.

'Now, the jacket, Leeev,' Dana said, interrupting Liv's thoughts to slide a three-quarter-length sleeved velvet bolero jacket, with covered buttons stitched on with silver thread, over her arms and bare back. 'And finally the veil.'

Liv found herself holding her breath as Dana floated a mist of finest net over her head, edged with the same exquisite snowflake motif, and then held it in place with a perfect crystal tiara.

As Liv looked at herself, once removed from reality by the veil that gave her features a soft focus, she felt certain that she wasn't looking at herself any more, but instead at some Snow Queen, one perhaps recently released from a set of wardrobes. And quite unexpectedly, she discovered that she did have a tear in her eye and, more than that, her heart was throbbing with a sudden urgent sense of loss. This was Anna's dress, the dress in which she would one day soon marry Tom. It was the final beautiful omen that Liv had to face to realise once and for all that Tom would never be hers. She'd told herself that a million times over the last eighteen months, but it was perhaps only now, standing here in Anna's dress, that she really understood it,

'It is perfect.' Anna's voice filled the air from the tablet, which Dana handed to Liv before exiting, sensing perhaps that the two women needed a moment to themselves. The veil hiding her tears from Anna, Liv took a breath and held the phone up at shoulder height so that Anna could see the dress reflected full length in the mirror.

'You see,' Anna whispered in her ear from three thousand miles away. 'You see why it has to be a Christmas wedding. Just like I always wanted a Christmas wedding, with my Christmas dress, and this is it. Just the way Mum and me drew it on that last Christmas.'

Liv bit her lip, willing the tears to stop falling, if her own heartbreak wasn't enough it was knowing that, despite everything, the one memory that Anna cherished above all others was that one happy Christmas she'd spent with her mum, the one when she'd been free of drugs for a few weeks, and they'd had a warm place to stay and even some presents. And how much, even now, Anna still loved that version of her mother, still steadfastly entwining her memory into her wedding, even though she hadn't seen or heard from her since she was nine years old.

'I completely see,' Liv said softly, wishing she could extend an arm and put it around her friend, as all sensible and rational thoughts about the marriage being the thing, rather than the dress and the party, evacuated her head in an instant.

'You look lovely in it,' Anna said, sweetly. 'Maybe a bit too lovely, come to think of it. I might have to have a word with Dana, make sure your bridesmaid's dress is a bit frumpier . . .'

'Don't be silly,' Liv chuckled. 'This dress would make anyone look good, but imagine *you*, with your hair, and your skin, and boobs that aren't extra-absorbent four-ply. Oh, Anna, you will be the most beautiful bride there has ever been. Sod Tom. If we can't get hold of his stupid wife and get her to divorce him I'll just find someone else to marry you. You need a Christmas wedding and I'm going to make sure you have it.'

Anna laughed. 'Thanks for doing this, darling,' she said, and when Liv looked she saw Anna's eyes were sparkling with tears again. Confident that her teary moment had passed, at least for now, she ever so carefully lifted the veil off her face so that she could see Anna more clearly.

'You don't have to thank me,' Liv said. 'I know you'd do the same for me, and for God's sake don't cry! Look, this will work out somehow, I know it will, because I know you. You are unsinkable.'

'What, like the *Titanic*?' Anna half sobbed and half giggled. 'No, seriously though. I know it's a pain for the world's last dedicated pedestrian to get to the far side of Surrey in one morning. All those trains and buses, all that public transport, it must have taken you hours.'

'Oh no, we drove,' Liv said, remembering a little bit too late that she probably shouldn't mention to Anna that it was Tom waiting outside in the car for her. Normally, the superstition prevented the groom from seeing the gown before the big day, but under their present tricky circumstances Liv was fairly certain that Anna wouldn't want to take any chances with Lady Luck. Or perhaps she was wrong about that because although they'd been on Facetime now for over half an hour, Anna hadn't asked about Tom, not once.

'Drove, who drove you?' Anna asked.

'Kitty,' Liv said, referring to their seventeen-year-old work experience girl who had only recently passed her test.

'Really, you put your life in Kitty's hands? Kitty who recently food-processed her little finger?' Anna looked amazed. 'Well, fine, but my dress is not getting in a car with her. Ask Dana to have it delivered, would you? I'll pay the extra. And when it gets to the flat hide it somewhere where Tom will not be able to see it.'

Liv nodded, taking one last look at herself, supposing she would have to take the dress off now, and go back to being her usual, short, boyish self again. She would put her boots back on, ruffle her hair into some sort of semblance of style, and feel forever about age nine.

'Talking of Tom, is he OK?' Anna asked her finally, reluctantly, as if she wasn't quite ready to acknowledge that she was in New York looking for his ex-wife and things between her and Tom were decidedly uncertain. 'I'm assuming that as you came to try the dress on he hasn't called off the wedding or anything? I mean, you would tell me, wouldn't you, if he had?'

Perhaps it was the way they were talking, separated by the impersonal screens, but Anna looked frail, white and anxious as she spoke. Not unlike she had the day that she'd finally come to live with Liv and her family for good. Liv remembered her pinched little face as she looked around her bedroom, which had been freshly painted for her.

'Aren't you happy?' Liv had asked her then.

Anna had had exactly the same expression on her face as she did now when she replied. 'I'm not sure, not yet.'

'Of course Tom hasn't called off the wedding,' Liv said. 'He was in pieces when I turned up at his place last night. He really feels like he's let you down. Haven't you talked to him yet?' Liv hesitated.

'No,' Anna said. 'There hasn't been time. I only woke

up a few minutes ago.' She knew that Tom wouldn't mind what time of the day or night she called him, but for some reason she just wasn't ready to have another conversation with him yet, another exchange of sentences that gave her the distinct feeling that neither one of them really got the other one. Everything had happened so fast since she'd gatecrashed his secret meeting with Martha, she hadn't had a moment to think about how she really felt about it, so determined had she been to keep the wedding on track.

'Well, I know he's regretting that it wasn't him on that flight. You didn't really give him a chance to rise to the occasion did you? You maybe did rush into this a bit, you know.'

'I know I did,' Anna admitted reluctantly. 'And I know really that it's not going to work out, and I know I won't get my Christmas Eve wedding and that I'll have to put that dress away for at least a year. In my head, I know that. I'm just not ready to accept it, not yet.'

'And I completely understand,' Liv told her. 'Which is why I think that now is the time that you and Tom should be together, working things out. Not on opposite sides of the Atlantic.'

'I know, you're right,' Anna said, wanly. 'It was just yesterday it seemed like a good idea to get on a plane and save my wedding. I'm cursed with the need to sort everything out, right now, you know that. Now I'm here though, I do feel a bit stupid. Poor Tom, does he think I've gone mad? Or madder than usual?'

'Which brings me to the other thing we talked about . . .' Liv hesitated, wondering how to bring it up.

'Liv!' Anna prompted her anxiously. 'What other thing? If he's told you about another wife, in another city, wearing another set of tassels then I need to know now!'

'Don't be insane. The other thing is I was a bit surprised that you'd told Tom the public version of your story. And not the real one. I kind of accidentally spilled the beans, about your mum and everything, because I thought, you know, what with you being on the verge of marrying him you might have told him the whole truth about yourself, not that he told you the whole truth about himself either, it's just that I did sort of think that kind of fundamental honesty was one of the basics of marriage, call me old-fashioned.'

'Oh.' Anna said nothing for a moment, looking towards what Liv thought must be a window as her profile was suddenly flooded with muted white light. 'I know that *seems* like the logical thing to do, but if you were Tom, or the Tom I thought I knew, you know, the one who was a vicar's son and not the one who drunkenly got married in a topless bar, would you marry the abandoned daughter of a drug-addicted part-time prostitute? I have a hard enough time hiding the crazy as it is, I didn't want to put him off me in the early days, the days when we were telling each other stuff. And then it seemed too late to tell him the whole story. Come to think of it that's probably why he didn't mention getting married in Vegas.'

'Well, you both know everything now,' Liv said, with something of a heavy heart. 'And you both still want to get married. That must mean something. Although I still think the pair of you need to be in the same room, to really sort things out. I don't want to say it but . . . well, it smacks a bit of Regina Clarkson.'

'Yes,' Anna said. 'I know. I can't afford to stay here long anyway, but as I am, I might have at least a day here to clear my head, and then I'll come home and start to be normal again within my recognised parameters and start to rearrange the wedding. Let me see the dress one last time, would you?'

Obediently, and although she found it quite hard to walk in the skirt and the heels, Liv propped Anna back on the mantelpiece and took a few faltering steps backwards.

'Do a twirl,' Anna commanded her. 'And now the other way . . .'

'What you up to babe?' A male voice suddenly sounded from the iPad, causing Liv to spin abruptly on her heels and almost fall off them as she tottered towards the mantel.

'Who was that?' she said, but by the time she got there Anna was gone, and when she tried again her call failed. It must have been in her imagination, Liv thought, as she carefully tiptoed back to the mirror for one last look before Dana came to disrobe her. Or a crossed line or something, if that was possible on Facetime. Maybe Dana had some secret man holed away in her house, because if Liv knew one thing for certain it was that there was no way that Anna would be in a hotel room in New York with a man that called her "babe". Not unless hell had frozen over and there were pigs flying across the Thames.

Hearing the door open behind her, Liv turned around expecting Dana and finding Tom.

'Listen, Liv, we've got to go. I've got a meeting with . . .' Tom stopped mid-sentence as he took in the sight of his friend in his bride-to-be's dress.

'Christ,' he spluttered finally, prompting Liv to stumble and totter behind the nearest – thankfully floor-length – curtain, in a belated attempt to hide the dress from him.

'Tom!' she hissed, peering out from behind the floral material, stamping her foot hard against the floorboards. 'You *can't* see this! Anna must never ever know that you've seen this! Get out! Get out, before Dana comes back and gouges out your eyes with a needle!'

'Of course,' Tom said, but he didn't move an inch, he just stood there in the doorway looking at her.

'Tom!' Liv said, feeling acutely uncomfortable under his incredulous gaze, like some silly little girl caught playing dress-up in her mother's closet and the object of affectionate ridicule.

'It's just . . .' Tom blinked, as if he was coming back to himself after being in a trance. 'It's just that, Liv, I never realised before how beautiful you are.'

'Oh my God,' Liv said crossly, dropping the curtain without thinking in her instinctive and confused reaction. 'Oh my God, Tom, are you really so shallow that it takes a net skirt and bucketload of sequins to make you look at a woman properly? Are you really that thick, because . . . Oh fuck it, just get out! Get out now. I'll be ten minutes.'

'Why are you so cross with me?' Tom asked her, confused.

'GET THE FUCK OUT!' Liv yelled at him, bringing Dana into the room.

Dana shrieked, swore extensively in both English and Polish, and grabbed Tom's arm and threw him with some force out of the front door.

'We never speak of ziz,' she told Liv darkly when she came back into the room. 'The one to speak of this will feel much pain.' She drew her finger across her throat, making a convincing strangulated squelching sound to go with it. But she needn't have worried, Liv didn't need telling twice.

Chapter Eight

'What?' Miles said as Anna almost jumped out of her skin, her iPad flying free from her hands and skidding across the bed to where it was stopped, fortunately, by the pillow.

'You didn't even knock!' Anna protested, not sure of exactly where to look, because although now she knew for sure that Miles had kept his boxers on all night, it was only because he'd waltzed into her room wearing nothing *but* them, leaving the sheet on the sofa.

'I did knock, but you didn't answer and I could hear you talking and this girl's voice so I thought maybe you had company and . . .' Miles paused, looking down at himself, before realising that he was about to justify walking in half naked on a conversation between two women with what might be considered very dubious motives. A most satisfying blush that began on his neck spread downwards, across his torso, which Anna was doing her best not to look at. 'Fuck, I forgot I've not got much in the way of clothes on.'

'What if that had been Tom?' Anna asked, throwing a cushion at him, which he caught gratefully and held protectively over his man parts. 'What if I'd been in the process of patching up my badly shaken relationship with my fiancé and then you walk in in your pants? What then?'

'I didn't think,' Miles said, apologetically. 'You know I just woke up. I was in a bit of a muddle. I just wanted to say hi and . . . anyway I'll go and put some clothes on.'

'Thank you,' Anna said, forced to avert her eyes once again as Miles presented her with his backside. 'And by the way, I don't want that pillow back.'

A sudden horrifying vision coming to her, she scrabbled off the bed and shouted through the freshly closed door. 'I'm having a shower now. Do not, on any account, come anywhere near me.'

There was no sound from the other side of the door and, deciding it was safe to proceed, Anna went into the bathroom, taking a change of clothes with her, and turned on the shower. Exhausted she may well be, but that didn't mean she couldn't at least look her best.

Sometime later, after Anna had brushed out her long hair and blow-dried it as best she could with the inadequate hotel dryer, she slipped on a light-grey knitted jumper dress, over thick woolly tights, and pulled on her knee-length boots. She paused for a moment to listen at the door for any sign of Miles, but it was still silent, and she assumed that he must have gone out, leaving her free to relax as she applied a little moisturiser, mascara and a slick of lip gloss. Taking a breath, Anna looked in the mirror and nodded. She was New York ready.

She jumped a little as she walked into the living room, surprised to find Miles sitting on the sofa, reading a book, thankfully fully dressed in a fresh pair of jeans and a white shirt, which, although crumpled, gave him a clean, almost boyish appeal.

'What are you doing?' Anna asked him.

'Reading,' Miles said glancing up at her. 'You can't have a go at me for reading. Not when I've got my clothes on.'

'It's just I thought you'd have gone by now, to your audition or something.'

'Oh that's not for a couple of days,' Miles said. 'I do need to practise, and finish off my song, but I'm kind of stuck at the moment. It's supposed to be an edgy punk-inspired rock number about the futility of existence, but it keeps turning into this sappy love song. And I've got a hundred sappy love songs.' Miles smiled at her thoughtfully. 'So I thought I'd hang with you for a bit, help you out. Clear my head of the crap that's going round and round it and see if I can't get better at songwriting by Monday.'

'I don't need you to help me,' Anna said. 'We're not here together, are we? We are here doing separate things. Separately. Remember, we agreed? You write your depressing song and I'll look for my boyfriend's wife.'

'OK,' Miles said. 'So, out of interest, where are you planning to start looking for one person in this city of a little over eight million people?'

'Well,' Anna said, lifting her chin, as she mentally scrambled for a response. 'I was going to . . . I thought what I'd do first is . . . My plan of attack is to firstly get a map and then . . .' She didn't want to tell him that the main thrust of her plan to track down Charisma Jones was mainly to go shopping and hope that she somehow bumped into her.

'Why don't you Google her?' Miles asked. 'See what that throws up?'

Anna pressed her lips together as she looked at him, sitting there so easily on the sofa, his long legs crossed, one arm stretched out across the back, holding his clever-looking paperback casually between his thumb and forefinger as if being him was the most natural thing in the world. She was beyond annoyed that it hadn't occurred to her to do what was pretty much the singularly most obvious course of action for one person searching for another person to take since time began. But she did have an answer for him at least.

'Duh,' she said rolling her eyes. 'Tom already did that, it was the first thing he did. He said she's not on Facebook or Twitter, he said that there was nothing about her at all out there.'

Miles frowned, folding down the corner of the page of his book and closing it. 'Really? It's just . . . Really?

This girl's a dancer, a singer, a wannabe actress – if she really doesn't have any information out there on the internet then, well, I'm pretty sure she's either from another planet, the past, or dead or imaginary. Yep, I'm pretty sure that if there is nothing about her on the internet then Tom made her up, for reasons we can only guess at.'

'Fine,' Anna said, turning swiftly on her kitten heel to retrieve her iPad. She swished back to the sofa to sit down heavily next to Miles, noticing that he edged far enough away so that they weren't actually touching. Confidently, she typed the name into Google and hit search. Immediately more than ten thousand results came back.

'Well,' Anna said eyeing the list apprehensively, 'there are bound to be some hits. I could type "jazz singing frog dates pig" and I'd get a hit.'

'Yes, yes, you would,' Miles said, 'mainly because you've just described the Muppets, but still you're right. There's nothing to say that any of these Charisma Joneses are *the* Charisma Jones. May I?'

Reluctantly, Anna handed him the tablet, whereupon he went immediately to Images.

'If I know the internet,' he said, 'and trust me, I do know the internet, if there is an image or images of a lady called Charisma Jones who also takes her top off it will come up pretty soon in the search . . .' Miles paused for a long moment as he took in what he found before handing it to Anna. 'Or in this case first.'

Anna didn't take back the tablet, instead she just stared at the photo that Miles had found within a few seconds and presented her with.

It was of a woman, of around Anna's age, her shiny brunette hair styled in a retro 50s fashion, one finely plucked brow raised in playful come-hither suggestion, one manicured red-nailed hand holding on to the tiny top hat that sat jauntily on the side of her head, which also happened to be the most substantial piece of actual clothing she was wearing, for other than a slash of red lipstick, some high-heeled ruby slippers and the tiniest pair of red bejewelled panties that Anna had ever seen, she was completely nude. Underneath the photo ran a shoutline that screamed out 'Charisma Jones, Live at the Scarlet Slipper, three times daily!' and a link to that venue, which Anna guessed probably wasn't a library say, or a knitting circle.

'Whoa,' Miles said. 'I mean . . . No, it's no good, I mean whoa. Look at that body!' Anna glanced sharply at him. 'Not that you don't have a really great body. I remember thinking that about you when I first met you, and then later thinking it was really a shame that you are so not my type.'

Anna shook her head, brushing away his unintended insult in favour of the real point that the imbecile she'd been unwittingly lumbered with was missing.

'He lied,' she said, looking at Miles, because it was

preferable to looking at Charisma Jones' alabaster skin. 'He told me there was nothing on the internet about her.'

'Well, that's not strictly true,' Miles said, seeing the discomfort in her expression and returning to the original search. 'He said she wasn't on Facebook or Twitter. Well, there are a few Miss C. Joneses on both those sites, but a quick glance tells me none of them are your Miss Charisma Jones.'

'She's not mine,' Anna said. 'And that doesn't change the fact that he lied. You found her in seconds. He must have too. Why? Why is he keeping that from me? Is this all just one big charade? Maybe it's his way out, pretend he can't find her and then the wedding's off. He's off the hook.'

Miles nodded, thinking for a moment. 'It could be that, or it could be that he was trying to protect you.'

'Protect me!' Anna exclaimed. 'By lying to me?'

'By not thrusting a picture of a really hot, mostly naked girl in your face and saying, "By the way, this is my wife." I mean, you don't want him to know that you're sharing a room with me, do you? Because you know, I'm really handsome and irresistible to most women and even though you wouldn't touch me with a bargepole, if Tom saw my raw good looks in the flesh he'd probably find that hard to believe. Well, trying to keep you from looking up that babe is probably the same for Tom. He was probably worried that you would lay eyes on that incredible pair of . . . shoes and think how could any man with a pulse possibly prefer me over that? Her, I mean. Obviously I didn't mean to objectify her as a sex object. Although in this case I do think that's kind of her intention.'

Anna turned her face from him, desperate to contain her urge to cry before he noticed.

'What I'm saying is that Tom obviously loves you, and he wants to protect you. And look . . .' Miles waited but Anna did not look, so he went off anyway. 'If you click on the link to the club, Charisma's not on the bill any more. She's obviously moved on. In fact . . .' Anna waited, staring at an uncharacteristic chip in her nail polish until she willed the tears back into her head. 'In fact, she hasn't been on the bill for more than a year, and there isn't any more recent image or reference to her than that. Tom wasn't lying to you, Anna. She's not here. Not in any useful way. He just wanted to keep you from seeing this, and I'm just sorry that I didn't have the same consideration that he did.'

Slowly, Anna turned her head just enough so that he could see the edge of her profile.

'Do you really think that's the only reason why?' Anna asked him. 'And not because he is still obsessed by her? I mean, she is really beautiful and she looks so . . . exciting. I would have no idea how to be like that.'

Miles looked puzzled but did not respond.

'I truly, honestly, do think he was trying to protect you,' Miles said. 'Look, you saw the photo. The woman's hot, yes, but she's not got anything that men really want when they fall in love. No mystery, that's for damn sure, no vulnerability, no funny little hard-to-understand quirks, and in my experience women who feel the need to take their clothes off to get attention are usually pathologically insecure and a total nightmare to go out with.'

Finally, Anna turned to face him, treating him to a small grateful smile. 'Thank you.'

'No worries, see? I'm not always completely annoying, am I?'

'Not completely,' Anna admitted. 'Although your tongue did literally hang out of your head when you were looking at that photo.'

'In horror!' Miles said, charmingly, making Anna chuckle. 'Like yuck, eugh, bleugh, I think I might be sick, in that kind of way. Anyway, this is a lead. We can use this.'

'We?' Anna raised a brow.

'Go on, Anna,' Miles said, sweetly. 'Let me help you and keep my mind off the audition. Please?'

Anna twisted her mouth into a knot as she thought for a moment and then shrugged and nodded. 'OK, Sherlock, so tell me, how is this a lead if she's not been at the club for over a year?'

'Well, someone she used to know, even maybe still

knows, might work there and remember her. We go to the Scarlet Slipper and we case the joint. I will be your bodyguard, protect you from all those unsavoury types that hang out in strip clubs.'

'Haven't you ever hung out in strip clubs?'

'Well, yes, I know what to expect,' Miles said.

'You're quite enjoying this, aren't you?' Anna asked him, unable to resist a smile.

'There are worse ways of avoiding the terror and fear about what will probably be my last shot at really making it than having a bash at being a knight in shining armour coming to the aid of a damsel in distress, I will concede.' Miles nodded, smiling with one side of his mouth. 'Plus, you know, burlesque at lunchtime in December in New York. It's like all my Christmases have come at once.'

The first thing Anna thought as she stepped out into the crisp December day on West 44th Street was she really should have paid the extra £3.99 to Scotchgard her new knee-length dove-grey suede boots. Back home, December had so far been a bland, mild, grey, rainy month without much glamour and decidedly absent of snow, a fact that Anna had been counting on God to rectify by the day of the wedding, certain that after all the crap he'd dished out in her life he had to owe her at least one beautifully snowy day when she required it. But just in case, she had a special effects unit from Shepperton Studios on speed-dial with their snow-making machine.

Maybe this is it, Anna thought, looking upwards to where the skyscrapers disappeared into the sky that was gently wafting huge fat flakes of snow down onto them, as if they were trapped inside one of the snow globes that Anna had seen for sale at the airport.

'Wow,' Miles said, following her gaze upwards, and then looking around him with a delighted smile on his face, like a small boy unwrapping his long-dreamed-of Christmas present. 'My God, look at where we are, Anna. And it's snowing!'

'I know,' Anna said, unhappily. 'I didn't pack for snow, it's going to ruin these boots.'

'Shut up!' Miles said, mildly. 'Look around you, take in the moment. See how the snow's made the city pristine and new, even now, after hours of New Yorkers trudging up and down the street. It's adding another layer of pure white, just for us. And look at that.' Miles pointed down the street, towards Times Square, which was jammed bumper to bumper with predominantly yellow taxis, the weather causing a sudden upswell in traffic. 'Smell that exhaust, listen to those horns!'

Anna took a deep breath of cold tinny air, immediately coughing it back out again. 'I'm slightly asthmatic, you know.'

'Look,' Miles said, hooking his arm through hers, in

what Anna thought was a particularly overfamiliar gesture. 'Look, there are fairy lights in all the trees, Christmas decorations in every window. And the Scarlet Slipper is on East 46th and Park so it will take us across Fifth Avenue – we'll get to see all the Christmas lights, maybe do some window shopping. It's brilliant!'

Anna slipped her arm out of Miles's with some difficulty as he turned to her and smiled, happily. 'Do you know what, I thought you were probably a total pain in the arse, but as it turns out I'm actually quite glad we've ended up here together – it's a lot more fun to see and do this with someone, isn't it?'

Anna looked at him, as a fluffy snowflake settled starkly against his dark hair for a moment, before slowly melting away, his eyes seemingly all the brighter and, disconcertingly, even more blue in the white world they had stepped into.

'Can't we get a cab?' she asked him, feeling suddenly excruciatingly guilty to be standing in this particular place, at that particular moment, looking into those particular eyes, instead of with Tom, who she felt sure was the only man she should be sharing a peak experience with. 'My boots . . .'

'Goddam it, woman!' Miles said, taking her arm once again and dragging her in what Anna assumed was the correct direction. 'Live life in the moment for once. We're in New York, the world's most exciting city, we're on an adventure to save your wedding, not to mention your relationship, we're going to a place where ladies dance on tables wearing not much more than a couple of sequins and glitter glue! I seriously think this might be the best day of my life.'

'OK, OK,' Anna complied reluctantly. 'But I'm perfectly capable of walking on my own without you frogmarching me around.' Once again she removed her arm from his, causing Miles to shrug and thrust his hands deep into the pockets of the entirely inadequate battered-looking denim jacket he was wearing over a navy-blue hoody.

'So you say we're crossing Fifth Avenue,' Anna asked him. 'Not walking down it until we find Saks, going in and then basically buying everything we see?'

'Ha.' Miles smiled. 'We can do that after, as a treat.'

'As a treat for what?' Anna asked, having to hop a little to keep up with him as he strode purposefully through the crowds that all seemed to be going in the opposite direction.

'As a treat for pure, prim, innocent little Anna being brave enough to go to what is essentially a strip bar,' Miles told her.

'I'm not prim, I'm not innocent and I am certainly not pure! I've been to strip clubs before. I've been to hundreds,' Anna shouted after him, as he forged ahead without her. She stamped her booted foot in the snow, and realised just a little too late that she'd made her declaration right next to a pair of nuns queuing at a hot dog stand.

'Oh, um, sorry,' Anna said. 'I didn't mean . . . well, what I mean was that I'm not at all like he thinks I am. I haven't actually been to a strip club before, I was just . . .' Miserably, she looked up the street where she could still just about see Miles's head bobbing above the crowd.

'The Lord does not judge you, my child, he loves you, whatever your sins, as long as you repent them,' one of the nuns told her, with a twinkle in her eye which gave Anna the distinct impression that she was trying not to giggle. 'Now, go after that young man and don't let him go. He's fine.'

Anna tottered as best as she could through the crowds in her kitten heels, the snow turning to sludge under her smooth soles, which slipped treacherously, as she tried to keep her eyes on Miles's head in the distance. She was suddenly aware that, apart from him, as really very annoying and smug as he was, she was thousands of miles away from anyone or anything she knew. And besides, Miles had the map and if she got lost she would be too scared to ask any of these frightening-looking people who were barging past her with single-minded purpose for directions, for fear they might mug her at gunpoint. Taking her eyes off him for a moment to avoid an especially fierce-looking lady in a full-length fur coat, Anna was horrified to see that she had lost Miles in the crowd.

'Damn, damn, damn,' she muttered under her breath, increasing her pace, without looking at her feet, in the hopes of catching a glimpse of him, but he was nowhere to be seen. And then the inevitable happened. Anna was caught in the perfect storm of snow, busy people hurrying past, and her slippery, smooth soles. All it took was one good old-fashioned shoulder barge from a woman with improbably high hair on her left, an unintentional trip from a man wearing a coat with shoulder pads bigger than his head on her right, and before she knew what was happening Anna was being propelled forwards in what was certainly destined to be a high-speed face plant right in the middle of a pile of suspiciously yellow-looking snow. At least it would have been if a strong arm hadn't appeared out of nowhere and hooked her out of her fated trajectory, hauling her both to the side of the sidewalk and against a denim-clad chest.

'Bloody hell!' Anna said to her rescuer accusingly. 'Why the bloody hell did you rush off like that, I could have been murdered!'

'I thought you were next to me.' Miles shrugged. 'And "murdered" is a little bit strong. This is New York not Beirut. Plus I just rescued you from a painful and not to mention humiliating fall.'

'Yes, well . . .' Anna stopped talking as she realised

that Miles still had her body firmly clasped against his with the same strong rescuing arm that had pulled her out of her fall, and although her camel coat was reasonably thick, it was in no way thick enough for her not to notice that her soft curves were crushed against his lean hard body, the one with the muscles and those thighs and that bottom that she absolutely hadn't looked at this morning as he'd lain sprawled, oblivious on the sofa. A slow tingling heat had begun to spread upwards throughout her body, radiating from, well, from a place that a lady didn't like to talk about in public.

Suddenly furious, Anna pushed him away, taking a moment to steady herself, until the curious and novel sensation of being physically close to Miles seeped away. No way could she let Miles see how her body had reacted to the proximity of his, absolutely not. This strange rebellion by her normally placid and verging on indifferent body had to be a temporary glitch, something to do with jet lag most likely. Not even Tom and his finely muscled kick-boxer's body had ever had quite that impact on her, which was ridiculous, because everybody agreed that Tom was exceptionally handsome and about as sexy as any man could be. Never entirely sure what sexy was exactly, Anna had always simply taken it as read that Tom was it. Now though, she wasn't so sure and it was an uncertainty she was keen to be in denial about as soon as possible.

'Thank you for stopping me from falling,' Anna said

finally, deciding it would be best not to look directly at Miles until he'd successfully managed to annoy her again, and the unfamiliar feelings being near him stirred up in the pit of her tummy had gone again.

'Not a problem,' Miles said, taking her arm in his for the third time. 'Now, let me escort you properly. I'm starving and I'm thinking burger, possibly with a side of boobs for lunch.'

And there it was, normal service was resumed once again.

The Scarlet Slipper was not how Anna imagined it would be. She'd been expecting a dingy basement, at the bottom of a flight of seedy-looking stairs, behind a rickety railing, which you had to go down as if descending into the depths of hell. Instead it had its own smart entrance right on the street, a smart neon-lit sign hanging above it, featuring a single red high-heeled shoe flashing on and off, and tasteful posters of ladies in boas both live and feather, and not to mention balloons, posing coquettishly behind spotlight glass either side of the revolving door. Anna felt sick as she followed Miles into the lobby, which was swathed in a red carpet that seemed to smother not only the floor, but the walls and the ceiling too, knowing that although she was unlikely to find Charisma here, she was about to face women exactly like her, the kind of women that Anna imagined were ballsy, confident and that thing that she had so little first-hand experience of – sexy. All the things that Tom's first wife was and that she had never intentionally been, at least not with any notable success.

'Table for two?' A pretty young girl, dressed like a French maid, greeted them from behind the reception desk, making Anna blink and look studiously at the carpeted ceiling so that she wouldn't have to confront the girl's stocking tops, which peeped from beneath her lace-trimmed skirt. 'There's a show due to start in fifteen minutes, so it's best to order before then, as the waitresses don't take orders during a performance.' She smiled at Miles, ignoring Anna, as she showed them down some runway-lit stairs, and into the tiny intimate theatre and to a table right by the stage. 'You're in luck, we're not so busy today,' the girl told Miles, winking at him. 'Best seats in the house.'

'Actually,' Miles said, before the girl could leave, 'my friend here is looking for someone.'

'Really?' the girl replied, wrinkling her nose up at Anna. 'We're not that sort of establishment.'

'No I mean, a friend of hers . . . a friend who used to work here? About a year ago. Her name was Charisma Jones.'

The girl looked blank. 'And why would you be looking for this Charisma?' she asked Anna.

'She's a friend – an old friend from my dancing days

back in . . . Vegas,' Anna said. 'I'm in New York for a few days, I was hoping to track her down.'

'You danced in Vegas, it's true what they say, anyone can get work in that city,' the girl said, giving her a scathing appraisal. 'Look, I never heard of anyone called Charisma, but I've only been working here a few weeks. There's a pretty high turnover of dancers here, but you could try talking to Mimi – she's getting ready for the next show, backstage. She's been here the longest, as far as I know. She might know something about your friend.'

'Really?' Anna said, grateful for the opportunity to leave as the lights went down and a spotlight appeared on the stage. 'Come on, Miles.'

'Oh no, they won't let him back there,' the girl said, smiling at Miles. 'Too many weirdos and stalkers for us to let any guys backstage, but if you tell Tony, the security guy, that Liza said you could go talk to Mimi, then he'll let you go. Don't worry. I'll personally make sure your friend has a great time.'

'See you, babe,' Miles said, leaning back in his chair, and ordering a quarter pounder.

Anna wasn't exactly sure why she was so furious with Miles, as she hurried in the general direction of what she assumed had to be the backstage, only that she was. Which was better than finding him inexplicably alluring, she supposed. She was confronted with the person who had to be Tony, a very large gentleman whose considerable bulk spilled over the edges of the spindly-looking stool he was perched on, as he guarded the stage door whilst reading what looked like a well-thumbed copy of *American Psycho*.

'Hello there!' Anna squeaked brightly, sounding about as posh and as English as she had ever done. 'You must be Tony? Liza said I could go backstage and talk to . . . um . . . Mimi, is it? She thought she might know where I could find my friend, Charisma, Charisma Jones?'

Tony stopped reading a little after Anna had stopped speaking and, licking one fat finger, carefully turned down the corner of his page before finally focusing his yellowing eyes on her.

'You here for a job?' he asked her, gazing pointedly at her chest, which, as well covered as it was, still seemed to be his main point of focus.

'Most certainly not,' Anna said, pulling her bag protectively across her body, and reaching new heights of Englishness at the same time. 'As I previously stated I am here to see Mimi, and to ascertain whether or not she knows the whereabouts of one Charisma Jones. Please will you let me pass at once, my good man.'

'Sorry, ma'am,' Tony said, dropping his gaze as if he'd just been caught letching at the Queen. 'Go straight through, ma'am. Mimi's dressing room is the last on the right, the one with the star on the door. Ma'am.'

'And about time too,' Anna said primly, stepping smartly through what felt like a Looking Glass into a world that a great many people, Miles included, would certainly think of as the definition of Wonderland.

The first thing to hit Anna as the door closed behind her was the assault of a variety of perfumes that brought tears to her eyes, and then the very surprising silence. She'd been expecting a corridor bustling with dancers, in all manner of feathers and fans, covered in balloons about to be popped, strolling along clutching outsize champagne glasses, or preparing to writhe around in bubbles in time to the music. But in actual fact, apart from the pungent scent that told her that many a young lady had passed through this way quite recently wearing a good deal of cheap perfume, the dressing-room area was remarkably sedate. What doors were open revealed empty rooms, scattered with costumes, dressing tables laden with make-up and abandoned false lashes, waiting for the chance to flutter once again. Anna could not guess what lay behind the doors that were shut, but as she heard the sound of muted laughter and voices, she guessed it was acts preparing for that afternoon's appearance. As she reached the end of the corridor, she found what she assumed must be Mimi's dressing room, exactly as Tony told her she would, star pinned haphazardly to the closed door, with a definite look of the home-made about it, above a name plaque that declared MISS MIMI ME! complete with an exclamation mark.

Taking a breath and trying to remember exactly why she was here, Anna knocked quietly on the door and, after a few seconds of silence, knocked again.

'What goddam it?' A voice sounded from behind the wood.

'Oh, hello?' Anna said. 'Is that Miss Mimi Me? Um, hello, my name is Anna Carter and I'm wondering if it would be possible to talk to you for a few minutes?'

'Are you the Queen of Frigging England?' the testy response came back.

'Er . . . no, my name is . . .'

''Cos if you ain't the queen of frigging England, what the hell are you doing harassing me just before a goddam show, bitch?'

'Um . . .' Anna didn't have an answer to that one. 'Well, Liza said I should come back and talk to you about . . .'

'Liza, that goddam slut on reception? She in charge of my diary is she, that bitch, I'll rip her hair out and make her eat it.'

'OK then,' Anna said to the door, patting it placatingly. 'Sorry to trouble you, bye then.'

She was all but running back up the corridor when Mimi's door opened and one heavily made-up eye peered through it.

'What's it about?' she asked, scowling at Anna with all the welcoming charm of a hungry lion.

'What's about what?' Anna asked her, riveted to the

spot, never thinking she'd be anxious to see Tony the doorman again.

'What did you want to see me about, Lady Di?' Mimi asked. 'What does Princess fucking Kate Middleton want with me?'

'Oh! Nothing, really, just I think you might have known a friend of mine that I'm trying to track down. I think she worked here until about a year ago. Her name is Charisma Jones.'

'Carrie?' Mimi exclaimed, dropping her nasty nasal twang in an instant. 'You a pal of Carrie, well why didn't you say so? Come in you dumb bitch, pull up a chair.' Whereupon Miss Mimi Me opened her dressing-room door to reveal she was wearing a thick hot pink towelling robe, and a turban on her head.

'Um, thank you,' Anna said, feeling a lot like she was entering a lioness's den.

'Sorry, honey,' Mimi said, as looking around she found a chair, well hidden by a great deal of costumes, and perched on the edge of it. 'We get so many perverts and nut jobs round here, I forget sometimes that people are just people. Most of the time it pays to start out angry and work your way down from there.'

Anna nodded. 'I can see how it would be like that. I'm really sorry to have surprised you.'

'So you're a pal of Carrie's?' Mimi said with a pleasant smile, taking what looked like a very frail bathing suit, which seemed to comprise of nothing more than one string of tinsel and a couple of plastic holly leaves, off a hanger and doing some mysterious shimmying under her robe, which meant the tiny outfit did not reappear. 'How come? You're not a dancer, I can tell by looking at you, and Carrie never said she had any British friends.'

'Oh well, to cut a very long story short Charisma is married to my fiancé,' Anna said, seeing no point in stringing out her vague untruth. 'He married her in Vegas a few years back and sort of forgot to mention it when he proposed to me a year ago, and here I've been planning my dream wedding all these months to find out that actually, unless we get 'Carrie''s signature on the annulment really soon then my wedding is off!'

'Shit,' Mimi said. 'Oh my God, you must be engaged to Tom, British Tom. Yeah, Carrie talked about him a lot.'

'She did?' Anna said in a small voice. This was not good news. Not good news at all. If Charisma was still talking a lot about Tom just recently then what did that mean for her prospects of signing an annulment?

'Oh yeah, whenever she'd had a little too much wine, you know what I mean? He was the one that got away, I guess. We've all got one of those, right?'

'No, I haven't,' Anna said unhappily. 'Well, not yet, anyway. But Tom said she left him?'

'Really?' Mimi's smile was sphinx-like. 'Carrie tells

another story. Well, anyway, kid, I wish I could help you but when Carrie quit the Slipper she quit her old friends too. Guess she didn't want us tarnishing her reputation.'

'Her reputation as what?' Anna asked. 'An . . . erm . . . exotic dancer? No offence.'

'None taken,' Mimi laughed. 'No, she went for this audition for an acting role, in some off-Broadway thing, just before she left here. Only she did it under another name, oh what was it . . . Erica Barnes, that was it. Anyway, she must have been good, because she got the part. I said I'd go and see it, but it was some play about the mortgage crisis, and you know how it is, there always seems like something better to do . . . we lost touch. I don't know how long it ran for, or if she's done any other work since. I haven't seen her name up in lights on Broadway, I know that much. But she hasn't been back here either, so maybe things are going better for Erica Barnes than they did for Charisma Jones.' Mimi looked sympathetic. 'Not much help to you, am I, honey?' she said, apologetically.

'Actually a huge help,' Anna thanked her. 'Now I have a name and an idea of where to look, so thank you. I never actually thought I'd get this close.'

'I hope you find her, and I hope that if you do she isn't still carrying that torch for your man. Charisma's never normally the sort of person to give up on something she wants. And when that girl's claws are out, you'd better make damn sure you don't get in the way of them.'

'Super,' Anna said, brightly. 'Marvellous. Well, I won't take up any more of your time. I'll let you get ready for your next . . . appearance.'

'Thank you, honey,' Mimi said, slipping off her gown in one sudden movement, sending Anna's eye line skywards once again as she tried very hard to avoid looking. 'Tell me, what do you think of my Christmas fairy outfit? You couldn't just help me on with those wings, could you? And any idea where I should hang these baubles . . .'

Anna had run halfway up the corridor when she collided with a tall, suave-looking man in a very expensive suit. He caught her arms as she plummeted into him, and held her away from him as he greeted her, without, Anna noticed anxiously, letting her go.

'Well, hello,' he said, taking her waist in his hands. 'I didn't know I was interviewing today, but come to my office. For you, I'll make time.'

'Unhand me at once!' Anna said firmly, resorting to the most schoolteachery tone she could muster. 'I am most certainly not here for an interview, now let me pass, you . . . you . . . blaggard'

Blaggard? Anna felt the heat rising in her cheeks as the man regarded her with a good deal of amusement. 'You know what this club is missing, it's missing a feisty little English rose like you, darling. Come on, come with Max and let me see if I can get past those thorns.'

'No!' Anna protested, trying to twist out of his grasp and finding it impossible.

'Come on, little lady, it's Christmas time and I'm due a present to unwrap.' Max leered at her.

'I don't think so, geezer,' Miles said, his arms crossed as he stood in the doorway that should have been guarded by Tony. 'Hands off the lady, OK?'

'How did you get back here?' Max asked. 'Where's Tony?'

'Tony is reading a modern American classic, in the gents,' Miles said, who seemed to be having the opposite affliction to Anna, as he suddenly sounded like he should be related to someone named Kray, and as if 'the gents' was actually a euphemism for sleeping with the fishes.

'If you'll excuse me,' Anna said poshly. Max in the nice suit let her go and stepped aside, so surprised by the English princess and what appeared to be her bit of rough that for a moment he wasn't sure how to react. As they fled out of the lobby, Anna took Miles's hand for no other reason than it seemed appropriate. As they ran they heard Max yell 'Tony!' so loudly it seemed like it might rattle the building to its foundations.

Anna found herself laughing when they finally came to a stop, her hand still in Miles's.

'When did you become a Cock-en-knee?' she asked him cheerfully.

'When did you become all Mary Poppins?' he retorted, wiping the tears from his eyes, as he regained his composure. They'd somehow found themselves in a sort of courtyard, surrounded on three sides by mirrored glass, and on the fourth by a series of pillars that ran parallel to the street. Perfectly circular bay trees stood sentinel around the square, each one adorned with white Christmas lights, and a weatherproof red bow around their pots.

'That Max, one of the creepiest men I've ever met,' Anna gasped, seeing the funny side of the situation now that she was no longer in it. 'It's a good job you turned up when you did, I'm not sure Mary Poppins would have been enough to keep him at bay for much longer.' She smiled at him. 'What were you doing there, anyway? I thought you'd be enjoying the show.'

'Yeah, me too,' Miles said. 'It turns out that wondering what women look like under their clothes is a lot more interesting than when they just take them off and wobble about. Who knew?'

'I thought you did. I thought you hung out in strip bars all the time. Or was that an exaggeration?'

'Slight exaggeration,' Miles admitted, ruefully. 'I did go to a lap-dancing club once on a mate's stag, but I was so drunk I passed out, and don't remember a thing about it, except that when I woke up, someone had drawn . . . something quite crude on my forehead in permanent marker.'

Anna giggled, hooking her arm through Miles's, as they strolled back towards the street.

'So any leads?' Miles asked her. 'And discoveries?'

'Yes, actually,' Anna said. 'We need to get back to the hotel and Google Erica Barnes.'

Chapter Nine

'This is ridiculous,' Liv said out loud, even though she was alone in the flat, clearing the search history from her laptop, just in case anyone ever discovered that she'd been Googling breast implants. What was wrong with her? One pretty dress and a bra stuffed with tissues and suddenly she wanted to be Jordan?

'Tom is not not marrying you because you are only a C cup,' she told her reflection in the mirror, a little tipsily, because after the day she'd had, half a bottle of Merlot and no dinner seemed like the only sensible option. 'He is not marrying you because you are not Anna, you muppet.'

Liv stared at herself in the mirror, the same person, but so entirely different from the one that had been trussed up in the magic wedding dress earlier that day, as she stood there in her red cotton PJs with the cute penguin pattern and her bare feet. In the corner of her bedroom, her little Christmas tree twinkled humbly away in its tub. She had doused it in stringy tinsel and it was a little bit tipsy itself since she'd forgotten to water it for a few days and currently it tilted danger-ously to one side. Her little tree and Anna's monument to all things Christmassy – the tree that stood six feet tall in the living room, perfectly symmetrical, and tastefully decorated to within a inch of its life – could almost be a metaphor for their friendship. Anna, perfect, brilliant, impressive, strong, overcoming adversity Anna, who deserved to be placed in a bay window, curtain constantly drawn back, smugly declaring to the world, 'Look at me, passers-by, look how perfect I got this ribbon and bauble combination, and then go home and weep at your shoddy approximation of what a Christmas tree *should* look like.' And then there was Liv, nice safe middle-class family, never had to struggle for much, or try very hard at school, sensible shoes, no idea what to do with eye shadow, C-cup Liv who if she were a tree would be one that was in the bargain bin at the garden centre, less than a foot high, shoved in a corner where no one could see it and with a tendency to wilt unless she was often watered. That's why Liv had rescued the little orphaned tree – much to Anna's horror – because it looked so dowdy and forlorn next to all the others; it reminded Liv of herself.

Liv picked up her glass and took another long draught of wine. The thing was she didn't resent Anna for the brilliant things she'd done, or the way that she furiously chased whatever she wanted from life, no matter how great the odds were against her. Resentment was the last thing that Liv felt for her friend, her adopted sister. If anything it was probably true that if she hadn't brought Anna home that Christmas her own life would be much less impressive than it had been. She felt that keenly, even now, boyfriendless and big-boobless as it was. It was Anna who'd spotted her talent in the kitchen and encouraged Liv to develop her skills and confidence, Anna who made her take her CV to all the top kitchens in London and beg for work experience in the fiercely competitive and male-dominated environment. And it had been Anna who'd convinced her that her talent was a strong enough basis for them to start their own business. What saddened Liv was that with all the privileges and comforts she had grown up with, she didn't nearly have half the drive, ambition, confidence, sheer force of will or cleavage that her best friend had somehow acquired. Also she had a really stupid tendency to fall helplessly in love with men who were completely out of reach, mainly, Liv thought a touch miserably, because the men that were within her reach tended to be short, round and annoying.

When the doorbell sounded, it took Liv a moment or two to uproot herself from her spot on the sofa and trundle haphazardly to the main front door, where she peered through the spyhole to check she hadn't accidentally ordered a pizza or something and then forgot about it.

'Oh it's you,' she told the small truncated image of a man, who stood on the other side of the door. 'What are you doing here?'

It occurred her about eight seconds later and on his third insistent pressing of the bell that the best way to answer that question was to answer the door.

'Oh good, you're not dead in a ditch then,' Liv's brother Simon said as she opened the door, tipping first back with its momentum, and then forwards again into his arms. 'That text you sent me sounded positively suicidal.' He cast a withering gaze at Liv and her surroundings. 'Though clearly I've come with only moments to spare.'

'Did I send you a text?' Liv asked him, confused. 'I don't recall sending you a text.'

'Probably for the best. Come on, chicken, let's get you inside and you can tell your big brother why you're drinking yourself into oblivion in your pyjamas on a Saturday night instead of being out on the town with an array of handsome studs.'

'So let me get this straight,' Simon said, pouring Liv another coffee that she still didn't want. 'You're depressed because you put on some Barbie dress and felt fantastic. That's depressed you? It's like me when I was seven all over again.' Simon ruffled her hair, in that annoying way that her family, and ninety-eight per cent of the world, continued to think was appropriate. 'Darling, it's OK. You're a girl, you're allowed to like looking like a girl, no one will mind. Not even the miserable old feminists mind you putting on a spot of lippy and a bra these days, darling. It's postmodern, or something.'

'But that's . . . that not really it,' Liv said. 'I mean it is, but it isn't. It's more that it was only when I was dressed up like her that he . . . Oh God.' Liv dropped her forehead onto the kitchen table with an audible crack, which fortunately she was still too inebriated to feel.

'What? What are you talking about?' Simon asked her, wrinkling his nose as Liv wiped hers on the sleeve of her pyjamas. 'You're not really that upset about Tom seeing you in Anna's dress, are you? She'll never know, darling, and, to be honest, I think a pre-existing wife is much more of a bad omen than a bit of unscheduled dress-viewing. Liv, you've got to stop beating yourself up over everything. It's not your fault that Tom is already married. It's not your fault that Anna's run off to New York in an act of unparalleled mentalism. It's not your fault that Tom doesn't know never to enter a bridal fitting room. None of these things are your fault, sweetheart. Come on now, sober up. It's Saturday night, I could be out, dancing the night away.'

'Or in, making sushi and watching *Strictly Come Dancing* with your husband,' Liv retorted.

'OK, darling, let me live the delusion that I'm not completely middle-aged and married for just a little longer,' Simon replied, mildly. 'What is it, really?'

'I can't tell you,' Liv sobbed. 'I'm so pathetic, I hate

myself. I mean look at Anna. Look at everything she's been through, she's not sobbing at the kitchen table comparing herself to Christmas trees, she's in New York sorting everything out, kicking ass, being super-woman, while I'm . . . I'm . . . here wishing I had bigger boobs so that Tom would have noticed *me*.'

Liv was dimly aware that she was a very noisy crier, that she didn't silently sob with big watery eyes like Anna did, that she gurgled, and rattled and heaved and sniffed, that her eyes puffed up to four times their original size and her face went blotchy and red. As her poor confused brother, torn against his will from a rendition of *Madam Butterfly* on Sky Arts HD, rubbed her shoulders, Liv just knew he was looking at her and wishing with all his heart and soul that she would just blow her nose already.

'*You* have a thing for Tom?' Simon asked her, repeating the phrase a few moments later with an entirely different intonation, this time as it all made perfect sense. 'You have a thing for Tom, of course you do! You met him first, you became friends, you even wore that dreadful dress to Anna's party . . . the party where Anna met Tom! Oh my God, Olivia, you are a tragic heroine from a Victorian novel, without the crinoline!'

'I feel . . . so . . . so . . . stupid,' Liv wept. 'I really thought he liked me, we laughed about stuff, and he held doors open for me and asked me to go places with him, and not just the pub – we went to the cinema and I went with him when he needed to buy a new pair of shoes. We went to the cinema, Simon! That should mean something, shouldn't it?'

'Yes, darling, yes it bloody should,' Simon said sympathetically, although he was looking at her as if he had no idea what she was talking about.

'I thought he was shy . . . a slow burner, which made him perfect for me,' Liv said, scrunching her hair in her hands as her tears plopped one by one onto the tabletop. 'I thought he was building up to asking me out, kissing me and all that, b-b-but I couldn't have been more wrong, could I?' Liv's shoulders shuddered with a fresh outpouring of sobs. 'Because he had his tongue down Anna's throat within half an hour of arriving here! He wasn't building up to declaring his love, he never ever saw me that way. Except . . . except for today, for a minute, when he saw me in Anna's dress, with Anna's boobs, and then it was like he was looking at me for the first time. But, Simon, that was a lie, that's not me and anyway what is he even doing letching at another woman when he is about to get married? I hate him, I hate him, I hate him, but, oh I love him too. A lot. Oh God, just kill me. Kill me now. I'll leave a note. You won't go to prison, use that cheese grater that he gave me for my birthday, that about sums up my entire miserable pointless life. Go on, grate me to death!'

Simon was silent for a moment as he took it all in. And then finally he spoke. 'So you're definitely not a lesbian, then?'

It took a hot bath, three more cups of coffee and Simon threatening to sing the entire songbook of *West Side Story* to her, accents and all, for Liv to finally regain control of her senses and see that perhaps she was being just a little bit melodramatic.

'Your trouble is you live in Anna's shadow, and it's your own fault,' Simon said finally as he settled Liv, now wrapped in a fluffy pink dressing gown, on the sofa and fed her chocolate. 'You fell in love with her the minute you saw her, and ever since you've been in awe.'

'I'm not a lesbian!' Liv reiterated firmly.

'I know that now, darling,' Simon said. 'I don't mean that kind of love, I mean, well, who didn't fall in love with her the minute they met her. I know I did. It even stopped me crushing on the postman for a while, until I realised I didn't love her in that way. I loved her. I love her, because, well, she's fab, isn't she? I fell in love with her, just like you and Mum and Dad did. The difference is I haven't spent the rest of my life comparing myself to her, what's the point? We've got a mum who loves us, who may well have unwittingly attempted to ruin our lives by saying inappropriate things at the wrong time on a daily basis, but out of love. We've got a dad who loves us and kept us safe, and didn't have a stroke when I told him I was gay. We are cursed with a loving and tolerant family, that is so really very nice that they even took a scraggy little girl who had nowhere else to go and made her one of their own. Anna is a hero, yes, she is, but if you call her now and ask her if she would have chosen that life, the life she's had, over one with a mum that stuck around and a real dad rather than one whose name she never knew, well, I think I know which one she would pick. And that doesn't mean to say you are not a hero, or brave, or clever or beautiful, like her, because you are all of those things. You just go about them in a different way.'

'I know that really,' Liv said. 'I do. I just wish . . . Why him, Si? Why out of all the men I know, did I fall for Tom?'

'Darling, Tom is the only real man you know, the only normal one anyway,' Simon told her gently. 'The first one you've met in a long time that wasn't some steroid-pumped-up repressed homosexual with height issues.'

'You're talking about Barry, aren't you?' Liv asked him with a small smile.

'Yes, yes, I am. Listen, darling, you work with women, you work mostly for women, your mother will keep trying to fix you up with men with beards and your brother doesn't know anyone single who'd be impressed by anyone's boobs, let alone your miserable excuse for a pair.'

Liv's smile broadened as she dug her brother in the ribs. 'I'll have you know I'm a C cup!'

'Are you sure you are in love with Tom?' Simon asked her, gently. 'And not just pretending to be in love with him because it's better than realising your life is empty of all meaningful emotion?'

'I'm sure,' Liv said. 'Even now, even after finding out about his secret wife, even after his stupid dress comments, and even knowing that if he doesn't marry Anna in less than a week, he will in a year's time. Even then. Whenever I look at him it feels like my heart rate triples. He's the only person who can make me laugh so much my ribs ache, the only person who I just long to put my arms around and hug.'

'Oh dear,' Simon said. 'You've got it bad and there's nothing to be done about it.'

'No,' Liv said, forcing herself to sit up straight, and lifting her chin. 'But, on the other hand, I've lived with it for a year and half already, so I'm sort of used to the unremitting misery, and I do really want Anna to be happy. And Tom.'

'You should become a nun,' Simon said. 'Seriously, you're halfway there anyway. You'd be really good.'

'Oh shut up,' Liv said. 'I'll be fine. It will wear off eventually, I'll meet a nice man who isn't secretly gay with height issues and, when I do, I'll remember to tell him that I like him before he proposes to my best friend. And when I do get married, I'm going to get the biggest, fattest princess dress that I can find, dress up like a fairy and not give a hoot about what anyone thinks.'

'Good,' Simon said.

'You should go,' Liv said. 'It must be really late, hubby will be wondering where you are.'

'It's actually only just after nine,' Simon told her. 'Judging from the text you sent me you started drinking to forget at about four?'

'Oh God, I am so, so sad,' Liv said plaintively.

'Yes, darling, yes, you are, but you are my sister, and my hero, and I love you. So chin up, keep marching on, maybe pretend you are in a Noël Coward play, I find that helps me when I need to feel noble, and one day your prince will come. I promise you.'

Liv kissed Simon on the cheek as she opened the front door, to find Tom standing there with a bottle of wine cradled in his arms.

'Oh God,' Simon said.

'Hi, Simon,' Tom said. 'Everything OK?'

'No,' Simon said. 'Shouldn't you be on a plane, on your way to tell your loved one that you adore her?'

'I don't know . . . I thought . . . I thought she probably needed some space. Do you think I should get a ticket?'

Simon turned to Liv. 'Come home with me, we'll make you sushi and watch *Casualty*, you know how you love it.'

'I'm fine, honestly,' Liv said. 'You go. Go on. I'll see you soon.'

'Noël Coward!' Simon called as he left reluctantly.

'What's he on about?' Tom asked as Liv stood aside and let him into the hallway.

'The thing is,' she said. 'The thing is I'm really tired and it's been a long day and I haven't heard from Anna, so I've got nothing to tell you and . . .'

'I thought we should clear the air, after the dress thing,' Tom said, holding out the wine. 'I want to apologise. First of all, for being so stupid as to walk in on a dress fitting and put you in a position where you have to lie to Anna. And, secondly, for reacting to the way you . . . the way you looked, the way I did. It was completely out of order.'

'It was nothing,' Liv said, rolling her eyes. 'It was the dress, and the veil and the . . . tissues. You weren't really seeing me, you were seeing Anna. And I can promise you when you see her coming up the aisle in that dress, she will look ten times better than I did in it.'

'Anna will look amazing in it, if she is still going to marry me, that is, and not decide to stay in New York for ever, but that's not what I mean. I mean, you said that I thought you looked beautiful because of the dress. And it's true, part of me did think that, the man part. But I wanted you know, Liv, you are one of the most beautiful people I know, and not just on the outside. And it's important to me that you know I do see you, I see the real you every day. You are my best friend, and that's worth a hundred pretty dresses and sparkly crowns to me.'

Liv stared at him as he stood in the doorway, telling her almost everything she'd wanted, dreamed of hearing from him, and she realised that there was only one thing she could do.

'You have to go to New York,' she said. 'If Anna won't talk to you, you have to follow her, find her and make her see that you love her, and that it doesn't matter if you get married this Christmas or next. You have to go, Tom. Show her that this means as much to you as it does to her.'

Tom nodded. 'I know, he said. 'I know I have to go and find her. That's the other thing I came to tell you and to ask you something else.'

'What?' Liv asked, already knowing the question before it was formed on his lips.

'Will you come too?'

Chapter Ten

'Look!' Anna said holding up a Dolce & Gabbana dress and smoothing it down over her hips.

After their escape from the clutches of Max at the Scarlet Slipper, Anna seemed uninterested in going to look for Erica Barnes right away, and declared that she was going shopping. She hadn't asked Miles to accompany her, but accompany her he did, looking perhaps a little incongruous in his jeans and biker boots, as Anna wandered wide-eyed around the ground floor of Saks. The store was a perfect vision of New York-style Christmas cheer – chic little trees, with lights that twinkled in perfect unison, the scent of cinnamon and spices in the air. It mingled with the large quantities of expensive perfume Anna had sprayed all over herself with the sort of abandon that only a girl who'd once had nothing could display. She had delighted in riding the 'elevator', insisting they get out on every single floor, cooing with excitement at the toy department, complete with grotto and a very authentic-looking Santa. The grotto itself was built into the centre of a huge model railway display, complete with a tiny steam train that puffed and tooted its merry little way through tiny forests and over snow-peaked papier-mâché mountains.

In menswear, Anna had discovered a five-thousand-dollar suit that she thought would look amazing on Tom.

'If only he were here,' she grumbled, pressing the jacket up against Miles's shoulders. 'No it's no good, you're bit taller than him, and wider in the shoulders.'

'Am I?' Miles said, pleased with himself. 'Anyway, if you miss him so much, why don't you answer his calls or his texts? Your phone might be on silent but I've heard it vibrate in your bag about twenty times today.'

Abruptly, Anna put the jacket back on the rail and marched for the lift again. Shrugging, Miles had followed her, cramming his large frame into the tiny space, already full of women so groomed to within an inch of their life that they made Anna look almost shabby.

'All I'm saying is,' Miles began, while the lift's cohabitants did their best not to look at him, 'that the reason you're here is because you want to marry this dude, like soon. You've gone to a lot of trouble to make it happen, and, amazingly, you're in with a really good chance, so why don't you answer his calls, Annie? That's what I want to know.'

A lady with hair far too jet black for her years, which were clearly considerably older than her collagen-plumped lips, had turned around to look at Anna. She might have raised a curious brow if her face hadn't been frozen in time.

Anna had pursed her lips, staring resolutely ahead until the shiny brass doors slid open on womenswear, then gasped in delight at the veritable Aladdin's cave of designer fashion – fashion that she could probably just as easily find at home in Harvey Nichols or Selfridges, but which for some reason here, in this wonderful city, seemed all the more magical.

'What do you think of this?' Anna asked Miles about the dress, slipping her coat off and hooking the halter neck over her head to get a better idea. 'Oh if only I had three thousand and something dollars and was a size zero, or even a four, even a size four would be OK. I did try giving up carbs, but it was like . . . giving up sunshine.'

'Anna,' Miles said, 'answer the question. Why aren't you talking to Tom, filling him in on what's going on?'

Anna sighed, slumping down on the edge of a platform housing a size zero mannequin, the dress still hooked around her neck.

'I don't know,' she said, looking up at Miles. 'I want to talk to him, but then every time I'm about to answer my phone . . . I don't.'

'I get that you're angry and hurt,' Miles said, taking a seat next to her. 'But you still love him, because you want to go through with the wedding.'

'The thing is I have the most amazing dress,' Anna

told him, absently. 'Not that that's why I want to go through with the wedding, well maybe a bit, but not entirely. But it is sort of why I want to do it now, and not in the spring or the summer, because that's in my plan you see. My life plan. A Christmas wedding is one of the immovable things in my life, like the North Star fixed in the sky. Something I've dreamed of since . . .'

'Since what?' Miles asked her.

Anna shook her head. 'I will talk to him, just not yet,' she said. 'I feel like I need to meet Charisma or Erica or whatever she's calling herself first. See what I'm up against.'

'But, babe, this girl, she's not your competition. She's the past.'

'I'm not so sure about that,' Anna said, thinking of Mimi Me's comments about the one who got away. 'I've got the distinct impression from her friend that Charisma might have other ideas about what she wants.'

'What she wants doesn't matter,' Miles said. 'It's you and Tom and your wedding dress that are getting married, isn't it? I think you should talk to him, Anna. Hear the sound of his voice, and then you'll know how you feel about him.'

'I didn't say I didn't know how I felt about him,' Anna said, looking sharply at Miles.

'If you say so,' Miles said.

Remaining silent, Anna got to her feet and hung the dress back on the rail, her shoulders drooping as if suddenly the pleasure and delight she was taking in her surroundings had just drained out of her. Miles also climbed to his feet.

'And for the record, just so you know, size zero, or size two or four or even six and eight, not usually very sexy. I don't know what size you are – most men don't care about that sort of thing – but it's the right one, trust me.'

At any other point in their brief association Anna would have been offended and annoyed by Miles assessing the merits of her body so openly, but on this occasion she could tell that he wasn't trying some ham-fisted move, he was simply attempting to be kind and to cheer her up, and the funny thing was, it worked.

'It reminds me of that song,' Anna found herself telling Miles over an enjoyable plate of pasta in a little Italian they had found on the way back to the hotel. She was gazing out of the window, at the icy night outside, watching the Friday night crowds bowl past, the world rushing by full of a purpose and intent that for once she didn't feel privy to. Instead, ever since Anna had found herself one step closer to actually pulling off the impossible and finding Tom's secret wife in time for her wedding to go ahead, there had been something else. An almost overwhelming urge to just run away, somewhere very far, curl up in a ball and not come out again until spring.

'What song?' Miles asked her, sucking a piece of spaghetti up through his pursed lips like the Tramp from the Disney movie.

'The one by the hippy woman, with the high voice, where she wishes she had a river she could skate away on.'

'Joni Mitchell?' Miles asked her, surprised as Anna clicked her fingers and nodded. 'You don't strike me as a Joni fan. It's the way you describe one of history's greatest singer-songwriters as that "hippy woman" that sort of gives it away.'

'I'm not really,' Anna admitted with a rueful smile. 'Or at least I would be except that in my first year at uni they made me share a room with this girl who wore tie-dyed headscarves . . . Jessica Parkinson, bloody awful example of humanity. The sort of person who was destined to grow up, have four kids called Jocasta and kill foxes at the weekend, but was pretending to be alternative in the meantime, which is mental, because, you know, what sort of alternative person listens to Joni Mitchell in two thousand and five? But anyway Joni Mitchell was constantly on her headphones. All I could hear was this annoying tinny little voice in the background all the time, like there was a tiny mouse trapped somewhere moaning about big yellow taxis.'

Anna checked her impromptu rant when she noticed that Miles was laughing at her.

'Couldn't you have turned your own music up?' Miles asked, almost choking on a meatball.

'I didn't really have my own music,' Anna admitted. 'Liv was always the one who was into music, discovering bands and making me go to gigs. When I was small we didn't really ever listen to music, not even on the radio. And after I moved in with Liv, well, I suppose I just got into whatever Liv and Simon were into. I was never really bothered one way or the other. But I got so sick of this tinny little voice coming from Jessica's headphones that one day I asked her to just stick the CD on and play it out loud, which she did non-stop for the rest of the year until I finally escaped her and went to share a house with some Christian Scientist students, who weren't very fun, but very tidy. Anyway, I heard the same CD so many times that I suppose it was sort of like aversion therapy, after a while I actually began to love it, especially the "skating away on a river" song. I mean I hadn't broken up with a boy or anything, like in the song, but Christmas ...' Anna paused, gazing out of the window once more at the fury of passers-by. 'Christmas has always made me want to find a river to skate away on.'

'Why?' Miles asked, when she paused in her ramble. He leaned in towards her slightly, examining her profile in the candlelight, as she stared at her own translucent reflection in the glass.

'Oh, I don't know,' Anna said absently. 'I've always seemed to be on the wrong side of the glass, I suppose.' She straightened her shoulders and sat up, smiling brightly at Miles. 'Except for now, this Christmas will be different, because it's *my* Christmas and it's the Christmas where I get married to the man I love.'

'Hooray,' Miles said quietly, balling one fist and shaking it in a half-hearted salute. 'Good for you.'

'Anyway, enough about me,' Anna said, noticing that his good mood seemed to have taken a significant dip since they started talking about Joni Mitchell. 'What about you?'

'What about me?' Miles asked, polishing off his glass of red wine in one long draught and reaching for the bottle.

'Well, when is your audition? Isn't it tomorrow? And you haven't done a thing to prepare for it since we got here. Which makes me feel terrible, because you've mainly been helping me.'

'Ah yes, my audition.' Miles looked out of the window, craning his neck to get a glimpse of the snow-laden sky that lay low over the tips of the skyscrapers. 'I don't know if there is much prep I can do, really. I mean I'm not going to play, or sing any better tomorrow at two p.m. than I do now. I would like to have finished that song I was writing, shown them original material, but there's still time.'

'Still time!' Anna exclaimed. 'No there isn't, you need to go back to the hotel now and start working on it. This is your big break, your moment, your chance, you can't just shrug your shoulders and see how it goes, you have to be prepared!'

'I am prepared,' Miles told her. 'By twenty years of playing and writing. And besides, haven't you learned yet that you can't always be prepared for what life throws at you.'

'Surprise wives, perhaps not,' Anna said, leaning forwards a little across the table and brandishing her fork at him. 'But auditions, hell yes, you can. You've bet everything you've got on this chance, Miles. Don't stuff it up by hanging around with me. Which doesn't mean I'm not weirdly glad that you've been here, and that I don't realise that I wouldn't have gotten nearly so far so quickly without you, I do. You've been really . . . helpful. But this is your chance, you have to do every single thing you can to make sure you make the most of this opportunity.'

Miles watched her for a moment, in the candlelight, night creeping up on them as they ate, a small smile playing on his lips, as he tipped his head to one side.

'You really care about stuff, don't you? Even my stuff. That's nice. I like that about you.'

'I care about . . . getting things right,' Anna said,

surprised by her own passion. 'About not letting anything that fate might want to throw at you drag you down and back to . . .' She faltered to a stop, taking a deep breath and then a sip of wine. 'I care about trying your best. I suppose that's kind of old-fashioned.'

'What happened to you?' Miles asked, his brows furrowing. 'I know you were fostered by Simon's family, although the way he talks about you you'd never know you weren't his blood relation, but what happened before that to make you so . . . scared?'

'I'm not scared,' Anna protested, dropping her gaze from his, because that was exactly what she was, all of the time, every single moment that she was awake, and she spent a great deal of time making sure that no one, not Tom, not even Liv, ever noticed it.

'Maybe you aren't,' Miles said, not willing to force her to acknowledge what he felt was true. 'But do you realise that you refer to yourself as mad and weird and mental all the time, and that you imply Tom must be a saint for putting up with you because you are so awful?'

'No I don't!' Anna exclaimed. 'Do I? I don't know, I just know that I'm not . . . Liv. Simon's sister – did you meet her?' Anna didn't wait for an answer. 'She's my best friend, my sister really. Liv always knows exactly what to do and say and how to be and people always like her straight away. Tom did, from the first moment he met her. For a while there, when we first started dating, he talked more about her than he did about me. I was starting to get a complex. Actually I've got a complex. I know I'm not Liv, I didn't grow up knowing how to just be in the world the way she does. I know I'm not easy to like, like she is, because I'm prickly and difficult and disjointed.'

'You're doing it again,' Miles said. 'You aren't like that at all, you know. Not once you stop telling everyone you are. It's like you're scared to let anyone see the good in you.'

'No . . . really?' Anna said, thoughtfully. 'I don't really think of myself as good. I think if myself as . . . taxing.'

'But why? Because you like to make a few lists and you prefer it when things go your way? That doesn't make you weird, that just makes you you. And, by the way, you should realise that for a person to be really scared, and still get up and face the world every day with a sword-rattling battle cry, well, that makes them also really brave, and pretty amazing. What have you been through, Anna?'

'My mum died,' Anna said, trotting out the B version of her life, the one she always gave to strangers. 'My dad was already dead and I didn't have any relatives so I got put into care. I met Liv when I started a new school, and her family took me in. I've been so lucky really. I couldn't have asked for more.'

Anna smiled, the very same smile that she always produced when she finished that particular piece of fiction, a smile that was usually greeted with some relief from the person she was telling it to, relief that they weren't going to have to deal with someone who was *really* damaged by life. But Miles didn't have that expression of relief as he looked at her; instead his eyes narrowed just a little, as if he somehow detected the lie, before deciding not to press on it, something that Anna was grateful for.

'Well, I don't know Simon very well, but he seems like a lovely man,' Miles said. 'So I'm guessing you really lucked out with the rest of his family.'

'Oh I did,' Anna said, her smile broadening into genuine joy. 'I mean, Graham, who's sort of been my dad, he acts like the rest of his family permanently confuse him, but he's so kind, and so loyal, and always there. And Angela, my foster mum, is really quite barking mad, says whatever is in her head, even if it's twaddle, but she never treated me differently from her own children, not for a minute. And when we were sick she'd put cold flannels on our heads and bring us toast and Lucozade, you know the old kind with the orange twisty plastic.' Miles nodded, smiling. 'And Simon is funny and kind and never once minded that this cuckoo turned up in the nest and Liv . . .' Anna paused, her gaze resting for a moment on the string of trees that lined the sidewalk outside the window, glittering gently with their Christmas lights in the still cold air, the snow that had ceased to fall a few hours ago throwing the shadows they cast into sharp contrast and making her suddenly want to feel the chill of the air on her cheeks and in her lungs. 'Liv is the most beautiful, best, funniest, cleverest, talented, genuine, gorgeous person that I know. I'd love to be like her, she finds life so effortless. Honestly, she is so . . . amazing. And if it wasn't for her . . . If she hadn't decided to be my best friend and persuade her parents to take me in, then . . . well, put it this way, I owe her so much. She saved my life.'

Miles nodded, glimpsing just a hint of the truth that lay behind Anna's fake story, when he saw the genuine passion Anna felt for her friend and sister.

'You know what,' he said. 'You're right. I need to go and practise or do something to get ready for tomorrow. I don't want to come all this way for no reason, do I?'

'No,' Anna said, a little surprised at how disappointed she felt that their evening out in NYC together was coming to an end, but pleased nevertheless that Miles had listened to her. After they had split the bill and found their coats, they walked out into the cold night air, the city buzzing and vibrating with life around them. It felt wrong somehow to Anna, to go back their hotel room now, and spend the rest of the night insulated from all this living that was being done around them, and she realised that for perhaps the very first time in her life she felt like being adventurous, of taking a right turn instead of a left, of losing herself in the sparkle of a strange, magical city and just seeing what happened next. It had to be New York that was doing this to her, with her brazen come-ons, decked out in all her flirtatious finery. As Anna looked upwards, trusting Miles to guide her through the sidewalk packed with revellers, her arm tucked in his, she couldn't help but get the very strong impression that the city itself was inviting her to just let go, live a little and see what it felt like.

'That would be a terrible idea,' Anna said, out loud apparently, as it caused Miles to stop and look at her.

'What would be?' he asked.

'Oh, nothing,' Anna said, blushing inexplicably. 'I don't know, there's something about this place, it sort of makes you forget who you are, doesn't it?'

'Does it?' Miles questioned her again, gazing into her eyes a little more intensely than Anna was prepared for. 'Maybe that's a good thing, but the more I get to know you the more I think you don't quite know who you are yet.'

Anna paused, fixed in that moment, as a fresh fall of snow began to appear all around them, the traffic swishing along the wet roads, a group of office workers on a big night out engulfing them in their midst for a moment as they tripped their tipsy way around Anna and Miles. And standing there, in that moment, cornered by Christmas, Anna realised that Miles was right, she had worked long and hard for most of her life to appear to be someone who she wasn't even all that proud of. But was that anxious, controlling, difficult person even her? Or was it just a persona she'd adopted and begun to believe in, a little bit like Santa Claus? Anna wasn't at all sure of who she was any more, not really, only that the person she had been working so hard to be for so many years seemed very far away now, almost as if when Anna had boarded that plane she'd left her carefully constructed disguise neatly folded on the bed.

'It's a scary thing,' Anna breathed, her words crystallising in the icy air. 'If I'm not me, I'm not really sure who I am.'

'There's no need to be afraid,' Miles said, so quietly that Anna almost couldn't hear him over the roar of the traffic. 'Come on, this way.'

Miles took Anna's hand and pulled her in what she was sure was the opposite direction to the hotel.

'I don't think this is the right way,' she said, allowing him to leave his hand loosely holding hers.

'It is for what I have in mind,' Miles said, guiding her with single-minded determination.

'What do you mean – "for what you have in mind"?' Anna asked, half thrilled and half alarmed by the unexpected turn of events, but for some reason not surprised by them. 'What *do* you have in mind?'

'Well, while you were interviewing that naked lady, I got a bit bored by the stage show, so I had a look at a listings magazine that was knocking around, and it turns out there is an open mic night at this bar, just around . . . here.' Miles stopped in front of an older brownstone building with a cellar bar that was audible even from street level. The steps that led down to the entrance were garlanded in lights, and there was fake snow sprayed along the insides of the windows. Every time the door opened, a snatch of laughter, talking and music wafted out into the air.

'You're checking out your competition?' Anna asked him, confused.

'No, Anna. I'm going to sing. Back home I do this quite a lot if I'm working on a song and it's not quite there. I take it out, give it an airing and the way people react lets me know if I'm on the right or wrong track.'

'Oh,' Anna said, suddenly paralysed with nerves, that technically she wasn't entitled to. 'Oh that's what you've got in mind. But what if you're awful? What if I get that horrible cringy, want to curl up and die inside feeling that I get when I'm watching talent shows on TV and the contestants are clearly delusional?'

'Well, thanks for the vote of confidence, but I've only ever been bottled off stage once and that was because the crowd were expecting an Abba tribute band,' Miles reassured her. 'Come on, woman, tomorrow, both our lives might change for ever, let's have a little fun tonight.'

*

The bar was full, with a mixture of bohemian-looking types, many of them clutching an instrument, and suits desperate for a drink after work. There were glamorous-looking girls, in low-cut tops, with long hair tumbling down their backs, most likely stopping off on their way to somewhere much more glitzy, and men who looked intent on snaring them before they did. There were no tables free, but Miles secured Anna a place at the bar, bought her a beer that she didn't ask for and would never normally drink, before heading off towards the small stage area, presumably with a view to putting his name down on some list. Anna sipped the beer, feeling distinctly uncomfortable about what Miles was about to do. The idea of putting her head above the parapet, inviting criticism, derision and even ridicule was something she endeavoured not to do at all costs. Part of her life's work was to always get everything just right enough, to never be too showy (with the exception of self-designed snowflake wedding dresses) or over-confident, and to never ever attract the wrong kind of attention, which was difficult as her unknown father had made her tall and blonde. And yet somehow, here she was glued to a bar stool in terror as Miles prepared to do exactly that, to chance everything on a crowd of strangers who might easily hate and revile him. Liv was the one who didn't care what people thought of her. She was brave and original, and did as she pleased. Anna was constantly worried that people would see through her neat manicure, her brushed hair, her flawless make-up and see that scraggy little wide-eyed loveless orphan.

'Have you got anything stronger?' she said, gripped by panic, leaning across the bar to attract the attention of the barman. They hadn't been back to the hotel since they'd left it around midday, and Anna was suddenly finding her sweater dress a little too warm for comfort in the close, hot atmosphere of the bar. The beer that she didn't even like had gone down surprisingly easily and now she found she rather needed something to steady her nerves.

'This is a bar, sweetheart,' the barman told her, cheerfully. 'What do you want?'

'Um, a cocktail?' Anna asked him. 'Something New Yorky.'

'You English?' the barman asked her. Anna nodded. 'Then you want a Cosmo, English girls always want a Cosmo. One coming right up, honey.'

'And keep them coming, my friend is going up there to do a number and I think I might actually die of embarrassment,' Anna confided in the stranger on an unfamiliar impulse, although she discovered that she liked referring to Miles as her friend. It was a novelty to think that she might actually have more than one in the world.

'Ah, the more they suck, they more they love them in here,' the bartender told her amiably, setting one pink concoction down in front of her. 'Now, go easy on these. I make them strong, and you don't look like a big drinker to me.'

'I'll be fine,' Anna assured him as a faint-hearted round of applause smattered its way around the bar, barely audible over the chatter and laughter. 'My friend will make sure I get back to the hotel OK.'

When she turned back, she was horrified to see Miles sitting on the stage, fiddling with an acoustic guitar that he had somehow got hold of. He'd taken off his jacket and hoody, leaving only a white singlet, which clung to his well-defined chest and abs, and left those strong arms completely naked. Anna noticed that most of the women in the bar had stopped talking, and started looking, and she smiled to herself as she watched Miles, utterly oblivious to the attention he was getting, his dark hair falling across his face, concentrating on getting the sound he wanted out of an unfamiliar instrument.

'Come on, buddy!' some guy shouted from the back of the room.

'Hey,' a female voice responded. 'Leave him be. I've seen a hell of a lot worse things to look at and you're one of them.' A ripple of laughter and applause followed, as Miles, suddenly aware that most eyes in the room were now on him, looked up and smiled, which solicited a whoop from the female sections of the audience.

'Hello,' he said, his English accent causing an audible sigh of pleasure.

'Oh, he's British,' a girl standing just in front of Anna said. 'God, I love British men, they're so funny, and humble and great.'

'So, I'm over in this wonderful city of yours for a few days with a friend . . .'

'We don't need your life story, "mate",' the same male voice told him with a bad imitation of an English accent.

'We do want your room number though,' another female voice added to the chorus, making Miles laugh so that his eyes crinkled.

'Anyway I've been working on this song. It started just being about that feeling you get when you think you'd like to be in love and you imagine what it's like, and it's sort of there, waiting around a corner but you don't know which one or when you'll bump into it.'

'Bump into me, baby, any time you like!' Another voice, this time male, sounded from somewhere in the middle of the bar.

'And then, in the last few hours really, it's started to be about someone. A person, a real person I just met, or met again, I should say. And so anyway . . .'

Miles looked across the bar and smiled at Anna who was clutching her elegant drink in both hands, her eyes wide and terrified.

'Thanks, Anna. If this goes down like a lead balloon, it's entirely your fault.'

The barman handed Anna three cocktails in a row, which lasted at the rate of approximately one per minute, as Miles held the bar in his thrall, singing a song that he had implied was about her. The tune, which sounded nothing like the retro punk-rock fusion band that he was planning to audition with the following day, had an instantly memorable melody, and his voice had just enough of a raw edge to give its warm, soulful tones a roughness that seemed to catch at every listener's heart. The room fell entirely silent, as Miles played on, his eyes half closed, a smile playing around his mouth until a split second after he finished and then suddenly the applause was deafening. He really was very, very good, Anna realised.

'Did he write that song for you?' the girl who liked English men asked Anna, looking at her, wide-eyed and impressed. 'Man, he loves you! All that stuff about light and love and finally seeing the real you . . . that's like, way romantic. He loves you, you lucky bitch.'

'Oh no, he doesn't,' Anna reassured her. 'We're just friends. We barely know each other. In actual fact, I'm getting married next week to someone else, well, that is if I can track down his wife so . . .'

'You're not *with* him?' the girl asked her, incredulous. 'Really? In that case would you mind introducing me to him when he comes over?'

'Oh well, I mean I'm sort of with him, in that we are together as friends and, anyway, he's got an early morning so he probably should just go to sleep.'

'And next up we have Miles again . . .' The MC had to pause for the cheers. 'But this time joined by his fellow Brit, Miss Annie Carter!'

'What?' Anna said as the barman slid another Cosmo straight into the palm of her hand. 'What? No way.'

'*You* sing too?' the curious girl asked her. 'Are you in like a band?'

'Come on, Annie.' Miles grinned, beckoning her over. 'Come and sing with me.'

'I can't sing!' Anna said, her voice unheard over the din as she downed the latest cocktail. 'Miles, I have no musical talent whatsoever!'

But the bar began to chant her name: 'Annie, Annie, Annie.' And Anna found herself being propelled, quite against her will, towards the platform where Miles was waiting, smiling at her. And, worse still, she hadn't had time to drink the last cocktail that the barman had made for her, which was probably just as well, as her face already felt numb and she wasn't entirely sure she could remember where her feet were, neither of which things helped with the fact that the very, very last thing Anna Carter ever wanted to do in her life was to stand on a stage, no matter how small, and sing.

'OK,' Miles told her, slipping his arm around her

waist as she clambered, blinking under the lights, on to the stage. 'Here's a mic.'

Anna took the clunky-looking thing as if it were an object that had recently appeared from outer space. 'Miles, I can't sing,' she hissed, her voice magnified around the room, causing a ripple of laughter.

'Everyone can sing,' Miles said. 'You can all sing, right?'

There was a cheer of general assent.

'And so can you, Anna,' he whispered into her ear. 'Come on. You wanted me to take my audition seriously, to get in some practice to work on my song, and I've done that, thanks to you. I now know that the song I've got is pretty good. So let me do something for you.'

'Miles! Doing something for me would be letting me leave here at once,' Anna insisted, her voice tight with fear, her stomach lurching dangerously.

'Just sing,' Miles urged her, smiling into her eyes. 'It doesn't matter what you sound like, just sing it and feel every word and let yourself go, skate away, I'll be right here next to you.'

'So,' he addressed the crowd. 'We'll be singing the best Christmas song I know. "River" by Joni Mitchell, and I want you all to join in, OK.'

'Joni Mitchell!' Anna squeaked. 'No one can sing along to her. Her voice is so high that only dogs and some breeds of bat can hear it. And angst-ridden teenage girls.'

'You're funny.' Miles smiled. 'Now, shut up and sing.'

There was only one thing for Anna to do – she had to sing. However, she had not been exaggerating about her lack of vocal talents. She was an awful singer; for every perfectly honed note that Miles hit, Anna squawked, squeaked and squealed her way through ten more, pausing with inward breath to apologise to the audience, who, oddly, didn't seem to mind at all, and who in fact seemed to be enjoying the gusto with which she sang, if not the actual sound that she made. And Anna found that the more they laughed and cheered, the more she felt her shoulders relax, and a smile spread across her face as she gradually let herself go, throwing herself into the song and finishing off her performance with an ear-splitting note that would render most people deaf for at least ten minutes. And yet everyone in the bar cheered and clapped and laughed as Anna took an unsteady bow, firstly on her own and then, finding Miles at her side, taking his hand and bowing again.

'Oh my God!' Anna turned to him, her eyes sparkling, breathless with laughter. 'This was the best fun ever, I think I should go on *The X Factor*. I think I should be a pop star! They love me, those people out there, they love me, Miles!'

'Yes, they do,' Miles said and before Anna knew what was happening he'd swept her into those arms of his and was twirling her round and round until the room spun. And very shortly after that she threw up about six undigested Cosmopolitans on his sexy white vest.

'I am *so* sorry,' Anna said for about the thousandth time in the fifteen minutes it had taken Miles to get her out of the back of the bar, and for them to find a street they recognised again. They had started back to the hotel, finding themselves somehow at an ice rink at the foot of the Rockefeller tower. Anna was still a little dizzy and breathless, so Miles sat her down at the edge of the rink so she could catch her breath. The rink was still packed and, as she sat under the twinkling lights of the enormous and perfectly proportioned Christmas tree, Anna took in deep breaths of cold air until she could feel her lungs shudder, and her head finally clear.

'Oh God,' she said, burying her head in her hands. 'I threw up in front of thousands of people! I threw up on you! Oh God, oh God, oh God.'

'It was more like you spontaneously regurgitated a great deal of alcohol in the vicinity of maybe two hundred people,' Miles said chuckling. 'And most of them didn't see, because I was standing between you and them, so really, the worst that happened was that you ruined my audition top. Thank God that carbonara stayed down, that would have been nasty!'

'I'm so humiliated,' Anna groaned, clutching her head in her hands. 'What must you think of me? Why do I always do this? Why? Why?'

'Sing badly and throw up?' Miles asked her. 'It's not such a big deal, Anna.'

'Freak out, mess up, make a good situation bad,' Anna continued unhappily. 'It's just I wonder some-times, am I like my mum?' Anna took another deep breath. 'Because I was nine when she . . . went. I was nine and I was quite old, but I don't remember a lot of my life with her, just little snippets, like . . .' She looked around for inspiration. 'Like bright stars in a dark night, you know? Always happy memories, times when we were laughing or it was sunny, and she looked pretty, even though I know it was hardly ever like that. And I wonder if it's because I was nine, or if it's because I don't want to remember, because she was . . .' Anna paused, running her fingers through her hair, and the air suddenly became charged with the unhappiness and fear that Anna spent every single day fighting off. She looked up at Miles, who, seeing her misery-struck expression, knelt down before her.

'Anna, what is it?' he asked gently, taking her wrists in his hands, because her fists, he discovered, were knotted into two tight balls. 'You just got a little bit drunk, it's fine.'

'But it's not fine, is it? That's what she used to say, "I'm just a little bit merry, love, it's fine." And it was never fine. What if I am like her? Because . . . it's so confusing, Miles. I'm terrified that if I put even one foot wrong, I will become the same person that she did.'

Miles's brow furrowed as he tried to understand. 'Anna, what really happened with your mum?'

'I don't know how to talk about it,' Anna told him, her voice trembling. 'I don't *know* who I really am, because I never let myself find out. What if I am the sort of person who runs away, who never gets it right, who lets people down time and time again, no matter how much I try not to? What if all this –' she spread her arms wide to embrace the city, glittering around them as if it was a remote mythical celestial audience '– me racing over to New York, trying to sort out this wedding, creating a great big drama just so my diary doesn't get messed up, is just me trying to prove that *I'm* not going to let anyone down, *I'm* not going to let it get messed up, that I'm *not* my mother, because the truth of it is I've never loved anyone as much I loved and adored my mum, and she left me. What if I'm just not the sort of person who gets a fairy-tale wedding and a happy ever after?'

'Don't be stupid,' Miles said, both perplexed and touched by Anna's tears. 'Of course you are, and, well, if your mum wasn't that great a mum maybe it was because she was ill, or . . . worried.'

'She *was* ill,' Anna said. 'I understand that now, at least.'

'And if you only remember the good bits, well, that's not a bad thing, not at all,' Miles said. 'It takes a special person to only look for the good, a kind-hearted, generous person who deserves all the happy endings they want. And if it helps, I think you're pretty brilliant actually. Look at tonight: I put you on the spot and you rose to the occasion, magnificently. You didn't mess the moment up, you *made* it. Maybe you ruptured a few eardrums in the process and if Joni ever heard the way you sang her stuff, she'd put a hitman on you, but if you want to know the truth, seeing you singing your heart out, albeit really, *really* badly, made me . . .' Miles paused, looking away from Anna for a moment, and at the circling, dizzy skaters laughing under the lights instead, as he searched for the right word. 'Happy. Your singing made me happy. And slightly nauseous. Although not as nauseous as you made yourself.'

Miles laughed and found a faint tear-stained smile greet him in return, which gave him a curiously warm sensation in the middle of his chest, the exact spot where Anna lightly whacked him with her still balled-up fist. Just for a moment, she found herself forgetting everything that normally nibbled around her edges every moment that she was awake. Just for that second as she looked into Miles's eyes and found herself laughing . . .

'Thank you,' she said on an outward breath, almost without realising it.

'What for?' Miles grinned, holding on to her wrists again, having caught them as she'd made a half-hearted attempt to beat him up.

'I don't know really,' Anna said, suddenly becoming self-conscious, withdrawing her hands from his. 'For making me forget myself, I suppose, just for a minute or two.'

'Annie,' Miles said slowly and for once Anna didn't feel the urge to correct him. 'Look, it doesn't take a genius to see that there is more to you than you are letting on. And you don't have to tell me anything you don't want to, but just then, when you were talking about your mum? Did she die?'

Anna looked up at him, caught off guard by his intuition.

'No,' she said simply. 'Well, not when I was nine anyway. Do you want to know the whole truth?'

'Only if you want to tell me,' he said. 'If you think it might help.'

Anna took a deep breath of the chilled air, feeling it fill her lungs. 'I've never really talked about this to anyone except Liv.'

'You don't have to talk to me about it now, not if you don't want to.'

'But for some really odd reason,' Anna said, 'I do. There's something about you that's very . . . easy.'

'Are you saying I'm easy?" he joked as Anna smiled.

Miles got up from his kneeling position to sit next to her. They both gazed up at the sky beyond the further peaks of the skyscrapers for a few seconds before Anna felt ready to talk.

'I was nine,' she began at last. 'It was Christmas.' She looked down at the toes of her snow-stained boots as she talked. 'We had this flat, this tiny flat. It was a messy one-bedroom but it was *our* flat. We'd had it for a few weeks. It was the longest time we'd ever stayed in one place. My mum was a drinker and a drug addict. Heroin mainly. But whatever she could get her hands on at the time would do. Most of the time the rent money would go the minute she got it. We got thrown out of a lot of places. We slept on a lot of other people's floors. One night, we slept in the park under the trees. It was summer and warm I remember. My mum said we were camping. It was only years later that I realised we'd slept rough that night. After that though things got better for a bit. There was a social worker, and some housing benefit. She arranged for it to be paid directly to the landlord or something. I don't remember the details exactly. But for the first time we had a proper place to live. A place that belonged to us, a home. I didn't know any different, so I didn't really get that the flat was filthy, that other people's homes weren't like mine. She left her empty bottles and needles lying around. And I got to sleep in the bed with her if she didn't have company. If she did, then she'd make me sleep on the sofa, or in the bath. But it was just normal to me. I didn't mind.'

Miles said nothing, he didn't move, his expression didn't change, he kept his eyes fixed on the far horizon, up where the stars were struggling to compete against the brighter galaxy of New York city lights.

'So it was Christmas, and for once Mum made an effort. She cleaned out the flat, and dressed up. She even got me a new dress from somewhere. I remember it still had the security tag on but I pretended not to notice. I've still got it, you know. I keep it in a box under my bed. No one knows that, not even Liv. We had a chicken, ready cooked and cold, and some pasta salad on the side. It wasn't really a traditional dinner but I thought it was the best thing I'd ever eaten. And Mum had gotten these crackers, and we pulled a whole box between us.' Anna smiled faintly. 'I got to keep all the little toys inside, it was like . . . well, it was like Christmas. And that would have been enough for me, it really would. It was so special, the way it was just us two, the way we laughed, the way she looked and smelled. Clean, you know. Not of stale vodka and smoke. It was like someone had waved a magic wand and made life just like it was on the TV, in all the adverts. And then, in the afternoon, she brought me out this present. It was all wrapped up with a bow on it. It was a wedding dress Barbie, in a massive sparkly net dress. And I was . . . in love, completely overwhelmed. I'd never been that happy. Mum grabbed me and hugged me so tightly, I could barely breathe, but I didn't mind because I knew that right then, whilst she was holding me, that she loved me and . . .' Anna stopped, taken off guard by the tears that thickened in her throat once again. She shook her head, taking several breaths, until the moment passed, and she could regain control of her voice again. 'I remember the telly didn't work, so we spent the rest of the day making plans for my Barbie's wedding, and somehow that turned into my wedding, the Christmas wedding that I would have one day. We drew pictures of the sleigh, the reindeer, what Mum would wear, everything except the groom, but then again the groom didn't seem that important.' Anna pictured herself sitting on the living-room floor with a packet of felt tips, her mum at her side, their heads bent together, as she schemed and drew. 'But most of all we drew pictures of my special dress, and exactly what it would be like. We stayed up, until I fell asleep, I suppose. I woke up the next morning alone in Mum's bed. And when I got up, the sun was shining, it was a bright day and I felt so . . . so happy and safe. I went to the living room. There was an empty bottle of vodka on the top of the TV, and a five pound note resting under it.' Anna frowned, her fingers plucking at a loose thread on her coat as she relived what happened next. 'I waited. I waited all day for her to come back, and all night. And the next day. She didn't come. I was too afraid to go out, I didn't know anyone to phone, so I just waited. For four days, and after the third day, the electric ran out on the meter. So I waited in the dark and the cold.'

Miles kept staring upwards as she talked. He was unable to look at her, Anna guessed. Now that he knew everything, he would probably never talk to her like he had before or make jokes. He'd be careful, and, from now on, politely distant, because no one wanted to get to know someone so damaged, in case it somehow rubbed off on them. Saddened, she felt the loss of that one moment of lightness that they had shared together, that now would be impossible to feel again. And yet, now she had started her story, she knew she had to finish it.

'On the fourth day,' Anna said. 'There was a loud banging at the door. Mum told me never to answer the door, and I never did usually, but this time I thought it might be her. It wasn't. It was loan sharks after their money. I suppose that could have been the worst thing that happened to me, but it was actually the best. I got loan sharks with a heart, you see. One of them called the police, said they'd found an abandoned kid in a flat, and left the door on the latch before they left. A nice policewoman came, they took me to the station, they fed me, got me clothes, another social worker came, and I spent my first night in care. I got moved around a bit, and after almost a year I got moved to yet another school. That was the school Liv went to, and it was soon after meeting her that my life really began. I never heard from my mum again, and I realise now that that Christmas Day, that was her goodbye gift to me. One perfect day. It's the only thing I really have of her.'

'You never saw or heard from her again?' Miles asked her, astounded. 'They couldn't find her?'

Anna shook her head. 'They found her. About a year after I went to live with Liv and her family. In a bedsit in Bristol. She was dead. Overdose.'

'And what about your father?' Miles asked gently.

'I never knew who he was – there's nothing on my birth certificate. But ever since then I've had a list, a plan, a . . . map of where to go and how to be, and I know if I stick to it, to the letter, then I won't lose control like she did. I won't hurt the people I love.'

Anna turned to look at Miles, expecting him to be unable to look her in the eye any more, but instead he picked up her hand and smiled at her.

'It's nearly midnight,' he told her. 'Let's go back to the room. I want to finish my song, you need to Google Erica Barnes and we need to make sure that tomorrow is the day that changes our lives for the better, OK?'

'OK,' Anna said, uncertainly, letting him pull her off the step.

'Now, Annie, please will you sing to me again,' Miles said with a smile. 'The sound of your angelic voice is really all I want for Christmas.'

It took a moment for Anna to realise he was still making jokes. He was acting as if he hadn't heard a single thing she'd said and, oddly, Anna knew he was behaving that way because he had not only heard her, he'd listened. And it was the strangest feeling in the world to know that she had finally met a man who understood her, and stranger still to realise that he wasn't the one she was about to marry.

Anna smiled as she punched him lightly in the ribs, and the moon sailed above their heads, and somewhere a drunk with a far better voice than Anna's sang 'Silent Night'.

Chapter Eleven

Anna opened her eyes, and stared for a moment into the darkness, as she orientated herself. That's right, she wasn't at home, in her own bed, arranged neatly on the pillows like a princess, she was in New York on the verge of tracking down Tom's surprise wife. That would be why, even in the dark, the world seemed a little upside down and back to front. And the reason her mouth was dry and there was this tiny but insistent pounding ache in her right temple was because she had taken it upon herself to drink six Cosmopolitan cocktails in the space of about ten minutes. And, even though they had left her system almost as quickly as they had entered it, they had left their legacy behind in the form of an elegant little hangover. That would explain why the roof of her mouth was as dry as bone, but not why she had a crick in her neck, or why her pillow, which she was sure was made of goose down yesterday, was now hard, and muscular, and rose and fell with a steady rhythm and, not to mention, appeared to have a heartbeat.

Anna opened her sleepy eyes wide, her whole body tensing in an instant as she realised that she was not

asleep in her bed in the suite, but must have in fact
passed out sometime after she and Miles had got back
last night, and had spent goodness only knew how
many hours slumbering on his – thankfully clothed
– chest. Terrified of moving even one eyelash, Anna
assessed the situation as best she could from her prone
position. Miles was fast asleep, his head propped up
on the cushions, one arm and one leg trailing on the
floor. She, much to her deep horror, was curled
between his legs, her head resting on his chest. His
other arm was draped loosely over her waist. She also
was fully dressed, and thankfully her dehydration
meant she hadn't drooled on him, so technically
nothing untoward had taken place. Except that if Tom
had told her he'd fallen asleep in a hotel room in the
arms of another woman she would tear him limb from
limb and then mince him for good measure. Anna's
heart sank as she realised that, in essence, she had
cheated on Tom, she had betrayed him. OK, she and
Miles hadn't done anything sexual, but as well as
spending a really fun and interesting evening together,
where they'd eaten, laughed, sung – very badly in her
case – they'd talked about things that Anna had never
wanted to talk to Tom about. It was an emotional
betrayal. She and Miles had shared each other's time
with a kind of trust and willingness that Anna wasn't
sure she'd ever really had with Tom, not even when
things were going brilliantly, not even just after they

got together or just after he'd proposed, because . . . well, he hadn't mentioned his showgirl wife and she'd never told him the real story of her childhood. She'd allowed herself to relax with Miles in a way she never had with Tom, and that had to be at least a kind of cheating.

Anna closed her eyes tightly shut again, wondering if it might be possible to transport herself to the bedroom using the power of telekinesis alone, and finding fairly quickly that it was not. This was no good, lying here listening to the beat of Miles's heart. They'd crashed out on the sofa, that was all that had happened. And it wasn't infidelity, not really. Besides, Anna thought, she'd started to feel warm towards Tom again, even almost ready to talk to him. She remembered that after they'd got back into the room, they'd found a large brown envelope waiting for her in the hallway, which she'd opened to find the annulment papers that Charisma needed to sign, and a note from Tom, written in his oversized loopy handwriting, a single sentence taking up a whole sheet: 'Anna, I miss you, I love you and I can't wait to see you again, _your_ Tom.'

And he'd underlined the 'your' especially to emphasise that it was her his heart belonged to and not Charisma, or at least that was how Anna had chosen to interpret it last night in her tipsy state. She'd hugged the note to her chest and determined that tomorrow she would call Tom and that they would really talk, really sort things out and, with a fair wind and a bit of good luck, have their Christmas wedding after all.

She remembered also that Miles had Googled Erica Brown and jubilantly cried out that he'd found her. He'd discovered an advertisement for a play, called *The Long Dark Night of the Soul*, which featured, somewhere in the middle of the bill, 'Erica Barnes.'

The website had said it was at a venue called City Centre – Stage II, West 55th Street. The play sounded dire: it was a about a nun who was secretly in love with her adopted brother who was dying of cancer. She remembered Miles had made a joke then. 'Interesting casting, I can't quite see Charisma as a nun . . . well, not that kind of nun anyway.'

Anna had flopped down on to the sofa next to him, as he clicked through to a link that listed the actors' biographies. And there it was, a photo of Charisma turned Erica. She was still unmistakable, with her long dark hair, falling in glossy waves over half of her face. Just as seductive in its way as the last photo, only now, instead of being mostly undressed, she was wearing a plain white shirt and little or no make-up, and was sporting a catlike smile that seemed to say she knew something that Anna didn't.

'We've found her, Anna,' Miles had said. 'We can go in the morning, get her to sign your papers and you can be on a plane home to sort your wedding out by tomorrow night.' He'd smiled at her, although his expression hadn't quite matched the enthusiasm of his tone.

'It's mad, isn't it?' Anna had replied, looking back at the photo and then at Miles. 'I didn't ever actually think this plan would work. But, anyway, I'll go on my own. You've got to go to your audition.'

'Not till the afternoon,' Miles had said. 'Honestly, I don't mind coming with you. I sort of want to see it through, if you don't mind and, actually, I was sort of hoping you might return the favour, come with me to my thing? It turns out I could do with a bit of moral support after all and having a hot blonde on my arm won't hurt my image any.' Anna had smiled, rolling her eyes, knowing Miles well enough now to know that he'd drop in a flippant comment to divert attention away from himself at every opportunity. Nevertheless, she had been touched that he'd asked her, and glad to have a reason to return the favour that he'd done her.

'OK,' she'd said. 'You're on, it seems only fair.'

'How do you feel, about the prospect of coming face to face with your bloke's first wife?' Miles had asked her, as Anna dwelled on Charisma's new photograph.

'It's funny,' she'd said thoughtfully. 'I thought I'd feel sick and scared and jealous and anxious and stupid. But right at this moment, I don't really feel anything very much at all.' She'd put the iPad down and turned to him. 'Come on you, time to practise.'

Anna had sat on a cushion on the floor while Miles

played to her, a selection of songs he'd written himself, although not the one he'd sung in the bar, which Anna was sort of grateful for, because it raised a whole lot of questions she hadn't really wanted to dwell on. She'd clapped and cheered him, then, between them, they'd decided on his outfit for the audition, and then they'd settled down on the sofa at just before two to watch some rubbish TV. It must have been sometime during an ancient episode of *Cagney and Lacey* that Anna had fallen asleep, because that was the last thing she remembered.

Now, ever so quietly and slowly, Anna began to shift her body weight upwards, finding Miles's grip tightening unconsciously on her waist as she attempted to move. Sighing, she paused, and lifted the dead weight of his arm off her and onto a cushion. Sitting up with some difficulty because she didn't want to use any part of his body as leverage, Anna finally found herself perched on the edge of the sofa, her legs twisted to avoid touching Miles's other leg that rested, still in its boot, on the floor. Anna paused to look down at him, sleeping serenely in the half-light of the early morning, the glow of the city through the heavy net curtains all that illuminated the bridge of his nose and his high cheekbones, and thought two things. Firstly, that he really was a very deep sleeper and, secondly, that she really had to break the habit of watching him sleep.

*

'I'd kill for a coffee – a real one, not a plane coffee,' Liv said as Tom took her bag from her, and they emerged blinking into the early daylight at JFK International Airport. It was freezing cold, snow whipped around in the wind, with an altogether more wintery feel than the damp, grey, unenthusiastic December they had left in London. It was just after 8 a.m. and the reality of where they were and what they were doing was only just hitting Liv after several warm hours cocooned in a metal cylinder suspended in mid-air where there was nothing she could do about anything. Tom had barely spoken to her for the whole journey, partly because when they'd booked their flights they had been unable to find two seats together, but also, Liv thought, as she watched him stare blankly at the TV screen from several rows behind, although he'd asked her to accompany him, and she had agreed almost at once, it wasn't making conversation with or paying even polite attention to her that he was concerned about. Liv's best guess was all he could think about was Anna and Charisma and how to make these two disjointed parts of his life work so that the one didn't drag down the other. Somewhere over the Atlantic Liv had cursed herself for agreeing to come along on the trip so readily. What was she doing here, really, if not still following her doomed crush on him with the kind of insane doggedness that other people in similar situations found themselves on the wrong end of restraining order for? When, Liv had wondered bitterly, would she finally let her compulsion to do everything Tom asked her go, and start to live her own life again? Anna wouldn't thank her, either, for turning up in New York, when strictly speaking she should be unboxing and hanging her dress, and overseeing the creation of the pre-service canapés, and all the other endless small tasks she'd been driven to delegate to Liv in her absence.

Without replying to her request for coffee, Tom grabbed the door of the nearest taxi and held it open for Liv, who climbed in, sliding across the plastic seat with a distinct sense of foreboding as the angry snow beat against the grimy window.

'You know where we're going, right?' Tom asked her, because until that moment Liv had kept her word to Anna and not told Tom where her friend was staying.

'The Algonquin,' Liv told the driver, wondering how Anna would react when she saw them.

'I'm not even sure anyone will be there at this time.' Miles was now awake and seemed oblivious to their slumbering tryst on the sofa, much to Anna's relief and slight annoyance. After a refreshingly cold shower, Anna had felt a renewed sense of purpose and had collected the annulment papers and dragged Miles, now dressed in his audition outfit of a red checked shirt, new dark-blue jeans, new trimmed stubble and freshly washed hair, complete with his guitar, out of their hotel and into the freezing winter morning. 'We could have coffee and breakfast and mosey on over there after that?'

'I feel like I have to go now,' Anna said, jiggling on her toes. 'If we don't go now, I'll just spend the time thinking about what to say to her, how to act. I was up at six this morning worrying about everything. I'm ready to confront her.' She stopped sticking her hand out in vain for a cab, and turned to Miles. 'If I wait any longer I won't be able to go through with it.'

'OK,' Miles said, and whistled a taxi to a standstill. 'But if there's no one around when we get there, coffee and pancakes in the nearest diner are on you.'

Miles was right, the venue was tightly closed when they arrived. As they stared at the closed shutters, he pulled his hoody up against the whipping snow that bowled down the street at a ferocious speed, and Anna wrapped her arms around her body, hugging herself against the cold. Looking around, it didn't take them long to find a diner serving hot coffee and a very enticing selection of pancakes. Not that Anna could bring herself to eat hers: her stomach was still too thick with the anxiety of knowing that any minute now she'd come face to face with her nemesis. Others might have found that term a little overstated but when used in reference to one's fiancé's secret wife, Anna felt in her guts, along with the anxiety-induced acid reflux, it would turn out to be appropriate. Particularly as she had no evidence to suggest that Charisma would simply sign the papers, and that would be that.

'You do look nice!' Miles said, as Anna unwrapped her coat and shed a few layers of woollens. He'd said it with that tone of surprise that men use and don't understand why women find it annoying, as if the idea of them looking nice could be so novel. Anna had indeed put in extra effort with her outfit that morning, casting aside her usual palette of muted colours in favour of a postbox red, lightly woven woollen pencil dress she'd picked up on her shopping trip to Saks with Miles. It wasn't normally Anna's policy to choose a dress because it enhanced and accentuated the fullness of her bust, even revealing a considerable amount, for her anyway, of cleavage, with its square-cut neckline. Or an outfit that made the most of her waist, hips and frankly her bottom, because Anna wasn't the sort of girl who liked to draw attention to her figure, knowing well enough that her long blonde hair was usually enough for people to judge her. She didn't like to give anyone any more ammunition to write her off as a bimbo, as if hair colour and bra size could somehow be a decent indication of your brain capacity anyway. On this occasion, however, she was making an exception, and pulling out, as Miles would say, the big guns. Charisma was a woman of glamour, even in her newly invented guise as the elegant angst-ridden nun-playing

Erica Barnes, and she needed to see Anna as her equal, and not some naive little English rose who could be swept aside if she decided she wanted to entice back her estranged husband after all.

'Are you not going to eat that?' Miles asked, pointing at Anna's virtually untouched stack of pancakes, which she slid towards him.

'Here, knock yourself out,' she said, taking another sip of black coffee.

'You look really . . .' Miles hesitated as his gaze roamed over her face, and frankly the parts of her that fell just south of that, for a few seconds. 'No, there is no polite way of saying it, you look damn sexy, Anna. I mean, really hot. You're not going to let Charisma outshine you, are you? I hope Tom knows what a very lucky man he is.'

Anna looked up at him and for a moment they were silent as they watched each other over the table, and Anna found herself imagining what it would be like to sweep aside the stack of pancakes between them, climb over the table, entwine her fingers in Miles's hair and kiss him until her red lipstick was smeared all over his face and he was unable to stop himself from sweeping her up into his arms, throwing her down in the booth and making mad reckless love to her right there. And then the practical real her emerged as she thought how the tightness of the skirt she was wearing would make that almost impossible without splitting a seam, and that they'd almost certainly get arrested for indecent behaviour, but not before at least a little of the heat of what she had been picturing must have seeped into her eyes, because suddenly she noticed that Miles's cheeks were a blazing red, almost matching the colour of her dress, and that he could not look her either in the eye or the cleavage any more.

Guiltily, Anna excused herself and went to the ladies' room, where she reapplied her lipstick, noticing the flush that burnished her own cheeks. It was just stress, she told herself, and the whole being far away from home and Tom and normality that had made her think in an inappropriate way about a man who just simply wasn't her type, not even if she had been single. It was all of those things and her tight little red dress that momentarily made her feel like someone else, like the kind of woman who strode down the streets of New York City leaving men gasping with desire in her wake. All this silliness, all this falling asleep on sexy men's chests, looking at them whilst they slept and worst of all imagining them with you in compromising situations had to stop at once. Poor Miles had been nothing but kind and supportive to her, full stop. OK, their friendship had started out a little unsteadily, what with the near-death experience and his unwavering ability to completely annoy her, but in the last couple of days Anna knew that she'd been lucky to have him by her side. What she could not, and would not do, was to draw him any further into this mess than he was already. She could not let him catch glimpses of the strange feelings he seemed to be inspiring in her, because they were fleeting and, more than that, they simply weren't real. In a few minutes' time, when the box office opened at the theatre, she'd go and see Charisma, and get the papers signed. And then she'd take a cab with Miles to the Village, where his audition was being held, and, after that, she'd book the first available flight to London and go home to Tom, where in just under a week she would marry him, and that would be that. She'd never have to think about anything else to do with men ever again.

When Anna returned to their booth, she found Miles pushing her still uneaten pancakes around the plate, his head bowed, deep in thought.

'Are you OK?' Anna asked him. 'Nervous about the audition?'

He looked up at her, his ice-blue gaze taking her aback a little. 'Yes,' he admitted. 'And . . .'

He frowned as he looked at her, some internal struggle etched on his face, until eventually he shook his head, as if deciding not to complete his sentence, except that he did it in a way that caught Anna completely off guard.

'What time did you go to your room last night?' he asked, his steady gaze somehow preventing her from lowering hers.

'Oh, I don't know, late, I suppose,' Anna hedged.

'I missed you,' he said, causing Anna's heart to plummet into her shoes. 'When you went, it was cold and I missed you.'

'So that's all I am to you, a glorified blanket,' Anna laughed awkwardly, and Miles's answering smile wasn't quite up to his full capacity.

'Sorry, Annie,' he said. 'Didn't mean to make you feel awkward.'

'Anna,' Anna repeated her name, slowly and heavily. 'My name is Anna and if my watch is right, now I can go over there and get the signature on this piece of paper that means I can marry the man I love.' As Anna looked into Miles's eyes she knew exactly what she had to say for both their sakes. 'And given that that is exactly what I intend to do it's probably not a good idea to mention the fact we've been sharing a room or sleeping . . . falling asleep together to anyone, you do understand, don't you?'

'Course I do,' Miles said, shrugging a little stiffly. 'I know, I get that. Just answer me one thing.'

Anna nodded.

'They've been up in the UK for a good few hours now, have you spoken to Tom yet?'

Anna's eyes widened as she realised that she'd completely forgotten the promise she'd made to herself to call him last night. In fact, until Miles had forced the issue, she'd more or less forgotten Tom completely she'd been so busy thinking about what to wear to impress Charisma.

'Yes,' she lied, getting up. 'Yes. I spoke to him before we left. We're fine, he's so pleased that I found Charisma, and that I'm sorting it all. It was really lovely to hear his voice.'

'Good,' Miles said. 'I'm pleased for you, Anna, really I am. Now go get your annulment. I'll wait here for you.'

'You're not coming?' Anna said, a little crestfallen. She'd sort of got used to having Miles around as her sidekick.

'No, not this time. I think you need to do this on your own,' Miles told her. 'Go on, Anna, you can do it. I know you can.'

Anna nodded and, bracing herself against the freezing wind, she prepared to meet her nemesis head-on.

'No, they're not in their room,' a polite young woman, whose name badge declared that she was called Kimberly, told Tom and Liv as they stood at the impressively appointed reception desk in the lobby of the Algonquin Hotel. 'I think they went out pretty early. There's no one answering the room phone. Are they expecting you?'

Tom said nothing, his gaze remaining fixated on Kimberly, just as Liv knew that he was fixated on the one word that she kept innocently repeating. They.

'Um, no,' Tom said. 'It's a surprise. I'm her fiancé, you see. I don't suppose you could tell us her room number, so I could leave a note.'

'Oh no, sir,' Kimberly said. 'But if you want to write a note, I'll make sure they get it as soon as they return, I promise.'

'*They*?' Tom finally asked the question. 'Only I understood that my fiancée was staying here alone?' Liv thought of that snatch of male voice she'd heard at the dress fitting, and then dismissed it again. This was Anna they were talking about. Anna just didn't pick up random men and share hotel rooms with them. She just didn't. And anyway, even if she had had some sort of psychotic break and done exactly that, then she would have told Liv, of course she would have. They told each other everything.

'I'm so sorry, sir,' Kimberly said pleasantly, her be-discreet-at-all-times training suddenly going into overdrive, as she pushed some headed notepaper towards him. 'It must be my mistake. Here, why don't you write a note and I'll be certain Miss Carter gets it as soon as she returns.'

Tom took the paper and scribbled a hasty message on it before stuffing it into a thick cream envelope and returning it to Kimberly.

'So, what shall we do?' Liv asked, looking around the luscious lobby, trying to imagine Anna swishing back and forth through it all on her own, and failing.

This seemed like far too 'adventurous' an adventure for Anna and, to be honest, she had been a little surprised when her friend hadn't come back home on the first available flight. 'We can't really sit here all day, who knows where she is and how long she'll be.'

'Or they,' Tom said darkly.

'Tom.' Liv grabbed his arm and shook it, making him look at her. 'I don't know what that receptionist was talking about, but I promise you, there is no "they"! I know Anna, better than anyone, and I know that if anything like that had happened she would have told me about it. We always tell each other everything, we always have.'

'Then why . . .' Tom gestured towards the reception desk where Kimberly was booking in a new set of guests. He looked terrible, with dark circles under his eyes, unshaven. He looked like all he wanted from life was a hug and a decent cup of tea, and for someone to tell him everything would be OK. Unfortunately, Liv could only do one of those things at the present moment. 'I mean, she wouldn't, would she? For revenge?'

'Tom, don't you know Anna at all?' Liv grabbed his stubbled cheeks in both hands, making him look into her eyes. 'I promise you, if there was anything going on I'd know about it. And I don't. OK?'

Tom nodded. 'Her phone's just ringing straight to answerphone.'

'Right, well then,' Liv said, tucking her arm in his.

'You've left her a note. I'm sure as soon as she gets it she'll call. In the meantime, this is my first visit to New York and it's Christmas, and I can't help but be a little excited about it! Come on, I know we're exhausted, but what's the harm of finding a decent cup of coffee and something to eat, maybe even a little explore while we wait for Anna to call?'

Tom smiled faintly at the enthusiasm that shone in her eyes.

'No harm at all, I suppose,' he said, letting Liv drag him off to discover the greatest city on earth, skipping like a little girl as she went.

'You buying a ticket or not?' the woman behind the ticket booth asked Anna for the fourth or fifth time.

'Um, well, no, you see, as I've explained previously, more than once as it happens, I don't actually want to see the play. I'm trying to get in touch with Erica Barnes, we're old school friends and . . .'

'See this?' The woman, who had dyed her hair a bright red several inches of root ago, and who wore 1950s-style spectacles which swept up at the edges despite being no more than thirty, pointed at the sign above the booth she was sitting in, lodged behind thick bulletproof glass. The sign read BOX OFFICE.

'I sell tickets for the play,' she told Anna in a flat monotone. 'I don't make nearly enough to reunite long-lost friends. Shit, have you never heard of Facebook?'

'I know that,' Anna said, poshing up her accent once again in the hope it might give her extra gravitas. 'And I understand your point, but the thing is, just this once, could you maybe at least pass a message to her? Ask her to see me? My name is . . . well if you mention Tom Collins.'

'Are you buying a ticket for this evening's perform-ance or not?' the woman asked her, her arms crossed over her chest, staring blankly into space as she repeated the question.

'Yes,' Anna said, recognising defeat when she felt it. 'Two, please.'

'Forty dollars.' The woman pointed at the tray under the glass division, which Anna dutifully dropped her cash into, before punching out two tickets for a performance that began at seven.

'Have a nice day,' the woman said, already opening a magazine.

When she got back to the diner, Miles was no longer in the booth but sitting at the long counter, chatting to the pretty young waitress, whose big dark eyes sparkled and black glossy curls bounced when he said anything that made her laugh, which seemed to be pretty much every word he uttered.

'That was quick.' Miles turned to smile at her as she walked over, any hint of the tension that had lingered between them when she left entirely gone. 'This is Anna,' he said, turning back to the waitress, who was pouring him another coffee. 'And Anna, this is Inez. I was just telling her about your predicament. How did you get on, did you get the papers signed?'

Anna seethed behind the tight, polite smile that she gave Inez, who could not have been more than twenty and looked altogether far too pretty in her candy-striped uniform, but not because the woman in the box office had been so rude and unhelpful, or because Miles had seen fit to reveal her story to a complete stranger. No, for some reason that she couldn't fathom, Anna was annoyed that Miles had all of a sudden stopped calling her Annie.

'No,' she said, sliding on to the stool next to Miles. 'I had to buy tickets for tonight's performance. I'll have to try and find a way to sneak backstage while you keep lookout again.'

'Me?' Miles asked her.

'Well, you'll come too, won't you?' Anna asked him.

'I'm not sure,' Miles said, glancing at Inez who was still hanging on his every word even as she refilled the sugar, a few stools down. 'I was thinking about what you said, about how people might get the wrong idea if they knew about the time we've been spending together and, erm, about the sofa. I'm wondering if maybe now wouldn't be a good time to go our separate ways. I mean, you'll be flying home pretty soon anyway and who knows where I'll be next week.'

'Really?' Anna asked, uncertainly. 'I mean, of course,

if you think so, then yes, of course. So you won't want me to come to your audition then, like you said, and you won't come with me to the play and . . .' She trailed off, feeling suddenly bereft and, for the first time since she'd arrived, alone in a big and scary city. 'Of course, that's totally fine.'

Sliding off the stool, Anna smiled at him. 'OK, well, I think I'll get back to the hotel then. Perhaps I might go Christmas shopping or something to kill time before tonight. I have left it rather late to get gifts what with all the wedding planning, this could be my perfect opportunity.'

'Good idea,' Miles said, nodding pleasantly. 'I'll sort out another place to stay this afternoon if I have to and I'll settle my half of the bill before I go. So I'll see you around, yeah?'

'Yes,' Anna said. She picked up her bag and took several slow steps to the door, where the snow was still lashing down with unremitting force and there wasn't a cab to be seen in any direction. Every sensible bone in Anna's body told her to open the door and walk away, that she was more than capable of negotiating the subway if it came to it, and that leaving her acquaintance with Miles now really was for the better. Maybe it was the red dress, maybe it was the newfound sense of freedom that had somehow engulfed her since she stepped off the plane, but Anna Carter found that she was in no mood to be sensible.

Turning on her heel, she strode back to where Miles was still sitting, Inez leaning over the counter, her chin resting in her hands.

'Actually,' Anna said, 'it's not OK. It's not OK for you to more or less force me to let you hang around with me, for you to make me like you and trust you and . . . and tell you things that I never tell anyone if I can help it. It's not OK for you to write a song about me, to make me sing in public, have a really, really good time, then pour my heart out to you and then laugh all the way back to the hotel. Or to be helpful, and kind and the sort of person who I think could really, really be a friend and then just take it all away like a spoilt child because I won't be one of the millions of girls who are apparently stupid enough to be seduced by your eyes, and your hair and your –' Anna gestured wildly up and down '– other stuff. It's not OK, Miles, to pretend to be someone's friend, just because you fancy a bunk-up.'

'That's what you think?' Miles asked her. 'That's what you think I'm doing?'

'Yes!' Anna exclaimed. 'One minute it's all, don't worry Annie, we're in this together and then just because I suggest we don't make a fuss about one little falling asleep fully clothed on a sofa incident, I can't see you for dust, so yes, Miles, that is exactly what I think you are doing!'

Miles stood up suddenly, causing Anna to totter

backwards a step or two as he towered over her.

'You really don't get it, do you?' Miles said. 'I'm doing this for you!'

'For me?' Anna stamped her foot in indignation. 'How can just abandoning me in the middle of everything be for me?'

'Because . . . because you don't belong to me!' Miles blurted out. 'And I'm not yours to rely on and I think that for a little while we both forgot that.' There was a beat of silence, as Anna took in what he'd said. 'In a couple of hours I've got the biggest audition of my life, and I need to focus on that now . . . on that only and not . . . not you, Anna.'

'Oh,' Anna said. 'Oh God, Miles, I'm so sorry.'

'Sorry?' Miles looked confused.

'Yes, sorry. I've been so caught up in my own drama, and I've dragged you into it and completely forgotten why you are here. It's this place, it's changed me, for the worse. I haven't made one list since I got here, I've barely thought about the wedding and you were right, I didn't speak to Tom this morning, I didn't even think about him. I've been obsessing about this woman that I've never met, and it didn't even occur to me that I was trying to take over your life too.'

'No, that's not what I'm trying to say.' Miles shook his head.

'No, it's OK,' Anna said quietly. 'I know I can be overpowering, only somehow in the last few days with you I'd forgotten. I don't want to go Christmas shopping on my own, Miles, I want to support you, at your audition, like we said. And you don't have to come tonight, to the play, and you can check out of the room, if you like. And we never, ever have to see each other again, if you're really that sick of me. It's fine, but, please, after everything you've done for me, please let me be there for you today. I promise I won't talk to anyone, I won't look at anyone. I'll stay outside, in the snow, probably getting hypothermia. Just let me be the kind of friend to you that you have been to me, even if it's just for a little while. It really would mean a lot to me.'

Miles looked at her for a very long moment, his expression hard to read, and then suddenly smiling, breezy Miles was back again.

'OK, Annie. You can come to the audition, and I'll come to the play. You're right, we might as well make the most of the time that we have left to hang out together before you're an old married lady and I am an international rock star and we take different paths for ever.'

'Wow,' Liv breathed, standing on the very top of the Rockefeller tower, side by side with Tom. 'Wow, look!'

It wasn't perhaps the best view the vantage point had ever afforded. The snowfall hadn't subsided by even a little since they'd arrived, which made Liv think they were lucky that their flight hadn't been diverted. They must have made it into JKF by the skin of their teeth. Low, pregnant-looking clouds lumbered over the pinnacles of the skyscrapers as if they might at any minute release an even heavier deluge, if the tops of the buildings pressed too hard. Still, the view was enough to take Liv's breath away, even if they weren't allowed onto the deck, for fear the wind might whisk them over the edge. She glanced up at Tom who was staring broodily into the tumult.

'Still no call,' he said miserably, clearly not seeing the same view that impressed Liv so much. She sighed. Since the anticlimax of their arrival she had tried her very best to distract him from Anna's marked absence. Though they were both battling the exhaustion of some twenty hours without proper sleep, she was determined to force him to take in their surroundings, to enjoy where they were, instead of merely tolerating them as if they were in some particularly unpleasant holding area waiting for Tom's life with Anna to begin again. So far nothing had really worked.

Liv had even sneaked off at one point and tried Anna's phone herself several times, but it just rang through to voicemail each time. Now the greetings message that Liv must have heard at least a thousand times was actually starting to sound sarcastic and mocking, giving an overtired and overemotional Liv the distinct impression that Anna was lost somewhere in this city living the high life, instead of picking up the pieces left in her wake. Finally she sent Anna a text: 'Tom & I in NYC, will meet you at your hotel. Call as soon as you get this . . . Anything you're not telling me?' That, she thought, might solicit some response from Anna, who hated even the idea of being in trouble over something she hadn't done, but still nothing came back.

And now here they were standing on what felt like the top of the world. It felt like a lifetime moment, and Liv, despite the reasons they were here, was desperate to enjoy it but Tom was *still* sulking.

'Oh, Tom, give it up,' she said irritably, crossing her arms.

'Give it up? Give what up? Worrying that my bride-to-be is lost in New York? That I've ruined everything, and that I probably deserve what I'm getting?'

'Yes!' Liv said, rolling her eyes. 'Yes, give it up and stop worrying. Anna didn't know we were coming. It's hardly fair of you to think the worst of her just because she wasn't sitting in her room alone, waiting to be rescued. She's out somewhere being proactive – doing what you didn't offer to do. And it's what she's best at. She's not the sort of person to let life happen to her, if she can possibly stop it in its tracks.'

'OK, OK,' Tom muttered. 'I'm enjoying the view.' He looked around with a heavy sigh. 'Let's talk about something else then. Anything else – take my mind off Anna. I know, what about you?' Tom said, turning to look at her suddenly.

'What about me?' Liv said, caught off guard by the question.

'You never talk about yourself much,' Tom said. 'Not any more. I was thinking on the plane, when we first met at the club getting you to talk to me was like getting blood out of a stone.'

'Was it?' Liv asked him, uncertainly. She hadn't been aware of him trying to squeeze words out of her particularly, mainly because she'd been hiding around corners willing her skin not to come out in scarlet blotches every time she walked past him, offering a casual 'hey'.

'Yes,' Tom said. 'You'd scurry off after a class, and be home before I could catch you, for ages.'

'Were you trying to catch me?' Liv asked, confused.

'Yes!' Tom laughed, rolling his eyes, momentarily distracted from his misery. 'Oh, Liv, you are funny!'

'Am I? Am I funny?' Liv asked, without very much mirth, before adding the inevitable question. 'Why?'

'What do you mean, "why"?' Tom asked her, puzzled. 'Do you really not know?'

'I really don't,' Liv said. 'I mean because I'm such a great kick-boxer? Or because I know all the best bars in London or . . . why?'

'Because I fancied you, you muppet,' Tom said shaking his head. 'I don't know how you don't see all the attention you get from men, I really don't.'

'You fancied me?' Liv repeated the question, rather testily. 'Me? Wait – what attention?'

'Yes, I fancied you!' Tom said. 'How many girls does a bloke meet who fight like a motherfucker, drink like a boy and look like Audrey Hepburn? Of course I fancied you! Almost every red-blooded male who meets you does.'

'You never said!' Liv spluttered, weighing up her sense of loyalty over even discussing the matter of attraction between her and best friend's intended. 'Why did you never say?'

Tom stared at her then, his face suddenly serious. 'Because we hung out, for ages,' he said. 'We did stuff, went places, went to the cinema even, and you never, ever, not once gave me any sign that you fancied me back. I can take a hint, you know ... eventually. Anyway, never mind, it all worked out for the best in the end.'

'I never gave you a sign that I fancied you back,' Liv repeated in disbelief. 'What sort of a sign were you looking for? My tongue down your throat, whipping my bra off in the middle of the latest *Mission Impossible*? What?'

'Either of those would have worked,' Tom said slowly, puzzled by her angry response. 'But you were just ... You've always just treated me like a mate, so I thought that's what you wanted us to be ... Wait, are you telling me you *did* fancy me?'

'No!' Liv said quickly, her heart and shoulders

sinking in unison. 'OK, yes, yes, Tom. Yes, I did fancy you, and all those drinks and shopping and cinema trips we went out on, I was waiting for *you* to make the first move, you know like boys are *supposed* to? But you never did, so I had a birthday party, just so I could invite you, so I could try and make something happen. Only you met Anna and . . . fell in love with her and you would have met her anyway, I suppose, even if we had . . . done something. And presumably you would have fallen in love with her anyway, wouldn't you? So . . .'

Liv wasn't really sure where to go with that particular train of thought. It seemed to her that if you were about to marry someone then they had to be the person you were destined to be with from the beginning. Even if she and Tom had started seeing each other, as soon as he met Anna it probably would have been game over. He'd have fallen for her – how could he not? And things would still be the same as they are now, only she might have got to kiss him a lot first. Though, actually, Anna would never have gone out with someone her best friend had previously gone out with, so there would have been no Tom and Anna, no wedding, no emergency visit to New York. Tom would probably have drifted out of both of their lives by now and . . . Liv forced herself to stop thinking about what might have been. The idea that fate could be so fickle scared her. She'd always comforted herself with the idea that

Anna and Tom were meant to be together; the thought that their relationship was somehow accidental was no comfort whatsoever.

'Oh my God.' Tom turned his back on New York City, leaning hard against the window, clearly not getting quite the same melodrama from the situation as Liv was. 'That's so weird, because that was my plan too. My plan was to come to the party and get up the courage to kiss you and see if you hit me or not. And you know what, I think if you'd opened the door instead of Anna, I probably would have kissed you right then and there, because I was too nervous to wait. Only you didn't, Anna did.' Tom shook his head. 'Funny how things work out, isn't it? If things had been different, I'd have been dating you instead of Anna.'

'Yes, it's funny,' Liv said quietly, returning her gaze to the view.

'I wonder what we'd have been like as a couple,' Tom said, chuckling. 'I mean it would have been odd, wouldn't it? I wonder how long we would have lasted, what we would have been like together, I mean. I can't imagine it now, can you? Funny!'

'Hi-fucking-larious,' Liv said, turning on her heel and heading suddenly for the lift.

'What? Wait, Liv, hold up!' Tom caught up with her in two easy strides as she was forced to come to a standstill outside the bank of lifts.

'Stupid tall buildings,' Liv muttered under her breath.

'Who needs more than four floors for anything, anyway, bloody stupid city, and stupid lifts.'

'Liv!' Tom said her name. 'What have I said? Come on, this isn't like you. You don't do that girly thing of getting all cross with a man, and not telling him why. That's one of the things I love about you.'

Liv's head snapped round to look at him, her eyes narrowing dangerously at his casual usage of the word that had been plaguing her more or less since she set eyes on him all those months ago. Fortunately, she heard a gratifying ping behind her as the lift door slid open, hissing her response.

'If you don't know then I'm not telling you,' she said stepping inside, and tapping the doors closed button furiously. 'Get the next lift. I'm not talking to you.'

'But what do you mean? Why?' Tom called through the ever narrowing gap in the door. 'What about the skating, do you still want to . . .?'

The door slid shut, and Liv found herself mercifully alone for a few minutes at least. The idea, the very idea that she'd come so close to being with the man she hadn't been able to stop thinking about ever since meeting him made her want to beat her fists against the wall, punch Tom on the nose and go and find Anna and rip all her hair out for accidentally getting in the way of Tom's fleeting interest in her. Except of course really the only person she could be angry at was herself.

After all she'd had countless opportunities to give him that one particular look or touch that would have absolutely – with no room for doubt – shown him how she felt about him. Even if she'd had no idea how to do that. She'd also been the one who'd invited him into the home she shared with her taller, curvier, blonder flatmate, the one who always outshone her, even when she didn't mean to. And most of all it had been stupid, moronic, idiotic her who'd persisted in feeling the same way about Tom even though she now had concrete proof that he was as dumb as a bag of rocks.

When the lift finally reached the ground floor, the doors opened to reveal Tom standing there. His lift had somehow beaten hers.

'I caught the express,' he said, by way of an explanation.

'Oh,' Liv said, shouldering her way past him and marching towards the lobby exit.

'Liv, I've worked it out, why you are pissed off,' Tom said.

She stopped dead in her tracks. 'Have you?'

'Yes, of course you are, you have every right to be. And I'm sorry.'

'Sorry for what?' Liv said, turning round very slowly to look at him. *Sorry for not kissing you first, sorry for not realising it's you and always has been*, were the words running through her jet-lagged head. She lifted her teary eyes to his, dimly hopeful of a Hollywood ending right then and there. (Even if there was still Anna to square away.)

'To put you in such an awkward position, talking about fancying you when I'm about to marry Anna. I know that must seem disloyal to you, and you're right. I'm completely out of order. It's Anna I've got to think about now, Anna above everything else and it was crass of me to even bring it up.'

'Oh, right, well, yes it was,' Liv said, wondering exactly how many times Tom could unwittingly crush her to smithereens without her actually turning to dust. 'Make sure you don't do it again.'

'I will . . . I won't, I mean,' Tom said. 'Are we friends again? Because I don't think I could take falling out with you now, you are just about all there is holding me together. What I was really trying to say, before, up there, is that things might not have worked out romantically for us, but you mean a lot to me.'

'Do I?' Liv said, any remaining ice chips in her heart melting in a moment.

'Course you do,' Tom said, dropping his arm around her shoulders and kissing her on the temple. 'There's no one else in the world I can talk to the way I talk to you. So, come on, there's nothing we can do until Anna gets in touch. How about ice skating, then lunch, then maybe several gins in the bar at Anna's hotel until she finally shows up and we can get things back to normal?'

Trouble was, Liv thought, as she rested her head against Tom's shoulder for a moment, getting things back to normal was the last thing she wanted.

Chapter Twelve

'This is not at all how I imagined it,' Anna said as she followed Miles into the Bowery Ballroom, where he was about to audition for the New York Rock Department. It was an impressively shabby old variety theatre on Delancey Street, which had clearly been a club for some years. The gold paint was cracking and peeling off the plaster and a wooden floor had been scuffed and scratched by decades of dancing feet. Both gave the venue an atmosphere of authenticity added to by the faint but lingering scent of stale beer.

The Bowery was decorated for Christmas with equally old, vintage-looking decorations: 70s-style big-eyed, plastic light-up reindeer; strings of yellowish fairy lights with huge sections hanging in limp darkness. There were plastic stars – mostly bald of the silver glitter that had once gilded them – hung from the vaulted ceiling, held in place with determined drawing pins, which marked the already pitted surface of the ceiling. With the snow driving down past the windows in the lobby, it felt a little to Anna as if she had stumbled back in time or perhaps through some magic wardrobe where a permanent Christmas party rumbled on, despite whatever the world was doing outside.

'How did you imagine it?' Miles said tightly, as he approached a bored-looking girl, with a record label ID round her neck, sitting behind a trestle table in front of the double doors in the auditorium. The sound of very loud music vibrated the glass in the doors, and made the swirls of ancient carpet beneath Anna's feet hum and vibrate.

'I pictured a recording studio, I suppose,' Anna said. 'And you in headphones behind a glass wall and a table with a lot of buttons and slidey up and down things. This seems much more . . . intense.'

'The NYRDs want someone who's good live, who can blend in with the band, and still bring something new. It's all about the vibe,' Miles said, his tone short and tense, his nerves clearly visible in his clenched jaw and the throbbing vein in his temple. It was the only time in their – admittedly very short – acquaintance that Anna had ever seen him any less than utterly relaxed and at ease in his body, and somehow this unexpected vulnerability made her like him all the more.

Nevertheless, despite his nerves, he managed a near perfect smile as he greeted the girl, whose ID tag revealed she was called Cheri Mortimer.

'Hi, I'm Miles,' he said, extending a hand to her.

'I know who you are.' Cheri smiled at him, visibly perked up by the sight of him. 'I love your stuff. It was me who suggested you when they were brainstorming for replacements. I showed the bosses your YouTube stuff too.'

'Really,' Miles said, a little awkwardly, two bright spots of colour appearing on his cheekbones, as he was confronted with a bona fide fan. 'Thank you . . . I don't know what to say.'

'Oh, don't say anything,' Cheri told him cheerfully. 'I might have got your name in the conversation, but my opinion doesn't count for much round here, not yet anyway. Your music is what got you here, and you're the last of the five they are seeing, so go for it. The guys need someone to really rock it out now.'

'They're only seeing five people?' Miles asked her, as she handed him a pass with his name and photo on it.

'Oh yeah,' Cheri said. 'Yeah, it's going to be one of you guys, just depends which one. The label wants looks and charisma, the band wants talent. I guess whoever has both is the winner. It's that way through to the auditorium. The last guy is just finishing up, so you can sit in the back and watch him if you like.' Cheri smiled at Anna, who'd been hanging back, doing her best to be discreet. 'I shouldn't really let your girl-friend go in with you, but as long as she sits at the back it should be OK.'

'Thank you.' Anna smiled at Cheri as she followed Miles into the theatre, realising as the doors opened to blast them with unadulterated hard rock at top volume that neither one of them had done or said anything to contradict the girl on her status as Miles's love interest.

Anna perched on the very end of the back row, Miles standing by her side as they watched the band, and the other potential new singer, perform one of their songs together. It was very loud, a world away from the song he'd sung for her on the open mic night. Full of screaming guitars and thundering drums that, if Anna was honest, mainly hurt her ears and made her dream of some benign elevator music. When the other audi-tionee sang it made her wonder if all the dogs in the vicinity were howling and all the cats running in the opposite direction. Still, maybe that was how it was supposed to be, all loud and shouty, and, as a girl who mainly listened to the sort of boy bands whose edgiest move was getting up from a stool and walking forwards in response to a key change, she acknowledged that she wasn't best placed to sit in judgement.

'Is he any good?' she repeated twice before realising she'd have to stand up and whisper the comment in Miles's ear. She rested her hand on his shoulder as she put her lips very close to his ear. Caught off guard he turned to face her, and suddenly their lips were very close together indeed, their noses actually touching. In all the noise and din, Anna caught her breath as she looked into his ice-blue eyes, her hand still on his shoulder. And then before Anna could move, or even react, Miles leaned forwards and kissed her, very gently, very briefly on the mouth.

'For luck,' he said, as the track came to an end, and suddenly the room was almost silent again, silent enough for Anna to be able to hear her blood thundering in her ears. 'And no, he was terrible. I'm going to kick his arse from here to the moon and back, just for you, Annie Carter.' With one last smile at her, Miles grabbed his guitar by the neck and strode towards the stage.

'Thanks, man.' The bassist shook the other guy's hand. 'We'll call you later, yeah?'

Anna watched as Miles leaped onto the stage with athletic ease, shook hands and exchanged man hugs with the other musicians, talking and laughing about something she couldn't make out, but the truth was even if she hadn't been right at the back of the auditorium she still wouldn't have been paying any attention to what was going on, because at that moment, and for quite a few moments afterwards, all she could think about was that Miles had just kissed her, albeit briefly, for a matter of seconds and with no more sexual intent than a peck on the cheek. Which begged the question, why was her heart threatening to pound its way out of her chest and why had her knees turned to jelly?

Miles was now performing serious rock music, wielding his electric guitar with more than a little theatrical aplomb, and a fair amount of phallic implication. It was quite a different spectacle from the one he'd given in the little bar, when he'd sung just for Anna and, more than that, it was quite a thing to behold. Anna sat down with a little wobbly-kneed bump, after the first NYRD track that Miles had had to learn kicked in, and found herself unexpectedly swept up by the driving guitars and, more pertinently, by Miles. She found it was impossible to take her eyes off him as he strode across the stage, interacting with the other musicians like he'd known them all his life. It was if he owned that few square feet of rickety, dusty wood, which became the very centre of the known universe as long as he was standing on it. Whereas the last candidate had all but screamed the lyrics – which seemed to have something to do with whisky, fast women and Armageddon – into the microphone, Miles's rendition was altogether more tuneful – he actually sang the words and, as a result, Anna realised she could almost detect a melody that was verging on catchy. Entranced, she watched as his fingers flew over his guitar like . . . well, like a well-practised lover who knew exactly how to make his instrument cry out. Anna smiled as he smiled, filled with the sheer joy of what he was doing, grinning at the other musicians on stage as they listened to each other play, catching each other's enthusiasm. For a total of five numbers, Anna sat on the edge of her faded red velvet seat, entranced, as Miles gave everything he had. She delighted in every arrogant toss of his head, each provocative thrust of his hips, and particularly the way he slid on his knees from the back of the stage to the front during one particularly challenging solo. And as she watched him perform, Anna came to a conclusion which somehow, deep down, did not surprise her: it was very easy to be sexually attracted to a man with an electric guitar.

And the truth was that, after forty-eight hours in his company, she was undeniably, and very strongly, sexually attracted to Miles. The man she'd assumed to be an idiot with a propensity for unwittingly selecting near fatal beverages, the man she'd dreaded sitting next to on a plane and fully hoped never to see again had somehow become irresistible. Which, Anna realised with a heavy, heavy heart, was very bad news for someone with a life plan.

Anna waited as Miles clasped hands with the drummer, pulling him to his chest in a weird sort of macho hug. 'Great playing with you, man. We'll be in touch real soon. Stop by Bill, our manager, on your way out, he wants to check your availability, other commitments.'

Miles leaped off the stage with ease and grace, and spent several minutes bent over an iPad, as he talked to a huge man with long hair that flowed down his back. It was a hairstyle at odds with his expensive-looking, tailored suit. The other candidate had left without stopping to talk to anyone, so this had to be a good sign, Anna decided, discovering she was just as anxious that Miles did well as he was. Finally, after some more handshaking, Miles bounded up the aisle towards her. Anna hoped that her newfound attraction to him didn't somehow show on her face.

'How'd I do?' he asked her, his face flushed and his voice a little breathless.

'Really good,' she said, grinning. 'Really amazing!'

'That's what I thought,' Miles said. 'Thanks, Anna. Thanks for coming, for making me see sense and letting you come. It meant a lot to me that you were out there. I think I played better because I knew you were.'

'Oh well,' Anna said, feeling like giggling and blushing but telling herself at the same time not to be so ridiculous. After all she was not some thirteen-year-old groupie. 'That's what friends are for.'

'I know,' Miles said. 'And you are a good friend. The best impromptu New York Christmas friend I've ever had. And even if our lives take us in opposite directions after this, I'll think about this time. Always.'

'So do you think you've got it then?' Anna asked as they walked back to the subway, the snow crunching under their feet, the cold making their cheeks ruddy and fingers numb.

'I don't know,' Miles said. 'But you know what, in some ways, Annie, it doesn't matter.'

'Really?' Anna asked him. 'Why not? What about the equipment you sold to get here?'

'Well, when I was up there playing today and last night in that little bar, singing, if that is what you can call it, with you, I realised, I love doing this, I love it. And as long as I am doing it, one way or another, in a stadium or a pub, it doesn't matter. Music was what I was meant to do, and I get to do it every day, sometimes even for money. That makes me very lucky.' He stopped for a second in the middle of the pavement. 'Yes, right now I feel like a very lucky man. Now, how about something to eat, and then we can go and hunt down that bitch that married your fiancé.'

Anna found herself grinning happily as she followed Miles down the steps to the subway, thinking how very wonderful it must be to be so certain about something without the need for lists, and counter-lists and footnotes and contingency plans and colour-coded highlighters, and how amazing it must be to just know something, know it with all your heart, with absolute certainty and never ever doubt or second guess yourself. Just once, just once in her life, Anna would like that moment of certainty to belong to her.

The Long Dark Night of the Soul was not exactly easy viewing, a fact that became apparent about ten minutes into the production when one of the nuns hanged herself from a scaffolding pole, the dramatic impetus of the moment being somewhat reduced by the deceased nun continuing to cough for several minutes after she was pronounced tragically dead. Anna would have laughed if she wasn't so compulsively polite, and Miles did laugh, sniggering into the back of his hand like an unruly little boy, which earned him a furious glare from a very pious Mother Superior onstage.

It was a small auditorium, one of several in the theatre complex, and much less glamorous than the one that Miles had rocked out in just a few hours earlier, for all its similar brand of vintage decay. There was no stage to speak of, and no set beyond what was already there. The seats were built on scaffolding that surrounded the performance area, rising in a steep pitch that looked like they could accommodate maybe four hundred people. Anna only realised as they arrived that she had bought front row tickets, and that apart from perhaps twenty other people, the theatre was empty, which perhaps wasn't surprising as suicidal and sexually confused nuns were rarely traditional Christmas viewing. (It was clearly not *The Sound of Music*.) Still, Anna was full of anticipation and a sense of dread: at any moment she knew she would be inches away from Charisma Jones, almost within touching distance of her husband-to-be's current wife.

Miles had been on an incredible high after the audition. His usual funny and charming self but pumped full of extra energy, he'd taken Anna for some Greek food in a place that Cheri from the record label had recommended to him on the way out, and Anna had spent pretty much all of the meal in happy silence, laughing as he told her a series of anecdotes from his life as a musician on the road, trying not to notice how his blue eyes sparkled or how much she wanted to run her fingertips over the smile lines in his stubble.

It's fine, Anna had told herself, leaning her chin into her hands as Miles re-enacted the time he and his bandmates had to go on stage soaking wet because of a dare involving a lamppost and a fountain and how he'd almost killed himself and shorted out all the electricity onstage in the process. All she was experiencing was a teenage crush, and teenage crushes were perfectly normal. OK, perfectly normal in teenagers, usually, but, as Anna reminded herself, she had not been a normal teenager. Whilst Liv had been mooning with obsessive dedication over an assortment of moody-looking pop boys, who'd lined the walls of their bedroom from around the age of twelve, Anna had not had time for crushes. She was intent on getting perfect grades in her GCSEs. Which meant that her and Liv's school lives complemented each other quite well, the pair of them always opting to stand with their backs against the wall at school discos: Liv was a wallflower because the idea of talking to boys she liked made her want to kill herself and the boys she didn't fancy only ever wanted to play football with her anyway. Anna had been regularly asked to dance to the slow ones by the same opportunistic ranks of boys who were hopeful of getting their hand up her top. But, soon after the Regina Clarkson incident, her English teacher had told her that to get distracted by boys now would be the ruin of her academic career, one that she had to work hard to keep up, because brains didn't come naturally to her. And so Anna, being Anna, had all but stifled every single hormonal impulse that her body threw at her, with the one notable exception that led to the Regina Clarkson incident, and she preferred never ever to think about that.

All that was happening now, with these unplanned urges towards a man that in any other situation she would find positively irritating, was that her hormones were finally catching up with her and she was having her first ever teenage crush. It didn't mean she didn't love Tom, that she didn't still want to marry him and live the rest of her life with him, it was just her body having one last – or to be fair, first – fling with fantasy, before she settled down to married life. And somehow, New York City at Christmas, thousands of miles away from home, made it seem all the more reasonable. It wasn't as if anything was going to happen between them. After all, the very reason Anna was sitting here, enduring nun angst by the poorly scripted bucketload, was to make the wedding – her perfect winter wedding – happen, not to ruin it with a rash sordid fling. And yes, as the lights came up on act two, she realised that not only had she still not spoken to Tom since she'd left England but she hadn't even noticed that she'd left her phone in the hotel room until just before the play was due to start and she was about to turn it off. For a few hours she'd completely forgotten about the wedding, her list, her life plan and her husband-to-be. But now that exhilarating, temporary sense of freedom was about to come to an end, as Charisma Jones took to the stage and Anna found out what she was really up against.

It would be fair to say that the atmosphere in the small auditorium, which until that point had been flat and bored, changed the moment that Charisma/Erica walked onstage. There was something about her, even in her nun's outfit (which featured a rather tight black poloneck sweater, an A-line calf-length skirt, some sensible shoes and the traditionally unflattering head-gear) that simply outshone everyone around her. She had chosen her first stage name all too well – she clearly had charisma by the bucketload, enough charm to overcome even the clunky script and the awful acting of her colleagues. Glancing at Miles, Anna noticed that his eyes were riveted to Charisma every single second she was onstage, whether she had any lines or not. And it wasn't just him. The men in the audience seemed to be following her every move, including one gentleman Anna noticed whose hands were suspiciously active underneath the raincoat that was neatly folded on his lap.

If she wasn't exactly Dame Judi Dench, Charisma

was still the best actor on the stage and evidently her costume and apparent lack of make-up couldn't hide her beauty. Anna found herself dwelling on the other woman's chocolate-brown eyes and her coppery-hued skin. In the world of show business, Charisma was no spring chicken – she had to be around Anna's age – but her skin was flawless and glowing with a sort of internal heat. It was as if she'd just absorbed a whole lot of tropical sun, even in this snowbound city, and was returning it to the world through every pore. Anna tried to imagine her as the glamorous showgirl that Tom had met and fallen for, and was dismayed to discover it was all too easy to do. But that was years ago, Anna reminded herself unhappily, and Charisma had left Tom, and he had left Vegas. He'd forgotten her, so completely in fact that he'd all but forgotten he'd even married her, so really and truly there was nothing for Anna to worry about, not rationally. Except she couldn't help but be relieved that it was she who was in New York, about to ask Charisma to sign the annulment papers, and not Tom. Who knew what feelings a glamorous actress in a nun's habit might stir up in her fiancé, if the two were to ever meet in person again.

'What do you think of her?' Anna asked Miles, as the players took their final bow to a room of half-hearted applause.

'She's got something about her,' Miles said,

thoughtfully, turning to look at Anna. 'Yes, she's got something.'

The actors walked off stage, the house lights came up and the scant audience began to file out.

'Right, this is my chance,' Anna said, her eyes on the wings.

'Let's go for it,' Miles said, half rising from his seat, but Anna put her hand on his shoulder.

'This is something I need to do alone,' she said, partly because that was how she really felt and partly because it felt like Charisma might be some kind of sultry Medusa, turning all men she met rock hard with one devastating look, and Anna found she wasn't willing to see Miles be impressed in person by Charisma. Miles paused and nodded. 'I'll wait in the lobby.'

Taking a deep breath, Anna crossed the stage at a trot, conscious of her heels clicking on the black and white floor.

'Excuse me, miss?' A rather uncertain-looking young man, dressed all in black and wearing a set of head-phones, stopped her. 'Are you looking for the restroom?'

'Anna Carter,' Anna said, holding her hand out, with more confidence than she felt. 'Theatrical correspondent, *The Times* of London.' She was surprised how easy the bluff came to her. 'I'm doing a piece on rising stars of fringe theatre and I would very much like a few words with Char–Erica Barnes. I thought her performance was outstanding.'

'Really?' The young man took her hand and shook it warmly. '*The Times* of London, you say? And what about the writing? The script? Did you enjoy that?'

Sensing that this young man was more than just the lighting engineer, Anna nodded enthusiastically. 'Oh yes,' she said, fluttering her lashes. 'It put me in mind of early Pinter.'

'Really?' He beamed at her, as he showed her backstage. 'I'm Christopher Underwood, the writer, director, jack of all trades.'

'How lovely to meet you, Christopher.' Anna beamed at him. ' Do you have a card? I'd love to talk to you before I file my article.' Happily, Christopher handed her what looked like it might be his one and only card, and rather guiltily Anna tucked it into her bag. 'And where might I find Miss Barnes?'

'First on your left. We're a collective so there are only two dressing rooms, one for guys and one for girls, although they don't always stay that segregated. Nice to meet you Miss Carter of *The Times*.'

Much to Anna's surprise, Christopher did an awkward little curtsy, and then his face flushed beetroot, as he turned on his Cuban heels and raced away at speed. Opening her bag, Anna took out the envelope with the papers in it and brandished them aloft like Van Helsing might wield a crucifix against a vampire. She knocked once on the dressing-room door before opening it. Fortunately, there were only two women in the dressing room. There was the sour-looking Mother Superior, now lounging in a bright yellow kaftan, smoking with industrious intent just underneath the NO SMOKING sign, and Charisma, now dressed in a pair of low-rise jeans and a waisted pale-blue shirt over a white vest trimmed with lace. And now that her mane of glossy chestnut-brown hair had been freed from its wimple she looked even more beautiful, if positively demure compared to the first picture Anna had seen of her.

'Hello,' Anna said pleasantly. 'Erica? My name's Anna Carter, Christopher Underwood showed me back here. I wonder if I could have a word with you.'

'There's an accent,' Charisma said pleasantly. 'I *love* the English accent. How can I help you, Anna?'

Anna glanced at the other nun, who was sitting with one bare foot propped up on a stool, puffing away with relish, as she sipped what smelled like cheap brandy from a mug.

'Do you think we could talk alone?' Anna asked her, winsomely apologetic as if she was ever so sorry for the inconvenience.

'Depends,' Charisma said, suddenly guarded. 'What's it about?'

'Tom Collins,' Anna said, watching Charisma's face closely, as her expression flared with . . . what? It was impossible to tell exactly how she'd reacted to the mention of her husband's name, because she'd composed herself again within a fraction of a second, smiling blandly at Anna, as if she had never heard the name before in her life.

'Fine, yes, of course. Leila, would you mind giving us a minute?' Charisma asked the older woman who sighed, stubbed the butt of her cigarette out on the Formica tabletop and gave a very brandyish burp.

'See you in the bar?' she growled, her poor Irish accent replaced by a deep gravelly tone that John Wayne would have been proud of.

'Sure, see you there,' Charisma said, shutting the door on her colleague and turning the lock. 'When hell freezes over.'

'Who are you?' she asked Anna, taking a couple of steps towards her, the intent in her eyes so fierce that Anna wondered if she wouldn't have been safer with Leila.

'Anna Carter,' she repeated, holding out her hand as if it might somehow ward off Evil-Showgirls-cum-Actresses. 'Pleased to meet you.'

Charisma looked at her hand, but didn't take it. 'What do you want to know about Tom for?'

'I don't,' Anna said. 'I already know Tom, very well. I'm engaged to be married to him.'

Charisma sat down suddenly on the ripped stool in front of the mirror. 'Tom's getting married?' she said at last over her shoulder, as she stared at her reflection in the mirror, her pretty brown eyes widening as they took in the news.

'Yes,' Anna said. 'Christmas Eve, in fact. Or at least, I hope we will be. There is one little technical hitch, however.'

'Me,' Charisma said simply, unzipping a bag of make-up and beginning to apply a little foundation to her already flawless complexion, perhaps because she'd been planning to, but more likely, Anna decided, because she was a warrior princess and this was her warpaint.

'Yes,' Anna said, unsure if Charisma really understood. 'Because . . .'

'Because we're technically still married,' Charisma said. Strangely, given her vivacity and the energy that had seemed to emit from her while she was onstage, she was suddenly flat and two-dimensional, her voice monotone, almost uninterested, as she began carefully to blend a palette of bronze and gold eye shadows on to her lids. 'You know, I always hoped I'd hear from Tom again one day. I didn't think he'd send his latest girlfriend to do his dirty work.'

'Not his latest,' Anna said quite firmly. 'His last girlfriend, his current fiancée and the woman that he will marry in a church whilst sober in a few days' time.'

Charisma sucked the air in through her teeth, turning on her stool to look at Anna, one eye heavily lined with liquid eyeliner drawn along the upper lid, finished with a catlike flourish.

'You may speak like the Queen but you fight like a bitch, I like that about you,' she said, before turning back to the mirror.

'Look,' Anna said carefully, drawing herself up to her full height, pushing her shoulders back, doing her best to be as beautiful as the original Charisma Vegas showgirl, who was gradually appearing in the mirror before her. 'I haven't come here to fight you over Tom. There is no fight to be had. You and he had a fling, years ago. Long before we ever met. You both made a foolish mistake. One, from what I can gather, that you both soon regretted.'

'He said that?' Charisma asked her, as she carefully inserted false lashes into her own, already fairly luscious set. 'That we both regretted it?'

'He said you went to look for your dream, and he wasn't part of it,' Anna said.

'Interesting,' Charisma said, fluttering her newly thickened lashes at her own reflection.

'And he said that he was relieved you'd gone. That once you left him he got back to the life he was meant to have.' It was, perhaps, a harsh way of putting things, but Anna was in no mood to be tactful with this strange, mercurial creature who had been Erica Barnes when she walked in, but who was fast transforming herself into exactly the exotic blast from the past that Anna had hoped to avoid.

'I see,' Charisma said, slicking on sticky red lipstick

without bothering to blot, so that it shone on her full lips. Without warning, she stood up and turned around, unpopping the buttons on her shirt, and pulling her camisole over her head to reveal a sensible black soft cotton bra. Knowing what was coming next, Anna turned her back on Charisma as she unhooked the bra and slipped into some lingerie confection that Anna suspected was much less comfortable and much more Charisma.

'So anyway,' Anna continued to talk to the wall. 'Tom had actually forgotten you two were married, which was why I only found out a couple of days ago. Now, my wedding, my dream wedding that I have been waiting for all my life is only a few days away. I have everything in place, every single little detail covered, but it can't go ahead unless you sign these papers. Then a judge will annul your marriage. And that's why I came to New York, to find you, to ask you to sign the papers and let Tom and me get married on Christmas Eve just like we planned.'

There was a moment of silence behind Anna's head in which she imagined Charisma coming at her with something heavy and blunt. But instead of being moved to murder her, Charisma seemed positively blithe.

'Impressive,' she said, the sound of a zip being sharply pulled up punctuating her comment. 'It takes some kind of broad to take a plane to another country to make sure she gets her man right where she wants him.'

'Oh, he's already where I want him,' Anna said, turning around slowly to find Charisma in all her full-bodied glory, wearing a draped pewter metallic dress with a plunging neckline, teamed with a pair of suede knee-length high-heeled boots. Her mane of chestnut hair was spread luxuriously over her shoulders, and she was standing with her hands on her hips, one of which was cocked in an if-you-want-it-come-and-get-it-bitch stance. Channelling Joan Collins circa 1987 for all she was worth, Anna raised a determinedly unimpressed eyebrow back at her.

'All this,' she said gesturing at Charisma. 'This is just admin.'

Anna braced herself, expecting Charisma to fly at her, grab her hair and pull her to the ground in a frenzy of female violence. And with very little idea about how to catfight, outside of the Regina Clarkson incident, which it was fair to say she didn't exactly come out on top of, Anna wondered if she would come out of this alive. It wasn't her life that flashed before her eyes, but images of her never-to-be-worn wedding dress languishing in a charity shop window. Though maybe she could be buried in it. Would there be time to tell someone she wanted to be buried in her wedding dress before Charisma gouged her eyes out with that French manicure? Steeling herself as Charisma took two swaggering steps towards her, Anna prepared to meet her fate. Which was when Charisma dissolved into a fit of girlish giggles, almost doubling up in laughter and leaning one hand on Anna's shoulder to steady herself.

'Oh my God, that was brilliant,' she gasped, clutching her jiggling chest, as tears of mirth threatened her immaculately applied mascara. 'Very *Dy-nasty*. I can see why Tom has fallen for you, you are an Amazonian, babe!'

'I beg your pardon?' Anna asked her, blinking.

'Defending your man, you were magnificent,' Charisma said, holding out her arms to Anna as if she actually expected some sort of hug. 'I'm sorry, darling. I couldn't resist seeing exactly what kind of woman it was that had finally, legitimately got Tom when he was sober and willing. I was messing with you, silly! Come on, come and hug it out and we'll sign those papers and get you on your way down the aisle!'

Anna remained where she was. 'Is this an elaborate ruse in order for you to lull me into a false sense of security and then break my neck when I'm least expecting it?'

'Darling, if I'd wanted to do that you'd be dead by now!' Charisma exclaimed. 'Now come here and let me kiss you. Ooh it's like you're my sister wife! We're positively Amish!'

As it happened Anna didn't need to move a step to be engulfed in a flurry of perfume and hair as Charisma hugged her, with far more familiarity than Anna was comfortable with. Nevertheless she tried to respond with the same level of generous friendship that her nemesis seemed to be gifting her with, even though she just couldn't shake the feeling that she was being hugged by a predator, a predator biding her time before striking.

'You know what this calls for,' Charisma said, picking up what looked like a real fur coat from the back of a chair, and a handbag that, if it was real, would cost about eight hundred pounds. 'This calls for you and me to get ourselves a drink, baby!' Anna opened her mouth to decline, but was promptly shouted down. 'No, I won't take no for an answer. Manhattan brace yourself, Tom's wives are out on the town.'

With Charisma's arm hooked determinedly through hers as they headed out of a fire exit at the back of the theatre and into the freezing night, Anna felt a little bit like she was being kidnapped and wondered about the possibility of ending up sleeping with some fishes at the bottom of the Hudson wearing a pair of concrete slingbacks.

Since announcing her plans for Anna, Charisma had not stopped talking about where she was going to take her new best friend and how they were going to celebrate this particular momentous event in both of their lives, and where they could go for breakfast at dawn, sweeping Anna along like some piece of flotsam doomed to trail in her wake.

Just in time Anna remembered Miles. 'Miles!' she

said, stopping dead, so that Charisma stumbled a little over her heels in the snow.

'Miles?' Charisma fluttered her lashes at her. 'Your feet hurt already?'

'No, my friend Miles. He's waiting for me in the lobby. He came with me tonight. For moral support.'

'You have a friend with you, a man friend?' Charisma asked her, intrigued. 'Does Tom know?'

It seemed counterproductive to say no, so Anna just laughed by way of explanation and let Charisma lead her around to the front of the venue, which was now locked up, its metal shutters firmly drawn down. Miles was sitting on the one dry step under the porch, his head bowed, clutching his phone in his hand, staring at the space between his boots. Every angle of his body told Anna that something had happened.

'Hi?' she said, uncertainly, as she approached him, prising Charisma's fingers from her arm, grateful that Charisma seemed to understand the need to hang back for a moment. 'Miles? Hi? Are you OK?'

Miles looked up at her and Anna gasped to see that his eyes were brightened by tears. Without a moment's thought she knelt in front of him, barely aware of the wet snow steadily melting through the material of her skirt.

'Oh God, what happened?' she asked, putting her hands on his knees as she looked up into his face.

'They called, Anna,' Miles told her, his voice thick

with emotion. 'The management company called about the audition.' He covered her hands with his own, which Anna noticed were trembling and freezing cold.

'Look, it's OK,' she said, sliding her hands out from under his, and putting her palms on his rough cheeks. 'It's fine, because, remember, you said it wasn't about success or money or fame, it was having the chance to do something that made you *so* happy, and that won't change, even if they did turn you down.'

'But they didn't,' Miles said, so quietly that Anna didn't hear him at first.

'And anyway,' she continued, 'at least this way you won't be travelling around the world for ever and ever, living a soulless life on the road, populated with endless hotel rooms and women throwing themselves at you and maybe we can even hang out again and—'

'Anna!' Miles grabbed her hands once again with his freezing fingers, and kissed them in turn. 'You are not listening to me! I got the job. I got the job, Anna! I'm the new lead singer and guitarist for the NYRDs!'

Before Anna had a chance to speak, Miles had swept her up in his arms, staggered down the steps with her and was spinning her around and around, the pair of them laughing until they were giddy, a world of Christmas lights flashing by in a neon swirl. 'This is going to change *everything*,' Miles told as her as they spun. 'This is where it all begins.'

Finally, he set her down unsteadily on her feet, the street still lurching around her, and hugged her so tightly to his chest that Anna could feel his heart thundering through her coat.

'I'm so glad you were here for this moment,' Miles said into her hair. 'I can't imagine wanting to share it with anyone else.'

But before Anna could think about what he'd said or what it might mean or how she might feel about it, Charisma made her presence felt, letting her coat fall open as she smiled at Miles.

'The lead singer of the NYRDs, huh?' she said, looking him up and down with naked admiration as he and Anna finally disengaged from their embrace. 'Well, if that's not a reason to rock this town tonight, then I don't know what is.'

'How are you holding up?' Tom asked Liv when she returned from the ladies' room after freshening up as best she could. After a day of jet lag and emotionally confusing sightseeing, she'd been determined to change for dinner, and to feel at least halfway human again, retiring to the restroom to slip into a teal-green sweater dress she'd picked up in Banana Republic, and applying some of the make-up the nice lady in Macy's had sold her, even though she didn't know she needed any. Just a little dark grey glitter gel on her lids and a sweep of lash-lengthening mascara, complemented with a dash of gloss that brought out what the nice lady had said was the natural cherry red of her full lips. At least now they got to sit down for a few hours, and, if not relax, exactly, as they waited for Anna to make an appearance, at least rebuild their reserves of energy with some good food and alcohol.

Tom had bargained his way into the Round Table restaurant at the Algonquin, which was supposedly fully booked, by unleashing the full extent of his charm on the flustered and easily impressed young lady at the front desk. She had taken pity on them and squeezed them on to a tiny two-seater table right at the back of the room, where Tom was constantly in danger of having his nose broken by the swing of the kitchen door as it bounded open every few seconds. Liv didn't mind where they were sitting though, it was exciting enough to be here in the very place where Dorothy Parker and her cohorts had once sat around being funny and wry and cynical about life. As a teenager Liv had always liked to think of herself as a sort of Dorothy Parker of the Home Counties. She was convinced she had been the nearest thing their school had had to a rapier wit and bold literary talent. At least in her head anyway. Her literary ambition hadn't got much further than Tom's quest to be the first Englishman to write a great American novel; much less further in fact, when she discovered that what she was really good at was creating sauces and jus and not rewriting *Pride and*

Prejudice for the umpteenth time, only minus the sexual tension and wit.

Still, now she was seated here, in this historic place where so many conversations had gone before, crackling with life and laughter, and the smell of really good food, Liv was quite content to slip into that fantasy again, casting Tom as her F. Scott Fitzgerald. In her head they were a pair of doomed lovers finding solace in each other's arms as their worlds fell apart around them. Except, of course, Tom's life was only just getting going and Liv's was the same as it ever was. It came to something, she thought wryly as she weaved her way through the tables to the back of the room where Tom was waiting, when the most exciting and impulsive thing that's happened to you all year is rescuing someone else's relationship.

'I'm fine, actually,' Liv told him as she squeezed into her seat, very grateful for the large gin and tonic that Tom had ordered her and which was waiting, quietly fizzing away, when she returned. 'A little knackered and I sort of wish I had a bed to sleep in tonight, I really thought there'd be at least one room free.'

'There is,' Tom said confidently. 'There's Anna's room. She'll be back sooner or later and it might be a bit of a squash, but you girls can share the bed and I'll sleep on the floor. There will be room at the inn tonight!'

'Yes, but not exactly the romantic reunion you were hoping for?' Liv asked, watching him across the rim of her glass, as she felt the gin fizz through her veins to her exhausted fingertips and then straight to her head. It was going to be very easy to get drunk tonight, in fact this one drink might do the trick. 'Obligatory best friend playing gooseberry just when you two should be engaged in a passionate clinch!'

'The thing with me and Anna though,' Tom said unconcerned, as he perused the menu looking for the closest thing to his usual steak and chips, 'is that we've never really done all that romantic stuff, which isn't to say I don't feel that way, it's just you know. Long looks, hand-holding, big gestures, grand speeches, that's not really us.'

Liv and Tom watched each other across the table for quite some moments before they each recognised the irony of the situation and Liv buried her face in her gin once more.

'What I'm trying to say,' Tom blundered on, his cheeks suddenly flushed, 'is that we don't need all that "tinsel" to make our relationship seem real. And that's what it's all about, isn't it? When you are about to marry someone, spend the rest of your life with them, it's not supposed to be about the thrill, or the romance or even the sex, is it? It's supposed to be about whether you can know for sure in your heart that you will still feel the same way about another person in ten, twenty, thirty years' time. It's about whether you'll make a good team, with the right skill sets for a nice life. And me and Anna, we make a good team. We have the right skill sets.'

'Except you weren't thinking about the next thirty years when you married Charisma,' Liv couldn't help pointing out. 'Although to be fair she might have quite different skill sets,' she added a tad cattily.

'That's my point exactly,' Tom said, not rising to the bait. 'I wasn't thinking about anything when I married Charisma, except where my next shot was coming from and how to keep her interested and entertained, so I could hang on to her a little longer. She was already slipping away from me, the fantasy was almost over, I knew it and I wasn't ready to live life in the real world again, so I married her in a topless bar. I know it seems silly now but I was . . . young.' Tom looked up, catching Liv's expression as he realised exactly what he'd said. Before, in the café with Martha the slutty lawyer, he made it seem as if it had been Charisma that had more or less coerced him into going through with what he'd thought was a joke ceremony. He hadn't said anything at all about just wanting to keep hold of her for as long as he could. This time it was Liv's cheeks that flared with colour as she felt a surge of irrational jealousy over Tom's willingness to make grand romantic gestures for this strange woman and not her best friend.

'Look,' Tom stumbled on, 'what happened between me and Charisma, it's not the same at all as what I have with Anna. My relationship with Charisma was an infatuation, it was a crush, my brain had nothing to do with anything I said or did, I was crazy about her. And when she left . . . well, I was heartbroken, sure. But it didn't take long for me to see that being with her had been like drinking a bottle of tequila every day, I had no idea what I was doing until she was gone and I had a chance to sober up.' On impulse, Tom reached across the table and covered Liv's hand with his own. 'It's not like that with Anna. She's beautiful and smart and sensible and she knows what she wants from life, and it's the same things I want too. And so what if she doesn't make me feel drunk or out of control, that's not what matters in the long run, is it?'

Very slowly Liv withdrew her fingers from under Tom's.

'You know what,' she said, slowly and carefully. 'I think we should stop talking about Anna now. She's not here, and it's not fair. And we're both tired and a little drunk and very far away from home and I . . . I'm worried that everything that seems so sane back in London seems insane here in New York and everything that seems so foolish back at home, seems like a good idea here. So let's stop talking about Anna, and let's get another drink and some food, OK?'

Tom nodded, gesturing for the waiter to come and take their order.

'I'm sorry,' Tom said, after the waiter had gone with

instructions to bring them steak and more gin. 'I don't mean to put you in an awkward position, it's just . . . Well, the thing is, Liv, there isn't anyone in the world who I can seem to talk to the way I talk to you.'

'Podium!' Charisma shouted, after their fifth shot of tequila, doing her best to pull Anna up, against her will, onto what was in fact a bar and not a podium, in some neon-lit club that hummed with bass and seethed with writhing clubbers. Not usually one for nightclubs or dancing of any sort, Anna remained with her feet firmly on the slightly sticky ground, feeling impossibly prim and overdressed in her red pencil dress, surrounded as she was by scantily clad young people.

'Come on, doll!' Charisma urged, shouting to make herself heard over the pounding beats. 'Let's dance for the rock star!'

Anna decided it was probably best to ignore her and, glancing over her shoulder, saw Miles, more than a little high on life and the alcoholic by-product of cactus, dancing with a passing redhead whose eye he'd caught. He had that ability to make women stop and look at him and, if it was bad now, it would be worse when he was officially a rock star. Anna tried and failed not to imagine the hundreds of sexually adventurous women that would be throwing themselves at him morning, noon and night when he was famous, and how much he'd love it. It was hard to feel that Miles had sort of been hers for a little while, and now he would belong to everyone.

'Get up here and grind!' Charisma hollered again, making Anna look back up at her. 'You need to move it if you want to keep him interested!'

'Are you kidding, in this skirt?' Anna said, still not drunk enough not to think about her seams splitting. 'And I don't want to keep him interested, he can "grind" with whomever he likes.'

'Ah, watch me then! Miles, Miles!' Charisma bellowed across the din, so that Miles looked up and laughed when he saw her frenzied gyrating, making the most of her years of exotic dance training. Leaving the redhead to stamp her foot and skulk off alone, he crossed over to where Charisma danced, and Anna stood looking up at her, in awe of and a little bit horrified by the powerhouse that was the woman that Tom had married first.

Miles dropped an arm around her shoulder as he joined her.

'She's quite something, isn't she?' he said, right into her ear because it was the only way to make himself heard. Anna shivered, feeling his breath on her neck. 'It's a good job she and Tom didn't last more than five minutes, I think a couple of weeks with that lady would probably be enough to kill any man.'

'Hey, Miles!' Miles looked up as, improbably, Charisma swung a black lace – and rather large-cupped

– bra around her head three times before draping it over Miles's head, leaning down just low enough so that he could get more than a glimpse of what was now unbridled beneath her pewter dress.

'That's an impressive move,' Miles said, picking up the bra and looking at it quizzically, before placing it rather formally on the bar.

'Pah, I can do that, that's *Flashdance* 101,' Anna said, before she knew it, blushing when Miles turned to look at her, his arms crossed as if waiting. 'I'm not going to though!'

'I know,' Miles said. 'Pleased to hear it too, that's not really the sort of move a nice girl makes.'

'So you prefer a nice girl to . . .' Anna nodded up at Charisma whose bra stunt had earned her a small crowd of male admirers, clamouring around her feet. 'Her. Because you know she's very much after you.'

'I know,' Miles said grinning. 'But not because of my great personality, or even my newly acquired rock-star status.'

'Oh, just your incredible body and amazing good looks then,' Anna said, realising a little late that she was fluttering her eyelashes at him and smiling flirta-tiously, the tip of her nose almost touching his.

'*That* would make the most sense,' Miles conceded. 'But no. She's after me, not because she wants me, but because she doesn't want you to get me.'

'Um?' Anna wondered if the tequila was taking its

toll after all, because she hadn't followed anything that Miles had just said.

'What I mean is Charisma Jones is not a woman's woman,' Miles said. 'She's the kind of girl who is always in competition with other women, and who always wants to win.'

'Don't be silly,' Anna said, turning again to where Charisma had finally persuaded some poor suited man to join her on the bar, where he bobbed about awkwardly as she wound her body around him, all the time checking to make sure that Miles was watching her. 'Charisma knows that I'm here for Tom. So that we can get married. She knows there's nothing going on between you and me.'

'That won't stop her trying to make me notice her instead of you though,' Miles said, leaning across the bar and gesturing for their shot glasses to be filled again. 'And you can bet your life that when it comes to it, she's not going to want you to have Tom either.'

Chapter Thirteen

Anna had continued to believe that she was as sober as a judge until her sixth shot of tequila whereupon she became suddenly very, very drunk all at once.

Thankfully they had left the club at that point, Charisma having dragged them to a little cabaret bar she knew, coercing a pair of fur-trimmed velvet Santa hats from a passing office party with a good deal of sexual manipulation and some kissing under fake mistletoe that Anna was certain included tongues on the way. Having perched one hat on her head, making it an instantly sexy accessory, she jammed the other on Anna's, which looked a whole lot less alluring, what with the brim covering her brows and forcing her ears to stick out at an odd angle. Anna looked more like an actual elf.

The bar was a welcome relief after the noise and heat of the club, and Anna couldn't help but take some pleasure in skipping past the lengthy queue that shivered outside, down the metal steps that led into the basement venue and getting direct VIP access via Charisma's apparently close relationship with the doorman. Inside, the tiny venue was packed with large round tables, each lit with small red tassel-fringed lamps, and every available space in between filled with stylishly dressed people, chatting and drinking as a very plausible Judy Garland drag queen sang 'Have Yourself a Merry Little Christmas' with exactly the right amount of melodrama and watery mascara.

'Sweet,' Miles said, as Charisma somehow obtained three stools at the busy bar and ordered them their sixth round of shots.

'Do you know,' Anna said. 'I'm always going to drink tequila from now on. I feel fantastic and I'm not in the least bit drunk.'

And that was when she fell off her stool and into a giggling heap on the floor.

Laughing, Miles helped her up and slid her back onto the seat, his hands helpfully remaining on her waist to secure her in a seated position. Judy finished her number with a flourish and was taking a bow when Charisma was struck with an idea.

'Want to do something really fun?' she asked Anna, leaning towards her.

'Yes!' Anna said, wide-eyed at the notion. 'Is it drink more tequila, because you know I'm completely sober on tequila. It's like magic.'

'Dance with me,' Charisma said. 'Oh come on, it will be wild.'

'There doesn't seem to be a dance floor,' Anna said, looking around. 'Or a floor . . . Is it me or is the room going uphill . . . and anyway I can't dance.'

'Come with me.' Charisma grabbed her hand, telling Miles, 'We're just going to the ladies' room.'

'Is there a dance floor in the ladies' room?' Anna asked, teetering along behind Charisma who marched purposefully down a black-painted corridor and walked unannounced into a brightly lit dressing room where Judy was peeling off one set of lashes.

'Judy!' Charisma shrieked, kissing him on a heavily rouged cheek. 'Long time no see, baby!'

'Carrie!' Judy turned in his chair and hugged her warmly. 'I thought you'd given up the life of sin for a life of God or a serious actor, both equally as celibate?'

'I have,' Charisma said. 'But just for tonight, I'm sort of celebrating, and I want to dance just once more, and so does my friend here.'

'No,' Anna said cheerfully. 'I'm a terrible dancer. I've got no rhythm.'

'You don't need rhythm for this kind of dancing, darling,' Charisma said, reaching into Judy's wardrobe and bringing out a sexy Santa outfit. 'I'm going to teach you the one thing you need to keep Tom happy. I'm going to teach you how to strip. All we need is a bit of tit glue, some tassels and you can make your debut right here . . .'

Anna didn't remember grabbing Miles as she fled into the biting cold, but she must have because he was there as she stumbled into the snowy night with Charisma hot on her heels.

'Wait! Wait up! I was only joking!' Charisma was calling after them.

'Only joking about what?' Miles asked when Anna, suddenly all at once out of breath and not at all sure which way was up, stopped, clinging on to a street light for dear life.

'She was going to get me to do that thing she does!' Anna accused, pointing at Charisma, who arrived a few seconds later giggling like a loon. 'That naked thing, in front of people. Like with the singing on the open mic night, but naked. I don't do naked and you –' Anna waggled her finger at Charisma '– are a very, very bad person.'

'Wow, Tom's taste in women has really changed,' Charisma said, sarcastically. 'Look, I wouldn't really have got you to dance with me. I just thought as tonight was a night for Charisma and not boring old Erica that I might let loose a little, have some fun, show Miles here a thing . . . or two.' Charisma managed to smile and pout at Miles simultaneously, a feat of co-ordination that Anna was very envious of, considering that she couldn't co-ordinate her own feet at that point. 'I knew you would never be daring enough to try your hand at burlesque. Besides you don't have what it takes.'

'I have what it takes!' Anna insisted, pulling open

her coat and thrusting out her chest, causing Miles to take a sudden interest in the sidewalk. 'I'm a thirty-four double D I'll have you know!'

'Oh, so that's why Tom likes you,' Charisma teased, chuckling merrily.

'No, no . . . he likes me because I'm . . . I'm . . .' Anna pointed at Miles, thankfully forgetting to chest thrust any more. 'Miles, why does Tom love me?'

'I don't know!' Miles said, suddenly exasperated by the two beautiful but drunk women who were besetting him with difficult questions and chest measurements. 'Look, we've had a great night, it's been a lot of fun. But I think maybe now it's time I got Anna back to the hotel.'

'Yes! Yes!' Charisma jumped on the idea. 'After-party at your place, room service, minibar!'

'I was thinking now would be a good time to say goodnight,' Miles said quite firmly.

'Goodnight?' Charisma asked dismayed. 'But we've only just started and it's not every day you get your marriage annulled, is it? You can't just make me sign something that important and monumental and then expect me to go home . . . alone?'

'The papers!' Anna exclaimed suddenly, remembering her precious cargo. Frantically, she began searching her bag and her pockets and for some reason down the front of her top for the large brown envelope. 'The papers have gone! Oh no, where have I left them?'

It took a further discussion for them to decide that they hadn't seen the envelope since the second bar they'd been to, where Charisma had grabbed it and waved it above her head like a flag, declaring that as soon as she signed the contents she would be open to offers of marriage. Charisma, they decided, must have left the package in that bar, shortly after their third shot of tequila.

'You did it on purpose!' Anna accused, listing heavily against the lamppost. 'You don't want to annul your marriage to Tom, you want to keep him!'

'Why would I want to do that?' Charisma asked her, seemingly genuinely perplexed.

'Because in all these years you never ever tried to get it annulled before!' Anna said.

'I've been busy!'

'Doing what, shaking your bottom about for perverts?' Anna challenged her.

'Pursuing a serious acting career, actually,' Charisma said, apparently amused by Anna's attempt at an insult. 'And as long as stupid guys pay to see me dance naked, then I'll do that too. It pays the bills while I'm waiting for my big break. And anyway Tom didn't even think about getting it annulled until it was too late. Does that mean he still secretly wants to be married to me?'

Anna lunged at her with more intent than accuracy, missing her target by such a wide angle that she instead landed in a mound of icy and dirty snow that had been swept up against a wall. Quickly, Miles lifted her to her feet, keeping his arms under hers to steady her.

'I think we're all a bit tired,' he said, sounding less like a rock star and more like a weary Nursery School teacher. 'Look, it's fine. We'll call the bar in the morning, pick up the papers, sort out the signature then. For now though, Anna needs some sleep.'

'But it's only just past midnight,' Charisma sulked, stamping one foot in the snow. 'I've been boring old Erica for so long, all I want to do is have a little fun. Hey, what about you and me take Miss Goody Two Shoes here back to her hotel and then head out alone. You're celebrating too, remember and I bet you and I could make some sweet music together?'

Miles sighed, wondering how best to take care of Anna and also keep control of Charisma at the same time. The worst possible case scenario would be to lose her in this city again, this time without any clue of how to find her. He didn't think somehow that her role in a third-rate play that nobody was going to see would be enough of a reason for her to stay put if she decided that now was the time to do another life and name changing flit.

'Let's go back to plan A,' he said, reluctantly, but unable to come up with an alternative. 'Come back with us. Have a drink, stay over and, in the morning, we'll find the papers, sign it all off and everything will be done.'

'Stay over you say?' Charisma said, widening her eyes at the suggestion. 'What will you and I get up to while poor old Anna sleeps off all that tequila?'

Miles looked Charisma firmly in the eye. 'Nothing,' he said. 'We will be getting up to nothing, Charisma, because I have only one rule: I never mess with married women.'

Charisma chuckled as Miles began to escort Anna back to the hotel, following in their wake. 'But nearly married women, that's a whole other story, right?'

Thankfully Tom didn't notice Anna passing them in the lobby, as he sat side by side with Liv on the sofa, because he had his head pushed back into the deep folds of the leather upholstery, and his eyes closed, finally giving in to the exhaustion and the after-effects of a good meal, wine and a large brandy.

It was Liv whose mouth fell open and then clamped very tightly shut again as a decidedly dishevelled-looking Anna, her blonde mane tangled around her shoulders, her lipstick smudged, her mascara dislodged, entered the lobby in a decidedly haphazard fashion, her arms around the neck of a man that Liv vaguely recognised. In their wake, grinning like the cat who'd got the cream, in a full-length fur coat, was a sultry brunette who couldn't be anyone else in the world but Charisma Jones. Anxiously, Liv sat in silence until the curious little ensemble disappeared into the lift, and then she tentatively shook Tom's arm, just enough to rouse him, but not enough to get him to open his eyes.

'Tom? I'm just going to powder my nose,' Liv said. 'Back in a minute.'

'Hmmm,' Tom muttered, clearly still half asleep. 'See you in a bit.'

Aware that she wasn't going to have much luck looking for Anna if she just ran up and down God only knew how many corridors shouting her name, Liv realised she needed a plan. Producing her lipgloss from her pocket, she approached the bellhop who was manning the lift that Anna had climbed into.

'Hello, that blonde lady dropped this,' she said, offering the tube of gloss as evidence. 'I just wondered what floor she got out on? I thought perhaps I'd try and catch her.'

There were a million holes of logic and reason in her flawed proposal, but the tired looking bellhop didn't care, probably deciding by taking one look at her that she wasn't an international assassin intent on dastardly deeds. 'Twelve,' he said languidly, pressing the relevant button as Liv stepped inside, biting her lip as she felt the elevator ascend. The way she saw it, she had about ten minutes to get to Anna, warn her Tom was here and find out what the hell was going on, before Tom realised she'd been gone much longer than a quick trip to the bathroom merited and came to find out what was going on. As soon as the doors slid open, she rushed out into the richly carpeted corridor, but it was now empty. And then she heard a peal of laughter from behind the double doors of a suite at the end of the hall, and Liv had no idea how, but she knew with absolute certainty that it was Charisma Jones's laugh.

'Anna?' She knocked firmly on the door, which was opened by the sexy brunette.

'You're not room service,' she said looking Liv up and down with marked disappointment. 'You're not anyone.'

'Liv!' The man that was just depositing Anna on the sofa caught sight of her and smiled warmly, which was when Liv realised where she knew him – he'd played at Simon's wedding, and then Simon had set him up with Anna. He'd been the one who'd almost killed her with kiwi. What on earth was he doing here?

'Miles,' Liv said with some relief that Anna wasn't exactly alone in a hotel room with a stripper and a strange man, although technically both things were true.

'What are you doing here?' Miles asked her as Liv entered the room tentatively to find Anna sprawled on the sofa, a cloud of hair covering her face.

'Funny,' Tom said from behind her. 'I was just about to ask *you* the same question.'

And it was at the sound of his voice that Anna sat up and opened her eyes just in time to see her fiancé be engulfed in an embrace by his current wife. And even in her less-than-sober state, she was fairly certain it involved tongues.

Chapter Fourteen

'You're here,' Anna said, blinking at Tom, who seemed to take an eternity to finally unpeel himself from his wife's embrace, dislodging her fingers one by one. Watching Charisma maul her fiancé as if from a great distance and behind a good deal of bubble wrap, Anna turned to Liv, who was rather incongruous in a scene occupied mainly by wives and wives-to-be. 'You're here too? Am I hallucinating? Is this tequila-related?'

'Tequila? You've been drinking tequila? What about you never drinking tequila again after that last time, on Sue's hen night in Madrid when you thought you'd gone blind?' Liv reminded her rather crossly, making Anna realise that her best friend and fiancé really were here, and, for some reason, rather than feeling overjoyed and delightfully surprised she felt somehow surprisingly resentful and quite inconvenienced.

'No, we are not a hallucination, sorry to disappoint you, Anna,' Tom said firmly, with the kind of scowl he usually reserved for days when his football team lost, which was most Saturdays during the season. 'But what the hell are you doing with a strange man in your hotel room?'

Tom pointed at Miles, as if there might be some confusion about which strange man exactly he was referring to. Anna looked to see Miles standing with his arms crossed, his shoulders squared, rather like he was getting ready to defend his homestead, or this instance a suite in a New York hotel.

'He's not strange,' Liv interjected from the doorway, the look on her face telling Anna that she was putting together the disembodied male voice that she had heard on the phone with the man standing in front of her. 'What I mean is, he's not a stranger – he's Miles, he's a friend of Simon's . . . He and Anna went on a date . . . once, ages ago. I don't know what he's doing here, but I know he isn't a stranger. Anna?'

'What?' Anna said, testily, as if she'd really rather be asleep than deal with all these questions, which to be fair to her was in fact the case. The tequila was sort of insulating her from the significance of the occasion, and the fact that Charisma and Tom were in the same room once again after eight years. Not that Tom had even glanced in Charisma's direction since her attempts to kiss him. Having been put firmly aside, she seemed quite content to watch on the sidelines, at least for the moment, her big chocolate-brown eyes taking everything in.

'What is Miles doing in your hotel room?' Liv prompted Anna, sharply. Wasn't it enough for her that the man Liv loved was rushing across the Atlantic to be with her? She had to have a hot rock god in her bedroom too?

Anna sighed. She could have tried coming up with some sort of excuse to explain Miles away that didn't involve cohabitation, even if it was mostly in separate rooms, but she was too tired, too fraught and too drunk, as well as too annoyed by Charisma's smirk and Liv's moral high ground, to be bothered.

'We're sharing it,' she said, rolling her eyes, and gesturing vaguely at Miles. 'We happened to arrive at the same time, we needed a place to stay, it made financial sense, blah, blah, blah, blah. At least I haven't accidentally got married and then forgotten about it.'

She raised an eyebrow at Tom who was still standing by the door, rooted to the spot, as if he still could not make sense of what he was seeing.

Charisma giggled delightedly. 'She has kind of got you there, babe,' she told Tom coyly over one shoulder. Tom simply refused to look at her as if ignoring her might somehow make her disappear.

'You were just sharing a room, and nothing was going on?' Tom asked, looking at Miles.

'God! Miles, tell him,' Anna said, furiously.

Crucially, Miles hesitated as he looked at Anna, the expression on his face unreadable and then, squaring his shoulders, Miles looked Tom right in the eye and shrugged, in a decidedly ambiguous fashion.

'What can I tell you,' he said, 'we hooked up at the airport.'

Which was when, out of the blue, Tom ran three strides forwards and sent Miles staggering backwards with a swift right hook that threatened to knock him right off his feet, and almost did.

'Oh my God!' Anna shrieked as Miles steadied himself, gingerly touching his hand to his jaw, tasting blood from his split lip. 'Oh my God, you hit him, Tom, you hit him!'

'Yeah, and I'll hit him again,' Tom said menacingly, narrowing his eyes. 'See these hands, pal? These hands are lethal weapons.'

'Tom, you do kick-boxing,' Liv reminded him under her breath.

'These feet are lethal weapons,' Tom added. 'Too.'

'I don't care if you've got an AK-47 in your pocket, that was a big mistake, my friend.' Miles shook out his arms, and bounced on his toes for a bit.

'What are you going to do – aerobics him to death?' Liv asked.

'You hit him!' Anna pointed at Miles, still quite clearly on the last page.

'Bring it on, mate,' Tom told Miles, assuming a kick-boxing stance, and giving Miles a little Bruce Lee-style beckon. 'If you think you're hard enough.'

Anna and Liv watched in horror, as ignoring the niceties of martial arts, Miles simply launched himself at Tom, and seemed to fly almost vertically towards him through the air, knocking him to the ground in something like a rugby tackle.

'What the hell are you doing?' Anna screamed as she watched Miles and Tom wrestle on the floor. Neither one was really hitting the other. It seemed to be more like a lot of angry grabbing, grunting and tussling.

'Get his head in a knee lock!' Liv called presumably to Tom. 'Crush his windpipe, cut off his air.'

'Liv!' Anna was horrified, her body numb and slow to respond to what she was seeing.

'What, presumably you are on Tom's side?' Liv asked her archly.

'I am on the side of justice!' Anna said, although she wasn't entirely sure what she meant by that.

'How does it feel to have two men fight over you?' Charisma said with mild interest, as the men continued to wrestle each other, any iota of training they might have forgotten in the primeval need to simply roll about, pointlessly. 'They're both pretty hot, so that's a plus, it's just a shame they have clothes on and that they aren't very good at it. For a really good brawl you need Texans. English men are too polite.' She paused thoughtfully. 'What are the chances we might get them to take their clothes off?'

Unable to watch their red, distorted stupid faces for a second longer, Anna clumsily threw herself into the fray, attempting to separate the two by grabbing at the first thing she could find in the tangle of men. It happened to be Tom's hair and he yowled. The momentary break in his concentration allowed Miles to bloody his lip in return with an unexpected elbow jab, which was probably more of an accident than intentional.

'For God's sake, stop it, you're hurting him!' Anna said, not sure exactly who she was defending, but knowing that whoever it was, this was not a good thing for the other. Desperately, she tried to insert herself between them and lever them apart. She found herself, for one confusingly exciting moment, in the grip of both men, a moment intensified when she realised that the sound of material tearing was actually the neckline of her dress, revealing a good deal more of her red lace bra than she should probably be showing to anyone in that room, except her fiancé.

'Oh, let them get on with it,' Charisma said, trying to drag Anna away by her wrist. 'It's funny and God knows why they're fighting over your sour little ass, but you should be pleased. You don't look it, but you must be one hell of a lay.'

'I beg your pardon?' Anna said, thinking in that exact moment that she sounded more like a nanny chiding a cheeky child than a woman, in a ripped dress, about to embark upon a catfight. Still, undeterred, she jumped up with what she considered to be verging on ninja-like speed, particularly considering her levels of intoxication, and slapped Charisma so smartly around her face that her chin whipped over her shoulder, leaving a wake of hair across her face.

'Take that back!' Anna demanded, thinking that Joan Collins would have been proud of her. But the moment of self-congratulation was short-lived as Charisma, recovering quickly, grabbed a handful of Anna's hair and started dragging her around the room, intent on yanking it out by the roots.

Anna wasn't sure for how long Charisma had her hands in her hair, scalping her, one golden thread at a time, or for how long she dug her nails into Charisma's wrists in an attempt to make her let go. Although it seemed like an eternity it must have taken much less than a minute for Liv to expertly break Charisma's hold on Anna, twist her hand behind her back and slam her up against the wall.

'You stay there,' Liv informed her. 'Otherwise I'll break more than a fingernail, got it?'

Impressed more than intimidated, Charisma shrugged, turned around and leaned back against the wall with a definite smirk on her pretty face, as Anna rubbed her sore head.

'And as for you two, stop it this second!' Liv yelled, with such authority that she didn't really need to knock Miles off Tom with a well-placed kick to his shoulder, and then stand over them, with her hands on her hips, like a latter-day Boudicca, as they lay panting on the floor, although that is exactly what she did.

'Put in some electric guitar and we'd have ourselves a porn film,' Charisma said happily, clearly delighted with how her reunion with her husband was going.

'You shut it,' Liv warned her. 'I am too tired, too bored of everyone else's crap constantly landing at my feet, to take a single second more of *any* nonsense from anyone. Now let's all act like grown-ups and get to the bottom of this, shall we? Fighting like children, honestly.'

Miles and Tom clambered to their feet, brushed down their clothes, straightened their dishevelled shirts and looked decidedly sheepish, as it began to dawn on them they'd both been brawling over nothing in particular, and had not been doing a particularly good job at either.

'Look at yourselves,' Liv said, disgusted. 'Anna, look at your dress. Do any of you even know what you are fighting about?'

The four of them stood there, three of them with their heads hanging, casting sideways looks at each other, Anna holding her dress together over her under-wear, while Charisma shrugged and said, 'Well, this is the most excitement I've had in ages. Sexually repressed nuns are no fun at all.'

'I wasn't fighting,' Anna interjected. 'I was trying to *stop* fighting until she got involved.'

'I think,' Liv said taking a deep breath, 'that we are *all* a bit overtired and emotional. Tom and I . . .'

'*Tom and I,*' Anna found herself repeating in a sarcastic tone, unfairly annoyed with Liv for being there, being sensible and most of all being sane.

'Tom and I have been up for hours waiting for *you*, Anna. Tom has come all this way for *you*. And because you haven't answered your phone or called anyone pretty much since you arrived, we didn't know that you were not here, you were out on the town with these two.' She gestured at Charisma and Miles, who exchanged the sort of conspiratorial smiles that made Liv feel cross. 'It seems to me that everyone has gotten into a pickle and overreacted. Let's just take a breath and remember why we are all here. It's so that Tom and Anna can get married in a few days' time. Not so that Tom and Miles can fight like a pair of toddlers after too many Smarties, and Charisma and Anna can scratch each other's eyes out like . . . like a pair of alley cats!'

Liv sat down heavily on the sofa, burying her head in her hands. 'Oh God, I need a life. Now, Anna, tell your fiancé why Miles is in your hotel room, preferably in a way that is not going to incite a riot.'

'Fine, but before I begin I want to say it's not as if I forgot to mention to my impending bride that I was already married . . .'

'How many times!' Tom exclaimed. 'I'm trying to get it sorted!'

'Fine,' Anna repeated, taking a breath and forcing herself to climb down from the combative stance she'd slipped into. 'So the reason that Miles is here is because *coincidentally*, he was on the same flight as me out here, sitting right next to me.' She turned to Tom. 'We had a really awful date, once, before I met you and, trust me, he was the last person I wanted to see on that day, after everything that had happened. But we talked on the flight and when we got here he offered to take me to a hotel.'

'I bet he did,' Charisma chimed in.

'To keep me safe,' Anna said firmly. 'And then it turned out there was only one room left in New York, and it cost a lot of money so we decided to share it. Miles *helped* me look for Charisma. There had been no inappropriate behaviour at all, he's been on the sofa the whole time.' She looked at Miles, whose swollen bottom lip oddly suited him, and smiled faintly. 'He's been a really great friend, actually.'

'Friend only?' Tom asked, looking at Miles. 'Be straight with me.'

Miles nodded, looking suddenly very tired. 'Friends only,' he told Tom, his shoulders dropping. 'I've been helping Anna find Charisma, while I waited for an audition. All she's talked about is you and how much she wants to marry you, and it's pretty clear the lengths she would go to for that. There is nothing going on between us.'

Tom's expression softened a little, as Anna wondered if that was strictly true, because there was *something* going on, in her heart, and her body, whenever she looked at Miles, or was near him. It had crept up on her during the hours they had spent together and now seemed to have some sort of hold. And even if it was just physical, some kind of chemical reaction that her heart had no control over, it was still *something*. Would Tom be able to sense that, see it in her face? Or worse still, would Miles?

However, Anna realised it was Liv who was watching her intently, probably sensing that something was up. She would certainly want to know why Anna hadn't told her about Miles when they had spoken on the phone. The trouble was Anna wasn't sure that she had a very good answer.

'Look,' Liv said, sending Anna a coded 'we'll talk later' look, 'Anna and Tom obviously need a minute to . . . say hello, so shall we just . . .' She gestured to the door. 'Give them a bit of space, and go and have some strong coffee in the bar? At least you lot are less likely to start a riot in a public space.'

'Hold on a second, honey,' Charisma said, pushing herself off from the wall where Liv had told her to stay. 'I get that you're defending your friends here, and I like it. But you're not the boss of me, and that's my husband there. I might not have seen him in a very long time, I might not have wanted to, but you don't get to just tell me to skedaddle until we've had words.'

Charisma walked over to Tom and took a long time looking him up and down.

'You look good, Tom,' she said, holding out a hand. "I'm sorry I inappropriately kissed you. I was a little drunk, and a lot more pleased to see you than I thought I was going to be.'

'It's fine,' Tom said, shrugging awkwardly. He smiled at her. 'You look good too, Charisma. Although I'm sorry we're still married.'

'It's not all your fault. It's not like we didn't both have plenty of time to sort it out.' Charisma smiled warmly. 'Every time I thought about doing it, over the years, I'd look back at the time we spent together and realise that it was the happiest I've ever been with a guy. I was just waiting to be that happy again before I finally let my last little connection to you go. What's your excuse?'

Tom pressed his lips together, before admitting, 'I forgot about it. And actually I didn't ever think we were legally married until quite recently. Sorry.'

For one moment, Charisma's big brown eyes were filled with sadness, but it was a moment so fleeting that if you hadn't been looking for it, like Anna had, you would never have known that it was there. Charisma laughed, slapping Tom hard on the shoulder, tossing her hair back as she turned to smile at Anna.

'Well, then, am I pleased you're marrying this little firecracker, because if we'd left it up to your lazy ass, then I would never have seen you again, eight years older, with quite a lot less hair, and I would have pined for you for at least another eight years.'

'So you will sign the papers then?' Anna asked her. 'Without any games or attempts to get Tom back by taking your top off?'

'Look,' Charisma said, the persona she'd been wearing all night dropping off her as easily as a tie-at-the-sides thong, 'I won't say I haven't thought about you, Tom, or wondered if I should have just walked out on you the way I did. Sometimes over the years I have dreamed about what it might have been like if I'd stayed. But I didn't stay, and actually, having seen you fight, I'm glad I didn't. You are way too British for me. But I'm glad I've seen you again. And met Anna, and this cool scary chick here. I'm not evil, I just couldn't resist pranking you a little bit, Anna. Of course I'm going to sign the papers. And then, you know what, I'm going to get on with my life, just the way I planned it.'

'Then thank you,' Anna said, managing a smile at the beautiful woman who'd just solved all of her problems in one fell swoop. 'You didn't have to be so helpful.'

'Oh, darling,' Charisma said, dropping a light kiss on first Anna and then Tom's cheek. 'I was never going to stand in your way. Now, you rock god, you can buy me a drink. That girl might be scary, but she's way too short to scare me sober.'

With one last long look at Anna, Miles took a breath, found a smile, picked up his guitar and walked past Tom, towards the door.

'Come on, babe,' he said to Charisma, 'let's go start a country sing-song in the bar of the Algonquin.'

'Take your time,' Liv told Anna and Tom just before she closed the door behind her. 'Not that you need me to give you permission to take your time. I mean take as long as you need . . . I mean . . . See you later!'

Anna and Tom were alone at last, and although it had only been a few days since they had last been together it felt like an age, almost like another life since they had been intimate. And as Anna stood there, looking at the man who she'd once been so certain was better than she ever could have deserved, she wondered if she had done the right thing by coming to New York to save their Christmas wedding day. Because one thing could not be denied, she was a very different person now than she had been when she boarded that flight.

More than a year and a half they had been together, but there was so much they still didn't know about each other, even now. There was so much that Anna felt she still didn't understand about Tom and there were certainly things that Tom didn't know about her, especially not the new and hard-to-understand feelings that Anna felt whenever she was near Miles. Or the odd sensation that she had that the two of them had become closer, understood each other better in less than forty-eight hours together than she and Tom had in all the time they'd been together. It was Tom who hadn't thought to tell her about Charisma until it was almost too late and Tom didn't know the truths and secrets that she'd so readily told Miles. Yet this was the man she was moving heaven and earth to marry in a few days' time, and Miles would soon be in the grip of his exciting new life and she wouldn't even be an afterthought for him. All of this was artificial, Anna reminded herself sternly. A set of extraordinary events, taking place in her snow globe, a fragile little bubble that had nothing to do with the real world. In the real world she was going to marry Tom, and that was what she had to stay focused on, because apart from anything else she was certain that Miles wasn't sitting in the bar, brooding over her.

'I'm sorry I hit Miles,' Tom began, cutting across her train of thought and breaking the silence between them. It was obvious that he thought that was the last bone of contention between them. 'It's just that you left, almost without saying goodbye, without giving me a chance to think about what was happening.'

'There wasn't any time to think!' Anna said. 'Sometimes you just have to act.'

Both of them were very aware that that didn't sound at all like the normal sort of thing Anna would say.

'Fine, but you haven't answered any of my calls since you got here or tried to call me. And then when I walk in and there's a man here . . . in your bedroom, and you're really drunk, and you don't normally get really drunk, and then suddenly there's Charisma, who I haven't seen in years and . . . I just couldn't work out what was happening. I don't blame you for wanting to punish me, but I overreacted by taking it out on Miles.'

'I wasn't trying to punish you,' Anna said, her hands hanging limply at her sides, when she knew she should be reaching out to her fiancé, pulling him into an embrace. 'I just . . . I needed a bit of space. I know I should have called you as soon as I got here, I meant to. But, I suppose I was more shocked about Charisma than I realised, and then I found her photo on the internet when *you* said there was nothing, and it felt like if you hadn't been straight with me about that, what else had you lied about?'

Tom dropped his gaze to the floor. 'I didn't mean to lie to you, I was trying to protect you.' He finished the sentence uncertainly, unsure that Anna would buy it. 'I knew how much it would hurt you if you saw photos of Charisma in all her glory. I was worried that you wouldn't understand, but she is my past. I decided nearly a year ago now that you are my future, the rest of my life. And I'm not the sort of man who goes back on his promises, even if I am the sort of man who has messed it all up really badly.'

'Miles said you were protecting me,' Anna said. 'Miles made a lot of sense about a lot of things, actually.'

'Did he?' Tom rubbed his hands through his hair. 'I guess I just don't know what to think about you hanging out with another man, Anna. In your hotel room, behind my back.'

'And I guess I don't know what to think about you being secretly married to another woman and then even when you do tell me, mainly because I made you tell me, by following you, not telling me everything!' Anna retorted, finding herself increasingly sober. 'I *guess* I don't really know what I think about *that*. I guess I'm still angry about it, and worried that it's changed things between us and maybe that's why . . .'

She had been about to say that maybe that was why she was having confusing reactions to Miles, but she stopped herself just in time.

'Maybe that's why I didn't call you, or answer your calls.'

'Nothing has changed between us,' Tom insisted, taking a step towards her. 'Please, Anna, it hasn't. I know I handled it all wrong. I know that. But that doesn't mean everything can't go ahead as you planned, does it? You've done it, you've found Charisma, you've made the wedding possible, and now, because of you, everything can be exactly like it was before. We can get married on Christmas Eve, Anna!'

Anna's gaze slipped to the window where earlier

Miles had drawn back the blinds to make the most of their panoramic view. It felt like the city was crowding round on the other side of the glass, peering in, to see what happens next.

Anna wondered why it was that she wasn't rushing into Tom's arms and kissing him madly, the way a girl should be doing when a boy has done such a good job of making a romantic declaration. And yet she was still there, her arms still hanging at her sides, no longer aware of her torn dress, nowhere near ready to embrace him. Tom took another step closer, and Anna resisted the urge to back away.

'Anna? Come on, please,' Tom pleaded, sweetly, with those Labrador eyes that Anna had never been able to resist before. 'Look, I know I landed a massive bombshell on you out of nowhere. And I know I was less than supportive about your idea to come out here and look for Charisma. I know that I was wrong about that. But, darling, I've been so cut up about it. Liv will tell you, we've been together the whole time since you left. She's been brilliant helping me make sense of it all. If she hadn't been by my side through all of this, I don't know what I would have done. It wasn't that Charisma was a secret, it was just that she was from a life, another universe, where I don't exist any more. The person I was then with her, he doesn't exist any more. That made sense in my head, although admittedly the relevant authorities probably wouldn't take the parallel universe excuse as a valid reason for committing bigamy.'

Tom stopped himself talking, taking the final few steps between him and Anna.

'Can we put this all behind us now?' he asked her, as if he were offering her a once in a lifetime deal. 'Pick up our lives where they left off?'

'Yes.' Anna nodded, mustering a weary smile, because, really, there was no other answer but that one. It was the answer she had given him almost a year ago when he'd proposed, and no matter how confused and churned up her feelings were right now, it was a commitment she was determined to abide by, and knowing that suddenly made everything else seem wonderfully simple.

'Yes,' she repeated. 'After all we're getting married in a few days.'

Smiling, his expression flooding with relief, Tom closed the last few inches between them, and took her in his arms, holding her body close against his. Anna looked up into his lovely eyes, his kind familiar face that had become so important to her over the last year and a half, and waited to feel even a tenth of the electricity that had surged through her when Miles's lips had brushed against hers for that fraction of an unexpected moment.

The fact that it didn't come didn't mean anything especially, she decided with detachment, as Tom pressed his lips against hers, gently opening her mouth with his tongue, in what had become his familiar kissing routine. It was only that she had gotten to know Tom well, that their kind of intimacy was solid and real, absent of the sort of, probably one-sided, sexual tension that being holed up in a hotel room in New York at Christmas might artificially create between two people. Concentrating very hard, Anna made herself stop thinking about anything except Tom, aware of exactly how important this moment was.

This was the moment the lovers reunited after hitting some serious bumps in the road, this was the moment when Charisma, and Miles, and last-minute flights that separated them by thousands of miles, were long forgotten, the moment that everything fell into place and they became one again.

Relaxing her body, Anna finally wound her arms around Tom's neck and kissed him back. She let her chin tilt back as his mouth travelled to her jaw and her neck. Closing her eyes, she sighed as the stubble of Miles's dark beard tickled her neck, and his hand, his beautiful, clever guitar-playing hand, caressed and cupped her lace-covered breast, running his thumb over her nipple until she moaned. And then Anna remembered this wasn't Miles she was kissing, it wasn't Miles touching her that way.

Panicking, she pushed Tom away as if it was Miles himself she was rejecting.

'What?' Tom asked her, with some dismay, flustered

and clearly in a state of arousal. Suddenly self-conscious, feeling like she was betraying someone, but not exactly sure who, Anna covered herself, crossing her arms over her chest, to keep her dress in place, half turning away from Tom to hide her confusion.

'I thought we were OK now?' Tom said. 'Are we not OK now?'

'We are,' Anna said, 'Of course we are, it's just . . .'

This couldn't be happening, she couldn't come all this way to save her wedding to Tom to suddenly transfer her affections to the first man she bumped into, that was just not the sort of thing that sensible, careful-never-to-put-a-foot wrong Anna Carter would do. It was the sort of thing her mother would do though, Anna realised. Rip everything that was supposed to be solid and good apart on a whim or a fad, because she never did grasp the importance of seeing things through, least of all parenting her only child. Anna simply would not allow herself to be that person. Whatever stupid feelings might suddenly be manifesting themselves now, they had to be repressed and stamped out at once, because Anna would not let this happen to her now, at this point in her life when almost everything was just as she had planned it to be, her careful, vital life plan, that was all that stood between her and the world of chaos that she had escaped.

It was Tom she loved, Tom she wanted, Tom she would marry. She knew that when she had got on the plane to New York, and she was certain that as soon as she was out of this heady city, as potent as a field full of poppies, then everything would fall back into place. Stealing herself, she went back to her fiancé and put her arms around him.

'It's just . . . they're all downstairs, and I bet they're waiting for us. It feels weird that we are up here, as if they would know if we were . . . you know.'

'You want to wait for a better moment.' Tom nodded understandingly. 'Yes, you're right. It would be kind of wrong to abandon Liv with two virtual strangers, after everything she's done. And I'm pretty sure if I leave her around that Miles for too long he'll try to seduce her too.'

'Oh Miles is all wrong for Liv,' Anna said with determined casualness, as she let go of Tom and walked towards the bedroom. 'The last thing she needs is to fall for a man who's about to go off around the world and make a career of having women throw themselves at him.'

'Really?' Tom said with a touch of jealousy.

'Yes, that was why Miles was here, for his chance at a big break, and he got it too. A whole new life is about to start for him.' Anna paused, realising that there were not very many more hours left until the last minute that would tick away to the moment where she would never see Miles again. And just then, standing in her ripped dress in a suite in the Algonquin, it made her feel excruciatingly sad. 'Anyway, let me get changed and let's go down and join them. After all Charisma is still your wife.'

'Anna, I thought . . .'

'We are fine,' Anna told him. 'Honestly, everything is fine. I'm joking!'

Anna was very clear about what she had to do next.

'We get the papers back,' she said to Tom. 'We watch as Charisma signs them and we get the first flight back home. The sooner we are back where we belong in the real world the better.'

As Tom waited in the other room for her to find another dress, Anna slipped off her ruined frock and hugged it against her chest for a moment as she took several deep breaths. A few more hours and she would be safe again, her carefully ordered life would be back on track and Miles would be miles and miles away, out of her life for ever. All she had to do was to get through the next twenty-four hours and it would be as if Charisma or Miles had never happened. She would leave them both – and any residual feeling she had for Miles – behind as she and Tom headed home.

Chapter Fifteen

'Silent night, holy night, All is calm, all is bright!'

Distracted by her attempt to glue on her first ever set of lash extensions, Anna paused and looked over her shoulder to where Charisma Jones was lying on her bed, having consumed most of a bottle of pink cava, in readiness for Anna's belated hen night. It still came as a shock to Anna that Charisma had not disappeared from her life as neatly as she'd predicted, but then she did only have herself to blame for Charisma's presence.

'Why are you here again?' Anna asked her, shaking her head. It had been three days since they had arrived back from New York en masse, three days since Anna had said goodbye to Miles and somehow acquired herself a former wife as a wannabe bridesmaid.

'Because *you* invited me,' Charisma said, sprawling herself all over Anna's lovely cream quilt like she was on a *Playboy* shoot. 'Because once you had my signature on your papers you flung your arms around my neck, said, thank you so much, Charisma, you've been amazing, I know, why don't you come to the wedding?'

'Yes, but I didn't actually mean it,' Anna said. 'I was

merely being polite. I thought you were far too busy being a sexually confused nun to pay a fortune for the last flight out of New York before Christmas and come and move in with me.'

'Pah, that pile of crap was never going to make me famous,' Charisma said cheerfully, opening Anna's bedside drawer and peering inside. 'Funny, I felt sure this would be where you kept your vibrator. Anyway, when you offered, I decided it must be fate. London, this is where it's at – the West End, Lloyd Webber, *Les Miserables* bastards! I want me some cool Britannia.' Charisma pushed herself up on her elbows, tipping her head on one side to regard Anna's futile attempts to wear fake lashes, one of them now glued rather securely to her cheek. 'You know what, it's a shame I signed those papers. I'd have found it much easier to get work if I was married to a Brit. Maybe it's not too late to recind . . .'

Anna picked up her tinsel halo headband provided courtesy of Liv and threw it vaguely in the direction of Charisma, who, giggling, hung over the far side of the bed to scoop it up off the floor, revealing her bare behind.

'Can I just say,' Anna said, 'that before we go out that door you are putting on panties. This is England, we do things properly here. In underwear, mostly.'

'All right, guv'nor, keep your drawers on,' Charisma said in the terrible cockney accent that she had insisted on using with almost everyone she had encountered since she had moved herself into Anna and Liv's flat. 'Apples and pears. Chim-chimmeny, what a palaver!'

Anna couldn't help laughing. If there was one thing she could say about her unexpected house guest it was that she was very entertaining. And although it was true that Anna had impulsively invited Charisma to the wedding, there were mitigating circumstances.

The morning after Tom and Liv arrived in New York, Anna had woken up early in bed with two other girls – Liv and Charisma. Liv had taken the middle spot in the king-size bed, to prevent any more brawling, and Anna could tell by looking at her best friend that she was only pretending to be asleep, which meant she didn't want to talk. They still hadn't talked properly since Liv had arrived, and Anna knew she was cross with her, although she wasn't entirely sure why. So, deciding that she had enough on her plate to deal with and desperate for a breath of fresh air and some strong coffee, Anna had pulled on a pair of cream leggings, a deep-green sweater dress, grabbed her coat and, after stopping to stick a note on the suite door explaining where she was, crept out of the room and made her way down to the lobby and out into the bright, freezing morning.

The snow had stopped falling sometime in the night, which had to be good news when it came to booking a flight home, and the sky was a vivid blue, domed above the looming tops of the skyscrapers, like a bell ready to ring out for Christmas. Shuddering against the cold and wrapping her scarf around her neck, Anna headed for a coffee shop across the street that she and Miles had passed a few times since they had arrived. It didn't take long for her to notice as she stood in the queue that Miles was already present, sitting in the furthest corner of a booth, picking a paper napkin to pieces. Just the sight of the back of his head was enough to send her heart thundering away and for a moment Anna considered pretending that she hadn't seen him, turning around and going in the opposite direction, but then she told herself it was foolish. Her crush on Miles had to be faced and sent packing. There was no real reason to hide from him, no real reason at all. And after all, this was her chance to say goodbye.

'Hello,' she said, a little tentatively as she approached him. 'Mind if I join you?'

He looked so sad, even when he smiled and nodded, that Anna thought at once that something must have happened.

'What is it?' she asked him, concerned. 'The band haven't changed their mind about you, have they?'

'No, no not at all, they're very keen. I'm just . . .' He ripped open a tube of sugar and poured it into his coffee, then discarded the wrapper with at least four more that he'd already opened. 'Oh, you know how it is when you finally think that you've got everything you ever wanted and then you find out there's something else you want even more?'

He looked up at her on the last word, and the look in his eyes took Anna's breath away.

'You mean that your new career as a world famous rock star isn't enough?' she asked him in a very small voice, terrified but desperate to know what he was going to say.

'I don't think anything will ever be enough if I don't have you,' Miles said.

Anna gasped in a breath. Did he really just say that? Did he mean it, or was it just another symptom of their little snow globe Christmas fantasy where nothing was quite real and everything was edged in glitter?

'Pardon?' Anna managed to say, just about.

Miles smiled wanly. 'Oh ignore me. It's because I'm artistic – we artistic types are never happy. Still, I will be able to write some great songs about how I came to New York for a career and met an incredible girl who was about to get married to someone else. I can see a life of doom-laden miserable music ahead of me, just what NYRD fans love.'

'That's funny,' Anna said carefully, 'one of the things I always liked about you was your cheerfulness, even when you'd almost killed me with a kiwi you were remarkably chipper.'

The two of them smiled at each other, challenging

the other one to hold their gaze.

'There are a lot of people in our hotel suite, aren't there?' Miles said. 'It feels sort of . . . wrong. I suppose I got used to our own little snow globe, and then along comes Tom and Charisma – and your mad mate – and they shake it all up.'

'You think of us in a snow globe too?' Anna asked, sensing something dangerous building in the air between them, like the promise of a storm just before the thunder rumbles.

'Anna, I've got to say it,' Miles said.

'Don't, please.' Anna was suddenly scared. 'I don't want you to say anything.'

'But I have to,' Miles said. 'I know it won't end well, not for me, anyway, but I can't let you go without saying what we both know is true . . .'

'You could you know, it would be absolutely fine.' Anna looked away from him, towards the door, expecting Tom to come through it any moment, having found her note and decided to go and join his fiancée for a coffee, not expecting for one moment that she would be engaged in a secret tryst.

'Something's happened between us, Anna,' Miles said, sliding his hand across the table so that just the very tips of his fingers were touching the very tips of hers. And even that slightest of contacts made Anna close her eyes and catch her breath. 'Look at me, please.'

With some force of will, Anna opened her eyes and

looked into Miles's, terrified and enraptured by the naked desire that she saw there, a desire she knew was clearly visible in her own.

'When I'm anywhere near you,' Miles told her, his voice low and urgent, 'I long to touch you, to wind my fingers in your hair, to kiss you, to hold you close enough to be able to feel the beating of your heart against my chest. But it's not just your incredible beauty and your amazing body that make me feel that way about you, Anna, and I have *never* felt this way about anyone. It's what's inside, behind the hair and the outfits, the girl who hides behind all the certainty and plans. You let me see a little glimpse of the real you, and in that second I knew you were the girl for me. What you don't seem to realise is that nothing frightens you, Anna, you who've had so many reasons to be afraid, that's what made me fall for you.'

'Everything frightens me,' Anna said, her voice barely above a whisper. 'You sitting here, saying these things to me frightens me, more than I can say.'

'But you want me to say them, don't you?' Miles asked her. 'I can see it in your eyes – you have feelings for me too.'

'Miles,' Anna breathed. 'I'm getting married . . . I can't just . . .'

'I know, I know,' Miles said. 'And I'm not trying to stop you, I'm not. But if I let you go to your wedding without telling you how amazing you are, how much better and more special than you think or know you are, then . . . I could never forgive myself for not letting you know how very much I want you, Anna, how very much I long for you. I just had to say it. I don't expect you to run into my arms. I just hope you know that you deserve to be happy and I really hope you are with Tom. Although it's hard to accept that any other man could make you feel as happy as I know I could.'

Anna looked at their hands, grazing each other on the tabletop, and thought of her mother, closing the front door quietly so that she wouldn't wake Anna up when she walked out on all the promises she'd made her. A pair of beautiful blue eyes and a touch that set her alight was not reason enough to turn her back on Tom.

'I'm getting married, and you are going round the world,' she said.

'I know,' Miles said. 'And I know I can't ask anything from you, or kiss you goodbye but . . .' Miles leaned across the table, a little closer to her, his eyes so magnetic that Anna found herself mirroring him, as the tips of his fingers ever so lightly ran the length of hers. 'But if I could kiss you, Anna, then I would trace the outline of your beautiful mouth with my fingertips. I'd hold your waist, fitting my hand into the curve of your hips, and I'd pull you close against me so you could feel exactly how much I am burning for you. I'd put my lips against yours, so soft and warm, and, once we started kissing, I know I wouldn't be able to stop, that if I kissed you for a million years, it still would not be enough. If I could kiss you goodbye, Anna, it would be the kind of kiss that you would never be able to walk away from and neither would I.'

Abruptly, Anna drew her fingers away from his, breaking the hypnotic connection that buzzed in the air between them.

'Miles,' she repeated, trying desperately not to picture what he'd described, not to feel his lips on her skin, his hands in her hair. 'I'm getting married in a few days. I've been planning getting married on Christmas Eve since I was nine years old and it's happening, despite everything that has been thrown at me, it's happening. And the man I'm marrying, he is a good man. The only man who's ever been able to put up with the mess that I am. And I can't . . . even if I do feel . . . *things* around you – strong, strong *things*, I can't be the sort of person who would throw away everything I've got with Tom for . . . what? We know nothing about each other, not really.'

'I'm not asking you to leave Tom for me,' Miles said, so bluntly that it caught Anna off guard. 'I wouldn't do that to you, Anna. I know that you need certainty and nothing could be less uncertain than what might happen next between us. I'd never ask you to risk all of that for me.'

'Oh,' Anna said. 'So you are not asking me to leave

Tom for you, then? Just to be clear? It's just that . . . well then, why all this talk of kissing?'

'I needed you to know how much you moved me,' Miles said. 'How much you mean to me, right in this moment, and that I don't think any man has to "put up with" you because any man would be lucky to have you in his life. And if you weren't about to get married then you bet your life I'd be asking you to run away with me. But even though I'll be thinking about you for a long time, Anna Carter, I would never try to break you and Tom up now.'

Anna had pushed her coffee away untouched, as it dawned on her that what Miles was really saying was, in an exceptionally erudite way, that he quite fancied her and if she'd been free he'd have given her a spin, seen how it worked out. Feeling foolish and hurt, tears suddenly prickling at her eyes, she stood up abruptly.

'Right, well, thank you,' she said. 'Thanks for letting me know. I'd better get back now, go and see my fiancé.'

'You don't get it do you?' Miles asked her, rising out of his seat as she left. 'Is it that you *want* me to steal you from Tom, is that what you want?'

'No,' she said, turning back to look at him. 'No, that's not what I want. All I want is to get married on Christmas Eve just like I always have since I was a little girl. Thank you for everything, Miles. I truly do hope you have a nice life.'

It was only when she arrived back at the hotel after

that last meeting with Miles that she'd discovered that Tom had taken a cab to the bar they'd been at the night before and recovered the annulment papers. As a result, she returned to the suite to find that Charisma had signed the papers without any drama at all. It felt like fate telling her what she should do and she had been so relieved to have that one decision taken out of her hands that she had invited Charisma to the wedding on an impulse, and incredibly Charisma had accepted.

'Round yon Virgin . . .' Charisma gestured at Anna as she uncrossed and re-crossed her legs *Basic Instinct*-style. 'Who should lighten up . . .'

'Cab's here!' Liv popped her head round the door, resplendent in a little Christmas fairy outfit, her face and hair covered in glitter, a pair of net wings bouncing chirpily on her shoulder blades.

Since they had gotten back, plus one, Liv had gotten into the swing of making the last-minute arrangements for the wedding and the catering, deciding to sort out a hen night, which Anna didn't even especially want, stating that some of them needed a party whether she liked it or not, and no the wedding did not count as a party. It was Liv who embraced Charisma's presence first, inviting her to stay in their flat with what Anna thought was almost relief, as it meant the two of them would not have to be alone in the run-up to the wedding. And as it turned out, Liv and Charisma got on surprisingly well, the former showgirl slash wife making Liv laugh almost as much as Anna did, to the point where Anna felt a little bit left out. It was to be expected though, Anna told herself. Soon she would be married to Tom and living in his flat and Liv did need to move on to a certain extent; a new friend was a good thing, even if it was Tom's ex and even if it meant things between them were not quite the same as they had been before Anna had run away to New York. Anna just wished she could work out exactly what it was that she had done to put this small but clear distance between her and Liv, sometime before the wedding.

'Where are your wings, Anna?' Liv asked her impatiently as the taxi driver beeped his horn again. 'You know we're sexy Christmas fairies, you have to put your L-plate wings on, and your flipping halo, it took me ages to glue on all that tinsel.'

'What if I don't want L-plate wings and a halo,' Anna protested, slipping on the offending articles reluctantly. 'A fancy dress hen night was not in my plan, Liv, you know that.'

' Well,' Liv said, putting her hands on her waist, 'believe it or not, the world does not revolve around you. You have friends, amazingly more than just the people in this room, and whether you like it or not they want to send you off to your wedding in style. So you are having a Christmas-themed hen night – to go with your Christmas-themed wedding – whether you like it or not.'

And that was how had it been since the moment they had gotten back. Liv didn't seem angry with her exactly, but neither was she her usual fun, sweet, easy-going self. There hadn't been the right moment to talk about what had really happened in New York. There had been last-minute wedding errands. There had been Charisma as a house guest. And so Anna couldn't tell Liv about her near miss and mixed emotions over Miles. And curiously Liv didn't ask. She seemed wrapped up in her own problems and equally intent on not discussing those with Anna either. And without that crucial private moment, almost everything Liv said came with a barbed comment and a distinct air of reproach. And as for Anna, all she had been doing was focusing on her life plan, her lists, her flip charts, her files, blocking out the kiss she never actually shared with Miles, the invitation to run away with him that he had never actually issued, and the more she tried the better she got at accepting the fact that marrying Tom was what she was meant to do – what she wanted to do.

She hoped that perhaps tonight – somewhere amongst the karaoke, crackers and Christmas stocking tops – there would be a chance to get things between her and Liv back on an even keel, to iron out the little niggles that remained, because nothing felt right when she and Liv weren't completely as one.

'Go on now go!' Liv was singing at the top of her voice, standing on a table at Rowan's Bowling Alley in Bloomsbury, a curiously unexpected venue in such a normally sedate and serious part of London. Karaoke blasted out side by side with the bowling and a seriously retro disco, and reams of stags and hens danced their last nights of freedom away to Abba. Liv was currently belting out Gloria Gaynor as if every single syllable meant the world to her. They were several hours into the night, the girls from work had taken it upon themselves to sing Queen's greatest hits one by one, Angela had done Tom Jones's 'Sex Bomb', much to the hilarity and embarrassment of her daughters. So far the only two people not to sing were Charisma, who was wearing the skimpiest Christmas fairy outfit, so tiny that it barely constituted a bikini, and Anna herself, who was watching Liv's passionate reinterpretation of 'I Will Survive' with some alarm.

'Anyone would think she'd just been dumped,' Anna said.

'Must be her time of the month,' Angela said. 'We've always been martyrs to her PMT, yours too, and when the pair of you synchronised, well let's just say it was a minefield. And it cost me a fortune in chocolate, Nurofen and feminine hygiene products.'

Angela put her arm around Anna and hugged her. 'Are you OK, my love? You look a little bit . . . not quite yourself.'

'I'm fine, Angela, honestly,' Anna reassured her.

Anna had wondered about how wise it was to bring her foster mother on the hen night, particularly because no one aggravated Liv more than her mother, but Angela had assumed that she was invited and no one had the heart to tell her otherwise. And besides, Anna liked having her there. Although Liv had opened the door, it was Angela who had made a strange little girl so welcome in her family. Anna had never been exactly sure how to say thank you for a gift of such magnitude, and so she'd never really said anything. Having Angela along on her hen night was a small gesture towards acknowledging that she was the nearest thing to a true mother that she had ever known.

'She's never usually this snippy,' Angela continued cheerfully. 'It's sexual frustration probably. I don't know when she last had sex. Perhaps I should get her a male prostitute for Christmas. Or a female one. Which one do you think she'd prefer?'

'I think that's probably not quite what she needs to cheer her up,' Anna said, as Liv – whose singing was almost as bad as hers – forced the girls standing closer to her to press their hands over their ears and cringe at the same time as they laughed.

'She's in love, that's her problem,' Charisma said, dropping into the conversation uninvited, while flirting shamelessly with a group of men in Santa hats a few tables down. She perched on the edge of the sofa, next to Angela. 'Unrequited love, there's nothing worse for putting you in a bad mood.'

'Oh no, it's not that, dear,' Angela said. 'If Liv had met a boy she'd have said. She tells me everything, you know. Me and my girls, we are more like sisters really, aren't we, Anna?'

'Um . . .' Anna grinned, kissing Angela on the cheek. 'Yes.'

'Now, tell me,' Angela asked Charisma, staring pointedly at her breasts, 'how do you to get that material to stick to your boobs, is it tit tape? I've often wondered where you get tit tape. I think I'd like some. I imagine it can come in awfully handy.'

'I use a roll-on glue,' Charisma told her sweetly, dipping into her purse and producing a tube. 'Here, have it, I have tons of the stuff. And yes, Liv is in love, the poor sweetheart. She's got it real bad, about as bad as I've ever seen it, poor, poor girl.'

'Liv is most certainly not in love,' Anna objected. 'You've been her friend for five minutes, I've known her most of my life and, trust me, if Liv was in love then *I* would know about it. I would be the *first* to know about it. Most likely I'd know about it even before she did, because we are *that close*.' Anna crossed her fingers and waved them in Charisma's face to illustrate her point.

'Really?' Charisma's grin was so knowing that it would have given Alice's Cheshire Cat a run for its money in terms of smugness.

'You know the only reason she likes you is because you lent her your stripper shoes and they make her feel tall,' Anna said.

'All of my shoes are stripper shoes,' Charisma replied. 'And the reason you don't know about Miss Olivia's broken heart, my dearest sister wife, is that she is far too good a friend to ever let you know that she's secretly in love with the man you are about to marry!'

When Charisma sang, she drew quite a crowd, which was nothing to be surprised about; after all she was a trained performer and practically naked. The moment she dropped her inflammatory little observation into the conversation coincided exactly with Liv taking a drunken bow, falling to her knees and literally shouting the last few words in the manner of someone who perhaps should be taking a break in the sort of institution where you might also get unlimited medication.

'My turn.' Charisma beamed, taking the mic off Liv as she stormed back to where Anna and Angela were sitting.

'Oh you poor darling,' Angela said, engulfing her confused daughter in a hug. 'I don't know how I didn't see it, it all makes sense now, and there you've been carrying this burden alone for so long. So tell us, how long have you—'

'Been hiding your light under a bushel,' Anna cut over her foster mother before Liv realised exactly what Angela was trying to say. 'Wow, Liv, you were brilliant.'

'No, I wasn't brilliant, I was drunk,' Liv said, turning back to the stage where Charisma was doing everything short of taking her top off, keeping a room full of men in her thrall. 'Look at her, this must be the only hen do in London where the stripper is also a bridesmaid.'

'She is not a bridesmaid,' Anna said. 'I don't care how delusional she is, if she has to be there at all, she can stay at the back, shackled to the font. Although she'd probably like that.'

'I think she is terribly refreshing,' Angela said, kissing Liv on the temple and hugging her again. 'And she was the only one to spot your little secret, you poor dear lamb.'

'Mother for the very last time,' Liv said, downing a random drink from the collection that had accumulated on the table in one go, 'I AM NOT GAY!'

Liv's outburst happened to coincide exactly with a moment of complete silence that just for a second engulfed the club, as some ancient pieces of wiring failed briefly before kicking back in.

'Oh no, dear, no, not *that* secret,' Angela said. 'The secret about you being in love with Tom, you poor darling, you should have told me. Anna would have understood and I could have helped you get through it. Of course, Charisma hit the nail on the head, now everything makes sense, your sulking, the weight gain . . .'

As Liv stormed towards the toilets, Anna raced after her as best as she could in her crystal-encrusted high heels. As she charged through the crowd, she saw Liv rush straight past the ladies' and through the fire exit into the freezing night.

'Liv,' Anna said, propping the fire door open with a box of toilet rolls that were languishing in the corridor. 'Don't let your mum get to you, you know what she's like. She doesn't mean any harm. And anyway it's not her fault, it was Charisma who said you had a thing for Tom. That woman can't resist stirring up trouble. Come on, Liv, please, tell me what's really up, so that I can say sorry, or change, or do whatever it takes to make you happy again.'

'That's impossible,' Liv said so quietly that Anna wasn't sure she heard her right.

'Pardon?' She tilted her head to one side.

'I do have "feelings" for Tom,' Liv said, sitting down on the frosty step with scant regard for her bare upper thighs. 'I liked him from the first moment I met him and, for a little while, I think he sort of liked me back.

And then . . . then he met you. And I thought it would stop – the me having feelings for him part, not the him loving you bit, but it didn't. And then you got engaged and I tried to get rid of the feelings, but they just wouldn't go away.'

'No,' Anna said. 'Sometimes secret feelings do have a terrible habit of hanging about.'

'But I was doing OK, I was coping. And then the secret wife came out and you . . . you ran away to New York and left me to pick up the pieces. You left me on my own with Tom when he really needed me. And that made the feelings a lot worse, and now they're almost impossible to live with.'

Anna didn't know what to say or how to react so she did neither, and simply stood in the doorway, the heat and noise of the club at her back, the chill and damp of 22 December nibbling at her fingers and the tips of her ears.

'It's like Regina Clarkson all over again,' Liv said at last.

'It's nothing like Regina Clarkson,' Anna said. 'How is this like Regina Clarkson? Regina Clarkson was a bitch. And you are not a bitch.'

Liv looked up at Anna. 'I'm not Regina Clarkson in this scenario.'

'You're saying that I am a Regina Clarkson? For what? For not knowing that you have a crush on the man I'm planning to marry?' Anna spluttered, bewildered. 'Is this why you've been so pissed off with me since New York, because I found Charisma, because I got my wedding back on track and Tom and I are still getting married? What, does that mean you don't have enough time to steal my boyfriend? If anybody is Regina Clarkson in this scenario, Liv, it's you.'

Liv said nothing as she sat shuddering on the step.

Looking over her shoulder, Anna discovered a large mouldering coat hanging on a hook outside the gents', and though she suspected it of having a past that involved some sort of flashing, gingerly took it off the hook. Checking it for insalubrious stains and signs of animal infestation, she took it outside and draped it round Liv's shoulders. As she huddled next to her on the step, the fire door slowly nudged the box of toilet paper out of its path, clicking shut and locking them both out.

'You aren't really Regina Clarkson,' Anna said. 'Regina Clarkson was the meanest, cruellest nasty girl ever to stalk the corridors of any school ever and it's her fault I got suspended for three weeks and nearly put back into care. Although with this coat on you do smell like her.' She was gratified to see the curve of Liv's cheek show the hint of a smile.

'Although everything you've said is technically true, on that one occasion it wasn't her fault, and anyway Regina Clarkson didn't smell,' Liv said. 'Well, except for Impulse and the enormous amount of hairspray it took to keep her flick in place. God, how I envied that flick, even when she was extorting our dinner money I used to admire that flick. You know full well that she was the prettiest girl in the school. Except for you, which is mainly why she hated you. And me because I didn't hate you.'

'Yes, but I didn't count because I was also the poorest girl in the school,' Anna said. 'Even after I starting living with you and had a clean uniform every day and proper shoes, everyone called me a skank or a gyppo.'

'Not everyone, just the girls who were jealous . . . well, just Regina Clarkson really. And her friends. They were scared not to do what she told them to. Remember how she flushed Wendy Aylett's head down the loo because she wouldn't give up her shoes. I mean her actual shoes off her feet.'

'It wasn't one of my finer moments though,' Anna said. 'Going ballistic and attacking her with a pair of scissors.'

'No, it was a little bit psycho of you,' Liv said. 'Even if you did think that Regina Clarkson told Gregory Peters that you had an STD.'

'He was my first love!' Anna said.

'He was a prick!' Liv reminded her. 'He was only interested in you because of your boobs.'

'I know, I knew that then, really, but it didn't matter. You are the only person who can know what it meant to me, the skanky ex-care home kid, to get asked out by one of the hottest boys in school. That one lunchtime when he held my hand and kept trying to get me to go round the back of the boiler house with him and let him put his hand up my top, that was the proudest moment of my school career.'

'What, more than your seventy-eight GCSEs?' Liv asked her, sceptically.

'Yes, because for that one lunchtime, I'd made it. I was utterly normal.'

'And then you went crazy with a pair of scissors,' Liv mused. 'Even I was scared of you.'

'Because by afternoon break someone had told him I had an STD!' Anna protested.

'Yes, but not Regina Clarkson.'

'No,' Anna admitted. 'Not Regina Clarkson.'

'Even though it was her you grabbed by the ponytail, dragged over the back of her chair and hacked off her lovely locks in one.'

'Really, craft scissors shouldn't be that sharp,' Anna said.

That had been the first time – and the last – that Anna had ever really lost control. Told by her boyfriend of five hours the reason why he was dumping her, something in her, that part of her that usually kept her head down, never complained, never spoke out of turn, never tried to be special or different, so that she could fit in with everyone else suddenly snapped. All at once she was filled with a rage that she had never experienced before. Perhaps it was all the anger she'd ever felt – anger towards her mother for leaving her, anger at her father for never even knowing her; anger that she was a part, but not really a part, of a family that loved and took care of each other in a way that she had only ever dreamed of – finally erupting out of her in a volcano of rage. But before she knew what she was doing she'd pretty much scalped Regina Clarkson in the art room.

'In my defence I was really, really . . . I don't know. I was hurt, I was so, so hurt.'

'Regina Clarkson was hysterical,' Liv said.

'It's not surprising really,' Anna said, with some remorse. 'I mean before, at the beginning, she probably did hate me unfairly. But after I went nuclear on her arse and cut off her ponytail and she had to go to the hairdresser's and have a pixie cut which made her look like a troll . . . then she probably did have reason to hate me.'

'But it wasn't Regina Clarkson's fault, was it,' Liv said, turning to look at Anna. 'Gillie Lampter told Gregory Peters you had an STD,' Liv reminded her. 'In actual fact Regina Clarkson was completely innocent of the downfall of your love affair. Regina Clarkson was in band practice for the whole of that afternoon.'

'I scared myself that day,' Anna said thoughtfully. 'It made me think that I didn't really know myself. How can I know what I inherited from the man that fathered me, what kind of a man he was, except that there was a good chance he wasn't a very nice one? And as for my mum, well, one minute she'd be the sweetest most loving woman, and the next she'd be cold, angry, desperate, depressed. It was like this stranger burst out of me, this angry, confused, impulsive stranger, and I was so frightened that she was the real me, the me my parents made. I nearly got put back in care, I nearly got taken away from you and Angela, the whole family, because of one stupid angry rash moment. That day changed everything. That was the day I started making lists. I vowed never to lose control of even the tiniest detail of my life again.'

For one second an image, or more of a feeling, of how the tips of Miles's fingers touching hers felt flashed across Anna's memory with a heart-wrenching jolt, and then it was gone again.

'You're not really Regina Clarkson,' Liv said, nudging Anna with her shoulder. 'Mainly because I caught up with her on Facebook a while back, and she lives with thirteen cats and a woman called Hilda in Milton Keynes. I should tell Mum, she'd be so pleased that I know a lesbian. But also because even if she wasn't guilty of breaking you up with Gregory Peters, she was a bitch. You are many things, Anna, but you are not a bitch. And that girl with the scissors, that wasn't you either. Not the real you. That was the part of you that had been dumped and hurt. That part of you needed to cut off someone's ponytail. Thank God they didn't have the power drills out in art that week.'

There was a moment of silence between them as they listened to the sound of traffic rushing by, of drunken revellers singing 'Last Christmas' somewhere in the distance and the dull thud, thud, thud of the disco on the other side of the fire door.

'Liv,' Anna said, preparing herself, 'are you really in love with Tom?'

'Not really,' Liv said. 'Not in a "never going to get over it" sort of way. I know he loves you and that you're meant to be together. I'm sure that in about ten or twenty years I'll be totally fine.'

'Oh Liv.' Anna held Liv close to her, her own confused feelings about Tom now thrown once more into disarray. She knew this was her moment to tell Liv about Miles but for some reason she couldn't. Liv had enough to deal with. Nothing was how it was supposed to be, nothing was certain. She had no idea what to do about it for the best.

'Look, I know I'm making a mountain out of a molehill,' Liv said, turning back to Anna. 'It's shameless attention-seeking on my part. Just ignore me.'

'If you tell me to, I won't marry him,' Anna said quite seriously, half wishing her friend would make the decision for her. 'I wouldn't ever do anything that would hurt you – you're my best friend.'

'Don't be ridiculous,' Liv said, brushing the offer off

with a flick of her hand. 'You flew across the Atlantic to save your wedding, you are certainly not going to give up because I'm having a bit of sulk.'

'But, Liv, I—'

'I suppose the thing is,' Liv cut across her, 'being your best friend can be a bit of a full-time job. Maybe it's because your life is so much more interesting than mine, but what it boils down to is that I'm jealous, Anna. I'm jealous of you, and of the life you are going to have, the life I haven't found . . . yet.'

'*You're* jealous of *me*! Don't be mental,' Anna said. She shuddered and, considering it safe, took one edge of the enormous coat and draped it over her shoulder so that the pair of them sat underneath it, like particularly glittery twin hobos. 'Me, the girl who can't get out of bed without making a list, the girl who pairs tights just to be on the safe side, the girl who can't function unless every single thing goes according to plan. I look at you, and you are so strong and certain and free, and I would give anything to be a tenth of the woman you are, I really would.' Anna thought for a long moment and repeated her offer. 'Anything you asked me now, I would do it for you.'

Liv looked at the firmly shut fire exit. 'Get me back inside so I can thaw out my arse?' she asked, at which point the door slammed open, and Charisma stood there.

'That's where you got to! Come on, Anna, your song

is up! It's "You're So Vain". I tried to find one called "I Have an Enormous Backside", which would have been so perfect for you, but it hasn't been written yet.'

Anna helped Liv to her feet and held her hand as she hopped over the icy paving slabs and back into the welcome heat of the club. But before she could follow Charisma back into the full onslaught of the din and laughter, Anna stopped Liv.

'I'm not really sure what just happened,' Anna said. 'But I do need to know, Liv, are you going to be OK?'

'Do you love Tom?' Liv asked her, her dark eyes searching Anna's.

Anna thought for a moment, back to that brief conversation with Miles, their almost kiss. Every second she had shared in New York with Miles was burned in her memory, but they were also shrouded with confusion and ambiguity, and at no point had he ever said 'I have fallen in love with you, Anna, please run away with me.' Which was not reason enough to marry Tom, but it was reason enough for Anna to consider very seriously whether or not she did truly love him, and then she'd finally come to a conclusion: the answer was yes. Tom was a very decent man, in a world where men like him were hard to come by. He was gentle and steadfast and loyal and, yes, Anna did love him very much.

'I do,' Anna said.

'Well, then, that is enough for me. Now, come on.

Let's get back to the party and see if we can get to Mum before she starts singing "When I Think About You I Touch Myself".'

But they were already too late.

Chapter Sixteen

Anna had been up since five, at the window of her hotel suite, looking out into the cold night, waiting for the sun to come up, waiting for her wedding day to begin.

The manor house was old and creaky, and a little cold. As she sat at the diamond-paned glass, her breath misting its surface, she watched and waited. Christmas Eve was here and even this early in the morning, with the sky outside still densely black, that special gloss of magic that this one special day gilded everything with was already in the air. That sense of expectation, that childish optimistic hope that this would be the start of something magical, the last day of hoping and wishing before at last every dream you ever had finally came true. For most, Christmas Day was the real day of magic, but for Anna it had always been the night before. The night before Christmas was when you could imagine for just a little longer that everything would be perfect.

It was just as the sun began to rise, sending its molten glow across the frost-encrusted grounds, burnishing everything in its path with copper, that it began to snow. It was just a few flakes at first, but before the sun could rise above the horizon, thick, heavily laden clouds blotted it out, as the snow began to fall in earnest. It was snowing on Christmas Eve, snowing on her wedding day. With her dress hanging on the wardrobe door behind her, her sleigh with reindeer on the way from the zoo, everything was perfect, just exactly as she had always wanted it, and yet . . . Anna didn't feel the way she had always expected to.

That last Christmas Eve, the last one with her mother, Anna had felt it then, the magic. They had brushed each other's hair, and her mum had sung her songs, pop songs that she liked from the radio. It was the one time she could remember music in her childhood before she went to live with Liv. She remembered then how her mum had gotten up and danced round and sang into their hairbrush, making Anna laugh so much that she couldn't breathe. And they had talked about all the things that Anna would do when she was a grown-up, and how her life was going to be special, because she was Mummy's special little girl and Mummy loved her so very much.

Anna knew that those two special days her mother had given her on the last Christmas they'd spent together were meant to be her real present, her parting gift. Two days in which Anna could taste the kind of childhood that she should have known. She was sure that her mother had meant that time to be something that Anna would look back on fondly, gratefully. And yet it had been those two perfect days that had haunted Anna ever since, knowing how fragile, how temporary that perfection and sense of order was. But also always leaving her wondering right into adulthood if there had been anything she could have done or said that would have made her mother choose her – choose to stay – instead of . . . oblivion. And today, this perfect day, with every single detail pinned down with absolute precision, including the weather, was meant to be the day she finally said goodbye to all the fear and anxiety her mother had left in her wake, the day she got to say at last, 'Look at me, Mum. I did this all by myself, in spite of the crappy childhood you gave me. I don't need you any more.'

Anna had expected to feel happy, excited and nervous. Perhaps fluttery, cross, stressed and demanding, but mainly happy. And yet as she sat there, waiting for the world to wake up to her pre-ordered winter wonderland, all she felt was flat. Flat and empty, like the pristine whitewashed world outside the window, a blank page.

A quiet knock at the door made her jump, and when Anna opened it she found Angela in her dressing gown, her handbag slung over one shoulder, outside the door.

'Hello, darling,' she said, engulfing Anna in a hug. 'I know it's early, but I knew you'd be up so I thought

I'd pop in before all your "posse" got here and have a quiet word.'

'A word?' Anna said, confused, even though she was pleased to see Angela, who, having swathed her in a red silk robe, went straight to the kettle on the dressing table and put it on.

'Well, yes, it's your wedding day and well, I know I've never said it, and you've never called me it, after all those years of fostering you, but I hope you know I think of you as a daughter. And maybe you think of me – well at least a little bit – as your mum?'

'You've always been so kind to me,' Anna said. 'And I've always been so grateful.'

'You don't have to be grateful, you silly girl,' Angela said. 'I love you, since that first Christmas when you came to stay with us, and you bought me that little plastic compact mirror, more of a toy than a real thing, but you'd spent what little money you had on it and wrapped it up and gave it to me. And I thought if after everything she's been through she can still think of other people then . . . well, I fell in love with you that day, you know.' Angela paused. 'I suppose I should have told you more, perhaps asked if you wanted us to adopt you properly, but no matter how I tried you always kept yourself a little bit apart, and I suppose I thought I ought to let you do what you thought best. But not today. Today, you need a mum, and I am it. Here, let me show you something.'

Angela reached into her handbag and produced the little plastic compact, resting in the palm of her hand. Anna smiled at the long-forgotten object, a rush of memories flooding back. How scared she'd been, how uncertain. How she'd wanted to make a good impression on these strangers who were being so inexplicably nice to her.

'It came free off the front of *Jackie* magazine,' Anna confessed. 'It wasn't even my *Jackie* magazine, it was Liv's.'

'Well, never more has the phrase "it's the thought that counts" been more appropriate,' Angela said gently.

Anna nodded, pressing her lips together, determined not to cry.

'Good. Now then,' Angela said, as she slipped an arm around Anna's shoulders, 'you can't have red and puffy eyes on your wedding day, that won't do. So don't cry about it. You're part of this family and whatever happens you always will be, as long as you know that there's nothing to cry about.'

Anna nodded, making herself smile away the tears.

'So, anyway, do you have any questions?'

'Questions?' Anna asked, finding her voice.

'You know, about being a married woman. I know that you young women have done it all these days, full sex, fellatio even, but there are lots of things you encounter *after* marriage that you might not be expecting. Erectile dysfunction, for example, or a sudden interest in BDSM. When Graham began his bondage phase, well, at first I was horrified and then we got a whip off eBay and it was laughs all the way. I said no to swinging though, it's not that I'm against group sex, it's just other lady parts I don't like the idea of.'

'I think I'm fine on the sex front, actually,' Anna said, shocked and awed by Angela's indiscretions, even though she knew she should be used to her foster mother's blunt talk by now. Although, to be honest, since they had returned from New York Anna had barely even seen Tom, let alone had sex with him. It was hardly surprising given that Charisma had moved into her flat, or the many number of things that had to be done in the last few days before the wedding, that Tom hadn't been to the flat to see her, or that she hadn't managed to go to his place. He had stayed at his parents' house last night, and he would be there now, with his mum cooking breakfast, his dogs lying on his feet, hoping for snippets of bacon. That would be her official life too, after today, Anna realised. Family holidays in that house, Sunday roasts with his mum and dad. When they got back from honeymoon she'd go back home to Tom's flat, let her own out to Liv and whoever she chose as her new flatmate and from that moment on everything would be plain sailing.

'Good, now what about the doubts you are having?' Angela got up and poured boiling water onto two sachets of instant coffee. Anna took the cup that was offered to her.

'Doubts?' she laughed. 'What doubts?'

'It's written all over your face, dear,' Angela said. 'I'm not one to pry, it might just be a case of wedding jitters. I had wedding jitters when I got married too. I woke up on the morning of the wedding and I thought, God help me, I'm marrying an utter prick. And I told my mother about it and she said don't be so ridiculous, I've paid for the hall hire, you're getting married. And I did, and after a year or two everything settled down and by the time my darling Simon was born we were in love again. So for me, it really was just jitters, but I vowed to always make sure my children weren't going through the same thing. I asked Simon too, even though it was clear how certain he was, and one day, when it's Liv's turn, I'll ask her the same thing. But for now, I'm asking you. Are you sure you want to marry Tom?'

Anna opened her mouth and then closed it again, turning her face away from Angela for a moment. 'Yes.'

'Look,' Angela said, covering Anna's hand with hers, 'I know you children think I'm borderline nuts.'

'Not borderline.' Anna smiled, causing Angela to lightly tap her on the back of the hand.

'But, I know you. I know you and Simon and Liv better than anyone else on this planet. Don't look at me like that; just because you came to me when you were nine doesn't mean I haven't obsessed about and worried about you just as much as I have my natural born children. Weren't you listening to me when I said that I'm your mum?'

Anna nodded, wishing with all her heart that she could accept once and for all the offer of family love that Angela never tired of making her. What wouldn't she give to look at the kind, caring, loving woman and truly think of her at last as her mother? Yet, even now, even sitting here on her wedding morning, it was the ghostlike memory of her real mother that haunted her. When she was alive nothing meant more to her than feeding her addictions, but even now, years after she had finally succumbed to them, it was her that Anna longed to both impress and escape, as futile as it was to want either.

'Now,' Angela continued, 'something doesn't seem quite right, not any more. Before this whole New York escapade and you found out about that lovely young stripper girl, you were so certain that this was the right thing. You were like a great white shark homing in on its prey, preparing to rip it to shreds, nothing could distract you.' Angela gnashed her teeth ever so slightly to illustrate her point. 'But now, ever since you got back, it's like you are detached from everything. Like someone's gone and fished you out of the sea and popped you in a whopping great tank and now you are just a spectator watching the action sail by and you don't really care if you are part of it or not.'

'You really are brilliant at analogies,' Anna said, as kindly as she could, hoping to deflect the fact that Angela had pretty much hit the nail on the head. She was right, it wasn't that Anna had felt doubts, or fears or even had any negative feelings for Tom since she got back from New York, it was just that she hardly felt anything at all.

'I'm not going to sit here and lecture you,' Angela said, despite it being apparent that that was exactly what she was going to do. 'But I just want to say that it doesn't matter that this wedding cost you a ridiculous amount of money that you wouldn't let us pay anything towards, and it doesn't matter that the dress you had made can only be worn on one day of the year, and is frankly – though gorgeous – very over the top, especially for you. Nor does it matter that your friends and family are risking their lives to get through the snow today to make it to your wedding. None of that matters: if you are not sure about marrying Tom today, then don't do it. All you have to do is let yourself feel what it's like to be happy, and follow that feeling and never ever stop, even if I do have to freeze a ton of canapés for the next year or so.' Angela leaned over. 'Or do it, you never know you might get lucky like me and find out after a few years that it wasn't a terrible mistake at all. There, hope that's helped.'

'It has so helped,' Anna lied, but needing her foster mother to know how much it meant to her that she had come at all. Before Angela could get up to leave Anna flung her arms around her and hugged her very tight, taking not only Angela but also herself by surprise.

'Thank you,' Anna said. 'Thank you for coming here and being bonkers and showing me how much you care, again. I just . . . I want you to know that you caring about me has made the world of difference to my life. It doesn't matter that you never adopted me, it just matters that you have always been there and . . .' Anna hugged Angela once more. 'Finally, I think I understand that, so thank you. Thanks for everything, Angela', she said. 'Thanks for everything, Mum.'

'Just pull it tighter,' Anna said, as Liv and Charisma, who even now was still trying to wrangle herself a job as bridesmaid, pulled at the lacing on her corset.

'It fitted me fine at the fitting,' Liv said, as she heaved one last time on the ribbons. 'Maybe you had too many burgers in New York.'

'Oh my God do you want to die?' Anna exclaimed, over her shoulder. 'If I could move right now, you would totally be dead.'

'Here.' Charisma nudged Liv aside and, sticking her knee in the small of Anna's back, braced herself and yanked so hard that the corset finally closed, and Anna, though possibly turning slightly blue, had exactly the waist that she wanted as Charisma double-tied the bows.

'In the world of burlesque you have to know how to do up a corset,' Charisma said, looking pleased with herself. 'Now, how about you sack that ugly stick insect girl from your wedding party and give me her dress. I know I've got bigger tits than her, but I promise not to upstage you with my incredible cleavage. Well, I don't promise, it's hard to defy such a force of nature.'

'Are you talking about me? You're talking about me, aren't you?' Liv said, laughing and outraged at once.

'No, you are the hot bridesmaid,' Charisma said. 'Or at least you will be until Anna gives me a matching dress, then you will become second hottest bridesmaid, second most likely to get laid. I mean sack the one with the teeth and dead-fish eyes.'

'No,' Anna said. 'I will not sack Tom's cousin Kathryn from the wedding party even if she does look like she recently kissed a prince and turned into a frog. She is *less* pretty than me and the main criteria for bridesmaids is that they are *less* pretty, *not* that they are sluts who can't stop getting their tits out. Or ex-wives!'

'So you're saying that I'm less pretty than you?' Liv pretended to be offended.

As the three women laughed, just for a moment Anna felt the happiness bubbling in her chest and she got the feeling that everything was going to be all right after all. She was going to marry Tom, just as she had dreamed of, and the rest of her life would be one peaceful, beautiful flat horizon, without a single corner or bend in the road for anything unexpected to hide behind.

And then dead-fish-eyed cousin Kathryn put her head round the door, and proved that life never went that way.

'The wedding band bloke is here to see you, something about the set list?' she lisped through her crooked teeth. 'I said Tom was dealing with that, but apparently he needs to talk to you about your song choice. Something to do with Joni Mitchell's "River"?'

Anna stopped smiling. 'Tell him to fuck off,' she said, turning her back on Kathryn. 'Go on, tell him to fuck off and don't come back.'

'That's a bit extreme,' Liv said, as Charisma snorted a laugh of surprise. 'Do you want me to go and see him? Or at least tell him to see Tom. I must say, he's here early, I didn't think the band arrived till five.'

'It's not the band,' Anna snapped. She lowered her voice and hissed in Liv's ear, 'It's Miles.'

'Miles, what's Miles doing here?' Liv forgot to whisper.

'Shit,' Charisma said. 'Miles is here. Now this is what I call a wedding.'

'Who's Miles?' Kathryn asked.

'Just tell him to FUCK OFF,' Anna said.

'If you want to be so rude you can tell him yourself, I'm sending him in.' Kathryn pouted and, before Anna could stop her, she was gone.

'What does Miles want?' Liv asked her. 'Today of all days!'

'I don't know!' Anna exclaimed. 'How the hell would I know?'

'Well, you know enough to want him to fuck off, so what is it you think he's here for? Did something happen between you in New York? Were you lying to me all along, because if you've cheated on Tom . . .?'

'No!' Anna insisted. 'Nothing actually happened. We didn't do anything. All we did was hang out and talk and . . . and . . . he talked about kissing me, about what it would be like and how much he'd like to, but we didn't actually kiss. And then he said he wasn't going to ask me not to marry Tom and he left and that's it, so I don't know why he is here now.'

'Maybe he wants to talk about having sex with you,' Charisma said. 'I wouldn't mind listening to that.'

'And do you have feelings for him?' Liv demanded.

'No!' Anna said. 'No, I don't think so. I know I don't think so. He got me muddled up, but then I came back and I got things straight and I don't want him to muddle me up again, so go out there and do your duty as my bridesmaid and tell him to fuck off!'

Anna whirled round to find Miles in the doorway, dressed in his trademark tatty jeans and boots, a battered leather biker jacket and his windswept hair giving the impression that he'd just arrived on a Harley.

'Miles!' Anna exclaimed, stamping her foot so that

her full skirt rustled and fluffed. 'Why are you here?'

'You look amazing,' Mile said, with a lopsided grin. 'Wow, that is some dress. You look like a really beautiful toilet roll fairy.'

Charisma laughed out loud, and Liv had to cover her mouth. It was only Anna who did not crack a smile.

'Go away!' she told him, pointing at the door. 'Fuck off!'

'No.' He shook his head, coming into the room. 'Look, I was in Texas, *Texas*, when I realised. And I have taken three planes for the last two days, and seriously risked my very new, very dream job to come here and say to you what I should have said to you in New York and didn't. Every day since you left, I've been replaying over and over the things I said, and the things you said and wondering why I couldn't just put it down to experience and move on, and then I got it. And I asked for forty-eight hours off a job I'd barely started and flew pretty much the wrong way round the world to get here, now at this precise moment, to say it right, before it is too late. So if you want me to go, you will have to throw me out.'

Anna looked from Liv to Charisma, who were waiting with bated breath.

'Give us a moment, please,' she said.

'What!' Charisma exclaimed. 'No way!'

'Liv! Please?'

Caught between her loyalty to Anna, and her very

real need to know what the hell was going on, Liv decided she wouldn't find out unless she let Anna say whatever it was she had to say to Miles. She grabbed Charisma's hand and tugged her towards the door.

'Anna,' she said just before she left, 'you have five minutes to get your make-up on before you are due to leave for the church.'

'And that's a forty-minute job to get you looking halfway decent, at least,' Charisma added.

'I know. I'll be two minutes, I promise you.' Anna sent Liv a pleading look, and reluctantly, her face full of concern, Liv began to close the door.

'Tom is the finest man I know,' she said, just as she drew it shut. 'Remember that.'

'Get on with it then!' Anna gestured impatiently at Miles.

'You are much less impressed by my grand romantic gesture than I thought you would be,' Miles said.

'Is that what it is? A grand romantic gesture?' Anna asked him. 'Why, Miles? Why are you here, when . . . you and I, we are nothing to each other?'

'That's not true,' Miles said. 'We are something to each other. We might not know that we are meant to be, we might not be sure that there isn't another person in the whole world for us, yet. But, Anna, the early signs are very good.'

'"The early signs are very good",' Anna repeated. 'Miles, this is my wedding day!'

'I know, and I wouldn't be here if I didn't think . . .'

'That I should throw all of this away and see how dating you goes, while you're on a world tour, and I'm working in London. Is that what you're proposing?'

'When you put it like that it doesn't seem so appealing . . .' Miles began, running his fingers through his hair, searching for the right thing to say.

'Look, Miles,' Anna said, 'you and me in New York, it was . . . it was wonderful, actually. Being with you was . . . well, I was different with you. And I liked the person I was. And maybe, maybe if you hadn't bought me that kiwi cocktail, and maybe if we'd actually gotten round to talking to each other that evening, then perhaps who knows, things might have been different. But we didn't. We missed our moment. New York was just a . . . a detour . . . a pit stop. And now I'm getting married and you are going on tour and there is nothing else to be said.'

Miles stood perfectly still for a moment, and Anna watched as the determination and adrenalin seeped out of his body.

'You're right,' he said. 'What am I doing here?'

'Well, there you go then,' Anna said, surprised by just how deeply the ease with which he gave up his foolish quest stung her, but glad at least that now she knew.

'I mean, why did I come all this way if I wasn't prepared to go for it and say how I feel for once, instead of hedging my bets, sitting on the fence, playing it safe?

This is no time to play it safe. This is the rest of our lives.'

'What are you talking about?' Anna asked him.

Taking two swift steps forwards, Miles took Anna's hand and dropped to his knees.

'What the . . . !' Anna exclaimed.

'I love you, Anna,' Miles said, stopping her in her tracks. 'I can't claim to have loved you from the moment we met – the time I nearly killed you – but definitely from the second you sang with me onstage, and you were so terrible – I've definitely loved you since then. I tried not to fall in love with you, I tried really hard. I mean you're complicated, and I've got this job and, oh yeah, you're getting married in twenty minutes. But it's happened, and I'm not going to lie about it or try and be cool any more. I love you, Anna. So don't marry Tom. Get out of that dress, come to Texas with me, come on tour with me, never ever leave my side again. I know I should have said all this in New York but I'm saying it now. I love you, Anna, don't marry Tom. Come with me.'

Anna snatched her hand from Miles and took two tottering steps backwards until her thighs collided with the bed and she sat down with a thump.

'Miles,' she said, finding that she wanted to say his name over and over again, but forcing herself not to. 'You have to go. I'm leaving to get married in four minutes and . . .'

'Don't send me away because you need make-up,' Miles said, still on his knees. 'You don't need make-up, you look stunning just as you are.'

'I'm not sending you away because I need make-up,' Anna said. 'I'm sending you away because a year ago I promised to marry a man who I . . . I love and respect. And who apart from forgetting to mention his first wife, has never done me any wrong. He will be a good husband to me, and a great father to my children and I know exactly what our life together will be like. It will be good, and calm, and friendly, and secure and . . . I can't back out on him now Miles. I just can't. I' not brave enough.'

'You're the bravest person I've ever met,' Miles replied, but Anna shook her head.

'Even though you love me too?' Miles said.

'I never said that,' Anna told him, but even as she said it, she reached forwards to touch his face. 'I never said I love you.'

Miles got up. 'OK, I'm going,' he said. 'It's fine, I get it. Maybe you need some time for all this to sink in. My flight leaves in just under two hours. So, I'll be at Luton Airport until then, that's when I catch a connecting flight to Paris. You know where to find me and if you don't come then I'll know how you feel. And I'll know that at least I told you everything that was in my heart. Goodbye, Anna.'

'Goodbye, Miles,' Anna said in a very small voice.

'You won't come, will you?' Miles asked her, his voice thick with emotion.

'No,' Anna said. 'I won't come.'

Anna sat very still on the bed after he went, and looked towards the window where the snow floated downwards, flake after flake. She was alone in her snow globe now.

Chapter Seventeen

Liv was pacing up and down the vestibule, the little room to the side of the church where Anna was arranging her veil. The sleigh had pulled her and Anna, Angela and Ray the short distance through the snow to the church, much to the delight of the local villagers, especially the children who'd clapped and cheered them all as they went past. Anna, looking radiant after having decided to leave her hair long and loose around her shoulders, and with just a touch of glitter on her eyelids, was perfectly calm and serene. It was thanks in no small part to the little white pill that Angela had made her take just before she climbed into the sleigh. She claimed it was just a herbal stress remedy, but ever since Anna had digested it she had felt wonderfully floaty, like she was filled with helium.

It was when they were ushered into a side room by Tom's dad, due to some unknown delay that Liv really realised how decidedly un-Anna-like she was being – so Zen. Tom's dad, who looked like he was putting a decidedly brave face on things, told Anna not to worry, which normally would have been enough to send her into a spin of panic. But oddly, being shown into the vestibule and told she'd have to wait for her wedding to begin because of some unnamed hitch didn't seem to worry Anna at all.

'Look at it coming down, be careful what you wish for,' Anna said, referring to the weather outside the stained glass window, where the driving snow was fast thickening on the narrow lanes that led to the church so they would quite soon be impassable. She'd sent the sleigh back to pick up as many guests as possible in a shuttle service from the hotel, and the rest were begging and borrowing wellies from the local villages and trudging here on foot. 'I tell you what though, I wish I hadn't had that last coffee, I could really do with a pee.'

'Do you think it's Miles?' Liv asked her, wondering why Anna wasn't freaking out more, desperate to know what it was Miles had said and what Anna had said back to him. 'Do you think he found Tom and told him about you and him?'

Anna shook her head, rolling her eyes. 'There is no me and him, Liv, nothing happened. Nothing real.'

'He said he loved you!' Liv had managed to crowbar that piece of information out of a surprisingly mild Anna when she returned to the room. 'That's massive!'

'It's not, because it's irrelevant,' Anna said. 'I realised it when he was standing there saying all that stuff. I realised, it doesn't matter what he says because I am marrying Tom today, just like I've planned to since I was a little girl, and nothing is going to change that. Nothing.'

'So you don't love Miles,' Liv asked her.

Anna shook her head. 'I wouldn't marry Tom if I did.'

Liv nodded, feeling a little deflated. Just for a moment she had thought that perhaps her Christmas wish might come true after all, but now she just felt guilty and sordid for even thinking that Anna might want to marry another man apart from Tom, let alone for wishing it would happen.

'Great news!' Charisma arrived in a full-length faux fur leopard-skin coat she had found on one of her many shopping trips since she'd arrived. 'I sexually intimidated the farmer guys in the pub into getting out their tractors, there's a whole fleet of them on their way here with your guests now. It's so sweet. I may sleep with one of them later, I don't know his name, but he has the cutest ass. And if I'm not a bridesmaid now then there's no justice in the world.'

'Anna!' One of the ushers, a guy called Jim, from Tom's five-a-side pub team, stuck his head round the door. 'He's ready, the church is half full, do you want to kick off or wait for the rest of your supporters?'

'I guess we'd better get it done,' Anna said. 'Canapés are due to be served in an hour, wouldn't want them to go cold . . .'

Then this had to be the right thing, Liv decided, as

she picked up her bouquet, smoothed her cranberry silk dress down over her hips and followed the bride to the top of the aisle where she would be giving herself away. If Anna and Tom had got to this moment, despite secret wives, impromptu trips to New York, declarations of love from rock stars in waiting, terrible weather and everything else, then this wedding had to be the right thing, it was written in the stars, it was fate. And when, in years to come, she watched Tom and Anna grow into their lives together, then at least she would be able to know that despite the terrible ache in her heart as Anna began to walk alone down the aisle, she had been right to do nothing to keep the man she loved from marrying her best friend.

The church was filled with the scent of lilies and lit with what seemed like a thousand candles, and it was so dark outside that it almost seemed like a night-time wedding. As the organist played 'Winter Wonderland', it didn't matter that the church wasn't completely full; everyone who was there, including their mum and dad, was beaming from ear to ear, and, as Anna progressed, the door behind them kept opening and closing, bringing in a little cold flurry of snow each time, as the church filled with latecomers behind her. Just over Anna's shoulder Liv could see the back of Tom's head, staring towards the altar. He did not turn around to look at Anna, nerves probably, or perhaps he was worried he'd become overemotional and cry. Swallowing her own sob, Liv pressed her lips together and lifted her chin. This was the right thing, all the fates agreed, it was time to accept it.

It wasn't until the very last second that Tom turned around and for one split second, before he looked at Anna, his eye caught hers and Liv could not believe what she saw there.

'Oh no,' she whispered.

'Dearly beloved . . .' Tom's father began.

'Dad,' Tom said.

'We are gathered here on this very special day, the eve of the birth of Jesus Christ, to celebrate . . .'

'Dad,' Tom repeated.

'Now, son, we talked about this.'

Liv watched in disbelief as Anna, seemingly completely oblivious to what was happening, stood at Tom's side waiting patiently for the ceremony to begin.

'No,' Tom said. 'This isn't right. This is . . . it's our lives, Anna.'

Liv shook her head as Tom took Anna's hand.

'Anna, we need to talk.'

'Tom.' Tom's dad was firmer this time.

'Now?' Anna asked him, mildly. 'Or afterwards? There should be about twenty minutes of alone time, while the guests are congregating in the ballroom, if they can get back there in this weather that is.'

'Now,' Tom spoke quietly, leaning his head towards

Anna, but at her shoulder Liv could hear every word.

'Anna, why didn't I fly to New York, like you did?'

'Because you are a lazy-arsed sod,' Anna said. 'But that's OK,' she added quickly, 'because you're *my* lazy-arsed sod. Also you thought I was crazy and you were right. It should never have worked out, but it did.'

'That's not why,' Tom said. 'And I didn't tell you about Charisma until the last minute because I forgot I was married. Liv talked me into getting on a plane to come after you for a reason. And last night I finally worked out what it was.'

Anna blinked at him as what was happening slowly began to dawn on her. 'You're about to jilt me at the altar, aren't you?'

'Yes,' Tom said, sending a gasp around the swelling congregation.

Tom flinched, probably preparing himself to be beaten senseless with a hand-tied bouquet of roses, but instead Anna just laughed, laughed so hard that if she could have bent in the middle wearing that corset she would have doubled up with giggles.

'Brilliant,' she said, staring up at the vaulted ceiling of the church. 'Really priceless. You are chucking me. That really is special.'

'Tom!' Liv pushed in front of her friend. 'What the hell are you doing? You are going to break Anna's heart! You know how much this means to her!'

'Yes,' Tom said, 'I do, which is why I can't go through

with this. She shouldn't marry me, I don't love her. Well, I do, but not the way that I love you, Liv.'

Another gasp rushed around the church. The congregation were enthralled, a whispered commentary hastily bringing those who were still arriving up to speed.

'Thomas Collins,' the vicar snapped at his son. 'You will not make a mockery of marriage in my church!'

'I'm not, Dad, I'm doing the opposite of that,' Tom insisted, tears standing bright in his eyes. 'I'm putting marriage before all of this, and I'm putting the life of a woman I truly love, and her happiness, over making the mistake of marrying a man who loves someone else.' Tom turned to Anna. 'Because I do love you, Anna. The first night I met you, I was dazzled by you, and as I got to know you I loved you more and more, but I think you know too, it's not the way it should be between us. And I've been trying to figure out for a while now what the problem is. For a while I thought it might be that I still wanted to be married to Charisma, but then when I saw her again, I realised that wasn't it. And when you went to New York, I thought that I must be such a fool to have doubts about marrying a woman like you. I mean you are incredible, but I didn't chase after you. I wasn't even that jealous about Miles. I only hit him because it seemed like I should be jealous. You found Charisma and everything worked out and I thought this has to mean we're meant to be married, but that doubt I had,

the past for ever, and you know what? It has. I am free, because now I know that plans, and lists, and colour-coded socks don't make a blind bit of difference when it comes to controlling what life has in store for you. And this *is* the happiest day of my life because suddenly I get it, I can rip up my life plan and start again and you know what? The world will not end.'

Anna turned to the riveted guests.

'There's going to be a really great party at the manor today, please do go and dance and eat and get drunk on me and Tom. And don't feel bad for us, really, because we are both going to be fine.' She stood on her tiptoes to find the sleigh driver waiting at the back of the church. 'Can your reindeer get me to Luton Airport in under thirty minutes?'

'Well, if there's no other traffic on the road we can try.'

'Right, then,' Anna said. 'I'm off to take a chance, wish me luck.'

She paused, reaching out both hands to touch Liv and Tom on the arm.

'I love you two, you love each other. One day we will laugh about this. But, Liv, make him suffer for a little bit first.'

And with a swish of tulle, and a jingle of bells, Anna ran up the aisle, prepared to risk everything, including her heart, on a man she'd never even kissed.

*

It turns out that given the right weather conditions, a free road, an expert driver and a decent sleigh, reindeer can make pretty good time. Maybe not quite as quick as the team that deliver all the toys around the world overnight, but quick enough for Anna's hair to whip out behind her as she sailed along the country lanes, screaming the whole way as she clung on to her seat for dear life, with snow churning up in her red raw face, her skirts billowing around her in a sub-zero gust of wind. There was a moment, when they turned a sharp bend at maximum velocity, that might have sent Anna tumbling like a lace-trimmed snowball through the air, if she hadn't clung so tightly on to the railing, feeling her lower body momentarily suspended in mid-air, as she came face to face with a tractor still ferrying guests to the church. For one terrifying second Anna wondered if the last thing she would ever see would be the look of astonished horror on the tractor driver's ruddy face, and then, with about as quick a reaction as was possible at the fifteen-miles-per-hour maximum speed, he drove the great green beast out of the way of the oncoming traffic and into a ditch. A fleeting image of Tom's Aunt Nancy's undergarments flashed by as the impact tipped her backwards in the trailer. The expertly driven reindeer team galloped through the tiny gap that was left, pulling ahead as if they sensed that the race was truly on.

'Thank you!' Anna called over her shoulder into the wind-whipped snow to the tractor driver who had climbed out of the lopsided vehicle and was standing in the road staring after them, dumbstruck. 'I'll send you my insurance details! And tell Aunt Nancy I'm very sorry!'

As they ploughed on through the snow, with Anna's soaking hair clinging to her freezing face and shoulders, it seemed that more and more people were there along the way waiting for them, cheering them on. Little girls jumping up and down in their wellies, little boys hanging out of bedroom windows, whooping. What Anna didn't know was that as she'd left the church, a flurry of texts, phone calls and tweets followed her, until the news of her journey overtook her, unfurling before the curious little party, and lining the roads with unexpected supporters who were there to cheer them on, take in the spectacle, or just be part of something that so oddly summed up the optimism and magic of Christmas: a woman in a wedding dress, careering through the snow on a reindeer-drawn sleigh, hoping to make a wisp of a wish come true.

'What's going on?' Anna shouted to a group of cheering teenage girls, tinsel hanging round their necks, standing atop a flat-roofed garage, filming her on their phones as they whizzed by.

'You're trending on Twitter!' one called after her. '#runawaybride! You're awesome!'

'Oh no,' Anna thought, realising that her determination to never be noticed had been well and truly blown and then feeling rather wonderful about it. If there was ever a way to start a new life then this was it.

It was only when they came to the first main road, running through Dunstable, that the reindeer man had to pull them to a slow trot and eventually into a lay-by.

'Oh no, what's going on?' Anna asked him, clambering out of the sleigh with some difficulty, her sodden skirts feeling like they weighed a ton. 'We're nowhere near yet!'

'I'm sorry,' he apologised. 'If we go any further, the animals will get scared. They don't normally do this sort of thing. They normally pootle round the zoo with a few kids onboard. There's lorries and all sorts on this road, if I take you any further it would be unfair on them.'

'That's OK.' Anna stroked the lead deer on the nose and kissed him between his eyes. 'Thank you, you have all been amazing,' Anna told the driver breathlessly before turning back to the road. 'And I've got fifteen minutes left so . . .'

Anna must have been quite a sight star-jumping in her muddy wedding gown at the side of the road, desperately trying to flag down a car, but clearly not the whole world was connected to their social networks that day, as several went by without stopping. It was the fifth or sixth one – incredibly a canary yellow Ferrari – that finally pulled over and, as soon as he did, Anna could see why. If anyone was going to be up for picking up a bedraggled Christmas bride, it would be these two. The driver was a very good-looking man, dressed as Santa, which might have given her cause to wonder if he was a Christmas-themed pervert, except that there was a young woman sitting next to him, dressed as an elf, and she was wearing a wedding ring. They had to be off to a fancy dress party or something.

'Hello.' The woman opened the door. 'You look like you are very much in need of a Christmas miracle.'

'I don't suppose you can get me to Departures at Luton in ten minutes?' Anna asked the couple. 'I'd be awfully grateful.'

'No problem,' Santa said. 'Amy will hop in the back, and you can slide in the passenger seat then you can make a quick exit.'

'Although I'd quite like to point out that if I slide anywhere in these trousers I will build quite a considerable charge of static electricity.' His wife – Amy – grinned at Anna as she crammed herself into the tiny back seat. 'You'd think they use quality material at the North Pole, wouldn't you, but no apparently there's a recession on there too.'

Anna laughed as she bundled herself and several metres of soaking muddy tulle into the car.

'I'm really sorry about your upholstery,' she apologised.

'Oh, it's fine, I'll get the elves to detail it later.'

'I think you'll find car washing is not in our job

description,' Amy called cheerfully from the back. 'Do it yourself.'

The husband was really far too handsome to make a convincing Santa, but they seemed like a nice enough couple and really, she would have considered getting into a car with an axe-wielding maniac if he'd agreed to get her to the airport in time to catch Miles.

'Thank you ever so much,' Anna told Santa as he pulled away. 'You don't know how much this means to me.'

Santa nodded as the reindeer began to trot off in the opposite direction. He saluted their keeper as he passed, as if they might know each other. 'It's not a problem, and those chaps are all very well and good.' He smiled at Anna. 'But sometimes you need a little bit of horsepower and a V8 engine to get the job done.'

They skidded to a halt right outside the departure lounge, and Amy leaned over the back seat and helped push Anna, hoops and all, out onto the pavement.

'I hope your Christmas wish comes true,' she said by way of goodbye.

'Good luck, Anna!' Santa added through the open window just before he and Amy sped off into the snow. Anna gave them a hurried wave, wondering exactly when in their short journey she had mentioned her name . . .

There was no time to lose though, as Anna realised that she was seconds away from Miles going through to catch his flight and possibly never seeing him again. Searching the board vainly, she realised she had no idea where he was going, because there were no direct flights to Texas from Luton, no flights to the USA at all, which meant he had to be changing somewhere, somewhere he could catch an international flight . . . then she remembered he'd told her his first flight was to Paris. Anna picked up her skirts and ran as best as she could, considering that due to her corset her lung capacity was now at about ten per cent and her dress felt like it weighed fifteen stone all by itself. It was, however, an unforeseen benefit of careering around an airport in a wedding dress that people tended to get out of her way.

'Final call for flight zero seven six zero to Charles de Gaulle, Paris,' a pleasant female voice came over the tannoy. 'Final call, check-in is about to close.'

And then she saw him, or the back of his head at least, about to go through security.

'Miles!' Anna meant to shout his name, but nothing came out. She'd used up all of her puff, running in wellingtons. Taking a second to pause, she knew she had one last chance and, mustering up every last ounce of breath she had, she shouted his name: 'Miles!'

Anna watched, disbelieving, as he disappeared through the security gate and vanished from sight.

Sinking down onto the muddy and damp airport floor, Anna deflated into the billows of her skirt and wept for the first time. It didn't matter to her that she'd ended her relationship with Tom – or rather he with her – that her dream wedding had disintegrated around her, or that she'd more or less ruined her perfect dress beyond repair, or that even now, somewhere her best friend and sister and former fiancé were working things out between them for their future. All of that seemed right, it seemed fitting. What Anna could not accept was that she had let Miles go, that despite her best efforts – and those of assorted reindeer and Santa himself – she had not made it to the airport in time to tell him that she loved him too.

'Why are you crying?'

'Because you left before I could . . . Oh!' Anna looked up to find Miles standing over her. 'You haven't left? Did you hear me calling for you?'

'No,' Miles said, holding out a hand to Anna and pulling her to her feet. 'I heard the people behind me talking about a crazy chick running about in a wedding dress, and I hoped there wasn't a spate of runaway brides. But it is you as it turns out. You came.'

'You missed your flight!' Anna said, apologetically.

'It's OK, I'll get another one, maybe . . . although it is Christmas Eve and probably all the flights are booked up, but anyway . . . You are here.'

'Tom jilted me,' Anna said.

'Tom jilted you!' Miles looked dumbstruck. 'So is that why you're here, I'm plan B?'

'No, oh God no. I was going to marry him because he was nice, and kind and I like him about as much as I've ever liked anyone, and Liv wouldn't tell me not to and I thought he seemed keen and I've never been in love before, so I wasn't sure that it was really for me, all the chaos and uncertainty and the up and downs, I like to know where I stand and what's going to happen next, or at least I thought I did.'

Miles frowned. 'Sorry, not sure I followed all that. Am I plan B or not? Because if I run I might just . . .'

'You're something I didn't plan at all,' Anna reassured him, taking his hand. 'Something wonderful. It turns out that actually I am a little bit like my mum. But not the one who left me and never looked back, not that poor sad woman, she's part of me, she made me, but she's not my mum. My real mum came to see me today and she said that all I had to do was let myself be happy, let myself feel what it's like to be really and truly happy and then I will know what to do. Miles, when I'm with you, I feel that way. I feel light-hearted and happy. I got a sleigh, pulled by reindeer, to get here to tell you that . . .Well, me too.'

Miles smiled. 'I went there, you have to as well.'

'I love you too,' Anna said, simply, a huge smile spreading across her face. 'Now are we going to do any kissing or are you only any good at talking about it?'

Miles dropped his backpack to the floor, then traced the tips of his fingers along Anna's jawline. He cinched her waist in the firm grip of his hand and, as their lips met, a spark of electricity vibrated through them both. Winding her fingers in his hair, Anna kissed Miles back, and somewhere, far away, a brass band began to play 'Rudolph the Red-nosed Reindeer'.

'Are you going to come and run away with me?' Miles asked her, grinning from ear to ear, as their lips finally parted.

'For a while I will,' Anna said happily. 'Let's just see what happens. Suddenly the future seems much more exciting and full of possibility now that I don't have to stick to a plan.'

Twenty Months Later

Epilogue

Thank God they'd waited until August. The summer had waited almost until the end of July to make an appearance, but now it was here it was in full force. Heat sizzled outside the open French windows, the hum of bees busying themselves in and out of the lupins, the chorus of birdsong making it a perfect summer morning to get married.

'You look wonderful,' Anna told Liv. 'Really, you know how to be a bride, none of this massive frock nonsense. Look at you.' And it was true. Dressed in soft ivory chiffon, with a simple slash neckline, which made the most of her subtle curves, and fresh flowers garlanding her hair, Liv looked stunning, beautiful and best of all radiantly happy.

'I never thought I'd see the day,' Angela said beaming at Liv. 'Well, I thought I might see the day, but I thought it was more likely to involve Doctor Marten boots and a rainbow flag, not that I would have minded.'

'Mum!' Anna and Liv said at once.

'One thing we know for sure,' Anna said happily, 'is that when Tom sees you coming down the aisle, he's not going to freak out and run away this time.'

'Don't joke about it!' Liv said horrified, although she knew that too. There had never been a more certain thing in her life than her love for Tom and, now he knew what his feelings for her meant, his love for her. Which was why after a year and eight months together Liv didn't have a single doubt that marrying him was the right thing to do.

'Don't worry, darling, I think if he bailed out of a second wedding in his dad's church he'd get excommunicated or something,' Angela said, winking at Anna. 'Certainly disowned.'

'I do wish you were here though,' Liv said taking her iPad off the mantelpiece to look into Anna's eyes, or at least as much as she could through Facetime. 'What's it like in Japan anyway?'

'Crazy mad,' Anna said. 'But so worth it. And you and Charisma have made such a success of our business, Liv. Who knew an ex-stripper and failed actress would be so good at marketing. I should have become a silent partner much sooner. I'm much better suited to managing tour logistics anyway. I have a suitcase full of Post-it notes. A suitcase, Liv, I'm in heaven.'

'And it means you get to see Miles a little bit more.' Liv smiled. 'Which is what it's really all about.'

'Yes,' Anna said, grinning. 'There is that fringe benefit to travelling constantly around the word that I never thought of. However, I'll be coming home as soon as this tour is done, for a few months anyway, and then

Miles and I are going to live in New York while the NYRDs write a new album.'

'Coming home?' Angela said. 'Well, about time too. Are you going to be staying with us? I could clear out your old bedroom. Dad calls it his dungeon now, but that's a load of stuff and nonsense, if you don't mind the manacles. They are screwed to the wall, and I don't want to spoil the wallpaper, it's Laura Ashley, you know.'

'Why are you coming back?' Liv asked her, concerned. 'I thought you loved life on the road.'

'I do,' Anna said. 'But this one might not . . .'

She panned the iPad down to show the small but unmistakable swell of her pregnant belly.

'Oh my God! You're having a baby!' Liv said, delighted. 'Or you've given in to cake, one or the other.'

'It's a baby!' Anna laughed.

'Is Miles the father?' Angela asked. 'I've heard about these rock and roll tours.'

'Yes, it's Miles's. And I was trying to wait until after the wedding to tell you, but I couldn't keep it in any longer. You will have a niece or nephew in about six months' time.'

'Trying to upstage me as usual.' Liv smiled, delighted.

'As if I could.' Anna smiled too, placing the tips of her fingers on the screen. 'I miss you, Liv.'

'I miss you too,' Liv said.

'Now, go and get married and start your happy-ever-after. I know mine started on the day I *didn't* get married, but that's just me, devil-may-care, footloose, take-life-how-it-comes, roll-with-the-punches me. We can't all be so rebellious.'

'Liv!' A male voice sounded in the background and Miles's face appeared over Anna's shoulder, his rough cheek rubbing against hers. 'Have a great day, babe,' he added. 'I wish we could be there, but this gig's been booked for two years.'

'It doesn't matter as long as you are giving Anna the happy ending she's always dreamed of,' Liv said.

'Ending?' Anna laughed. 'Oh, Liv, this is just the start of my happy beginning.'

Enjoyed *Married by Christmas*?

Turn the page for a sneak peek at
The Night Before Christmas
also by Scarlett Bailey

Prologue

4 December

Lydia Grant hadn't meant to find the engagement ring intended for her, on that dank and drizzly December morning, but she had. Her boyfriend, Stephen, had got up long before the crack of dawn, leaving Lydia with the luxury of the middle of the bed. A rare treat that she relished by assuming the position of a starfish and tapping the snooze button on the alarm clock four times, dipping in and out of sleep with delicious, dozy abandon until 6.50 a.m., when she had sat bolt upright and remembered who she was.

By night, she was a serial romantic, taking every precious spare second she had to lose herself in the golden age of the Hollywood romances that she'd loved so much since she was a young girl. She could fall in love over and over again with Cary Grant or Trevor Howard; and even occasionally – but not quite so much recently – her own boyfriend.

But by day – a day that should have started at 6.30 sharp – she was Lydia Grant, Junior Barrister, a career-hungry, hard-as-nails crusader for justice. And, in just over an hour, she had to be in court representing a forty-six-year-old surgeon's wife who stood accused of credit card fraud running into tens of thousands of pounds. Having only been handed her client's brief at eight-thirty last night, Lydia needed to get a move on if she were to get to court in time to meet and talk over the case with the accused before the start of proceedings, and reassure Mrs Harris that everything would be all right. After all, if there was ever a barrister who could make a judge see that a woman needed two hundred pairs of designer shoes, it was surely Lydia Grant. Failing that, she'd go for diminished responsibility. Who hadn't gone mad lusting over a pair of shoes they could ill afford at least once in their life?

Running dangerously late, Lydia thanked her lucky stars that Stephen's Holborn flat – hers as well now, she reminded herself, though somehow, despite living together for the last six months, she couldn't stop herself calling it 'Stephen's flat' in her head – was only a fifteen-minute walk away from court. She leaped out of bed and allowed herself five minutes in the shower, before bundling her long, dark, chestnut-brown hair into a neat chignon with practised ease. Slipping into a smart white shirt and an authoritative black trouser suit that she'd set out before going to bed, she gave her lucky Gucci killer-heeled boots a quick polish. Taking a moment for a quick glance in the hall mirror – and pulling a face at her reflection – she told herself out loud that today she needed to be a strong, confident and capable woman; a woman who was never in doubt, not even for one second, that she'd show the judge and jury how ridiculous the charges were, and that her client was the true victim in this case, a victim of a wealthy husband who refused to buy her sufficient shoes.

It didn't help that Lydia couldn't find any black socks in the drawer Stephen had ceremoniously cleared out for her when he'd invited her to move in. 'After all, Lydia,' he'd told her when he'd casually handed her the key to his flat, 'it's about time we moved things along, don't you think?' Perhaps it hadn't been the most romantic moment in Lydia's life, but it was a bench-mark, nevertheless. A step towards commitment that, until quite recently, she would never have thought possible, even if it was commitment that afforded her just one drawer.

She could find training socks, pop socks, a pair of pink glittery socks that her eleven-year-old step-sister, from her father's third marriage, had got her for her birthday, plus a quantity of tights all tangled up in one big bundle, but no suitable socks to go under her lucky boots. Verging precariously on the edge of acceptable lateness, Lydia had done what any strong, capable, confident woman would. She'd decided to borrow a pair of her boyfriend's socks, yanking open his top drawer only to find the shock of her life sitting there, right on top of his neatly paired socks, blatantly out in the open, without even a minimal effort to hide it.

It was a small, square box in unmistakable pale greenish turquoise, with the words *Tiffany & Co* printed in black on the lid.

Without even thinking about what it might mean, Lydia grabbed the box and opened it, like a greedy child ripping open a packet of sweets. And there it was, winking at her in the electric light required on the dark, winter morning.

A one-carat, platinum-set, Tiffany Bezet princess-cut diamond engagement ring. Lydia sucked in a long breath. It was perfect. It was beautiful. And most importantly, it was exactly the ring she'd always dreamed of, chosen by a man who had taken some considerable time and care to discover her taste exactly. A man who knew that she always carried a battered and dog-eared copy of *Breakfast at Tiffany's* in her briefcase, and that since her early teens, her idea of the pinnacle of romance was to receive just such a ring, presented in that wonderfully distinctive box. It was a ring chosen by a man who cared enough about her to get it exactly right. By a man Lydia was now certain must love her very much to get it *so* right, and who knew that proposing to her at this special time of year would make another dream come true for her, because finally Lydia would get to have her own happy Christmas.

Which was why the second thought to pop into Lydia Grant's head that morning, as she stared at the ring, was rather surprising.

Lydia Grant wasn't at all sure that she wanted to get married.

Chapter One

21 December

Lydia glanced sideways at Stephen, who had been finger tapping the steering wheel since the last service station.

'Looks like we're going to beat the worst of the weather, anyway,' she said, briefly squinting out of the car window at the voluminous leaden clouds, hanging low over the horizon, pregnant with the promise of snow. 'The forecast said dangerous driving conditions, snow, snow and more snow – but look, it's only just started to come down.' Lydia nodded at the windscreen, where the first few delicate flakes of snow that had begun to waft down were settling briefly before being brutally wiped away in an instant.

Stephen said nothing in reply.

'So are you going to sulk about this for the whole three hundred miles?' Lydia asked him impatiently. 'God, I said I'd pay the toll on the M6.'

'It's not that and you know it,' Stephen said, keeping his eyes on the road. 'This is our first Christmas.'

'No, it's not.' Lydia sighed. 'It's our second Christmas,

or wasn't that you drunk and wearing a Santa hat at my mum's last year?'

Lydia grimaced as she remembered their actual first Christmas together, her mother, who had started on the Bailey's at breakfast, sitting on her step-father's lap, chewing his face off while the Queen gave a speech in the background and Stephen worked his way through an overcooked turkey and undercooked potatoes.

'It is, it *was*, going to be our first Christmas alone,' Stephen said. 'No family this year, you said. No trekking from Kent to Birmingham in the space of forty-eight hours just to make sure that you see all of your various parents and multitude of step-siblings. This year, I distinctly remember you saying, we're going to do as we please, by which you obviously meant do as you please. Silly me.'

'Various parents?' Lydia complained. 'You make me sound like a Mormon or the child of some sort of hippy commune. It's called a blended family these days, Stephen, which you of all people should know, Mr Family Law.'

'You know what I mean. What was it last year? Your mum and Greg on Christmas Day, practically having sex on your gran's reclining easy-up chair. And then we had to get up first thing on Boxing Day to make it to your dad and Janie's in time for lunch, where you have so many half siblings, and half-half siblings, it's like visiting a crèche. I mean, how old is your dad? How does he have the energy?'

'I don't know, perhaps you should ask him,' Lydia muttered under her breath. 'You know what my family's like.'

Lydia's childhood had been far from perfect, something she'd been at pains to express to Stephen since they'd first started getting serious, knowing that sooner or later he'd have to meet them. And love them as she did – most of the time – they weren't exactly the sort of family a girl looked forward to introducing to her most serious boyfriend ever.

Her parents had had a whirlwind courtship – marrying a month after they'd first met, and only discovering once they'd conceived Lydia that they hated each other's guts. The Christmases of her childhood were far removed from her beloved screen versions, where it always snowed, everyone always loved each other and it always turned out all right in the end. Lydia's childhood Christmases had a nightmare soundtrack of angry words, bitter recriminations and slammed doors, until Lydia was twelve and her father had walked out on her and her mum for good on Christmas Day. It had easily been the worst out of a lifetime of disappointing Christmases, and for the next few years she'd become a bargaining chip in the increasingly spiteful war between her parents, alternating holidays between the two of them and not feeling at home anywhere.

Since then, her mother had remarried, perhaps a little too happily for Lydia's liking, given the incident last Christmas, and her father seemed to be competing in some world record challenge for most-married man.

'Dad's got issues. He's been having a midlife crisis all his life. At least you met him in the Janie phase. I actually quite like her. His second wife was a proper cow. She always used to call me "the girl". Never used my name, just "the girl", with a sort of bad smell expression. I used to dread it when it was their turn to have me for Christmas . . .'

Lydia always did her best not to blame her dad for the Karen years – for leaving her alone in the living room in front of the telly for Christmas lunch, for never remembering to get her a gift, even though he always spent every penny he didn't have on Karen. And for agreeing, as soon as Karen demanded it, that Lydia did not have to come at Christmas at all, or Easter, or at any time, for that matter. Lydia resolved not to blame her dad for letting Karen edge her almost completely out of his life, because after all, he had left the witch before it was too late. And after that, he'd made a token effort to rebuild their relationship. At least he had until he'd taken up with the very buxom, though far more personable, Janie. Either way, Lydia was glad that Karen was gone. Janie made her dad happy, and she always remembered to get her some smellies from Lush, which was something.

Noticing Stephen's expression softening slightly, Lydia reached over and rested her hand on his thigh for a moment. 'Anyway, it's not as if we're doing family, is it? We're not trekking from Broadstairs to Birmingham. We *are* having a proper grown-up Christmas in the stunning surrounds of the Lake District, just the two of us.'

'Just the two of us *and* all of your friends,' Stephen muttered. 'I told my mum we weren't going to hers this year because we were doing our own thing, because . . .' Stephen stopped himself from saying more, and Lydia, hearing alarm bells in the vicinity of her heart, thought it best not to press him further. Having met his mother on a number of occasions now, she could honestly say that she'd rather gouge out her own eyes with a rusty nail than have to endure any more of the those 'you'll-never-be good-enough-for-my-only-son' looks again, something that would be tricky if she married Stephen. Mentally, Lydia added 'Stephen's Mum' to her list of pros and cons for marrying him, slotting it very firmly under 'con'. His dad was nice, though, in that quiet, unassuming, had-all-the-life-and-joy-sucked-out-of-him-by-the-cow-he'd married sort of way, which, all things considered, Lydia didn't think could be counted as a 'pro'.

'Look, I'm sorry I said yes to Christmas at Katy and Jim's without exactly running it past you,' Lydia apologised, not for the first time. 'The thing is, when Katy phoned, she was all over the place. It's been six months since she and Jim and the kids bought the hotel, and . . . well, reading between the lines, I think it's been a bit of a money pit. I don't know what possessed them . . . After all, Jim used to be an investment banker, and the nearest Katy's ever previously come to running a boutique hotel in the middle of nowhere is making us all toast after a big night out when we were students. They've poured every single penny they have into Heron's Pike. If it doesn't work out, they're stuffed. Katy said that they're fully booked for New Year's Eve and she needs to practise on someone. Who better than her three oldest friends and their lovely, handsome, sexy men?'

Stephen said nothing, keeping his eyes on the road as the falling snow began to thicken. Lydia turned to look out of the window, a shiver of anticipation running down her spine as she thought of the photos of the house Katy had sent her. Heron's Pike looked like the setting for a perfect Christmas. 'Besides, think of it, Stephen,' she continued, 'it's the Lake District, and Heron's Pike is a beautiful Victorian manor house, a stone's throw from Derwentwater Lake. It's got its own little boathouse and Katy says the village down the road looks like a picture postcard.' Lydia sighed. 'It will be just like the bit in *Holiday Inn* when Bing sings "White Christmas" and I always cry. And, look – it's going to be a white Christmas, too, a real one with snow, and open fires, and food, and wine, and people that actually like each other, for once. I, for one, can't wait to spend it with you and my best friends. I just wish you loved them as much as I do.'

'It's not that I don't like your friends,' Stephen began, carefully. 'Alex is great, although she is quite possibly the most frightening woman I've ever met, especially now she's pregnant. And David's okay if you don't mind talking about Romans or Normans, or whatever it is he lectures in. I've only met Katy and Jim at Alex's wedding, and I didn't get to talk to them too much because – if you remember – Katy got over-excited by the free champagne, burst into tears and then passed out in her dessert. But I'm sure they are a lovely couple. Just as I'm certain that their kids and their grandparents are charming. But Christmas with Joanna Summers? The queen of TV shopping? I'm sorry, Lydia, that is so low down my Christmas wish list that it comes below being stranded on a desert island and forced to eat my own legs to survive.'

'Harsh!' Lydia chuckled, despite herself. 'I know Joanna is an acquired taste, but the four of us have been friends since we met at university, and she's been a good friend to me, the best.' The four girls had met in the first week of their first term, thrown into the random mix of being on the same corridor in their hall of residence. And sharing a house in their final two years – through boys, exams, assorted family dramas and one very real tragedy – had cemented their friend-ships for life. 'Besides,' added Lydia now, 'if Joanna hadn't let me live with her rent free while I was studying for the bar, then I'd have been sunk.'

'She's just so up herself, strutting around like she owns the place.'

'That's her TV image, not what she's really like. She's had to be tough.' Of all of them, Joanna had found it easiest to adapt to student life and living away from home for the first time. She might joke about having been raised by wolves but, in truth, she'd been dumped by her parents in various boarding schools from the age of seven. She'd had to cope. 'You need a lot of guts to do her job. All that drama and confidence, that's more about keeping up a front than anything else.'

'She's so superficial,' Stephen snapped back. 'She sells cheap tat to people who can't afford it on a shopping channel, Lydia,' he added. 'How does blathering on incessantly about how you can own a genuine fake diamond ring for forty-nine ninety-nine, in two easy instalments, require guts?'

'God, you are such a snob,' Lydia retorted as the snow began to fall in earnest, and the last motorway sign flashed up a new fifty mile per hour speed limit. 'Not everyone can charge about saving the world like you, you know.'

'No, but *some* people could do a little more to try,' Stephen said, glancing pointedly at Lydia. Lydia bit her lip. She did her best to keep up with him, his charity work, all the legal aid stuff and the weekend volunteering, but it never seemed to be enough to please him. He forgot that, while he was at a comfortable, secure stage in his career, she was really still only starting out in hers. She had to do the work that chambers gave her, when it came in, and that barely left her time to breathe let alone spend every spare minute doing good, in the relentless way Stephen did.

'Besides' – Lydia decided to ignore his jibe – 'I'd like to *you* see present live TV. She has to think on her feet all the time. That's why she's the best at what she does, not just because she's beautiful. Sometimes, if I've got a case I'm particularly nervous about, I think of her, and that gives me courage.'

'Who knew that flogging crap could be so inspiring,' Stephen muttered under his breath, but again Lydia let it pass. While she loved Joanna to the depths of her shallows, and would defend her to the hilt, secretly she was rather glad Stephen hadn't instantly been utterly charmed by her stunning, long-legged, titian-haired friend. A fair few of her past boyfriends had rather let her down in that respect, and although Lydia knew that Joanna would never, ever break the golden rule when it came to pinching a friend's beau, she had not been quite so certain of some of her ex-boyfriends. Lydia did sort of take after her parents when it came to bad romances. In the past, she'd fallen in love at the drop of a hat, and her eternal romantic optimism had seen her disappointed in love more than her fair share. That was until she met sensible, stable, Stephen. After a moment's reflection, Lydia added, 'Did not fall for Joanna' to her mental list of pros.

'What I'm intrigued by is this latest guy Joanna's bringing along,' Lydia went on. 'Alex says she's mad about him, she says he's definitely the one she's going to marry.'

'Definitely the one she's going to marry until after she's collected a big, expensive engagement ring that most certainly hasn't been purchased on BuyIt! TV,' Stephen said, cynically. 'Then I'm sure he'll go the way of her other short-lived fiancés, and she'll simply have another obscenely large diamond to add to her collection.'

Lydia wriggled in her seat, yanking at the seatbelt that, after too many hours sitting in one position, had started to grate on her neck. The conversation was also beginning to sail just a little too close to the wind for her peace of mind. For the last two weeks, Lydia had felt the presence of the engagement ring in Stephen's top drawer like a ticking bomb in a bad B-movie. But Stephen had proven himself an expert at keeping his plans to propose to her a secret. Even when she'd dashed his suggestion of a country cottage hideaway just for the two of them, begging him to let them spend Christmas with her friends instead, he'd hid his disappointment well. Before they'd set off this morning, she'd made an excuse to run back into the flat and check, but the bomb was evidently coming with them. And all this talk of rings seemed loaded with unspoken meaning that she was keen to steer clear of.

'I think it's brave of her not to marry a man just because he asks her or it looks good on paper. It's brave to hold out, pause and take a breath. She always realised that something wasn't right and she changed her mind. I wish my parents had done the same; they would have been a lot happier, a lot sooner.'

'Well, I don't,' Stephen said, taking his eyes off the road for a second to smile at her. 'If they had, I wouldn't have you. I just hope this latest poor sod knows what he's getting himself into with Joanna. Still, I suppose if he survives Christmas with the four of you girls in one piece, then he's pretty much capable of surviving anything.'

'We're not that bad, are we?' Lydia asked him, although she knew that, when she and her friends were all together, they seemed to simultaneously regress about ten years and drown out any other noise within a five-mile vicinity, each one clamouring to be heard above the others, just as it used to be on a daily basis in their overcrowded student house.

'No.' Stephen looked a little chastened. 'No, you are not bad at all, not even Joanna, I suppose. It's just . . . it's just that I thought this year it would be different, no family, no friends, just you and me. That was how I pictured it.'

'I know, and that would have been lovely, it really, truly would,' Lydia said, suddenly consumed by guilt at her deliberate decision to avoid spending anything that could be described as 'potential romantic proposal time' alone with Stephen, just in case he popped the question and she wasn't ready to answer yet.

Here he was, sulking because she'd persuaded him to let them spend Christmas with her friends, but little did he know that she was doing this for him. Far better for her to be able to answer confidently when he finally proposed to her, rather than, 'Um, well . . . the thing is, I'm not sure, can you give me a month or year or two to mull it over?' Most of all, before Stephen produced that beautiful ring, Lydia wanted more than anything to have talked herself into saying yes.

Yes, because Stephen was certainly handsome, with his Nordic good looks, pale blond hair, light blue eyes and square manly jaw, and he would make a splendid contribution to the attractive children Lydia had vaguely pictured herself having one day. Yes, because he was genuinely a nice man, the kind of man who cared about what happened in the world and worked to make it a better place. But, most importantly, yes, because she loved him.

This hesitation wasn't at all like Lydia. When it came to love, she usually rushed in where even fools turned back. After all, she'd met Stephen out of the blue, allowing herself to free fall into a relationship with him without a second thought, and she'd been content enough with their relationship for over a year. So why pull up short now?

Perhaps it was the memory of her mother's face, staring unseeingly at the burnt turkey languishing in the sink on the day her dad had finally left home, that was putting her off making that final commitment to one man. Or the string of boyfriends Mum had brought home, in the years before she'd finally met Greg. It seemed at the time like there was a new one sitting at the head of the table every Christmas, while her mum fawned over him with unseemly gratitude, expecting Lydia to treat him like a member of their tiny, disjointed family. Her mum had always been so sure that the next one was *the one*, that this time she would be happy. In reality, though, it had taken her a great deal of broken eggs to make her omelette, and if her mother never knew when she was making her latest monumental mistake, then how would she?

If she were being strictly honest, though, Lydia knew that it was her more immediate past that was holding her back. Not least of all the fact that, when she'd first met Stephen, she had been horribly, utterly – and very dramatically – on the rebound.

Also by Scarlett Bailey:

The Night Before Christmas

All Lydia's ever wanted is a perfect Christmas . . .

So when her oldest friends invite her to spend the holidays with them, it seems like a dream come true. She's been promised log fires, roasted chestnuts, her own weight in mince pies – all in a setting that looks like something out of a Christmas card.

But her winter wonderland is ruined when she finds herself snowed in with her current boyfriend, her old flame and a hunky stranger. Well, three (wise) men are traditional at this time of year . . .

Praise for *The Night Before Christmas*

'Loved it!' Miranda Dickinson

'A delicious Christmas read!' Trisha Ashley

'This feel good rom-com is perfectly festive and great fun.' *Closer*